THE MOUNTAIN of IMMODERATE DESIRES

By the same Author:

MOURNING IS NOT PERMITTED
MALEFICE

THE
MOUNTAIN
of
IMMODERATE
DESIRES

———

Leslie Wilson

WEIDENFELD & NICOLSON

LONDON

First published in 1994 by Weidenfeld & Nicolson,
an imprint of the Orion Publishing Group, Orion House,
5 Upper Saint Martin's Lane, London WC2H 9EA

A catalogue record for this book is available from
the British Library

ISBN 0 297 81371 4

Typeset by Deltatype Ltd, Ellesmere Port, Cheshire
Printed in Great Britain by
Butler & Tanner Ltd, Frome and London

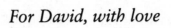

For David, with love

My destiny I create for myself, my fortune I seek for myself.
  (*The Book of Odes and Documents*, translation in: *Three lives*,
          Martin Palmer, Kwok Man-Ho and Kerry Brown)

All Truth is a shadow except the last, except the utmost; yet
every Truth is true in its kind. It is substance in its own place,
though it be but a shadow in another place (for it is but a
reflection from an intenser substance); and the shadow is a true
shadow, as the substance is a true substance.
                                             (Isaac Penington)

ANCHORAGE, MERCHANT SHIPPING

MAN OF WAR
ANCHORAGE

China
Sugar
Refiner

VICTORIA
BAY

Queen's Road
Caine Road
Bonham Road
Robinson Road
Police Station
Kennedy Road
Victoria Peak
Bowen Road
Pokfolum Road
Chinese Cemetery
Tramway
M © Co
RC
PR
P

Mount Kellet

KOWLOO BA

■ Government House

© Cemeteries
Mohammedan
Roman Catholic
Protestant
Parsee

The **TOURIST'S GUIDE** to **HONG KONG**,
with **SHORT TRIPS** to the **MAINLAND** of **CHINA**

REFERENCES:

—— Roads.   ···· Hill-paths.   ✿ Land-marks.

PROGRAMMES.

Nº						
1	From	the	Peak	via	Pokfolum to Clock-tower	about 6 miles
2	"	"	"	"	Magasine-gap "	" 5 "
3	"	"	"	"	Peak Road "	" 2½ "
4	"	"	"	"	Aberdeen & Pokf'm "	" 8½ "
5	"	"	"	"	" " Wanchai "	" 6½ "
6	"	"	"	"	Little Hong Kong to Stanley	" 10 "
7	"	"	"	Clock-tower via Quarry Bay to Tytam & rtn.		15 "
8	"	"	"	"	Shaukiwan " " "	17 "
9	"	"	"	"	Bowen Rd to Happy Valley	5 "
10	"	"	"	"	Kennedy Rd " "	3 "
11	"	"	"	"	Wongnei Chong to Tytam	8 "
12	"	"	"	to **KOWLOON** trip.		5 "

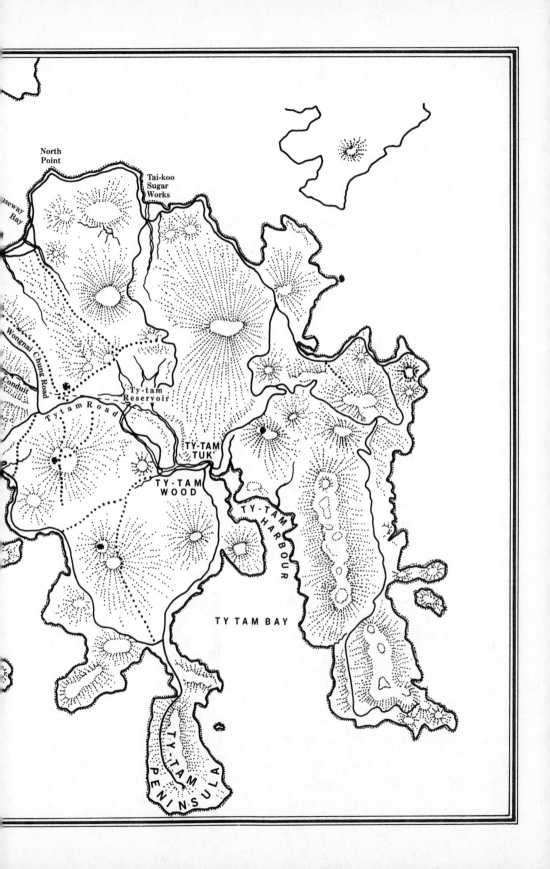

North
Point

Tai-koo
Sugar
Works

seway
Bay

Wongnai Chung Road

Conduit

Ty-tam
Reservoir

Ty tam Road

TY-TAM
TUK'

TY-TAM
WOOD

TY-TAM HARBOUR

TY TAM BAY

TY-TAM PENINSULA

I

SAMUEL
Dorset 1881

SAMUEL rode a black horse: it was only made of wood but he rose in the stirrups as if it was alive. Now and again he brushed his damp fair hair out of his eyes and rubbed the moisture off the downy fuzz of his new unshaven moustache. He hoped it was growing longer.

There were mirrors set round the inner drum of the machine: he was travelling too fast to see himself there. He caught sight of a man-eating tiger, a rajah on an elephant, a Chinese mandarin, a paddle-steamer. For a moment he let himself believe he was being carried round the world, but he could see his tutor beside him on another painted wooden horse. Reynolds and he were riding a tiny circle of Dorset land, that was all.

It had been a lark, a piece of wildness to run away from the dank oilcloth-floored corridors of the rectory and come to the fairground. The Rector had told him the fair was a haunt of cheats, the stallholders all swindlers, and it was true: Samuel could see that. At least it was honest, straightforward cheating. You knew the coconuts were nailed to the cups, you knew the rifles at the shooting gallery were made to aim crooked.

The hoarse voice of the organ pumped out popular tunes, and there was a smell of food and burning coal.

'The fair,' had said the Rector, 'is a dangerous place to go. It corrupts all those who visit it.' (Reynolds had winked at Samuel, as if to say: Who dares?) The Rector said: 'You will not go there, Samuel.'

That was enough. The boy wanted so much to see the world, the bad as well as the good. Reynolds said purity was for cowards. He was disappointed in the fair now he'd come. Though the rise and fall of the machine brought on that wicked excitement he dared mention to no one and –

'There's a pickpocket,' said Reynolds, pointing, grinning under his sandy moustaches.

'I've seen them before,' said Samuel, 'on market-day.' As for the other thing, he was getting used to it.

'So you think your father was wrong about the corruption?' asked Reynolds, grinning again. His horse was bright scarlet, and its mouth was wide open, showing all its teeth: it took him up when Samuel was down, then dipped him to look up at Samuel on high.

'He's not my father,' said Samuel, 'you know that.'

'I meant to say, the Rector,' said Reynolds. That was part of the game, the game of escape. They got out of the house at night, through Samuel's bedroom window, down the drainpipe, out into the night-time countryside.

Reynolds's thick sandy hair fell back as he looked up at Samuel. His grinning mouth was wide open.

'We shouldn't have come,' said Samuel, 'people will tell.'

'So?' asked Reynolds.

Samuel said: 'The Rector might send you away.'

'He won't,' said Reynolds. 'He doesn't really care. You know that. He only moralizes because he thinks he has to. All he wants is a quiet life.'

Samuel was fifteen years old and his own life was contained inside a framework of pretence; the forms of address he had to use to the people around him; the Rector's rules, which he and Reynolds must appear to keep.

Five miles away, at West Burton, the rectory kept its chilly early-bed quiet. The Reverend Henry and Mrs Pink lay awake in their separate bedrooms while the servants fell into exhausted sleep in the attics. The window in Samuel's bedroom was open, but no one was going there to see if he was lying in his wormy four-poster bed.

At the Abbotsport fair Samuel sat on the galloping horses and caught glimpses of the pickpocket stealing. He said to his tutor: 'He's really not my father, is he?'

Reynolds said: 'One day, the ambassadors will come to claim you. They'll tell you whose son you are.'

'The child of the Archduke,'

'Or the King. They'll take you back to your kingdom.'

Samuel said: 'That's why he didn't buy the portrait the man made of me. Because I'm not his son.'

'Only I'm your faithful servant, and I've told you the truth.'

Samuel said: 'It's not all a game, is it? They are lying to me. He's not my father. Or he would care for me. He'd do more than just give me tracts to read.' He shut his mouth on the bitterness.

'Don't be angry with him,' said Reynolds. 'He's not worth it.'

Samuel said: 'He treats me like a lodger in the house.'

There was a china dog for sale on a huckster's stand: its nose sneered up into the air, its eyes picked Samuel out for especial disdain. Because the dog knew what he was, knew what was really behind the games. There was only one reason for leaving a child with foster-parents.

The pickpocket slid in and out of the crowd: Samuel saw his clever hand slide into a young woman's reticule and come out with her purse. He was such a gentle thief: none of his victims felt him. The merry-go-round whirled Samuel and Reynolds away and when they came back the man had vanished.

The gallopers stopped.

'Do you want another ride?' asked Reynolds.

'I suppose so,' said Samuel. 'Nothing much else to do.' Reynolds winked at the girl in charge of the shooting gallery, and she giggled. Most of the other customers were getting off and a new lot coming on. None of *them* looked bored with the fair. It was the usual crowd of countryfolk delighted with the garish colours and the moving brass arms of the steam engine. Samuel wished he was one of them. They looked happy.

The music began to wheeze again and the machine turned slowly. The man came with his leather bag to collect the halfpennies: the young lad next to Samuel hunted for his money and couldn't find it because the pickpocket had forked him ten minutes ago.

The money-collector took the lad by the collar and accused him of cheating his way to a free ride. The lad protested that he'd had his pennies out and counted them before he got on to the machine. He made a big show of his indignation, but he was pale and frightened: the engine of pleasure turned faster, braying at his distress.

I could pay for him, said Samuel to himself, but he didn't move. And the money-collector shouted for the merry-go-round to slow down, shoved the lad off while the other merrymakers, who didn't know what was happening, hallooed and booed their disapproval. They wanted to move. Samuel thought he might cry – but he couldn't make a fool of himself in public. He found his own halfpenny and slapped it down on the back of his wrist: heads I'm a bastard, tails I'm not. The coin came down heads, but it wasn't conclusive evidence. The Queen's aquiline profile looked up at him.

'I'll pay,' said Reynolds.

'I'll have to find out, somehow, whose child I am,' said Samuel. 'I have to know.' The fairground heaved away from them: the pickpocket filched a gold watch from a stout farmer and slid off into the darkness that curled around the fairground like a black cat.

'Two shots a penny!' shouted the girl in charge of the shooting gallery, looking at Reynolds. 'Lovely prizes!'

There was the excitement again. And freedom, and danger. Samuel hoisted his leg over the horse's back to sit sideways, pitting his balance against the centrifugal force of the moving drum.

'You'll fall,' said Reynolds.

'No,' said Samuel. He still had the coin in his hand. The white spaniel sneered at him again.

'Look at the Queen's head on the coin,' said Reynolds from behind him. 'Hold on tight. Don't you think it looks like you?'

Samuel looked at the coin, then twisted his head round to the mirror. He saw his profile for a moment, before his body began to slide forwards.

Then he was falling, falling away from the merry-go-round, from Reynolds and the other riders and the sneering spaniel, and there was still the thin flat hardness of the coin in his fingers, and then a dark roaring like the sound of an express train.

He was very ill. He lay in his bedroom with his head bandaged and endured six weeks of muzziness and pain.

In the daytime they had the windows open to allow the air in to him, but the curtains were drawn round the bed. The faded chintz flapped in the wind: you could just see a faint illusion of roses against the cream background. It was autumn. Now and again he would get up out of bed, go to the open window, and look out at cottages and a dusty road where chickens ran and children played.

The sun patterned through the yellowing leaves of the old horse chestnuts on the tiny green opposite the rectory, and a few leaves drifted down in the wind: then a salvo of conkers thudded into the grass. It made his head ache to watch them fall, and he felt dizzy: with difficulty, he found his bed again.

Reynolds hadn't been to see him all day, and he was worried the Rector had dismissed him after all. He couldn't concentrate on his worries, though. He couldn't read or think. He didn't know what to do with himself.

He slept, and woke to find Mrs Pink standing over him, plump and nervous, her chest pinned up with a brown cameo mourning brooch.

'Asleep?' she asked, laying a warm damp hand on his forehead – her hand was never cool. 'Poor child,' she said, then, sharply all at once: 'I hope you'll let this be a lesson to you. Do you know how much anxiety you've caused? You can thank me: I've brought you some lemonade.'

Samuel compared her face with his, though it made him feel worse to think. He didn't look like her. She had brown eyes either side of a snubby fat nose that crumpled her face upwards, like a pug-dog's, and her full chin cascaded downwards in a rumple of secondary bulges.

He asked: 'Where's Mr Reynolds?'

'He's had to go to London,' said Mrs Pink. She sighed.

'When I'm so ill?' asked Samuel. She looked at him strangely. 'When's he coming back?' he asked.

'I don't know,' she said, and shut her mouth tight.

He found himself wondering if there was poison in the lemonade. They would have waited for his tutor to go away before they did it, so that Reynolds wouldn't see his blue, convulsed features, his stiff hands and fingers, and call the police. Maybe they'd already killed Reynolds. He felt very lonely and unsafe.

He drank cautiously, testing his stomach for cramps. She was fidgeting as she waited to take the drink away.

'Why must you drink so slowly?' she asked, then put her hand in front of her mouth as if she could fetch the words back. 'Go back to sleep,' she said.

He knew – even if she wasn't poisoning him – that she was glad to have him asleep, quiet, still, that she was able to endure the inconvenience of his illness for the blessing of the silence in the house. He comforted himself that they must be getting money for his care, from his real parent – they certainly weren't looking after him for love – so of course they wouldn't kill him off. He stared at the bed-curtains and tried not to see menacing faces emerging from the shapes of the long-dead roses.

The worst thing was to be told nothing. To be left wondering. And why hadn't Mr Pink bought the painting of him and his dog?

The painter had been there on the green one day, a canvas bag slung over his shoulder, looking about him. The spiky green conker shells were filling out and the leaves were September-weary, torn at the edges. He'd watched Samuel come out of the rectory gate. He was a brown middle-aged man with bright eyes and dust on his clothes, and he was putting up at the Dog and Duck.

He wanted to paint Samuel. The Rector permitted it. So Samuel sat on the grass with his dog, and the painter told him stories of the East – he had been out there, to China, and there he had painted junks and mandarins and had only just survived a seafight with pirates, whom he held off single-handed with one revolver. Samuel listened, delighted.

'I'm going to find a dinosaurus,' he said, 'the cliffs are full of them, it's only a matter of time. Every time there's a fall of rock, I go to hunt. I want to be famous.'

The painter dabbed from palette to canvas, and Samuel and his black spaniel appeared there: you couldn't see how small Samuel was for his age, because he was sitting down. The painter saw and represented Samuel's wondering, rather naive face and small eager hands, the hint of bewilderment in his blue eyes. When he finished the painting, he took it to the rectory, and Mr Pink looked at it, thanked him, and refused to buy it.

The window blew shut with a bang. Samuel's head ached so much he thought he was quite likely to die.

There were paintings of the Rector's parents in the house, a miniature of Mr Pink as a young man, and a painting of Mrs Pink when she was a young wife. The Rector valued the family portraits, but he hadn't wanted to add Samuel to the collection. And why hadn't he been sent to school? The Pinks said he was delicate – but he was never ill. It was as if someone was keeping him prisoner here.

The Rector came in and offered him another tract: *On the right use of leisure, and the necessity of using well the talents the Lord has lent us.* The Rector might not be his father, might not love him, but he was a virtuous man. He visited and relieved the poor, and preached a sermon of his own every Sunday – an hour at least. He understood God. Samuel remembered Hell, and was frightened again.

'I'm sorry,' he said. 'I shouldn't have gone to the fair.'

'Is this real repentance,' asked the Rector, 'or are you only saying you're sorry you were hurt?'

The Rector was very tall: he had a thick head of iron-grey hair that had once been black, intense grey eyes and a thin face at odds with his heavy mottled and congested nose. The sea mists didn't agree with him. He couldn't stir without his handkerchief.

Samuel fiddled with his sheet. He asked: 'Why's Mr Reynolds gone to London?'

'Inquisitiveness,' said the Rector, 'won't help you get better. You'll over-tax your brain. Are you really sorry, Samuel?'

'Yes,' said Samuel. 'It was wicked of me.'

The Rector said heavily: 'What is beyond purchase, Samuel, is the knowledge of our own fallibility, our need for the saving grace of God.'

He left the room without saying goodbye.

Samuel lay in bed on Sunday evening, while the wind pulled at the trees outside and blew twigs and leaves against the glass. The church would be draughty and shivery. They were singing: he could just make out the melody.

> Eternal Father, strong to save,
> Whose arm doth bind the restless wave,
> Who bidd'st the mighty ocean deep
> Its own appointed limits keep:
> O hear us when we cry to thee
> For those in peril on the sea.

But the sea didn't keep its limits on this coast: it was dragging the edges off the land, and on nights like this it battered the clifftops. You could never forget the sea. The air smelt of it, even inside the church. He could hear it now, gnawing and grinding the Chesil Beach, overpowering the words of the hymn.

God wasn't here to protect him, He was in church with the rest of the household. It felt very lonely.

He shouted: 'Come out with it! Tell me the truth!' There was no answer. Then he was afraid of what the truth might be. It might burst out of the walls and drive him mad. He couldn't breathe.

Reynolds came into the room, laughing at him. He sat on the bed close beside Samuel and slapped his shoulder gently: Samuel thumped him in return.

'Where have you been?' he demanded.

'Away,' said Reynolds. 'Doing business.'

His face was cheerful and covered with freckles. He was a clever cricketer, a good sport, an indulgent and interesting teacher. He was Samuel's ally against the Pinks. Now he was back, Samuel was safe.

'I want to be better,' said Samuel. 'I'm tired of this.'

'You will be,' said Reynolds. 'Listen, I've got a book to read to you.'

'What's it called?' demanded Samuel.

'*Among the Cannibals*,' said Reynolds. 'It's frightening. Will you mind?'

'I like thrilling books,' said Samuel, 'and of course the hero gets away.'

'Of course,' said Reynolds, 'he always gets away. Doesn't he?'

2

THE SIXTEENTH
BIRTHDAY

SAMUEL had a wavy, vulnerable mouth beneath the young moustache: he tried to set it firm as he sat at the yew-wood table in the rectory dining room. Russet foxes' heads lay under the French polish and they looked up at him, wild and fearful, as if the hunt was out and after them.

Every one of Samuel's birthdays began this way: he sat in the dining room and was given his report for the year, from Reynolds, from the Rector. Then he'd be given money, and a present. His spaniel had come five years ago, ponies had arrived as Samuel grew. They were good presents, but there was a formality about them, as if the Rector's heart wasn't in them. This one was different: Reynolds had warned him. He was going to be told.

How would the Rector do it? Samuel wished he was taller. Sometimes, when he thought no one would notice, he pulled himself up on the furniture, standing on the points of his toes to add an inch or so to his height. He thought everything would be so much easier if he was tall. He caught Reynolds's eye, looking for reassurance, but Reynolds was biting his lip: he seemed to be as nervous as Samuel. He tried to smile, and Samuel was grateful for that.

He looked out of the window and saw the rectory cat crossing the lawn with a small fieldmouse in her mouth: you could see the thin tail stringing out beyond her whiskers. The mouse was alive, hoping to get away, but the cat would play it and torment it. The foxes kept quiet, motionless, deep down where they lay in the wood.

The Rector stood up and blew his nose. This was a noisy performance and hard work, but it showed he was about to speak. Samuel clenched his hands. There was a moment's silence. Mrs Pink

9

cough-coughed and tried to suppress it. Then the Rector put his handkerchief up and trumpeted again.

Samuel saw Reynolds take out his silver watch and wind it hastily, then turn it over to look at the initials on the back: it had belonged to his father, who was dead.

'Samuel,' said the Rector. Samuel looked at his knees. His mouth was hideously dry. 'Look at me,' said the Rector.

Samuel turned his blue eyes up to the man whose surname he bore. He wanted to ask the question for himself but he knew he mustn't.

The Rector's voice was unusually kind, forbearing even.

'Samuel,' he said, 'we have been parents to you for sixteen years, and you have been a good boy, by and large. You have some lessons to learn in the field of *obedience* – sometimes I'd call you headstrong – but I don't want to dwell on that. Not now. And you are easily influenced.'

For a moment, he looked pettishly at Reynolds. But it was a tolerant irritation. Reynolds even grinned.

'You see,' said the Rector, 'we are not your natural parents, Samuel. Your mother sent you to live with us. I can't tell you who she is. But she has sent a letter for you, for your sixteenth birthday. She directed that you should be told today.'

Samuel's face felt cold. He stared at the Rector.

'Does it come as a shock to you, Samuel?'

He said: 'So I'm a bastard.' It was what he'd feared.

'Not in the eyes of the world,' said the Rector, hastily.

Reynolds began to drum his fingers on the table.

Mrs Pink muttered something about her nerves, and fetched out her smelling salts. Her eyes watered. She said: 'I must lie down,' and left the room.

'You knew,' said Samuel to Reynolds. 'All the time.'

Hastily, the Rector said: 'Nothing has changed, Samuel. Your tutor will continue to educate you. You will attend one of the universities. Your mother and I – for we *do* regard ourselves as your parents – will keep you constantly in our prayers. Plans have been made for you. They are in this letter. You must read it.' He sat down. His dignity hadn't lasted him out: he was a fussy, agitated old man.

Samuel sat clutching the envelope, white and addressed to him in blue ink and a feminine hand.

Hurriedly, the Rector said: 'I must not be questioned, Samuel. That is all.'

He shambled out of the room, his clerical skirts cluttering his ankles. No one had said anything about presents.

'You knew,' said Samuel to Reynolds, 'and you fed me fairy-tales.'

Reynolds said: 'I'd have lost this post if I'd told you. And I told you you were right.'

Samuel said: 'You pretended I was the heir to a kingdom. Bastards can't inherit anything.'

Reynolds put his hand over his eyes. Samuel was glad to see him hurt, he wanted everyone to hurt. He wanted to share the pain the truth had surprised him with, in case, thinned out, it might be more bearable.

He stood up. I'm going down to the beach.'

There'd been a fall of rock down at the beach the day before but Samuel didn't go looking for his fossil dinosaurus. He was still clutching the letter from his mother: sooner or later he'd have to read it. He sat down among the grey crumble of decayed rock and round stones, and looked at the sea.

There was no one on the beach. He could see where the fishermen's boats had rested on the shingle, but they were out at sea. The sea and the sky were grey, and it was blowy. His fingers, scrabbling beside him, came up with a roundy object, ribbed at the side. It was an ammonite. He looked at it for a moment, then put it in his pocket. It was a good ammonite, and he should have been pleased with it, but it wasn't interesting any more. Fearfully, he opened the letter.

Dear son Samuel, now at last you have reached your sixteenth birthday, it is time for me to write to you, and I shall continue to do so. There are those who will inform me how your life is progressing, though there are good reasons why you must never write to me. You may find this hard. It cannot be changed: I am sorry if it causes you pain. Nor must you try to find out who I am.

You are the product of what some would call sin. It did not seem so at the time, and I shall not give it that name now. Your father is a good man, and your ancestry is one to be proud of. I cannot say more. You must be worthy of the attainments of your forefathers,

Samuel. My position demands that I keep your existence secret. I have duties to fulfil, work to carry out. But do not believe, dear son, that my heart has not often yearned for you.

You are to carry on your studies with Mr Reynolds. He will prepare you for Oxford. After that, you are to go abroad, either to India or to our Far Eastern colonies. The world is full of promise for young men who know how to work hard, and I have heard that you are intelligent. I am glad. You are to work hard and do me credit. We will never meet, but I shall write to you every birthday. I shall pray for you and hold you in my heart.

It was signed: *Your affectionate Mother.*

He saw Reynolds coming along the path to the beach, between the gorse-blossom where the bees fussed and fed. He had something in his hands: Samuel realized it was his father's watch. He came up to stand in front of Samuel, facing the cliff-fall and began to wind it again. The spring snapped with a small metallic snarl – Reynolds flinched.

'I've got an ammonite,' said Samuel, pocketing his letter.

'You've got a mother,' said Reynolds. 'She's going to look after you and make sure you're never in need. You'll have a good job, and people under you.'

Samuel swallowed. He said: 'I can't talk about it. Look at my ammonite. It died such a long time ago, and it's still here. It's beautiful.'

Reynolds said: 'So you won't need me much longer. I'll have to look for another job. You'll be at Oxford, and I don't know where I'll be.'

Samuel ran his fingers round and round the curve of the dead, fossilized ammonite, feeling the grooves. He said: 'I don't decide these things, do I? You can't teach me everything I need to learn. And you lied to me.'

'I didn't,' said Reynolds. 'Give me that thing.'

'No,' said Samuel, 'it's mine.'

'You're spoilt,' said Reynolds. 'You think you can throw me away.'

The sun came out, lighting the gorse-blossoms lurid yellow against the gloom of the further sky, and dazzling Samuel. Reynolds snatched the ammonite and began to run, his feet sliding and sinking among the stones of the beach. Samuel scrambled up and came after him, but it was hard to hurry. Reynolds went up the hill towards the clifftop, panting, but keeping his lead.

When he reached the top, he stood still, then, when Samuel was within a foot of him, he swept his arm back and bowled the ammonite, overarm –

'No!' cried Samuel, but it was too late. The ammonite swept forward in a neat clean arc like the red cricket ball, and was gone, lost in the dazzling unquietness of the water. Reynolds laughed.

'I hate you,' said Samuel. He grabbed the tutor's hard-muscled arm, and lobbed a punch straight at his face. But Reynolds parried him. It was easy for him to hold Samuel off: hadn't he taught him to box?

Samuel came back, all the same, determined to force the fight, desperate – not to win, but to hit someone, to hurt someone. Reynolds snarled, and took him on. He was angry enough to miss a few punches, but most of them he parried easily. Samuel felt his powerlessness. He was going to lose. The sun went away.

It began to rain in wet cold smacks on his hot body, and his courage and his guard fell away together. Reynolds's fist smashed into his nose: he found himself prone, blubbering and snuffling on the grass.

The rain came harder, soaking through to his scalp, enveloping him in a veil of confusion and despair. He was quite alone.

The stranger came out of the rain and fell on him, pinning him to the ground. Then his hand went roughly under Samuel to undo his trousers.

It hurt dreadfully. He wanted to vomit, but his face was too close to the ground. He held it in. He submitted, his nose smearing blood on the stiff windswept grass.

'You wanted this, boy,' whispered the stranger, close in his ear.

Samuel couldn't say anything. Then the weight went off his buttocks, and he heard footsteps going away. He was alone again. Presently, he curled on to his side, pulled his trousers up and fastened them: his mother's letter crackled in the pocket. The rain eased off.

There was a clump of wild thyme by his hand and he pulled some leaves off, bruised them and sniffed them, but there was hardly any scent. Perhaps it had been taken away from him: after all, he was illegitimate. He had no right to exist. Now he'd brought punishment on himself. He'd never suspected the depth of evil there was inside him. If he was a cannibal, he'd have been less repulsive. He felt he'd been marked, like Cain, only his mark was in a secret place. That made the whole thing worse.

'Is it possible to repent?' he asked God. 'Is there any saving grace for someone like me?'

He felt Hell all about him, and it was a cold place, full of icy sinners who'd have welcomed some flames to warm them.

Reynolds's voice came into his trance.

'Still there? What's happened to you?' He sounded concerned.

'Nothing,' said Samuel. 'I just couldn't get up.'

Reynolds said: 'You'd better forget about that fight. You shouldn't have gone for me, you know.'

He pulled Samuel to his feet and led him down to the sea, where he began to wash him in the salt water.

'No,' said Samuel, 'I'll wash myself.'

Reynolds sat on the shingle and watched him rinse the traces of violence off his face. He was still desperately cold.

'We won't say anything about it,' he said.

Reynolds patted his shoulder. Samuel gave a little shudder. Reynolds passed him his handkerchief to dry himself off. But he felt the uncleanliness inside his trousers.

'Do you know who she is?' asked Samuel suddenly. He could ask, while his feelings were frozen.

'Your mother?' Reynolds frowned.

'You do know,' insisted Samuel, 'don't you?'

Reynolds said slowly: 'I don't know if it's safe to tell you.'

'I can keep my mouth shut,' said Samuel. 'Whatever it is.' He made a tight fist of his left hand.

'You saw the coin, at the fair,' said Reynolds. He watched Samuel's face.

Stupidly, Samuel asked: 'The coin?'

Reynolds said: 'I'm employed by a solicitor in London. He handles your affairs. He had a letter from your mother on his desk. I didn't see the signature, but I saw the coat of arms.'

'Yes?'

'The royal coat of arms. I worked it out: the dates would fit.'

'I'm the Queen's son.'

'Yes,' said Reynolds, 'the Queen's son by her servant John Brown.'

Samuel remembered cartoons he had seen in the newspaper, a pamphlet he'd found lying around in the schoolroom:

Noble Britons, does it not shame your bulldog blood to think that you are ruled by the *Power Behind the Throne*? This drunken and insolent Highlander has acquired such influence over *Her Majesty the Queen* that he has prevailed on her to engage in a *Secret Marriage*, and more, the Authors of this pamphlet have discovered that she has born him a *bonny baby*!

He couldn't remember the rest.

Reynolds said: 'I expect they smuggled you out of Balmoral in a warming-pan.' He grinned.

Samuel said: 'She wrote that my ancestry was one to be proud of.'

'I wasn't lying, you see,' said Reynolds.

Samuel said: 'But I'm a bastard.'

'Will you show me the letter?' asked Reynolds.

'No,' said Samuel.

Reynolds said: 'You're the only one that's his. And as for the others – Bertie and Beatrice, Leopold, Alice, Louise, Alfred, Victoria – none of them can bear him. Probably they discuss you when they go out with their whisky and biscuits into the heather. Before they start whatever else they get up to there. The Queen's immune to cold, I believe.' Reynolds laughed. Then he said: 'I shouldn't have said that. I'm sorry.' He looked shiftily at Samuel. Samuel couldn't bear it and he gave him the letter to read after all.

He didn't want to ask Reynolds any more questions. He couldn't write to his mother and ask her. He thought of Burrows, the housekeeper. Her sister was in royal service at Osborne, on the Isle of Wight. But Burrows had a way of gossiping without opening her mouth – she pressed her lips together instead and an expression came over her face: *I know what I know*, that could set the whole neighbourhood ferreting after it. He mustn't say anything to Burrows.

Reynolds looked up from the letter: 'You see what she says – her position demands that you stay a secret. There's enough scandal about the Prince of Wales, and the scandal about her and John Brown is bad enough without anyone finding out you exist. She couldn't possibly acknowledge you.'

There would be no call, no kingdom for him. But wasn't there another calling? Samuel felt hope after all. Even though he had been punished so unspeakably, he was alive, he wasn't damned. And his mother would hear about his progress, the Queen would hear about his progress.

'I've got to grow up,' he said to Reynolds. 'No more games, no more going out at night. I've a lot of work to do.'

Reynolds asked: 'So that they make you Governor of India? Shall I keep this for you?'

'No,' said Samuel. 'Please give it back.'

Reynolds held onto it for a moment: Samuel's heart thumped and he felt sick again.

'Please,' he said.

'What you don't realize,' said Reynolds, 'is how lucky you are.'

The Rector gave Samuel missionary tracts, and told him about a man called Fawler, who had gone out to China from Abbotsport, a good man, the Rector said, though enthusiastic, not a gentleman, a Methodist. And you didn't have to be a missionary, said the Rector, to spread the knowledge of the Lord. All you had to be was a Christian.

'And what I do in anything,' quoted Mr Pink, 'to do it as for thee.'

Samuel was pleased to find his foster-father paying him so much attention, but then the Rector said exactly the same words in the pulpit at matins, and Samuel knew he had only been trying out his sermon. He dedicated himself, all the same, kneeling beneath the window the old Squire had put up in memory of his only son, dead in the Crimean War. After that he stopped jumping when the shadows moved at night.

'British trade,' said Reynolds in the middle of his Greek lesson, 'is reaching out to the furthest corners of the earth. British inventiveness is lightening the darkness of ignorance. British greatness requires that it be so.' He paused. 'Have you read the missionary tracts?'

'Yes,' said Samuel.

'You never used to,' said Reynolds, 'but I suppose you need to understand every aspect of the Empire.'

'What do you mean?' asked Samuel.

Reynolds said: 'The way in which religion is used.'

'How?' asked Samuel.

Reynolds said: 'First the Bible, then the sword, then the merchant. It's all to do with power. You persuade the poor devils, if you can, that your God is better than theirs. If you can defeat someone's God, you can defeat them.'

Samuel said: 'But there is only one true God.'

'Yes, of course,' said Reynolds. 'So we'll turn back to your Greek. You have to work hard at Greek. You'll need to learn languages, out there. To govern the natives.' He laughed. 'Xenophon, Samuel. *Anabasis* Four. The march to the sea. You'll miss the sea at Oxford, won't you?'

'I'm nervous about living in college,' said Samuel, 'with the other young men.'

'Don't worry,' said Reynolds. 'You're living in lodgings. Arrangements have been made. I'm coming with you. We won't be parted yet: aren't you glad?'

Samuel felt nothing. He found it difficult to believe that he'd go to Oxford anyway, let alone hundreds of miles across the world.

The Easter before he went to Oxford, John Brown died. Samuel's mother said nothing about it in her annual letter, but of course she was trying to keep the secret. She praised his progress in his studies and urged him to keep them up when he went to Oxford: *I have made sure*, she wrote, *that you will be kept safe from temptation*. She sent him a complete set of Virgil's work, calf-bound.

Reynolds said: 'She did that for the Prince. He wasn't allowed to live in college either. It didn't stop him getting into mischief, though.'

He grinned at Samuel.

'I mean to be good,' said Samuel. He said: 'My father's dead.'

'Do you think,' asked Reynolds, 'that he called her "Your Majesty" in bed?'

Samuel knew he wasn't safe from temptation, not with Reynolds making questionable remarks. At night, when the lights were out, he prayed for his tutor's soul, and his mother's. You couldn't pray for the souls of the dead, but he told the Almighty how much he hoped his father hadn't gone to Hell, which would have to do instead.

Everyone turned out to watch them leave for Oxford, the two housemaids, Burrows, the cook in her apron, the gardener, the gardener's boy, the Reverend and Mrs Pink. The retired schoolmaster whose hobby was photography came to take a photograph: he almost made them miss the train, and then the photographs came out blurred because of the old man's shaky hand.

Bright red berries of *Iris foetidissima* surrounded the front porch of the rectory: Samuel's black spaniel whined and begged to come too. He would be in lodgings, in Oxford, and couldn't take her with him. He was just seventeen. His heart ached for the dog, who was doomed to be abandoned. He felt treacherous. He wanted to leave.

The Rector said: 'Work hard and do credit to yourself. Do nothing you'd hesitate to do with your mother looking on.' Samuel wondered if he meant Mrs Pink or the Queen. The Rector pulled his gold watch out, and said: 'You'd better go.'

Samuel climbed up into the station fly, and Reynolds came in after him. The driver shook the reins and they were off, along the familiar road to Abbotsport, the sea almost always visible to their left, the cliffs rising to their height at Golden Cap in the distance. It was a clear day, and you could just see The Cobb at Lyme Regis.

The station at Abbotsport was quiet – a halt on a small branch line to the seaside. Then the train came in, all steam and dark metal and oiled arms moving the wheels back and forth. Samuel thought that he had studied Xenophon's *Anabis*, the *Iliad*, the *Odyssey*, Catullus' Odes, the Georgics, had learned from Virgil how to make bees swarm out of a dead horse, and yet was utterly ignorant about steam engines. The world stretched ahead of him, complex and alluring and a little frightening. He had no idea how any of it worked.

He was moving faster than he had ever moved before. He looked out of the window and watched the countryside run away. They changed at Maiden Newton and Bath. Maiden Newton was quiet, but the station at Bath was crazy Bedlam, pushing and shoving and shouting. Reynolds dragged him through the crowd to a packed waiting room where they drank tea between trains: the waiters made ribbons of their abdomens and squeezed through the cracks between the chairs: the tea ran over the trays and dripped on the seated travellers. They gulped their tea, stood up and forced their way out on to the platform to catch the connection to Didcot.

The train panted them along again between embankments blackened by smoke, charred in places where sparks had set the dry grass on fire.

Reynolds said: 'This is the great world, Samuel. Do you like it?'

It smelt nasty, got under your fingernails, and blackened them. The train shook with every joint in the rails. And yet –

'It's progress,' said Samuel. He knew that much, at least.

'Isn't it horrible?' asked Reynolds. 'Isn't it a juggernaut that throttles the humanity out of us? Well, it does *you* good. You'll be off to China, and I'll have to look for another badly paid job, in a family or a school. No progress for me. I'll stay what I am. A poor needy usher.' His voice was bitter.

'I'll write to you,' said Samuel helplessly. 'I didn't know you minded so much.'

'Didn't you?' asked Reynolds. 'I'm sorry to upset you.' He shuddered.

'Oh – ' said Samuel. 'It was my fault. I was inconsiderate.' He couldn't be princely and say he'd look after Reynolds, because he was powerless himself. He felt guilty, all the same. The smoke came grey against the windows and cut them off from the fields outside.

'I'm tired,' said Reynolds. He shut his eyes.

Samuel watched him for a moment: he was pale and all the freckles stood out on his drained sagging face: he's ugly, thought Samuel, I never knew how ugly he is, like an ugly poor person's child that gets slapped for asking questions.

Then he was ashamed that he'd watched his tutor and thought these thoughts. He shut his own eyes and the motion sent him to sleep.

He dreamed he was going through a jungle to hunt tigers. The jungle was lush and full of enormous toothed leaves and sprays of bright red berries. There were coconuts waving on trees overhead – and snakes – armfuls of snakes, whom he tried to kill with his revolver, but they wriggled out of the way and came after him. Then he found a dark maiden with her back against a tree and a tiger at her throat. He shot the tiger and it collapsed like a rug on the jungle floor.

The maiden was covered in jewels everywhere, they were in her ears, in her nose: they glowed green as poison. She began to topple: he caught her in his arms. He thought she'd swooned but she was dead. Though he couldn't see how, he knew he'd killed her. He held her in his arms: she smelt like a wilting rose with a whiff of rot about her. Her thick hair – seeded with pearls like the starry night – tickled him, and he saw how beautiful her glazing dark eyes had been, deep pools of darkness.

He began to cry. The snakes crept down out of the trees and clung round his shoulders, his neck, licked the tears off his cheek, but they had it in for him – he saw their yellow lidless eyes sizing him up. Any moment now, they were going to attack his throat.

Then the angel came. She was a wonderful creature in white with pale-gold hair and eyes like amethysts. She lifted her staff of silver and the snakes vanished along with the dark maiden's corpse.

He wanted to let his head fall on the angel's breast, he wanted to drink the ineffable milk of her boundless understanding, but she slipped away too. He woke up, frightened and shivering.

He wondered how his mother could want to keep him from temptation, when she refused to admit the sin of his conception. Because, from what she said in the letter, if she had married John Brown, it could only have been after the event.

3

THE OTHER CHILD
Lily, London 1883

———————

MR Jackson said: 'Lily, I'm going to tell you a story.'

Lily, who had been staring at the red chrysanthemums on her Japanese lacquer desk, raised her eyes to Mr Jackson's handsome old face. She glanced at him, half smiling, for a moment, no more, then lowered her eyelids.

'Good,' said Mr Jackson. 'Just like that.'

She could see her face dimly mirrored in the desk: she opened her black eyes again wide and caught sight of the languid, teasing expression he liked. But she couldn't see her downcast eyelashes against her jasmine-white cheek.

Mr Jackson said: 'It is the story of a Chinese man who wanted to live forever.'

'Can anyone live forever?' asked Lily.

Mr Jackson smiled at her with tender contempt; this was also part of the game.

'You're a butterfly, Lily,' he said, 'a beautifully made piece of delightful folly.'

Lily put her lips out to make them fuller still: she frowned and turned away from him. He put his hand on her shoulder, and she shook it off.

'Lily,' he said, 'Lily, you like stories, little flower, won't you listen?'

The shouts of children playing in the garden of the London square came through the window along with the sweet heavy smell of lime-blossom. Lily giggled suddenly.

'That's pretty,' approved Mr Jackson.

She took his hand, patted it, and said: 'Tell me.'

There was a scroll-painting of a mountain hanging on the dark brocaded wall opposite. Mr Jackson pointed to it and said: 'There's the story. Now I'll tell you what it's about.'

Lily opened her eyes wide. She listened.

Mr Jackson said: 'Once, a long time ago in China, there was a very wise man who had many disciples; his name was Chang. One day he took them to the edge of a cliff, very high up on the mountains, where the clouds hang. There was a single peach tree just as thick as my arm growing out from the rock, which plunged down so far you couldn't see the valley.'

The stylized clouds sat in perfect relation to the cliff which had been quickly, confidently brushed with the minimum of strokes necessary to indicate its precipitousness: the leaves and peaches on the contorted tree were the only part of the painting that the artist had coloured in. The wise man and his followers stood like ants on the cliff-edge.

Mr Jackson said: 'Chang told his disciples that any one of them who could fetch the fruit could learn the secret of immortality. Now, Lily, they all wanted to live forever, and that was why they were following the Master. But they were terrified of the abyss. They leaned down, and there were the peaches – but how could they possibly get down there to fetch them?' He paused. 'You're so pretty,' he said suddenly, 'sweet as sandalwood, and you're only thirteen years old, and I'm already sixty.' He sighed. 'I used to climb mountains,' he said, 'in Austria, and France, and in China, too. I was as surefooted as a mountain goat.'

Lily opened her eyes wide again, met his, and saw them suddenly full of fear. She dropped her own at once.

'The clouds came up all round them,' said Mr Jackson slowly. 'That made the gaping emptiness even more frightening. Their heads began to swim. They crouched there on the edge of the abyss, they became grovelling idiots.' He turned away from her and held on to the edge of his carved blackwood chair.

Lily said: 'Mr Jackson?'

He didn't answer.

Lily got up and came up close to him. She rubbed her cheek against his hand. Then he put his arm round her and his hand touched her chest where it ached nowadays, where the little points that had sat pale and meek for so long had just begun to grow fat and a little darker. She gasped, because he hurt her.

He said: 'Lily.'

She didn't care if he hurt her, if only he knew she was there.

She said: 'Mr Jackson?'

He said: 'Don't talk, Lily, don't ask questions. I don't like you to chatter, you know that.'

She closed her red mouth.

He said: 'I couldn't do it. I felt as if the mist was a new country. I wanted to walk out into it, straight off the mountainside. I couldn't. I wasn't brave enough. You know what happens to cowards, Lily?'

Lily said again: 'Mr Jackson?' His face had changed, was strained almost out of recognition. His thick white hair seemed to have thinned within minutes.

He said: 'There were two men who had the courage to go down. They got the peaches and escaped death.' He frowned. He said: 'Lily, come and sit on my knee.'

He had never invited her on to his knee before. But she came at once and sat down there, swinging her legs in her Chinese silk trousers. He held her light warm weight to his ageing body. She turned and smiled at him, all open and trustful. Then she tried out the teasing look again. He ran his hands over her back, stroked her firm little buttocks, her legs, her chest, flicking the swollen nipples.

'It hurts,' she said with a little sigh.

He said: 'Poor Lily.' He kissed her lightly on her shiny black head. He asked: 'You don't want me to die, do you?'

She hid her face in his Chinese silk robe, and whimpered. She mumbled: 'What would I do without you? I would be sent to beg on the streets.'

He said: 'Or to the workhouse. I have to stay alive, haven't I, for you? No one else cares for you as I do.'

Lily said: 'My nurse cares for me.'

He said: 'She cares for the money I pay her.'

'Mr Jackson,' she asked, 'couldn't you teach me Chinese?'

He frowned. 'Why do you need to learn Chinese?'

She stroked his arm to coax him. 'I might be able to go back to China and find my family.'

He said: 'How would you find them, foolish child? I picked you up outside the walls of Soochow. There was nothing on you to show you belonged to anyone. You were wrapped in cotton rags. They didn't want you.'

He stared down at her for a moment, then slapped her cheek. She wasn't allowed to long for her parents.

She said: 'You're so clever, Mr Jackson, and I'm stupid.'

He said: 'No. *I'm* stupid. Or not clever enough. How can anyone be clever enough? And no plea of mercy will get me off the punishment for my stupidity. I should have stepped off the mountainside. I cowered there instead, pressing my back against a rock. I thought the abyss was stretching its arms out to pull me into it. The cliffs went up and down as far as you could see, Lily, and further. I knew that. So I didn't dare. I managed to reach the valley when the mist cleared. Who knows if the peach tree was waiting for me, if someone else picked the fruit?'

'Mr Jackson,' said Lily anxiously. 'I love you.'

He said: 'I shall die, Lily. I shall die and they'll take you away.'

Lily knew she mustn't cry now: this terror was too big for tears.

She said: 'You're so strong and healthy, Mr Jackson.'

He held her tight, as if he was about to fall off his chair. She could hardly breathe.

He said: 'The two men who went down for the peaches were called Chao Sheng and Wang Chang and the Master taught them all the secrets of immortality. Because the Chinese believe it is possible, Lily. Who should know that better than I?'

He put Lily off his knee and stood up. He bent his knees and made a few strange movements, moving back and forth and holding his arms out.

'Of course,' he murmured. 'That was it.'

Lily asked: 'Mr Jackson?'

His long dark-brown eyes lay each under a fold of skin: his face was almost Chinese, but pinker than Lily's pale Chinese skin. His hair was quite white. He took no notice of her now.

Lily wanted to go to him and tell him he could touch her and hurt her as much as he liked, but it wouldn't make any difference, she knew that – and she must always be careful. She was there to do as he wanted. She was a foundling: he had saved her from scavenging dogs who would have torn her apart and eaten her.

Sometimes she wondered if she had been left behind by accident, if her mother had come back for her and wept and torn her hair to find her baby gone. She couldn't believe that for long. Mr Jackson was right. Her parents had left her behind because they had wanted her to die.

Mr Jackson muttered: 'Where did I put it?' He strode out of the

24

room. Lily ran after him, her long plaits swinging and bumping her shoulders.

He had had special shelves made for Chinese scrolls, and they filled up a whole wall of his library. He rummaged among them, throwing precious manuscripts down, sometimes even walking on them, though Lily tried to gather them up out of his way. They were all neatly tied with silk ribbon and labelled with the Chinese writing she couldn't understand. The butler came to tell them luncheon was ready, but Mr Jackson shouted at him: he said the food could wait. And at last Mr Jackson found the scroll he wanted, opened it, read a few lines, and then sighed with content.

'Now,' he said, 'now we can eat.'

He was usually tidy in his movements, skilled with the brush and the pen and his knife at dinner. He carved a chicken with careful, controlled cruelty. Today he told Lily the story of Cook Ting, who butchered so skilfully the animals didn't even know they had been killed.

Lily opened her eyes wide. 'So they wouldn't have time to run away.'

'Why should they run away?' asked Mr Jackson, giving Lily a slice of breast, a slice off the leg, and a wing. 'If the animals could run away, humans wouldn't have anything to eat. They're there to be eaten.' Then he paused, and frowned.

Lily ate her chicken. She was grateful that Cook Ting hadn't butchered it, or the wing might still have been fluttering in her mouth.

Mr Jackson sat down at his desk in the night and began to write: he always wrote between eleven and two in the morning, when the house was quite silent. The row of his scholarly works sat leather-bound on the bookshelves opposite him: his gilt name went across every spine. If he opened any of them, his own superannuated words would echo emptily in his mind. Now he was writing his autobiography: he thought it might as well be his obituary. He hated his publisher for suggesting it.

He wrote: *Providence, Fate, Heaven, call them what you will, seem to have destined me to the study of Chinese classics; now, sixty years from my birth I have translated almost every Taoist work I could find.*

'With one exception,' he said aloud. The scroll he had found that afternoon lay beside him on the desk. He had tied it up again, with a neat bow of black ribbon. He held it for a moment. The clock ticked the seconds away with a discreet, measured movement.

He dipped his pen in the ink again.

I was born the son of a merchant in the Chinese country trade: in these times when our sensibilities are more delicate it seems dangerous to admit that my father's large fortune was made out of opium, though the trade has not yet been outlawed by us. I place it on record that he was never known to pass off inferior products or engage in dubious business practices, and, indeed, left a substantial legacy to various benevolent institutions and the relief of poverty when fever overcame him in Macao at the age of only forty-five years. My unfortunate mother died shortly after this and I was left a young, wealthy orphan. I was educated at Winchester School and New College, Oxford, and then journeyed out to China: my trustees had left many of his investments as they had been, and thanks to an honest business partner —

Mr Jackson put his pen down on the blotting paper and stared at the clock. He stood up. He went to the bookshelves and removed all the books that bore his name on the spine. He made a tower of them: they reached about as far as his thigh. He pushed the tower over and the books sprawled on the Chinese silk carpet.

He sat down at his desk again and wrote:

Master Chuang Tzu teaches acceptance of death, of change. When Master Lai lay dying, Master Li forbade his wife and children to weep. He joked with Master Lai, asking him what he thought Heaven might make of him next, the liver of a rat, the elbow of a beetle. Man's life, we learn from this text, is carried away by the flow of change and there is nothing anyone can do to prevent it. Yet there are the stories of the Immortals. If a man is utterly within the Way, and has the courage to undertake what other men will not do
— He put his hand on the scroll again. Then he wrote, jerkily: *I am an old man. I am going to die. How many cargoes of opium could blot out that fact? And now I sit here in the middle of the night, I am alone — solitude used to give me pleasure — and I am afraid.*

I am afraid.

He unbound the Chinese scroll and began to read it. After half an hour, he stopped. Then he began to inspect the writing, the characters, the paper, scrutinizing them closely with a silver-framed magnifying glass.

Lily saw her face in the mirror, her long black eyes, her pointed chin, the lips Mr Jackson was pleased with, because they were full and beautifully shaped. Her nurse behind her pulled the bristle brush through her hair, counting the strokes up to a hundred.

'Just look at the gloss on it,' she said proudly.

'Nurse,' said Lily. 'I'm bleeding. I don't know why.'

She was frightened, but she didn't cry. The big things, the really dreadful things, you kept inside yourself. Something might come and eat you if you made a noise.

'Oh, my baby – ' said the nurse. She was a short, large-breasted woman with a growing moustache. She put her hands on Lily's shoulders. 'It means you're growing up. I'll give you the cloths to use. You don't have to be afraid, it happens to women.'

Lily said: 'Please, can we go now?'

That was all she said. The nurse washed the blood off her and put the cloths tenderly round her. She'd had them ready for a year now.

'Keep yourself decent,' she said.

Lily's eyes questioned her.

She said: 'Don't let a man touch you till you're married. Only a kiss, when you're engaged.' There was no conviction in her voice.

Lily noticed. She said: 'Mr Jackson has no wife.'

Her body fluttered as it sometimes did when he looked at her, as if there was a frightened butterfly caught inside her clothes, against her skin.

'Look,' said the nurse. 'I've got you a paper. *The Girls' Own Paper*. It's published by the Religious Tract Society. You'll always read the Bible, won't you, and say your prayers, the way I've taught you?'

Lily laid her head against the nurse's breasts. They were soft and warm. The nurse held the paper behind her, enclosing her with her arms.

'It says here,' said the nurse, 'Where a pure and healthy heart cries out for one of a like purity, the answer is generally forthcoming.'

Lily had always felt safer with her nurse than she ever did with Mr Jackson. She hadn't told anyone that. Her real feelings were locked in a tight dark place at her heart. Mr Jackson had taught her they must stay there. Mr Jackson with his slaps had become their custodian.

'He's going to send me away,' said the nurse.

Lily wouldn't cry. She only said: 'Nurse?'

'You'll miss me?' asked the nurse.

'Of course,' said Lily, sweetly, caressingly. She put her arms round the nurse's waist and held tight. She sniffed the strong harsh smell of mingled coal-tar soap and sweat.

Lily said: 'I try to be a good girl.'

The nurse said: 'Get what you can out of him. Look out for yourself.'

Lily sat reading the article from *The Girl's Own Paper.*

> The leading, guiding and controlling impulse of women is to render themselves agreeable and helpful to men, whether by beauty, gentleness, forethought, energy, intelligence, domestic cares, home-virtues, toil – assistance, in 'hours of ease', in sickness, or amid the perplexities, anxieties, disappointments, and labours that environ life; it is so, and ever will be so, in spite of the 'strong-minded' who consider and describe as humiliation that which is woman's glory, and should be her boast.

Downstairs someone called, and the butler told him Mr Jackson was not at home. Lily went to the window and watched the top-hatted, greatcoated old man getting back into a hansom cab. Mr Jackson was reading in the library.

He had given the nurse her notice and she was going in five hours' time.

Aloud, Lily said: 'I belong to Mr Jackson. I *will* make myself agreeable and helpful to him.'

Lily had got the cook to buy a white-covered Bible as a parting present for the nurse. She had filched the money, from time to time, from the bag under the nurse's mattress. She didn't think the nurse would miss the amount, and how else was she to buy her a present?

If I ever have money, thought Lily, I shan't keep it under a mattress. Mr Jackson has investments. I shall do that, too.

Mr Jackson had an ivory image of Kwan Yin, Goddess of Mercy. Lily went to look at her gentle face. She held in her hand a series of filigreed balls: they sat snug inside each other growing smaller, and as far as you could reach they would move inside each other if you touched them.

I am in her hand, thought Lily, trying to find my way through those ivory spheres. It's difficult, and complicated, and they slide away under my feet.

The nurse was packing her things upstairs, crying because she was leaving Lily. Inside Lily's heart there was a long stabbing needle of desolation and she smiled back at Kwan Yin who was the only person who could be allowed to know about it.

Mr Jackson came, smoking his Chinese bamboo and ivory pipe. He had hung a Japanese kimono ornament at his belt. Lily had played with it when it was sitting with the others on the shelves.

'The peaches of Immortality,' she said to him, putting her hand out to stroke the smooth dark wood.

'Lily,' he said, 'would you help me?'

'Yes, of course,' said Lily. 'Of course, Mr Jackson, when you're so good to me.' She gave him the look he liked. His dark eyes stared down into hers as if he was searching her. She felt the butterfly fluttering against her body again. It was too much. This time she dropped her eyes because she had to.

Mr Jackson bent his long shapely fingers over each other and seemed to look inward and down. He said: 'Thank you,' and his voice was uncertain and hoarse.

Mr Jackson had many ivory sculptures. There was a model pleasure-boat of ivory, all the detail finely carved, the crew with their pigtails under bamboo hats, the ladies walking on the deck with their parasols – even the rigging was carved out of ivory and you could see every detail of it against the dark case it sat in.

One day a housemaid broke a piece of the rigging when she was dusting. Lily saw her.

'Look what she did to the boat,' she said to Mr Jackson.

The evidence lay on the Chinese rug, on top of silken bats and peaches and dragons.

'Oh, please, sir – ' begged the housemaid.

Mr Jackson picked the little boat up by the mast and threw it down on the floor.

'Stamp on it,' he said to the housemaid. Lily put her hands to her mouth.

'Oh, please, sir – ' said the housemaid again.

'Go on,' said Mr Jackson.

The housemaid trembled. She sobbed. Then, since he stood there, waiting, she put her boot on the boat and ground it into the carpet. It was crushed into splinters.

'You've destroyed it,' said Mr Jackson to the housemaid. 'Now you may go. Without wages. Or a character. I don't give a character to clumsy bumpkins.'

The housemaid squeaked with distress and shed tears. Mr Jackson walked away.

The housemaid vanished from the house, into the pitiless and hungry world outside.

The nurse wrote to Lily about the new family she was with, five children and a darling little baby. Lily hurt, hurt, hurt in that secret chamber where all the feelings were locked tight and lonely. She tore the letter up and never wrote to the nurse again.

Samuel and Reynolds lodged in Iffley, at the house of a widow. Every morning before breakfast they walked along the towpath towards Christchurch and back, or in the other direction, towards Sandford. It was usually foggy at that time, so they only saw hints of the buildings, the yellowing trees and fields, a few dull feet of the river. There was often a scull emerging from the mist: if the rower was experienced, they never heard him coming, there'd be the sharp boat all of a sudden, gone in a moment, the man inside intent on his exercise.

'I'm surprised the young gentleman never catches a chill,' said the landlady, coughing suggestively, 'when you say he's too delicate to live in college. My late husband always said the Oxford air made a fortune for doctors.'

'It's his heart,' said Reynolds. He made a grave face at Mrs Waltham. Samuel stuffed his hands in his pockets and shut his mouth tight.

'Oh, I *see*,' she said, impressed. 'Heart cases don't catch cold, that's quite true. My brother had a weak heart, and he could go out in the snow without a greatcoat. How bad is it, poor young gentleman?'

Reynolds shook his head at her. She put her hand to her mouth and looked nervously at Samuel.

'I can't have a death in the house,' she said. Samuel suppressed a snigger.

'It's not that,' said Reynolds. 'His nerves aren't strong. He doesn't like to have his health talked about.'

Samuel left the room quickly: Mrs Waltham thought he was offended. He heard her apologizing to Reynolds as he hurried up the stairs to their rooms. She told the parlourmaid, who made sure the breakfast dishes kept quiet, tutting fiercely at them if they clattered.

The house was dark and muffled anyway, everything was draped and shrouded in dark-red velvet and widow's lace, in brocade and dripping bobbles, while on the walls there hung engravings of hunting: 'The View Halloo.' 'The Kill.' The gaslights were always turned low. They were something new to Samuel – there were oil lamps at the rectory – though not very exciting. You got used to them too quickly.

Reynolds took him into the colleges to listen to lectures, but he had his tutorials on his own, given by a college Fellow who came to the house. The learned Doctor never gave any sign that the procedure was unusual: indeed, he hardly gave any sign that he noticed Samuel at all. He was a grey man whose mind seemed incapable of taking in anything that wasn't written or printed on paper. It was infectious: Samuel had to write the Doctor's name down and put it in his pocket because he kept forgetting it.

The first weekend, Reynolds hired a punt on the river and gave Samuel a chance to take the pole. Samuel fell in, but he was a good swimmer and didn't get caught in the trailing weeds. Reynolds hauled him out.

'We'd better sneak in,' said Reynolds, 'so that Mrs Waltham doesn't see how wet you are.'

'I'm a fraud,' said Samuel, but he was getting used to that. He was content to be on the punt, zig-zagging along the river, learning to test his body against the current and the pole. He got the hang of it after a little while. It was a bright autumn afternoon and the willows were dropping woolly white seeds in the water: they stuck to the punt pole and his clothes were full of them since he fell in. There were other men punting in parties of four, five, six: real students, who didn't need to be hidden away and lied about. They fell in too. They drank beer and champagne and shouted. Samuel was jealous of them, and a little frightened.

'You're not allowed strong drink,' said Reynolds, 'but – '

'No,' said Samuel, 'no, I mustn't.'

Then he drank some whisky after all because Reynolds laughed at him. It seared his throat, but he liked it. So they went to public houses where Reynolds flirted with the barmaids. There was one night when Samuel got terribly drunk and was sick on Magdalen Bridge. He was almost arrested, but Reynolds persuaded the policeman he was ill.

'If you were in college,' said Reynolds, propelling him along the Iffley Road, 'you'd have to wear a gown and have the proctors look out for you. You've got more freedom, with me. And the Prince of Wales made sure he had fun.'

He was the best companion, thought Samuel, putting his headache in cold water next morning, the most loyal friend.

He worked hard, all the same – he was determined to get a First. He sat for hours at his desk, studying. When he looked up he saw patterns of damp spreading like maps over the wallpaper: like maps of the British Empire, colouring the world red. His mother's world, his world. He was England's son. Yet what should a man do with so large a concept?

Then they went back to Dorset for the Christmas vacation. Samuel hadn't grown at all, but everything seemed smaller. He ran with his dog and rode his pony, but a growing impatience and discomfort made the days crawl, though he worked as hard as he could.

He thought about the Queen at Balmoral. He hoped she might walk the rooms at night, stopping by the Christmas tree with its knobbly burned-out candles, wishing she'd been able to give him his present in person. She might shed tears for him. He thought he could sense that yearning dovelike maternity flying to him across miles of cold air. He took the last letter out and read it: it was already creased and soft with handling.

Dear Samuel, you are seventeen now, and have worked hard at your studies. You are ready for Oxford. I am proud of you. I hope you will remember this, and that you will also remember God, to whom I commend you every night in my prayers. Oxford can draw many young men off their course, but I have made sure that you will be safe from temptation. Mr Reynolds will do his duty by you.

I am a long way away from you – I can tell you this much – in Scotland. It is hard for me to imagine the seasons down in England, and yet once I knew it well. I have endured a great deal of sorrow, dear son, and have been supported only by the conviction that God cares for me and has work for me to do. So I can assure you that there is consolation, even in the darkest hours, but only religion and

work can supply it. Remember that, and that my love and care for
you are constant.

Your loving mother.

Samuel found himself in tears. It felt better that he could cry. He didn't stop even when Reynolds came into the room, and Reynolds, as soon as he saw Samuel, turned and went out again.

He used to go down to the beach and look at the sea. It gave him no tenderness, throwing up only a few jeering gifts: a bottle, fragments of wood, a decomposing crab or a stranded evaporating jellyfish. Then a freak tide came up and took everything away, stripped most of the pebbles off the beach and left coarse sand in their place.

The vacation came to an end and they went back on the train to Oxford.

'It's decided,' said Reynolds. 'You're going to Hong-Kong. You're to take the examination for the Hong-Kong government service when you've finished your studies here. You'll train for a year, in London, then leave the country. For ever.'

He took the lid off the kidneys and helped himself. Samuel held his breath: he couldn't bear the smell of kidneys. Usually Reynolds put the lid down quickly, but today he kept the dish open, wafting the reeking steam over towards Samuel, who began to retch.

'You're too fussy,' said the tutor. 'You're spoilt.'

'Put the lid down,' said Samuel.

'All right,' said Reynolds. 'You need to learn to give orders. You'll have power. I wonder how you'll use it?' His face was strained. Samuel noticed that his hair was thinning.

As if in a dream, Samuel said: 'It's the responsibility of the ruler to order everything for the good of those he rules.'

'You're such an idealist,' said Reynolds, 'I have to tell you, or everyone will take advantage of you. It's the responsibility of the ruler to maintain his power. That's what he's there for.' He filled his mouth with kidney and mushroom and washed it down with syrupy tea: he always took three spoonfuls of sugar. He was getting fat.

'But surely,' said Samuel, 'we've got to serve God, make the world a better place?'

Reynolds asked: 'Do you really think the world is becoming better?'

Samuel said: 'Look at railways, for example. Gas lighting. The products that are so freely available everywhere. Manufacturing industry – '

'That's what they say,' said Reynolds, his breath coming short. 'But what about the places where that industry is carried out?'

'Oh, I know,' said Samuel, 'there are slums, but even there – there are Board Schools now, there are Acts regulating the hours people can work in the factories, children no longer go down coal mines – '

'Slums,' said Reynolds angrily. 'Hell. Misery. In spite of those improvements. It's about power. Don't let them fool you. There's always someone being walked over.' He knew Samuel's eyes were searching for his: he looked down. The carpet had moved a little, exposing an area of unstained floorboards.

Samuel said: 'I'll have to believe in the goodness of what I'm doing.'

'What do you mean by goodness?' asked Reynolds, kicking the carpet a little further to see the bare dirty wood.

'Law,' said Samuel, 'religion, decency.' He got up and put the carpet back.

'And feeling?' asked Reynolds. 'You wouldn't have been born without illicit feeling, would you?'

'That doesn't make it right,' said Samuel.

Reynolds said: 'Do you remember the fun we used to have when we ran away to have our adventures?' His eyes met Samuel's now, childish, oddly wild. 'The smell of the night air, when we weren't supposed to be out?'

Samuel felt his face twitch. He rubbed it, but it didn't make any difference. His heart began to race.

'A man grows up,' he said, though he hadn't grown very big. But he had long moustaches now, and wore a bowler hat. 'And I shan't get drunk any more. I don't like it.'

'Oh, don't deny wildness,' said Reynolds passionately, 'don't take feeling away and put machines in its place. Look at Iffley Church. Then compare it with the jerry-built villas they're throwing up now in Oxford.'

Samuel said: 'But Iffley Church was built by craftsmen. They were organized in guilds, they had rules.'

'Go on,' said Reynolds, 'go on, tell me everything I say is wrong, tell me you don't need me any more. I've cared for you: doesn't that count for something?' He stood up, knocking a teacup on to the floor, spilling the sugar all over the tablecloth. He went out on to the street.

A few months before Samuel's Schools Examinations, Reynolds threw a book down on his desk.

'Engravings of China,' he said. 'There are one or two of Hong-Kong, too. It's out of date, of course.' Reynolds said this as if it served Samuel right. 'Come on,' said Reynolds, 'look at it. You can go back to your Greek later.' His face was flushed: he smelt of alcohol. He wasn't quite drunk, but his face and even his eyes were inflamed and red.

Samuel opened the book and saw a canal, buildings with extraordinarily shaped roofs, a tall pagoda with bells hanging from the eaves, and hump-roofed boats propelled by people with wide straw hats. It looked exactly like the old wallpaper in the sitting room at the rectory.

He said: 'It's not real.'

'Oh,' said Reynolds, 'you'll find it's real all right. When you get there, and you're miles away from home. And from me. Won't you be glad to get away from me?'

He placed himself behind Samuel's back and put a hand on each shoulder. Samuel felt his spine tremble. He didn't know what to say to make it better for Reynolds, and the man was suffering. He turned the pages till he found a coloured picture of steep stony hills slightly shaded green, and a small town with white walls and red roofs. Boats were being built in the foreground. If the hills hadn't been so steep, if the people building the boats hadn't been wearing long pigtails and wide-brimmed hats, he'd have thought it was Dorset. The picture was called 'Hong-Kong from Kowloon.'

The hands were still on his shoulders. He could feel Reynolds's breath hot and damp on the back of his neck.

'I'll be by the sea,' Samuel said.

'That's right, Samuel,' said Reynolds viciously, 'put a brave face on it.' He let go of Samuel and went out.

Samuel stayed looking at the engraving: he thought if he kept quite still everything might fall into its right place again. He couldn't see any pagodas or bells in Hong-Kong, though there were hump-roofed boats. He was disappointed and reassured at the same time.

He tried to imagine himself working there, walking the streets between the peaks and the sea. There would be a lot of Chinese, heathens to whom he was bringing the blessings of civilization –

and their lives *would* be so much better for it. They'd be grateful to him.

But the Chinese in his mind wouldn't do as he bade them. There were pirates. And the Hong-Kong he saw was such an insignificant town, defended by a handful of boats. The brave whites were assailed by hordes of angry yellow men, who refused to accept their defeat at the hands of the British. The sort of murderous natives who'd killed General Gordon last year at Khartoum.

He set up a small but determined garrison inside one of the buildings he could see on the lower hills. By now the pirates had the building surrounded, their ships in the harbour had overpowered the small British fleet and cut every sailor's throat. The garrison was running out of ammunition. The women – precious creatures accustomed to the boudoir and the drawing room – had to run to and fro, binding up wounds.

There was a wonderfully beautiful woman among them, with white-blond hair and amethyst eyes: she was the angel of Samuel's dream. Where she passed, the men felt new courage. Samuel himself was wounded in the arm, but she tied it up to stop the bleeding and he was able to fight on.

But at last he was the only man left, and the angel the only woman – the others had all disappeared out of his mind. He could die defending her, but that would leave her to the mercy of the Chinese. The best thing to do was to shoot her before they could get to her, but he couldn't pull the trigger. He held the gun to her head, she begged him to shoot, any moment now he'd be dead and unable to shoot her.

He thought: But wouldn't the fleet arrive and save us? Then I'd be glad I didn't shoot her. We'd marry.

He put his head in his hands and cried for a moment, because he wanted to continue: We'd come home.

At breakfast time, Samuel would pick what he wanted from the dishes on the breakfast table, bacon, kedgeree, egg, mushrooms. He didn't like sausages. Reynolds ate everything: he said life had taught him not to be choosy about his food.

'Were you so poor?' asked Samuel, wonderingly. 'What was your father's profession?'

'My father was a lawyer,' said Reynolds. 'But he put all his money into a bank and it failed. So he died.'

Samuel didn't dare ask how the elder Reynolds had died.

Reynolds stuffed his mouth with sausages and kidney. He said: 'I had an uncle who paid for my education, and for me to go to Oxford. Then he went bankrupt. I got my degree and had to look for employment where I could. I answered an advertisement in *The Times* and was sent to educate you. That's my story. My mother died when I was at Oxford. She never saw me graduate.'

'Poor Mrs Reynolds,' said Samuel, turning his face away.

Reynolds began to eat again, only faster this time. Food spilled out of the corner of his mouth, and he seemed to be shivering. He said: 'It won't happen to your mother – you won't be destitute. Unless of course – '

'What?' asked Samuel.

'Revolution,' said Reynolds thickly through toast and marmalade. 'It happened in France, after all.' Then he laughed. 'Don't look so serious. I worry about you, you're so easy to make fun of.'

Ten minutes after Samuel had turned over the paper for his last Schools Examination, sitting in the lofty cold hall in his gown and mortarboard, he understood Greek tragedy as he'd never understood it before. The subject was Oedipus. Oedipus who'd killed his father and married his mother in spite of his own best efforts to avoid that fate. It was the sort of understanding that drove you mad and made you bore your eyes out. He began to shake: he put his sharp pen away. He thought Fate had made him evil, had laid it down in his character before he was born. So he had desired the unspeakable, the thing he never knew he'd invited, the frightful pain and humiliation of the stranger's assault on the clifftop. So Oedipus, when he fought Laius outside Thebes, entered the city, and found Jocasta making eyes at him.

He picked up his pen and wrenched it downwards to point at the paper. He found himself writing:

What else lies in store for me? My mother is unregenerate, doesn't that mean I have to bear the burden? If only she'd repented, my mother, my real mother – wicked Victoria – she lay in her nightgown and there was a bottle of whisky at her elbow, I suppose she lay in a huge bed with the royal arms at the head – and John Brown in his kilt and nothing else. And then they – like the animals in the farmyard, like the cow and the bull, it's quite horrible. How can anyone do it, but when it was wrong, when they weren't

37

married, because she admitted they weren't, she said I was the product of what the world would call sin. And I was born, and they sent me away with their sin wrapped round me, it sank in through my skin. Does she think she's above everything? There might still be a revolution. They might make me the President. That would serve her right. I could have her summoned to my presence and make her say she was sorry. Only as long as she's not sorry, I'll have to be —

An invigilator passed him, swishing his gown, and the paper flew on to the floor some feet away. The invigilator bent to pick it up.

He'd have to read it, only because it would condemn Samuel to the straitjacket. Samuel, facing ruin, fell into the empty reaches of space between two ticks of the clock, where he recognized God, eternity: *this* was the moment of deliverance, this was when the angel flew in. And nothing was as he thought. It was plain as the shaft of sunlight dancing on the austerity of the church wall, and it was gone in a second like the sunlight. He knew a moment's enormous refreshment, till his heart crashed like a sledge-hammer and brought him back.

He forgot it at once. The invigilator handed him the paper without looking at it. Samuel took his pen and inked over the words so that no one would ever be able to read them. Then he crumpled the sheet into a ball and began work on the Theban tragedy.

But his unruly mind kept running back to his parents, kept finding them where no son should ever surprise his mother and father. He put his pen down on his paper: wasn't it enough that he'd almost betrayed himself? He tried to order his thoughts. He desired order as the hunted animal longs for water. It eluded him.

He thought: I shall rededicate my life to virtue. I shall never have a woman I haven't married.

When the bell rang for the end of the examination, he'd only completed about half the questions. He wouldn't get a First now.

He got a Second, which was better than nothing. He went back to Dorset to work for the examinations that were being held for two Hong-Kong cadetships. Reynolds coached him. He'd have to take the examinations in handwriting, précis writing, English composition, Latin, Greek, arithmetic, and French. He found the arithmetic most difficult. Reynolds was impatient with him. His mind went blank. He was dreadfully frightened that he wouldn't manage it.

He struggled through, forcing himself to understand the figures

– they demanded an ordered mind – he *must* have a mind to master them.

He hated working in the old schoolroom. He wanted to get away from Dorset and the rectory: both had begun to feel like a tight scratchy coat he'd outgrown. He began to understand the arithmetic.

4

THE PROCESS OF CHANGE

'CHINESE food,' said Mr Jackson to Lily, lifting the huge blue-bladed chopper he had that morning received from Hong-Kong, 'unlike Western food, which is based on the principle of stuffing as many indigestible and incompatible items down the gullet as the stomach will take – '

Lily, wrapped in a big white linen apron, half-listened and saw the flush of indignation on the cook's face.

'What, sir,' asked the cook – trying to be meek – 'do you use this metal bowl for?'

'You chop the food small,' explained Mr Jackson, 'and heat it as quickly as possible inside the wok. This metal bowl, Cook, is a wok. Of course, not all Chinese food is cooked in this way. You can have the triple-boiled soup for example, the hot-pot. There are delicacies, fish lips, bear paws, pea sprouts, many kinds of edible fungus which promote long life. Now, to cook rice perfectly – '

'Sir,' demanded the cook rather loudly, 'do you expect me to learn all this?'

'I don't think you could manage it,' said Mr Jackson. 'I intend to cook.'

'Then I intend to give in my notice,' said the cook.

'I'll give you a reference,' he said. 'You'd better leave today. Your kitchenmaid will help me – or do you intend to leave, too?'

The kitchenmaid said: 'If I'm to do all the work in the kitchen, then of course I couldn't do it at the wage I'm – '

'Of course not,' said Mr Jackson. 'I'll tell the housekeeper to pay you a cook's wage. Now, Chinese food, Lily, is based on the harmonious interaction of yin and yang, thus it is always in balance, the spiced with the bland, the sweet with the sour, the dark with the light, and the hot with the cold. I'll teach you which foods are heating and which are cooling. We have to balance them. In winter, of course, what sort of foods would you want?'

'Heating, Mr Jackson?' asked Lily.

'Not so foolish,' said Mr Jackson, and actually laughed. He ran his hand down Lily's back. 'But there are many other more subtle things to be taken into account. Goodbye, Cook. Thank you for your services. Oh – the housekeeper will pay you your money in lieu of notice. Tell her to double it.'

'Thank you, sir,' said the cook, half pleased, half outraged. She blew a kiss to Lily, muttered: 'Poor little thing,' and left.

The kitchenmaid smiled.

Mr Jackson said to Lily: 'The performance of generous acts can lengthen a man's life. Likewise when the yin and the yang are in balance – this isn't a static thing, mind you! When you breathe in, gathering, contracting – it is yin. When you breathe out, expanding, pushing forward – that is yang. How many times a day do we perform these actions, and are they ever done at the same time?'

Lily said: 'No, Mr Jackson.'

'Now in the seasons we have summer, which is yang – life presses outward in leaf and flower – and winter, which is yin – when life is stored deep in root and stem. And in the interplay of man and woman too this rhythm can be perceived.'

He stopped talking and looked at her intently. She dropped her eyes at once. She was afraid to see his face.

'The interaction of these essential principles produces *chi*,' said Mr Jackson. 'Slice these carrots.' He handed her another chopper. 'Carefully, now, it's razor-sharp. Which in some cases, can produce the immortal embryo in a man's body, so that at the moment of death – and you don't want me to die, do you, Lily?'

Lily said eagerly: 'No, Mr Jackson. I want you to live.' She began to slice the carrots wafer-thin, nervous of the blade. She thought it was after her fingers; it was too strong for her.

Mr Jackson said: 'He becomes an Immortal, leaving the old shell as the snake abandons its sloughed skin or as the butterfly leaves the chrysalid behind. You remember I told you about Cook Ting who was so clever at slaughtering animals? Give me that chicken – what's your name?' he asked the kitchenmaid.

'Saunders, sir,' she said. She passed him the chicken.

Mr Jackson turned the bird over in his fingers. 'Cook Ting,' he said, 'knew every cavity in a carcase, knew how to slice up through the interstices using a minimum of force so that his vital energy – his *chi*, Lily! was preserved. And his knife! After ten years his knife was as keen as ever, and he'd never had it sharpened.'

His face was alight. He looked at the chicken again, puzzling where to make the first incision. The loose, pock-marked skin clung to his fingers. It looked as if he was dandling a trussed dead baby. He laid it down and brought the chopper into the space between the leg and the breast, then he paused, feeling the resistance. A little gout of blood oozed out on to the wooden chopping board. The kitchenmaid started to cough and went out into the scullery.

Mr Jackson said: 'These are the men who know how to care for life. They observe the patterns of nature, not the formalities and pieties of Confucius or Mencius, or of Christianity. Such things are only for the vulgar.'

He searched the chicken with the chopper, finally pulled the leg away from the carcase, widening the gap he had already made, and chopped down into it. He was pleased to see the two part company neatly, though he had gone straight through the bone.

Lily cut an ugly triangle of carrot and made a gash in her finger. She stood and stared at the white wound. It took a few moments before the blood came welling up.

Since the nurse left, she had kept not only her feelings but her attention within herself, trying to know as little as possible in the hope of keeping herself safe. But it seemed hurt came after her, no matter how small she curled up.

'Foolish, clumsy child,' said Mr Jackson. 'Saunders! Bring a bandage. Now who's going to help me? You're not attuned to the flow, Lily, or you wouldn't have done that. Look how neatly I've got the legs off this chicken.'

Lily opened her mouth to accuse him of cutting her finger off, but she said: 'Mr Jackson, if I learned Chinese, perhaps I wouldn't be so clumsy.'

Mr Jackson smiled delightedly. He patted her shoulder while Saunders wrapped her finger up in a fat white roll of gauze.

'Not so foolish after all,' he said. 'I'll teach you Chinese – Mandarin, of course. When you've learned for a while, we can speak nothing but Chinese to each other. Why should I soil my tongue with English any more than I need? Maybe we'll even go to China.'

And find my family, thought Lily, chopping carrots again. Get what you can out of him, Lily. Look out for yourself.

'I need your help,' said Mr Jackson, pulling her to him while his other hand held the blood-smeared chopper. 'I can't do it without you. And what do I give you in return?'

'Life,' said Lily, rubbing her cheek against his shoulder. 'The dogs would have eaten me otherwise. I belong to you.'

Mr Jackson said: 'Look at me, then.'

She looked up at him and felt excitement rise in her – but he was still holding the chopper. She dropped her eyes and her head and wondered if the steel might have killed her already, without her knowledge.

There was everything, all over the house, that money could buy, the shell of the house had been decorated to his exact instructions when he returned from Hong-Kong with the infant Lily and supervised the work from his rented house. The rooms were dark, rich, the perfect casing for the treasures he put in them. He'd had the ceilings painted in midnight blue and the stars shone on them in real gold leaf. Money, taste and scholarship had created this wonder: now he understood that they couldn't give him everything. He had been blessed with good health, which had cushioned him from the knowledge of his mortality, but his fear of death had come up round him and was threatening to stifle him.

He gave orders that the admiring callers were to be kept out of the house, as if the butler would be able to send the bone-man and his scythe away: he knew he was acting crazily, but it didn't make any difference.

He had Lily to talk to: it was better. He had trained her not to argue. He decided she should learn Chinese – and she sat diligently at her desk with her brush and her inkstone and block of black ink, brushing ever more complicated characters. She learned fast. She was intelligent. He didn't quite like to admit this.

While she worked, he had his own brush and inkstone out, and his own roll of white rice-paper, everything of far finer quality than he gave her, of course. He wrote a poem, positioning each stroke in the right place, stopping from time to time to admire his work.

Lily brushed with pleasure and great determination, making her journey through the labyrinth of the Chinese language, each character guarding a new passageway, and she had already encountered and understood many more than Mr Jackson had predicted.

Somewhere, at the very heart of the labyrinth, her repentant parents were waiting for her.

Mr Jackson said suddenly: 'And the Western powers believe they have everything China needs: religion, industry, modernization. Pah!' He laid his brush down. 'Never realize what we might learn from China – they'll go in there and destroy it. The Chinese Emperors understood that. That's why they've always wanted to keep us out. And what do we teach in our universities? Latin and Greek.' He paused. Then he said: 'It might be just as well.'

'How, Mr Jackson?' asked Lily.

Mr Jackson said: 'Knowledge is only fit for those who are ready for it. I think I'm worthy. I hope I'm worthy.'

Lily said: 'Mr Jackson, if you aren't worthy, I don't know who is.'

She knew he was talking about immortality.

Mr Jackson looked her up and down. She was fourteen years old now. She sat in her chair with her legs crossed: her loose Chinese clothing hid her breasts, but he was intensely moved by the graceful line of her straight spine. And always that fragrance: it stuck to his hands when he'd stroked her body or her hair.

He passed his work to her: he asked her if she could read it.

She read:

> There is a sweet wilful girl in my house
> Her body sways like bamboo in the wind
> Her mouth pouts, asking for a thousand kisses.
> At night, silk sheets caress her jasmine skin
> Yet she knows nothing of love: I dare not teach her.
> She answers my fears with her foolish little hopes,
> She smudges characters on rice-paper.
> I have put pearls in her hair instead of my fingers.
> I have given her everything, and how does she repay me?
> She keeps me at bay with a smile.

Lily said: 'It's beautiful, Mr Jackson.' She found herself shivering ever so slightly. She asked 'Did I read it well?'

'You understood it?' he asked.

She looked down at the floor. He came towards her: she could just hear his soft Chinese shoes on the carpet. He stood beside her and her skin twitched to his nearness.

He walked away brusquely.

'I'm a scoundrel,' he said.

Lily said: 'I don't know what to say, Mr Jackson. I'm afraid.'

He slapped her. It was what she expected.

She said breathlessly: 'Mr Jackson, you're a good man. I'm a stupid silly child who belongs to you. Please don't reproach me, Mr Jackson, you only have to tell me what you want.'

He said testily: 'Not yet, don't you understand that? Read the poem again.'

She read it. Her heart pounded.

'Now,' he said, 'look at me. That's right. Now you can sulk a little, if you like. I wish I'd had your feet bound: there were women in China who could have done it for us, when you were small. You could have had three-inch golden lilies instead of those big feet of yours.'

Lily turned her face away and pushed her mouth out as he expected.

He said: 'Take your shoes and stockings off.'

She did as she was told, still sulking diligently. She was relieved to sulk: she couldn't have managed cheerfulness. He knelt on the floor and took a foot in each hand, running his fingers along the soles. Lily giggled for fright.

'That's right,' he said, smiling. She breathed more freely.

She still had the copy of *The Girls' Own Paper* that the nurse had bought her. She had bound it in white rice-paper to keep it nice. Every night, before she went to bed, she repeated to herself: 'I must render myself agreeable and helpful to Mr Jackson, whether by beauty' – sometimes she got up at this point and reassured herself by looking in the mirror – 'gentleness, forethought, energy, intelligence, domestic cares, home-virtues, toil – assistance, "in hours of ease", in sickness, or amid the perplexities, anxieties, disappointments and labours that environ life; it is so, and will ever be so. Amen.'

She had promised the nurse she would always say her prayers.

'T'ai chi ch'uan, Lily,' said Mr Jackson. 'The supreme ultimate boxing. Where you don't close with the enemy, indeed, you can practise it all alone. It's one of the mountain arts that lengthen a man's life. I learned it years ago, in China. Now I can remember the movements – that proves something, doesn't it?'

Lust, he thought, I ought to admit it, I lust after her.

He said: 'This one is called "Grasping the peacock's Tail", this one is "White Crane Spreads its Wings", this one is "Playing the Lute". I will teach you to play the Chinese lute – the *pi pa*, Lily – when I can get one sent from Hong-Kong. You can play to me. Watch, here we have: "Embrace Tiger, Return to Mountain". All the movement comes from the centre: there is a yin movement and a yang movement. What is yang, Lily?'

Lily said: 'Summer, day, the part of the plant that lies above the soil, everything that expands, is warm, that rises. Heaven.'

'And the male principle, Lily,' said Mr Jackson. 'What is the yin?'

'The female principle,' said Lily. 'Winter, cold, night. Earth. What lies under the soil, everything that contracts, gathers. But yin always turns into yang, and yang into yin.'

'That's right,' said Mr Jackson. 'The yin and yang are the pulse of life for everything – all the ten thousand things. Now see how it works out in t'ai chi ch'uan: yin is yielding, sinking, withdrawing' – he pulled himself back and sank into a movement – 'and you breathe in. This is a yang movement, conquering, rising, advancing – you breathe out. Each is necessary to the other. But a man is not all yang, nor is a woman all yin. This follows, since yang is not better than yin, only different, but men are superior to women.'

Lily said: 'Yes, Mr Jackson. A woman must yield to a man.'

Mr Jackson performed kicks into the air: an army of ghosts was closing in on him, but he warded them off slowly, inexorably, kicked them with movements soft as silk, left them lying on the floor.

'When you yield, Lily,' said Mr Jackson, 'you may also gain advantage.' He added hastily: 'But a woman mustn't try to gain the advantage over a man, since a man knows better than a woman.'

'Yes, Mr Jackson,' said Lily. 'I can gain by yielding, however.'

He said: 'Lily?'

'I can gain your love,' she said.

He stared at her. Not yet, he said to himself. She doesn't know what she's saying. He said: 'There's a Master of t'ai chi in China who has knowledge I lack. I must learn it. We must go back to China, Lily.' He looked at her sidelong and said: 'If I become an Immortal, I'll find your family for you, Lily, believe me. I'll be able to do anything, then. But you must help me, Lily.'

Lily said: 'Mr Jackson, I will, when you tell me how.'

Mr Jackson prepared to light his pipe. He said: 'I'll tell you when we get to China.'

He begun to practise t'ai chi ch'uan in the Square garden before anyone was up except the tradesmen and the servants. The housemaids leaned giggling out of the house windows to watch him when they were supposed to be doing their early morning chores. He had a sword sent him from Hong-Kong, and did exercises with that.

Then one day he met a neighbour's son collecting birds' eggs. The boy asked if he could play with the sword. At least that was what the boys' parents said had happened. Mr Jackson said the boy had insulted him and made fun of him.

Each side agreed that Mr Jackson had grown very angry and had chased the boy away, with his sword upraised. I was justified, said Mr Jackson. Needless savagery, said the neighbours, the man's mad, who knows what he might have done with his sword?

Mr Jackson might have been arrested and thrown into prison, if he hadn't been so rich and well-connected: the Lord Chief Justice was his cousin's brother-in-law. Instead he was politely requested to come to court, where he was bound over to keep the peace.

He stamped in the house, and stoked the fires of his fury. He said the neighbours were conspiring against him. He cursed the magistrate, the magistrate's parents and his children. Then he fixed the date of their departure for China. He decided that they would stay in Hong-Kong at first, and journey into China proper after six months or so.

So there were visits from tropical outfitters, and steamer trunks open in his dressing room and Lily's. A firm of shipping agents packed the choicest pieces from Mr Jackson's collection for transport to Hong-Kong. Mr Jackson supervised them, wearing his Chinese robe. Two trunkfuls of books were labelled: 'Wanted On the Voyage.' They were to sail from Southampton on the first of October.

Samuel might have expected London to be dirtier still than Oxford – the very pigeons were black as night with eyes that gleamed in their faces like burgled rubies. He hadn't, and though he'd known how much bigger London would be, he was astonished by the increase of filth, the solid quality of the fogs. He could imagine no end to the buildings when he was among them, yet there were acres of parkland, while the river had gobbled dozens of tributaries since he saw it in Oxford, and snaked through the city, enormously fat, powerful and menacing. There was so much of everything: it was the most populous city on earth and he'd known that, but the reality was greater and overpoweringly uglier than his expectations. Reynolds saw his amazement, and laughed at him.

Inside the grimy coating ran the machinery of Empire, his destined sphere of work. He came, briefly, in October for the Far Eastern Civil Service examinations. In November, they wrote him that he had passed. On the first of January he began work at the Colonial Office in Whitehall. He was employed there part time, but his main task was to attend King's College, where an erudite professor taught him Chinese. He wasn't alone: there was another cadet, Henderson.

He sat in gaslit rooms learning the exotic language, learning to service the Empire. He struggled on three days a week with a language that ran up and down the paper instead of from side to side, that began at the end of the book and finished at the front, and on the other days with the proper language for logging dispatches, the formats the Service used to reply to them. He had a third language to learn, the language young men used with each other.

Henderson was tall, broad-shouldered and handsome. He had brown hair that tumbled into his large, expressive brown eyes. Henderson was generous – to a fault, which meant he gave money to organ-grinders and beggars. Henderson took him out on to the night-time streets of London – Reynolds came too. Both of them seemed at ease, skilled: Samuel was the only apprentice.

'Pink doesn't know the world, does he?' Henderson asked Reynolds.

'Not a bit,' said Reynolds, 'he's got a lot of catching up to do.'

Samuel saw that they took freedoms he had no intention of allowing himself. He didn't despise them for this. It only proved his own greater need for salvation.

He did drink with them. He learned to smoke.

He roomed in Westminster, with Reynolds. They had a pair of bedrooms and a common sitting-dining room with all services laid on. Henderson ate there at least twice a week, when he always kissed the maid. Reynolds kissed the maid too: Samuel knew she was wondering when he would start. He didn't. The maid was surprised, perhaps offended, though sometimes he wondered if she was relieved. He thought she probably wasn't interested in him. He was a little man with a tendency to chubbiness, and it was going to get worse.

'Awfully amusing fellow, your tutor, ain't he?' asked Henderson.

He learned the articles of faith of the Service. There were ways in which things were done, ways a man didn't argue about, and these proprieties were a vital part of the civilization that the young men had to take out to the East with them. A man went where he was sent. His work was his only on loan: he was interested in a task for as long as it was his, then he had to transfer his interest to the next thing. He obeyed orders as a soldier had to. Samuel dreamed forms of words at night: they stood up like silver filigree patterns against the darkness. They had a serious, compelling beauty and they made him feel safe.

Safer than in the streets Henderson and Reynolds led him through, where the fog battled with the streetlamps at night. Someone might come up behind him in the dark, hit him over the head and steal his money. His nose ran grey and spoiled all his handkerchiefs. He suffered from headaches. He met other young men, friends Henderson had picked up since he came here from Northampton – other government employees or workers in banks. They lounged in smoky sanded bars and talked. Henderson sniggered about the eighteen tones of Cantonese. If you got the tone wrong, you'd end up saying something you hadn't meant to, and you'd make a fool of yourself.

'Something quite gross,' said Henderson to the rest of them and anyone else who might be listening, 'you'd be shamed for ever, the British Empire would be shamed for ever if you got your Chinese wrong like that. Pink won't. He's good at it. Perfect pitch, I expect. I'm the one who'll use the falling tone instead of the rising tone. I'll say "bum" instead of "nine", and the Mandarins'll demand my execution.'

Everybody laughed. Samuel was the fool for being so diligent and unable to avoid exposure. But it wasn't his fault: not everyone had royal blood to expiate.

'It's a life-sentence, of course,' said Henderson. 'Absolute life-sentence. Apart from the home leaves. Once a fellow's fluent in Chinese, there isn't anywhere else much they can use him, is there? They wouldn't want to. They'll need our skills – why waste us on Timbuktu?'

He got hold of the barmaid and kissed her, putting his hands round her waist, tickling her breasts. She didn't seem to mind. There was always so much kissing and touching women.

Henderson pushed the barmaid over to Samuel: 'Now you,' he said. Samuel flushed hot all over. 'Got to make the most of Old England,' said Henderson, 'before you leave it for ever, go on, kiss her. She's longing for you.'

'Leave him alone,' said the barmaid, giggling, 'he's a better man than the rest of you.' She went back to serve the other customers. Samuel knew Henderson had humiliated him for fun, but he'd have been able to protect himself, if he hadn't deserved it.

There was never any respite from the hard work of the daytime and the round of gaiety at night. Henderson and Reynolds trailed him round music-halls, to endless public houses and at last to a brothel.

'I won't,' he said.

'Don't be a prig,' said Reynolds roughly.

'I can't help it.' Samuel pleaded.

'Well then,' said Henderson, 'you can wait for us, can't you?'

So Samuel sat on a soiled cream velvet chair while the gaslamps hissed at him, and when the girls realized what he was doing, they came to point and titter. Yet he couldn't be angry with them. He felt dreadfully, painfully sorry for them. He'd have liked to rescue them all. The tears gathered behind his eyes: he got his handkerchief out and pretended he had a cold. He wished he was at work. He wished his mother knew how much she'd made him suffer.

The other two came out, flushed and self-satisfied.

'Have you often been to places like that?' he asked Reynolds before bed.

'Of course,' said Reynolds. 'How do you think I get relief?'

'But isn't it awful,' asked Samuel, 'touching them?'

'No,' said Reynolds. Then he said: 'You'll have to stand up to Henderson. I can't do any good by shielding you. You know that, don't you?'

The year drew on, taking them nearer to their departure. The days grew longer and the sun began to shine in London: the trees in the squares grew sooty leaves.

'Almost off into the unknown,' said Henderson in the pub. 'They don't tell us much. We go to Hong-Kong. We spend time there. We spend periods studying the language in Canton. They pay for our

50

quarters and our teaching as well as our salary. The rest is silence.'

Samuel said: 'No one seems to know much about Hong-Kong.'

'Only one thing,' said Reynolds, taking a drink. 'It's a white man's grave.'

At that, everyone began to laugh as uproariously as he could.

'We'll be martyrs,' said Samuel, 'to the white man's mission.'

The other men thought that joke was even better. He was the hero of the next five minutes, and yet he'd meant it quite seriously.

'*My dearest son*, wrote his mother to him on his twenty-first birthday: *this is a solemn year for us both. You will be going so far away, and indeed now it comes so close I would not be able to bear it if it wasn't for the fact that I must never see you. You cannot imagine how much pain that dreadful necessity causes me. At least I shall hear how you are going on: also I am confident that your father will watch over you. I cannot tell you how, but believe me, Samuel, it is true. And God will guide you, if you trust him.*

From heaven, supposed Samuel, she believes my father will watch over me from heaven. He was afraid Reynolds might see the tears in his eyes, but Reynolds was hidden behind a newspaper: Samuel noticed an advertisement for Dennistons' Fine Conserves and a headline about a murder in the East End. Samuel noticed marmalade on his hand and licked it off so that it didn't spoil his letter.

She was coming to London for the Jubilee, she wrote – well of course she would be. How could there be a Jubilee without the Queen? *I shall be nearer to you than I have ever been before – don't think it doesn't tear my heart. I shall be in the procession – I cannot tell you more. If only you could ride with me! Loneliness is my burden, dear boy. Always loneliness. I am consoled by the thought of your father, though I am parted from him for ever. I remember his tender love and will never call it a sin. Dear, precious boy, you must strive to be worthy of him. I have to stop writing, or I shall commit indiscretions I should regret. I shall write to you next year, in Hong-Kong. Work hard and make a name for yourself – alas that it can never be his who gave you life!* She sent him a gold watch, with his initials engraved on it, and the inscription: *from your loving mother* inside the lid.

He didn't go to the Jubilee. He'd have gone if she'd told him to, but she hadn't. He couldn't bear to see her borne past him for a few brief minutes. She'd look so indistinct, she'd see him as a blur among other blurred faces. The thought of it really made him ill, yet there was no escape from her face. The landlady bought a series of plates with her picture on them, which she arranged in the entrance hall. The crackers after dinner came up in a tin with Victoria on it, and the jam, which had always been spooned into a glass saucer, was now left in its jar – the special crystal jar engraved with her name, her face, the royal coat of arms, and Dennistons' own name, that the jam manufacturers had commissioned specially to celebrate the occasion. There were photographs in the newspaper.

'All you have to do is reign fifty years,' said Reynolds, 'and people think you're good.'

'She's my mother,' said Samuel.

'You have a reason to love her,' admitted Reynolds, 'but as for the rest of them – has anything really changed since six months ago, when they didn't think much of her? She's coming to London and giving them a show. It won't change the conditions of their lives.'

Samuel said: 'She's coming to see them at last. No wonder they're happy.'

The portraits were very severe, and didn't look like the woman who wrote the letters to him.

He did work hard and passed his examinations. So did Henderson. They went home in September, to spend a last holiday with their families. The rectory was dull and full of awkward silences: he spent most of the time out with Reynolds. His pony had been sold, but his dog was there. She was old now and couldn't go out to the East with him. She cried when he left, which was more than the Pinks did.

Reynolds was going to teach in a Manchester school: a good position, but he wasn't looking forward to it. His mood varied between frenzied hilarity and brooding silence. Now and again everything was all right and they were easy together, but only when both could forget what lay ahead of them.

'First Class,' said Mr Jackson to Lily as they sat in the reserved compartment on the train. Lily was dressed in Western clothes: she always wore them when he took her out and she found them very uncomfortable. Bones and stays dug into her everywhere and she could hardly see through the veil Mr Jackson had pulled down over her face. Mr Jackson said: 'They wanted you to go Second Class, because you're Chinese, but I have a large block of shares in the shipping company, so they made a concession. You'll have to stay in your stateroom throughout the voyage, that's the snag. You won't mind, will you? I'll be with you a lot of the day: we've lessons to do.'

Lily said: 'Thank you, Mr Jackson.' The countryside blurred past her and her vision was often doubly clouded by soot and smoke as well as by the veil. 'I should hate to be separated from you.'

'It wouldn't do,' said Mr Jackson, 'and you know I could hardly go Second Class.' He leaned back in his seat and took a drink of water from a silver flask. He said: 'The Third Class passengers on these trains sit just behind the engine in the open. Sometimes they get roasted by the sparks from the fire.'

Lily had dreamed, last night, that she was a baby in her mother's arms, trying to feed from her mother's breast. There was no milk in the breast. She was hungry. She cried for hunger. She heard a rough pair of hands take her away from the breast. A man's voice said: 'She is a husband-killer. The priest saw it in her horoscope. And another mouth – a useless mouth. Let me take her away. If you had born a son, now – '

Her mother said: 'Take her.'

She saw the ancient walls towering above her. It was evening, and cold. She cried for her father to take pity on her, to halt his hurrying soft-soled footsteps going away. She thought: he wrapped me up. Surely he won't abandon me? She could hear the dogs in the distance.

But the feet that came were hard-soled, heavier than her father's. A pair of enormous hands picked her up. The fingers pushed her clothes apart, spread her wide like an open flower.

The flower had been destroyed, she knew it, sitting now on the plush seats of the carriage, eating the sandwiches and drinking the tea Mr Jackson had ordered. The train pulled on and brought them to Southampton in the evening. Bone-white seagulls were crying from the rooftops and the air.

Samuel didn't realize that he'd carry England with him, that a particular effect of the light, a bad smell even, a drift of smoke or a trill of birdsong would be able to evoke England even when he was half a world away. Nor that his baggage contained a half-consoling, half-tormenting vision of an ideal country, fresh and rural and comprehensible: it was necessary equipment for a colonialist: it had slipped in with the solar topi and the white linen suit and in this respect, at least, Samuel was no different from the rest.

'Do you know what you're doing?' asked Reynolds. They sat in the huge hotel dining room: Henderson was staying at an aunt's house, and would be on the boat tomorrow.

'I'll have to do my best,' said Samuel.

'Do you even know what that means?' Reynolds ate, stuffed himself, as always. 'They'll destroy you, do you know that? They'll put you in their machinery and grind you to pulp. And use that stuff about doing your best to justify it. You'll exert power, but it'll be other people's power, not yours.'

Samuel said: 'I'll be doing *her* work.'

Angrily, Reynolds said: 'And the work of the tradesmen and industrialists who really rule this country. Stretching their claws out for China. Living off the starvation of the poor.'

Samuel said: 'You've dripped gravy on your waistcoat.'

He was afraid of Reynolds: he didn't know why, but he wanted to distance himself from him. He said: 'I will write to you from Hong-Kong. I promise.'

Reynolds said: 'I hope one day you'll find out what life's all about.'

'Oh,' said Samuel, 'I do want to know. I do want to understand.'

'Well,' said Reynolds, 'do your best.' He began to laugh: they both laughed for some minutes. Samuel had no idea what they were laughing at.

He said: 'The Rector's going to send me a copy of the photograph, with you on it.'

'It'll be blurred.' Reynolds lavished mustard on his steak.

'I'll be glad to have it,' said Samuel. 'And I'll go to see that Wesleyan missionary. Fawler.'

'And worship at the cathedral,' said Reynolds, imitating the Rector's voice, 'which is the only possible place for a gentleman.'

Samuel knew he couldn't eat any more, though he'd only had soup and a few mouthfuls of beef. After dinner they walked along the seafront in the wind and saw the boat that was going to take him away.

5

THE VOYAGE
Southampton–
Hong-Kong 1887

THE *Pearl River* made her way down the English Channel, keeping her distance from the coast of France. It was unusually calm weather for October. A coal-fed steam engine within her hull turned the massive propeller, while a small generator – also coal-fed – made electric light throughout the vessel.

On the first day out from Southampton, Lily stood flicking the brass switch on and off, on and off.

'It's clever,' she said. 'You don't need matches.'

'You're such a child,' said Mr Jackson, patting her shoulder. 'Do you like the flowers, and the mirrors?'

Lily stared at herself, still in her Western clothing. She had to wear it all the way through the voyage. It was made of cream-coloured wool and she felt like a sheep. She hated the scratchy feeling of wool next to the skin. When it grew hot she'd have wash silk and linens to wear, and then she wouldn't wear the fine woollen underwear the tropical outfitter had insisted was the best for hot climates. Or the corsets. Mr Jackson hadn't wanted to take a maid out with them, and she was glad. It meant she could dress as she liked.

'I don't look nice,' she said, pushing her lip out.

Mr Jackson smiled delightedly.

'Silly little girl,' he said, 'you'll be in your Chinese clothes again soon enough, it's only so that no one will look through the door when it's open and guess you're Chinese.'

She said: 'I wish I'd had my feet bound.'

He said: 'But your feet are very nice, Lily, very pretty, in spite of that – '

55

She interrupted him. She knew it was dangerous, she knew she was carrying things too far – what right had she to be in distress? Still she said:

'Then I wouldn't *want* to walk about.'

He said, warningly: 'Lily.'

She ran to him and kissed his cheek. She thought she was forgiven. She said gaily: 'I'll work hard and learn Chinese. Then I'll be able to speak Chinese to the other people in Hong-Kong.'

'No,' said Mr Jackson.

Lily asked; 'Isn't my Chinese good enough?'

'I've taught you Mandarin,' said Mr Jackson. 'In Hong-Kong they speak Cantonese. There are many dialects of Chinese, Fukienese, Shanghainese – '

Lily asked fearfully: 'So you'll teach me Cantonese?'

He said: 'You interrupted me. Why do you need to learn Cantonese? It's an ugly language. Mandarin is the best, the language of poets. I don't want to hear you talking Cantonese. It sounds like parrots squawking in the jungle.'

Lily asked: 'So you haven't learned Cantonese, Mr Jackson?'

'Of course I have, foolish child. I've learned as many dialects of Chinese as possible.'

He looked her over and liked what he saw: the cream colour set off her black hair and eyes and pale skin and emphasized the deep flush of her pretty full-lipped mouth. She was so slender that corsets were hardly necessary. She smiled at him and cast her eyes down. English clothes or not, she moved with Oriental allure. He left for dinner.

Presently, a stewardess brought her dinner in to her. She banged the tray down on the table and withdrew. Lily was left alone.

She took up her Mandarin texts again. Mr Jackson had given her a book of love poems to read. Lily wandered into their world and was taken up by it: she *heard* the forlorn, unvisited concubines, the ladies whose husbands had gone away, who lamented the emptiness of their lives among the cold winds and the white frost. She read about dancers signalling to their lovers – a lift of their moth eyebrows, an earring deliberately let fall, and the assignation was made. The lovers were beautiful young Chinese men with clean strong limbs clothed in silk.

Presently, she noticed that most of the poems dealt with deserted women and they'd almost all been written by men.

Blue, blue, she thought, the sea and the sky. Dull, dull my stateroom, my prison. Men leave women to cry, and then they write poetry about them.

Samuel sat in his stateroom, writing to Reynolds. He'd post the letter in Gibraltar.

I was placed opposite an extraordinary man at luncheon: he didn't say a word to anyone, except to introduce himself. His name is Jackson. He spent the entire meal playing with his food, but not at all at random. I watched him and I could see that he was dividing each dish up according to its colours and textures. Then he ate a little from each heap in turn. It took him a very long time. They say he's a famous Chinese scholar, and a great eccentric.

There are no other young men on the boat, but there is a rubber planter returning to Malaya, and a shipping man from Singapore. No government servants. There are six ladies.

Samuel had been put next to one of them: Miss Roper who had a port-wine stain all over her thin right hand and a hint of it under the stiff white collar that went round her neck. Samuel wondered how far it spread. She would chatter very fast, in a whispery voice that stopped him catching half her words, or else sit mute and white-faced, as if she was dreadfully ashamed of herself for opening her mouth. Samuel then had to ask her questions until the breathless chatter came on again. He couldn't bear her. Her shame touched his own: her fear cramped his stomach. She made him want to cry, just like the prostitutes in the brothel. She wasn't safe.

He wrote: *Four of the ladies are very plain, which is a disappointment* – he hoped Reynolds wouldn't jibe at this, hoped indeed that Reynolds would forget what he knew about Samuel and women – *one more is engaged to a missionary and the other one is married.*

There were three unattractive young ladies: one had red hair and a rash of freckles, the second was gap-toothed, the third was six feet tall, and they were all peeping at the men and sizing them up. The missionary's fiancée was plump and comely, and visibly amused by Samuel and Henderson's disappointment.

Samuel wrote: *They are going out to Hong-Kong to catch husbands: the 'Fishing Fleet'. They hope to make fools of us, but we shan't be trapped by them, mustn't get married for years, after all. The married lady is called Mrs Darley and she is the wife of the Surveyor-General in Hong-Kong.*

Henderson had been put next to her at luncheon. She was plump, small and beautiful with a cloud of dark hair: her skin had the bloom of a large ripe fruit. Miss Roper had looked at her and sighed resignedly. Henderson was absorbed in her, Samuel was listening to her instead of talking to Miss Roper. Mrs Darley had a deep voice with a hint of a laugh in it. He could hear it now: 'I've been visiting my poor dear children at school in England, so sad, the climate of Hong-Kong's so unhealthy for children – though things are improving, mind! My husband sees to that. Reservoirs and drains – ugh! but necessary, aren't they, Mr Henderson – and of course we'll have you up to dinner at "Isola Bella" – our house on the Peak, you know – you'll be working in Hong-Kong as well as studying in Canton and I love to entertain the cadets.'

'The Peak?' had asked Henderson.

'Mr Henderson, you'll know all this within a fortnight, I hardly need to tell you now, but it's the *dernier cri*, to go to live up on Victoria Peak – a little trying to get there just at present, though a sedan chair's so comfortable! But they're building the new High Level Tramway now, and it's going to be so convenient, soon, at least a degree cooler in the hot season, and secluded!'

Samuel wrote: *She seems to know many things which are of interest to Henderson and to me.* He looked over this last sentence, deleted the full stop, and added: *I mean about Hong-Kong and what goes on there.*

He wrote: *There was an empty chair at the table. I kept expecting you to come and sit down in it.*

After all, Reynolds was his family as the Pinks had never been – he might have bad moods, but he'd cared for Samuel, taught him, amused him.

I think I managed to entertain my 'Fishing Fleet' lady partner, though it wasn't easy.

'I'm reading a topping book,' he'd gabbled to Miss Roper. 'About a private investigator called Sherlock Holmes. It's called *The Sign of Four*. He lives in Baker Street and takes cases the police can't solve. He's wonderfully clever.'

He'd managed to talk for the rest of the meal. She had a nervous habit of putting her hand to her face, and she'd rubbed the powder off it, bit by bit revealing the ugly birthmark all the way up her cheek.

After luncheon the passengers always drank coffee and chatted. On the second day, Mrs Darley made Henderson bring Samuel over to be introduced. They talked London: she'd come to stay with a sister and watch the dear Queen's Jubilee: the Queen so *suitably* dressed in her black dress and her bonnet – diamonds, of course, on the bonnet, and her fingers *laden* with jewels apparently. Then she looked Samuel over, raised her eyebrows into even more perfect half-moons and asked if he knew he looked *exactly* like the Prince of Wales when young.

'Are you going to be as wicked as that?' she asked. 'I do hope so.' Her voice never lost the undertone of amusement: it made Samuel feel foolish.

He saw his mother's portrait on the wall: she looked stern and sad, hiding her own wickedness which he mustn't emulate.

He couldn't look Mrs Darley in the face. She bewildered him. She was too delicious, too lavish in everything. She smelt, close to, like an apple just fresh off the tree.

'There's one lady who's ill,' said Mrs Darley, 'poor thing, she can't leave her cabin. You saw the empty chair at lunch-time? Isn't it surprising her doctor allowed her to travel? I thought I'd go to visit her, to see if there was anything I could do, but she can't even have visitors. Isn't it a mystery?'

Samuel saw the title: 'The Unknown Passenger'. Mr Sherlock Holmes – or better still, Mr Samuel Pink – by using a cold and brilliant analytical brain – solved it, but not, of course, before thrilling and dramatic events had occurred. Only Mr Samuel Pink's brain wasn't cold or analytical and – unlike Sherlock Holmes – he wasn't indifferent to women. His skin prickled at the proximity of Mrs Darley's scented flesh.

'There are grave perils,' said Mr Jackson to Lily, 'in the desire of men for women.'

Lily said: 'Yes, Mr Jackson.' She sat with her hands on her knees, her eyes on the floor, but she knew he was watching her.

Mr Jackson said: 'The day I found you in Soochow, I bought an ancient text from a wandering monk. I've tested its authenticity to my own satisfaction' – his voice was austere, scholarly – 'and I believe it's right to give it to you to study now.' A different note crept into his voice, a rough heat that fluttered Lily's skin. The butterfly was there again, its proboscis testing the moist sensitivities between her legs.

59

She mustn't tell Mr Jackson she was afraid.

Mr Jackson knew how he sounded: he struggled to get the scholarly note back. He explained: 'If a man spends himself too much – '

'Mr Jackson?' said Lily.

'Speak up,' he said. 'I can't hear you.'

'I don't understand.'

'Little fool,' he said tetchily, 'how could you know? A man has a virile member – did you even know that? No matter. It contains within it the seed that engenders children, which is spilt within the woman in the act of procreation. The bulk of the human race spend themselves and die, leaving their children behind – and there's nothing dishonourable about this. To some, however, other insights are given. There have been many theories about the way to attain immortality: men have swallowed pills, have meditated, have helped themselves by seeking the love of virgins.'

'Virgins, Mr Jackson?'

'Young girls,' said Mr Jackson, his tanned face darkening, 'who haven't yet known a man. As a man knows a woman to produce children. Why don't you say anything, why can't you help me?'

Falteringly, Lily said: 'I *am* trying to understand, Mr Jackson.'

Mr Jackson shook himself. He said: 'If this energy is *not* spent in the procreative act – you will understand in time, Lily – then it remains within the man. The performance of certain disciplines can cause this energy – *jing*, to be transformed into the life-principle *chi*. What is *chi*, Lily?'

Lily said: 'The energy that gives life to all things, the offspring of the yin and yang.'

'You see,' said Mr Jackson, rather anxiously, 'you do understand part of it already. The procreative act itself is of course the intercourse of yin and yang. The man's yang energy is complemented by the yin energy of the woman. But it is our task to generate the immortal foetus at the base of my abdomen, which will then be expelled through my head at death – and I shall become immortal. Much of this part is my business, and mine alone. It will be for you to help me perform the exercises, which are all contained within this scroll. Its name is *The Jade Chamber and the Immortal Foetus*. I want you to work diligently, Lily. Do you love me enough?'

He came up close to Lily and put his hand on her neck.

Eagerly, Lily said: 'Yes, Mr Jackson, I do love you. You have been mother and father to me, and who else do I have to love?'

She looked up at him, opening her black eyes wide, fluttering her lashes for shyness, raising her moth eyebrows. Then she looked down, just as he had taught her.

Mr Jackson turned sheet-white. He almost ran out of the stateroom. Lily was left all alone. She was confused, but relieved. She wanted to read the text, and she didn't want him to watch her at it.

Mr Jackson stood in the passageway between her cabin and his, and remembered the child brothel he used to frequent in London. He'd patronized a twelve-year-old with painted eyes and slender limbs: she'd been skilled at her trade, and he'd always tried not to hurt her. He couldn't understand why the hint of arousal in Lily's innocent face had appalled him so much.

He shut the door of his own cabin behind him and said aloud: 'I could have had her when she was thirteen, God knows she was leading me on.'

'I come home in the summer,' said Mrs Darley to Henderson. 'I stay on, sometimes. You see, I have so little to go home for.' She looked up at him, half piteous, half defying pity.

'Your children,' said Henderson, looking at the dip between her breasts, 'you must miss your children dreadfully.'

'I do,' she sighed, 'and my husband – oh dear – ' she wrapped her shawl closer round her and gave a little, laughing shudder. 'Get me another glass of grog, dear Mr Henderson.'

Henderson fetched the grog for both of them.

'I have *such* a comfortable stateroom,' said Mrs Darley, 'Number Five, really this boat is the best-equipped I have sailed on, and the electric light, such a comfort! They say we'll have electric light everywhere soon, Mr Henderson, do you think it's possible?'

'The telegraph seemed impossible a few years ago,' said Henderson, smiling with masculine authority, 'or gas lighting in houses, or the telephone.'

'Of course,' said Mrs Darley, 'of course, you're right. And your family, tell me some more, your poor widowed mother especially, you must be terribly sad to be leaving your mother?'

'I am,' said Henderson earnestly, looking away from her, 'and I'll miss my sisters, but they have great hopes for me, I mustn't disappoint them.'

'Oh,' said Mrs Darley in her playful deep voice, 'you must never disappoint ladies. We don't take to it well.'

Henderson's hand moved, for a moment, to Mrs Darley's knee. Her eyes followed it. When she felt the warmth of his palm on the silk satin, she sighed and smiled, leaning back a little in her chair. Henderson shifted his hand up to her thigh, then removed it.

The *Pearl River* entered the Suez Canal and sailed along the narrow strip between stretches of desert: it was burning hot and the flies buzzed round them and stung. The passengers, in their white tropical clothing, stood sweating on the deck and looked out for camels and Bedouins: sometimes they encountered another ship at one of the Passing Stations and this interested them hugely because – though the canal was a miracle of progress – they were so dreadfully bored. The captain took them down to the engine room to show them the screwshaft that was driving them to Hong-Kong so much faster than a steamship would have done: it gave them something to talk about at dinner. Once, to everyone's delight – they saw a mirage, a ship sailing along in the air with the desert horizon and a portion of the sky visible below its keel. Henderson was going to bed with Mrs Darley. Samuel knew it. By day they flirted and made fun of everyone else. Samuel tried to bury himself in Cantonese studies, but the heat made him dozy.

Lily sat confined to her stateroom and made transcripts of the aged scroll, but it was far harder to read than anything else Mr Jackson had given her. When Mr Jackson was away, she fetched out her tattered single copy of *The Girls' Own Paper*, and read it again and again. She knew, by heart: one episode of a story about a girl called Kathleen, one about Elsie, the life story of a Scottish Queen, hundreds of years ago, some poetry (not to be compared with Chinese), an article about 'Literary Studies', a song-sheet and the Answers to Correspondents. You never saw the original letter, only the answer. One of the correspondents had inadvertently dyed her hair green, another was rapped over the knuckles for wearing gloves at dinner. At the very bottom was an answer directed at 'Anxious Alice'.

The position is one that demands unflinching loyalty to your knowledge of Right. You would be doing grievous wrong to go, and there is the greatest danger in corresponding with him or holding the least intercourse with one who has treated you so scandalously. Think of your own honour and reputation, and forget not to use the petition of our Master, 'Lead us not into temptation'. You have our sympathy and prayers.

Lily put the paper down and began to draw spirals on rice-paper: then long, apparently aimless strokes, to which she appended pointed leaves. Bamboo, the most difficult subject of all to paint, the sign (said Mr Jackson) of an untroubled mind. Aloud, she repeated: 'Lead us not into temptation.'

She set the brush down, picked up a transcription she had already made from the scroll, and read: *The man must enter her from behind for this exercise. He must move his jade member within her fifteen times and no more, then withdraw, being careful not to spill a drop of his seed.*

Some of the positions prescribed the number of movements, some said: *Stop when the woman is satisfied.*

Satisfied, thought Lily, falling into a dreamy state, running her hands over her breasts, brushing the nipples as Mr Jackson sometimes did. It felt so nice.

Then she began to cry. She was surprised by her tears: they came without her intention or consent, without sobs, rolling off her smooth young face. She put her arms round herself and held on tight.

When they entered the Red Sea, it grew hotter still. The captain announced that the mercury had reached 93 degrees. A dry uncomfortable wind blew across the desert and scattered sand all over the deck. The ship rocked in the waves as if it were in a trough of boiling water being dollied on washday. Most of the passengers were laid flat with seasickness.

Rich unavailing smells still drifted round, at breakfast time, at luncheon-time, at dinner-time, at tea-time, at supper-time. They tormented the sufferers through the closed doors of their staterooms. The showers of sand made it far too disagreeable for them to think of sitting out on deck.

Samuel wasn't seasick, and he walked the deck on the first day of swell, holding a hand over his face to keep the sand out of his eyes. He was rather proud of his sea legs: Henderson didn't have them. He could see an Arab boat a short way off, fishing perhaps? He had no idea.

The white lifeboats rocked on their davits, and a lady came towards him, dressed in white linen and a boater hat. It was Mrs

Darley. Her balance was excellent, and it was maybe the sand that she slipped on.

She clutched at the air, seemed about to fall in a colourless damp heap. Samuel ran across the deck, put his hand out for her, grasped her round the waist – now he thought she was fainting – felt, for the first time ever, the warmth of what a woman really was underneath the busking and corsetry and tidy clothing: the things Henderson knew all about, and why, he thought in anguish, wasn't Henderson here to catch her? Mrs Darley slumped round against him so that the boned hill that enclosed her breasts lay on his arm: he staggered under her weight – fortunately she came to herself: she was apologetic, she was confused.

She smelt sweet; he thought of the harvest at church. The wind from the desert blew her dark hair out of its bonds and whipped its musky scent against Samuel's face. The sea leaned her against him, then him against her. Inside those bony clothes she was all softness. He thought: women are like that, encased, veiled, you don't know what there is inside. Only their eyes look out at you. No wonder men have to find places to go where women can't watch them.

Frightened, he glanced towards the shade and thought he saw Reynolds lounging there, untroubled by the heat and idly lighting his pipe: his tutor winked. His heart whacked the breath out of him: Reynolds must have got in to the second class, stowed away even. He put a hand to his face, and the figure vanished. It had been a mirage, a confusion the heat had wrought in his roasted brain. He saw an osprey hovering above the murky Red Sea water: in a second it plunged beak first into the sea and was gone too. He didn't know what he'd been thinking about.

'You're ill,' he said anxiously to Mrs Darley. He didn't dare remove his arm. The wind blew a fresh spatter of sand over them. He ought to take her away to the ship's doctor.

'Oh,' she said, smiling round at him: 'only a moment's indisposition – the sun, you know – so unpleasant here, but one must have exercise – *dear* young man, so kind! If you could help me to my stateroom?'

'Of course,' he said. His mouth was dry.

She said again: 'Oh, how kind!' She leaned heavily on his arm and they walked together. It really wasn't far. He thought he would leave her at the door of the stateroom, but he found he had to walk her right inside.

She revived at once. 'You see,' she said, 'isn't it a dear little place? Here I sit when I want to be private in the daytime, and here' – opening the door – 'I sleep. It's not important to lock the door at night, don't you think? Not on a British ship.'

She had drawn him forward so that he had one foot over the threshold of her bedroom. He could see her maid putting away an armful of what looked like undergarments.

'Oh, Jane,' said Mrs Darley, putting her hand to her head, 'the heat, so intolerable – and this kind young man – draw the blinds down, will you?'

The maid, instead of hurrying to her mistress's side, did as she was told, muttered something about smelling salts and went away. Samuel was left alone with Mrs Darley.

There was an India-rubber folding bath lying in the corner of the bedroom. His lawless imagination set it upright, filled it with water, put Mrs Darley in it – he could just see her back, a hint of a breast, and a deliciously rounded arm – he knew how beautiful her arms were, he'd seen them naked when she was dressed for dinner. Behind the bath was a biscuit tin decorated with a portrait of the Queen.

1837–1887. Victoria the Good. Peace and Plenty.

'My eau-de-Cologne,' said Mrs Darley, letting him go, indicating the bottle and patting her thick dark hair – 'please, Mr Pink.'

'Yes,' said Samuel, wondering if anyone had seen him come in here, and when the maid might return, and what he might find to do if she didn't? He passed Mrs Darley the eau-de-Cologne: she stroked it over her face and slipped her hand inside her collar to moisten herself there. She smiled at him; she smiled invitingly; she had smiled like that at Henderson. The air smelt sweet.

Plenty, he thought wildly, enjoyment, and peace of mind while you took your pleasure. Plenty of men did it without thinking twice, and hadn't his mother done the same with John Brown? He thought he saw encouragement in her eyes. Of course, she thought immorality was justified by love alone. I'm a man, he said to himself. Henderson does this – this is the sort of thing that young men do. They seduce women.

It was going to happen now – if only he could manage it. Could he wipe out so many good resolutions in a moment?

Mrs Darley said softly: 'You *are* a dear creature – *so* grateful to you.' She came up close to him again, he was lost in a mist of

65

eau-de-Cologne, in the middle of which her lips met his, her tongue captured his. Sensation flowered down below his belt – he was melting with the heat and her hot close body – only she gave him a little shove. The maid came in.

'Now don't forget me, will you?' she asked, giving him an arch smile, and little creases smiled at the corner of her eyes, she was warm, and, he thought now, comforting, and welcoming, yes that was the word. He left, slipping his hands casually into his jacket pocket and holding it forward to conceal what was happening inside his trousers.

At the captain's table that night, she sat next to him and showed her breasts to him. Mr Jackson, austere, withdrawn, and immune to seasickness, sat opposite, picking his food over and arranging it as usual.

'Poor boy,' she crooned, 'going out all alone to the end of the earth: won't you miss your mother?'

'I couldn't miss anyone,' said Samuel eagerly, 'not sitting beside you.'

Mrs Darley laughed and hid behind her fan.

'Wickedness,' she said, 'such impertinence!' Samuel shrank a little from the word wicked: he wished she wouldn't use it.

Mr Jackson knew what they were up to. He wondered how anyone could desire such an old woman – she had creases at the corners of her eyes. He meditated on Lily's slender unawakened body and achieved a satisfactory erection in response. He got up from the table: he all but ran to possess her there and then.

He made himself go to his own room instead: everything had to be done carefully and in good order, and he hadn't yet learned not to spill his seed. The scroll instructed the aspirant to press his groin with his fingers, breathe out and grind his teeth fifty times. He usually spent at least twenty minutes of each afternoon nap time trying it on his own, before he fell asleep.

Immortality was his goal, not the satisfaction of a moment's thoughtless lust. He lay down and set to work on the problem, summoning up Lily's image to help him. Perhaps he wasn't grinding his teeth firmly enough. The trouble was, he was too proud of them, still so sound at his age. Yet he'd have a new set of teeth along with everything else when he became an Immortal. And he'd be Chinese.

He'd been wanting to be Chinese for at least thirty years.

Samuel and Mrs Darley sat on at the table, flirted, and sweated:

66

the ship was drenched in sweat, sweat ran all over it, dissolved in the ever-evaporating waters of the Red Sea, carried a thin oil of Mrs Darley's perfume down to the busy brilliant fish and the coral reefs.

'You're so wicked,' said Mrs Darley again, 'such a dear young man, tell me all about yourself.'

'I've led a quiet life,' he said, setting his jaw and trying to be wicked, 'my father's a clergyman in Dorset, but my grandmother was well-born, of a very noble family – a Scottish family.'

'Which one?' asked Mrs Darley with interest.

'The Campbells,' said Samuel at random.

'Argyll?' asked Mrs Darley, 'tell me – '

'I don't know anything about them,' said Samuel frightened into inventiveness, 'they wouldn't speak to my grandmother after she married my grandfather, and yet he was a very respectable gentleman.'

'How touching,' said Mrs Darley, 'how sad. We'll have to cheer you up.'

'Yes, please,' said Samuel. At that moment, he thought he could do anything.

But when night came, he lay in his bed: her scent was in his nostrils; she was all alone with the door unlocked; he knew he was missing his opportunity, but he was afraid something dreadful would happen to him if he went. He got up, knelt beside his bed and said his prayers.

The ship docked at Aden, and the seasick got up from their prone position. Henderson took possession of Mrs Darley, Samuel resigned himself to virtue and was relieved. Then they sailed out into the Indian Ocean and Henderson was laid low again. At least now the sufferers could lie on the shady side of the deck, and admire the flying fish while they kept themselves alive with hot soup. Mrs Darley walked round the deck in her boater hat – talked to Henderson, all motherly and consoling – walked round with Samuel – and kissed him behind the lifeboats. She was so calm, so cheerful: she was waiting for him and really, there could be nothing to it.

For three nights after they left Aden he got up and walked almost to her stateroom, for three nights he turned back at the door and went out on deck where he watched the huge tropical moon and felt the hot wind breathe on the back of his neck.

*

67

On the fifth night out from Aden, Lily got up from her bed, took off her white lawn nightdress and opened her curtains. She peered out, but she could never see the dolphins and phosphorescence Mr Jackson had told her about, or even the big waves, only the moonlight, all fractured into flakes, and, when the ship rolled, the rough shape of the moon itself. There was always too much water messing the glass.

The light came and went from the cabin: she turned to look at glimpses of herself in the huge mirror, her white body like the moon's child, thin shoulders, long black hair and pubic hair so scanty you could see the cleft through it.

She opened her wardrobe door and began rummaging for clothes – as few as she needed. She put on a dress but no pantalettes, shoes but no stockings. She found a big silk shawl, white embroidery on cream, and wrapped it round her head and across her face so that only her eyes were visible. She examined herself for a moment, in the mirror.

Then she opened her door and looked up and down the corridor. The first step she took out of the stateroom was the hardest to make: she put her foot in and out at least ten times before she followed it with the other foot.

She told herself that there was no one there. They'd all be asleep at this time. There would only be the people whose job it was to sail the ship, and they wouldn't be here. She stepped forward, testing herself against the movement, keeping to the side of the corridor for the stability of the wall. She guessed she'd have to go upstairs to get out on deck, so she went up the first set of wide, carpeted stairs she found. Her balance was improving: when she got to the top of the stairs she ran joyfully through the freedom the others took for granted. There were tables and chairs, armchairs – all fixed to the floor – she swung on them or pushed off from them against the waves.

She didn't care if she met anyone. She was too glad to escape.

'I couldn't breathe down there,' she whispered to herself in the empty saloon. The moonlight showed her a door that led to another door. She went through them both and there she was with the hot damp air blowing in her face. She clutched her shawl round her, then – looking round again – dropped it and knotted it round her shoulders. She put her face up to the moon and tasted the wind with her open mouth. She ran to the rail and looked over at the sea while the spray splashed her face. She saw a hump in the water, and another, and she was looking out at dolphins, playing in the foam around the ship. When they broke the surface it flashed.

The ship leaned into a bigger roller than the rest, pressing Lily's chest painfully against the rail. There was a wall of water only a few feet from her that looked as if it might engulf the ship any moment: she wasn't afraid of it. She was only afraid of being found out. But she didn't meet anyone, neither on the deck or on her cautious way back.

She might have met Samuel if he'd got up half an hour earlier. He walked on the same part of the deck, and went back to Mrs Darley's cabin. When he passed Lily's door he wondered, briefly, about the woman inside: the gossip now was that she was Mr Jackson's wife, sixty-four years old and determined to die in Macao where she had been born the daughter of a country trader. He had too much on his mind to give it much thought. Now at last he'd thrown off the bounds of morality, now he was going to have a good time with a woman. It felt like those wild nights of his boyhood, only far, far better.

As softly as he could, he opened Mrs Darley's door, and then the second door to her bedroom. And there was Mrs Darley lying on the bed in a one-piece suite edged with lace, frilled, and buttoned to the throat. She put out her arms to him – they were round and white in the moonlight – and he sat beside her, found himself lying on top of her, her sleeping suit was opening as if of its own accord – though he supposed her fingers had something to do with it, but they were also occupied with his clothing and slipping something on to his erect member: he wondered in his pleasure how many hands she had? She was so amazingly capable, it seemed there'd been nothing to worry about after all.

He swam up into her through his sweat and hers – 'you mean to say you've never – oh, how *delightful*, how *enchanting*! So *sweet*, young men, so *grateful*!'

He learned that her husband was *incapable*, totally useless, that she was hard done by, that she *had* to have a man ' – because never believe them, when they say a woman doesn't need your love and tenderness, dear boy, we need it in the *fullest* sense, I am not lying, believe me – ' and her husband was such a *boor*, such a *brute* – and her maid, such an excellent creature, such a *treasure*!

He ejaculated into her in a chrysanthemum burst of pyrotechnic pleasure that left him empty of any feeling except grateful satiety. He'd never imagined it could be like this. He felt safe, held, purged. Only once he thought the waves would throw him off her, but she put her arms round him and anchored him.

6

SCANDAL

I'VE had a woman, wrote Samuel to Reynolds: the letter could go into the post at Colombo. *I've had Mrs Darley.*

He'd dreamed of the angel when he came back from her cabin: 'Go away,' he said to her. 'I like Mrs Darley better.' She put her wings over her eyes and vanished.

Just think, I can do what I like with her, that whole lush body is at my disposal. It's such tremendous fun. Who needs prostitutes?

That would surprise Reynolds, shock him out of his skin. Samuel grinned. He'd jumped off solid ground into the waters of wickedness, and had neither drowned nor been eaten by sharks. He looked back on his earlier, earnest self with compassion. He thought he'd grown an inch. He was sure of it.

The weather continued rough. He gave the occasional pitying thought to poor seasick Henderson.

It calmed when they were one day's sailing out of Colombo and the rest of the First Class passengers got up and came to dinner. It was as if the social life of the voyage had never been interrupted: each knew, by now, whom they had to avoid, whom they must seek out. Henderson sought out Mrs Darley.

He was cold towards Samuel – well, he must have some suspicion – he made a wall of his back and penned Mrs Darley behind it. Mrs Darley acquiesced.

She had the right, of course. Samuel wouldn't have denied her anything – no, it wasn't true. He did want to deny her Henderson. His stomach which had been immune to seasickness griped with jealousy: *now* he was on his way out, back into loneliness, into childishness. No. He wouldn't have it.

He met Henderson in the gentlemen's lavatory.

He said: 'I'm in love with Mrs Darley.'

Henderson shook his penis – Samuel hoped, angrily – and drops of urine splattered the air.

'Oh,' said Henderson, jeering, *'there's* a challenge.'

Samuel was furious with Henderson who had used him as fool in London.

'I've been to bed with her,' he said vindictively, then hurried out to find Mrs Darley and get possession of her first.

Mrs Darley asked him to get her coffee. Writhing inwardly, he obeyed. He came back to find Henderson standing over Mrs Darley. They glared at each other.

'I always told my children,' said Mrs Darley, laughing slightly at them both, 'that they must learn to share. We used to have an old rocking horse, especially the two boys used to fight each other to ride it, you can't imagine the noise! So I said to them, boys, one of you rides one day, the other the next. And Alfie, you rode yesterday, so Charlie rides today. Is that understood? I said to them. Firmness solves so many problems, don't you both think?'

Sadly, Samuel prepared to walk away.

'Oh, Mr Pink,' said Mrs Darley, 'do stay. I was just saying, I told my boys, they could *stroke* the horse when it wasn't their turn, it was only the rides they mustn't have. Don't you think I'm a fair mother?'

'Of course,' said Henderson, treading accidentally on Samuel's foot.

Still, Samuel admired her. Her enemies should be his enemies, her allies – except for Henderson – his. She told both young men about Hong-Kong, dividing it into the socially acceptable and the social disasters: Mr Bradwell, the Colonial Secretary, such a *nice* man, and such a help to her husband; the Governor, quite the gentleman, but ineffectual, everyone said. The Postmaster-General was *irritating*, excessively religious, and there was Mr Philips the Registrar-General, a very *strange* man, far too fond of people like the Sassoons, Jews, after all – Mrs Darley had never understood why the Prince of Wales had taken them up – and the Rustomjees, and the Chatterjees, 'because after all, we *need* these people to help run the colony, but they must know their place. At least they aren't allowed in the Hong-Kong Club. And Mr Philips is often *very* obstructive to Mr Darley, and that makes my life harder, dear boys, because heaven knows he's not an easy man.'

'And Chinese people?' asked Samuel.

'Lord,' said Mrs Darley, 'they're servants and coolies. The better sort keep themselves to themselves. Only Mr Philips sees them socially – I think he despises his own people, I really do.'

Samuel got ready to hate Mr Philips. He practised by hating Henderson. He hoped Henderson would fail Mrs Darley that night: if Samuel's ill-will could do it, he'd run with dysentery for the rest of the voyage. He got out of bed at two in the morning, and went to stand outside Mrs Darley's door, in case he might hear something – he didn't. On the way back, he thought he saw a figure in pale clothing slip round a corner, someone who certainly wasn't Henderson. It frightened him: he thought it might be the angel who he'd rejected, stalking him. Then he drank whisky and forgot about it.

He played deck cricket with the other men, all but Mr Jackson. The ladies watched. He clean-bowled Henderson. Mrs Darley applauded along with everyone else. Henderson went out, showing his teeth in a not quite sportsmanlike grin. It was a relief to be malicious, to give up virtue. He even maligned Henderson to Mrs Darley, told her (in bed) that he was mediocre at Cantonese, that he'd needed Samuel's help to pass his examinations, that he'd been sick in the street one night when he was drunk. Mrs Darley laughed.

I'm not afraid of anything any more, he asserted to Reynolds, *I can snap my fingers at Fate and God alike. A man has to live, hasn't he?*

'To arouse the vital energy,' said Mr Jackson, 'to channel it within the body – read that last exercise to me again, Lily.'

Lily read out: 'The woman lies on the bed with her legs on the man's shoulders. He enters her and thrusts deep ten times, shallow another ten, then a final five times as he pleases. He must withdraw if he feels he cannot control the motion of his seed.'

Mr Jackson ground his teeth a little. Lily knew this was part of the exercise, but she still found it alarming: as if he was sharpening his teeth, as if he might eat her.

'Lily,' he asked, 'are you wearing a corset?'

'Yes,' she lied.

He came to stand behind her and ran his hands up and down her front, leaning her against him. She could feel his member moving against her, as if of its own volition, could feel her own body's

73

excitement. Then he let go of her, began to grind his teeth with something like desperation, panting and pressing his groin. At last he said: 'Ah!' smiled, and left her: he said he had to lie down.

Lily also lay down on her bed. She was tired. She had taken to roaming ever more freely about the boat at night, knew the whole of the First Class by heart now, knew the deck and the tropical night sky in cloud, in rain, and in the moonlight. Now she fell asleep. Mr Jackson came in later, found her there, admired her for a moment, and then slapped her.

'Get to work,' he said, 'idle little hussy, what do you think I keep you for?'

She was momentarily frightened, resolved not to go out that night – and went all the same.

Miss Sayer, slipping out of Miss Roper's room after a long night-time heart-to-heart, caught a glimpse of her.

'There's a lady who sleepwalks,' she said the next day at breakfast. 'I saw her last night. I didn't recognize her, but it must be one of us. What a terrible tragedy if she were to go on deck and fall into the water!'

Everyone was alarmed, but no one had any idea what to do about it.

Between Colombo and Penang, they ran into a frightful tropical storm. The ship laboured up and down enormous waves, shuddering violently with the effort of the screwshaft, while water leaked in everywhere: the passengers stayed in their berths and prayed.

It was Henderson's night for Mrs Darley, but he wouldn't go in this weather, so Samuel crawled out of his stateroom and made his way up the stairs towards the door of Mrs Darley's room. The ship's hard edges beat and bruised him as he went: he was only so much helpless jetsam in the turmoil. Still he kept on towards his goal.

He found Mrs Darley reading, though the electric light flickered and often went out altogether. Her face was quite calm and fearless. She put her arms out to Samuel. She said – raising her voice against the din:

'Dear boy. There could be no better way to die.'

He didn't doubt it. He'd never understood it, but now he saw that life and death went hand in hand: to be afraid of death was to refuse life. He felt how magnificent she was, sublime, greater than woman. He laid her bare: her breasts, her navel, her cleft that was deeper than the troughs of the ship's frightful path. The electricity went out altogether, and he had to grope for her in the blackness. Sometimes the violence of the waves jerked him clean out of her, and he had to re-enter. They laughed. At last they lay exhausted. Their passion was tremendous, but the wind had more staying power.

'Mrs Darley,' he said (she'd never invited him to use her Christian name), 'I lied to you, the other day.'

'When you said you loved me?' she enquired in the dark.

'Oh, no,' he said, 'never that – ' He kissed her and she laughed.

'I'm a bastard,' he said. 'I'm adopted. All that talk of Scottish noble blood – but there is something. I believe –'

He wanted to tell her, he was going to tell her. The ship was shaking apart, he *must* die with the truth on his lips.

'Oh, my eye,' she laughed, 'You're the Prince's bastard. I knew it!'

Samuel stopped in his tracks, sobered by her vulgarity. 'No,' he said quickly, 'only a nobleman. I don't know for sure. You won't tell anyone, will you?'

'Dear boy,' she said, 'my lips are sealed.'

He could have given everything away. He must have lost his wits.

'Leaving me so soon?' asked Mrs Darley. 'I won't tell anyone, I do promise. Don't you believe me?'

'I never said anything,' said Samuel desperately. 'Please – please let me go.'

He struggled out: the sleeping-cabin door leaned against him and he could hardly open it. Then – he couldn't understand it – the sea calmed. He opened the day-cabin door and the corridor lay flat ahead of him as if it was land. They were inside the eye, the breathless hour or so of quiet.

Lily thought the storm had come to an end. She got up at once, opened her own door, and stood out on the corridor. She didn't even trouble to look: there wouldn't be anyone about after a night like this. She ran forward and found herself face to face with Samuel. She cried out and tried to hide in her shawl.

Samuel – who had never encountered a Chinese person before – saw a pair of long black eyes above the shawl. They fled from his: for a moment he thought of the Arab women in Port Said.

He smelt a sweet scent: far sweeter than Mrs Darley, and there was something about her that made the very hairs on his arms rise in response: like the vibration of a violin playing unseen and below the threshold of sound. His heart was still beating a percussion accompaniment: he was sure it echoed in the quiet. The next thing he noticed was that she was as frightened as he was. Her hands shook as they held the silk shawl just under her eyes, her tears ran down into it.

'Please,' she said in the purest English (slightly muffled by the silk), 'don't tell.'

Samuel was appalled to see her get down on to her knees before him. Her shawl caught under her and tumbled on to the polished wood floor, revealing her face, and still he didn't see that she was Chinese.

'Who are you?' he asked. 'You mustn't kneel to me, please don't – ' He put both hands out and pulled her up on to her feet again. He didn't let go of her hands.

'My name's Lily,' she said. 'Lily Jackson.' Then she shut her mouth and stood there like the dumb heroine of a fairy-tale, incredibly beautiful and unable to explain anything, shivering. Her clothes hung on her in a bedraggled sort of way: as if she wasn't wearing corsets. When Samuel put her shawl round her shoulders, he realized, with a shock, that she wasn't. Her eyes were downcast.

'No,' he said, 'I won't tell anyone.'

There was no one else in the world, just the two of them in the quiet passage. A picture came into his mind from somewhere – he had no idea – light moving on a stone wall. His heart slowed.

'Then I'm safe,' said Lily. 'I don't know what they'd do to me if they found out.'

'Why,' asked Samuel, 'why would anyone want to do anything bad to you?'

'Can't you see?' she said with a sob, 'I'm Chinese. But Mr Jackson – Now you'll tell, won't you?'

'No,' said Samuel. 'No, never. I understand.'

She said: 'How can you?'

'I can't say,' said Samuel.

She said: 'I've got to go back to my cabin. I've been wicked. I shan't do it again. Mr Jackson would be so angry.' She shuddered.

Samuel wanted to kiss her hand: he did it with snatched, awkward tenderness. Then he let her go, and she slipped inside.

He stood there in the scent she'd left behind her, but it was fading fast. He wanted to knock on her cabin door and see her again. She was a being quite outside his experience, sensual, it was true, but unearthly. He'd read, in Plato, that the things of this earth were mere shadows of better things, cast from a deeper reality. Just for a moment, he'd seen what was outside the shabby cave of lust and domesticity. It wouldn't last, of course. He'd keep going to Mrs Darley.

But for a moment he thought he'd like to throw himself overboard: he might be united with the ineffable, if he did.

It was Miss Roper who exposed Lily, and all from the very best of motives. The weather had calmed, the *Pearl River* was making good headway, and they were almost in Penang: two nights more at most, the captain had told the diners at his table.

Lily knew she'd been lucky to meet the young man: anyone else would have told. She remembered the feel of his hands on her: he'd touched her with tenderness, as if she were a piece of Sung dynasty porcelain, or a rare scroll. And he'd said – which wasn't possible – that he understood. Lily felt the wonderful tug of the impossible. She thought she could tell him how she'd lost the habit of sleeping through the night, how she sat up in her stateroom and couldn't bear it that the only face she saw was her own in the mirror.

She went out.

Miss Roper woke from a happy dream of matrimony – and the port-wine stain had been bleached white by the wedding clothes, gone for ever – to the sad reality of her state. Coldly, she lay in bed and assessed her chances. Perhaps she should have stayed in England and learned to work a typewriter? But surely – in Hong-Kong with so many hideous Chinese women around – she'd show to better advantage? Except that Mrs Darley had told her there were also many pretty young daughters of English families – 'My dear,' had asked cruel Mrs Darley, 'didn't you *know*?'

Miss Roper walked up and down her day room. The ship tipped suddenly and violently. Miss Roper grabbed the edge of a table and steadied herself, waiting for the lurch in the opposite direction. When it came, she heard the sound of someone falling against her door. She held on to the table, panting. The ship steadied herself and continued as if nothing had happened: most of the passengers didn't even wake up.

Miss Roper felt it was her duty – as a Christian – to investigate the sound outside the door. It might be the sleepwalking lady. She hoped it wasn't Mrs Darley in some horridly revealing nightdress. She tried to remember how to deal with such cases. You didn't wake them. You took them by the hand and led them gently back to their bed.

Unlike Samuel, she saw at once that Lily was Chinese.

'Mr Pink!' cried Mrs Darley at breakfast, 'Miss Roper caught the sleepwalker, and think! She was a Chinese woman, a horrid Chinese prostitute belonging to Mr Jackson, travelling in the First Class. It's a dreadful scandal: I'll make sure my husband complains to the company. The Captain says they'll have to leave the ship at Penang, mind you, he knew it was going on.'

'She was so frightened,' said Miss Roper, 'and I called the stewardess, *she* gave her a slap, and wanted to know what she was doing out of her cabin. They were all in it, it's shameful. Then Mr Jackson came along, and *he* gave her another slap – '

She fell silent when she saw Samuel's face.

'Oh, Mr Pink,' said Mrs Darley teasingly, '*you're* not going to take her part against us, are you?'

'No,' muttered Samuel.

There was no need for him to be disappointed in her: he only desired her, and she had never expected anything from him but wickedness and vice. If she kept the secret of his bastardy it was more than he deserved. And Lily Jackson was a bad woman too, a thing to be slapped about and despised. He began to make jokes.

Mr Jackson and Lily were put off the ship at Penang, where they took refuge with an old friend of his, a merchant who lived there with his Malay mistress. The woman was kind to Lily, though they didn't speak a word of each other's languages.

'It's just as well,' said Mr Jackson, 'they were ignorant people, bad for my *chi*, every one of them. The food was bad, too. All the same, you deserved those slaps, Lily! You might have been ruined, if you'd met a man. Then how could you have helped me?'

Mr Walters had a Chinese cook – though Mr Jackson found the Singapore-style food too hot. Mr Walters also had a trading vessel just leaving for Hong-Kong. There was a limited amount of passenger accommodation on board her, and there they would travel.

Mr Jackson kept the key to Lily's cabin: he locked her in for the rest of the voyage. The first thing Lily saw when they arrived in Hong-Kong harbour was the *Pearl River*: she had arrived several days before. They disembarked and were transported straight to the house Mr Jackson had taken on the Peak.

The wave that had thrown Lily off-balance was the result of a volcano's underwater eruption. It swept on through the Pacific and devastated an island twenty-three miles square. It was a moderate monster, as tidal waves go.

7

HONG-KONG
1887

THE island of Hong-Kong had always been there, lying alongside
the mainland among a scatter of other islands: the South China
Sea that encircled it was coloured green-blue by yellow mud from
the Pearl river estuary. Yellow beaches had formed in the tucks of
the island's craggy shoreline, and here pirates once beached their
boats. At the north-west of the island, opposite the peninsula of
Kowloon where nine dragons lay inside the hills, there had been a
waterfall from which fisherfolk and pirates alike filled their
bottles.

There had been a few fishing villages along the side of the island, a
few paddy fields like thrown-down pieces of emerald cloth in the
lower laps of the bleak granite hills, and years of quiet days and
afternoons when huge black swallowtail butterflies fed on thrifty
flowers – till the British came in 1842 and began to build the city of
Victoria. Later, in 1860, they acquired the peninsula they called
Kowloon.

The British Government constructed a diplomatic and military
base, the merchants constructed a centre of shipping and trade.
Both needed an outpost from which they could reach into China
though the government wasn't prepared to intervene as often as the
merchants wanted. The place made money, and Chinese people
came in to participate. What only the Chinese knew was how much
importance the island had lost. It had been cast off from the Dragon
Empire and loosely anchored – though by the most modern means
of communication – to a small barbarian island seven thousand
miles away. Let it be never so built up and never so prosperous, let
the great trading hongs hold never so much state – Jardine
Matheson, Butterfield and Swire, Dent's – its frantic busyness

was no more significant against the ages of China than was an antheap against a mountainside.

The majority of its population was still Chinese. A large number of them had no idea who the Queen-Empress Victoria was, knowing only the Emperor of China, or, if they were better informed, the Empress Tzu Hsi who ruled in fact. They had their own names for the streets: they called Elgin Street 'Earth Street', Queen's Road was 'The Great Horse Road', and Gap Road 'The Severed Dragon' because the road, having been built without due regard to the principles of *feng shui*, the dragon who lay in the hillside had been brutally sliced in half. They looked down on the British.

The island had a circumference of twenty-seven miles and an area of thirty square miles, was about eleven miles long and from two to five miles wide, while the British part of the Kowloon peninsula comprised an area of three square miles. The peninsula was rugged and hilly, and the island itself little more than a range of hills emerging from the water, among whose scatter of scrub large granite boulders sat upright and stared out at the sea. The city sprawled over the lower northern slopes of Victoria Peak, but on the other side of the ridge it was the same island that it had always been: Deepwater Bay, Stanley, Shek O, Big Wave Bay, Little Hong-Kong, Aberdeen, Tai Tam Chuk, Pokfulam gave little indication of the white man's presence, except for the reservoirs he had built and the visits of picnic parties or hardy walkers. The southside water was Chinese territory, and all the other islands that could be seen from the shore belonged to China, Lamma, Lantau, Cheung Chow.

The island formed one side of a superb natural harbour, its surface spider-webbed by the white trails of steam-launches, of sampans, of steamers as well as junks of all kinds and purposes. It had a superb postal service, a telegraph service, 'expresses' came in at any time of the day and night and were posted in the Hong-Kong Club. Visitors had their choice of many fine hotels – if they could get a room. Christians could choose between six places of worship – for the Jews there was a synagogue, a mosque for the Muslims, to say nothing of temples for the Chinese population. Children were schooled, orphans put in institutions, the sick could go to hospital, the mad to the asylum, those in need of edification to the museum or the Botanical Garden. The banks, the shops, the Stock Exchange rattled with the sound of money turning over. When you came in by boat the first thing you saw was the brown smoke from the sugar refineries.

For John Darley and his wife, the first day passed as it always did; he had taken time off work to meet her and wished he was back there; they greeted each other with a mixture of fear and anger. He was a lean little man, leathern and yellowed through years of exposure to tropical sun. She always thought, when she saw him again after a long absence, that he was exactly like a jockey, but he had stopped riding her some years ago. His desire was for other things.

They were taken by sedan to where 'Isola Bella' (her choice of name) sat on a stone terrace on the steep hillside. Soon they'd be able to use the High Level Tramway which was at present only a line of exposed red soil. But neither of them really wanted Darley home earlier at night. They had nothing to say to each other.

He supposed she'd be thinking about the young men on the boat. He had caught them in the moonshape of his telescope lens: he used it to scan the harbour, to investigate the detail of junks, to see the rocks huddled on the hills opposite, or observe the movements of boat-builders and farmers. He'd seen the rounded vignette of a lady giving her hand to two gentlemen, one after the other, had felt the bite of apprehension in his vitals. He might have guessed – he knew her, after all.

He'd been living in a hotel while she was away, to be closer to his work. Arrived back at home, he looked round at its splendours as if it was another hotel – it wasn't real to him. She knew it. They sat opposite each other at a long table and she told him stories of the children. He listened, and nodded: the jockey again. Was he interested? She didn't know. He kept the words he might have spoken trapped inside his head: they might have been rats that he didn't want to release into the world, destructive gnawing beasts, spoilers of everything they touched. He would cock his head sideways if any escaped, watch them distrustfully, fearful they might turn and bite him.

It was the drains of Hong-Kong that ran John Darley's lifeblood. He was also intensely fond of carbolic – that is, of the idea of that cleansing, detoxifying liquid. As a surgeon might see a body completely transparent, the organs, veins, arteries and nerves exposed to delight him, the diseases apparent to enrage him and provide him with employment, so Darley saw, behind the white buildings and godowns, the secret drains and sewers under the surface of Victoria. Then his blue eyes would burn with the fire that had once captivated his wife: he didn't know how much it enraged her to see it.

The library was full of books about drains and public health, leather-bound, rubbing up against his wife's volumes of Sir Walter Scott's work. He wouldn't have them moved, except when his wife was away and they went down to the hotel with him.

She'd never been what he'd thought she was, when he'd come back on home leave and asked her to marry him. She was superficial. He thought, all the same, that he'd done his duty by her. He'd given her four children. Then he'd left her alone. He'd not interfered or reproached her.

She would have given anything to get him into her bed again.

There was no letter for Samuel from Reynolds or anyone else. Of course, the post would come after him: the *Pearl River* was a fast steamer. Any answers to the letters he'd sent would take still longer to come. On his second day, Samuel sat down, man-to-man, to write another one.

Picture me here, he began, rather proud of the throwaway tone, *surrounded by hordes of Chinese. You'd have thought I'd be used to natives by now – I walked round Port Said, for example, Penang, Singapore. This feels different. This is serious, no brief saunter round the town. This is journey's end. And you know, one can't help asking oneself what one's really doing here? No doubt I'll get the answer in due course.*

But this was disingenuous – he knew what he was doing here. It had come to him as soon as he'd seen the island.

I went to see the Colonial Secretary today: all Chinese clerks of course, and in spite of a year's teaching I still can't make out much of what they're saying. The junks have eyes painted on their prows, and that's what you feel, all the time: they're watching you.

I wasn't expecting it to be so cold – set in early, this year – and even though Mrs Darley warned me it still came as a shock. (I had a last night with her – you'd be surprised to see how well your pupil can acquit himself.) Anyway, I was telling you about the govern-ment offices: quite dilapidated, that was another shock. Somehow that drove it home to me that this is the place I'll spend the rest of my life. Dear old England is another world – now comes the real adventure: getting on top of the new one.

But he'd master it. He was going to be Governor, surely that was what his mother intended for him? He'd sit in her position, wield her authority: it was the closest she could bring him to the royalty that was out of reach.

There was a picture of the Queen on the wall of the office: it concentrated my thoughts on my duty. Though I intend to live a little, too. I've grown up a good deal since we said goodbye at Southampton.

The Queen's eyes had been watching him, she might have been wondering what he was turning into. He couldn't reassure her, it was other people's job to communicate his affairs to her.

He wrote: *When I went in to Mr Bradwell, he told me where to tread so that I wouldn't go through the floorboards. White ants, he said. It seems the whole building is riddled with them. Someone had been carving their initials on his desk. I had to sit in a rattan lounger that had lost its arms. At least there was a fire in the room, but that didn't comfort me for long. It made the place far hotter than we're used to in England. They say your blood thins in the heat. Mr Bradwell is a very happy-looking man, which I suppose says something for the life out here.*

'Been here twenty years now,' Bradwell had told him. 'Expecting a move soon – wherever they send me. That's the Service. We don't choose, do we? We let those above decide what's good for us. Quite right too. Didn't go to school, did you, some childhood delicacy, wasn't it? All gone now, I hope. You need a strong constitution out here.'

Samuel remembered the large drop of sweat that had formed like a tear in the exact centre of his back. It had run down his spine underneath his woollen combinations, had hesitated for a moment when it reached his buttocks, then run into the crease.

Victoria had been on the wall here too: she held a handkerchief in her hand and had an anxious expression on her face. He'd protested his physical strength, and thought he saw her look relieved.

Bradwell told me I'll spend a month here getting acquainted with the work of the government – and meeting people – then they're going to send me over to Canton to learn Chinese. He was very friendly and welcoming. He has a fine moutache but he's losing the hair at the back of his head – maybe the white ants nibble your hair at night? Samuel giggled at his own joke. *They say there are huge cockroaches everywhere in the hot season. He asked me how my cricket was: I said I hoped he'd find me a tolerable bowler. Then it was a polite enquiry about my lodgings, and I left. I'm sharing a little house in Caine Road with Henderson – good enough for a pair of bachelors, and of course we'll be in Canton half the time. But you sense, at once, that great things are expected of you. I only hope I can live up to that. I'm looking forward to getting a letter from you. I hope you're well yourself.*

He sealed the letter without reading it through and asked the servant to post it: he was going out now to walk round the streets with Henderson. He brushed his hair and moustache, checked his appearance in the mirror and caught himself straining up on to his toes to look taller. He got down on to his heels and vowed never to make such a fool of himself again.

Mrs Darley had told him that the city of Victoria looked like Italy, and Samuel, who had never been there, took it on trust. It was true that the streets were beautiful, the white buildings with their red roofs and the leaves all fussing round them – they must be evergreens – and the brilliance of the winter sun on the harbour was enchanting. There were still too many Chinese.

They weren't like Lily – Samuel wondered when she and Mr Jackson would get to Hong-Kong? These Chinese were streetworn, bulky with layers of wadded clothing, pigtails swinging as they walked. Raucous market women smoked pipes and cried their wares: they were burned dark by the sun. They were coarse and ugly.

'Safe part of the town,' said Henderson, who seemed to know a great deal more than Samuel – had Mrs Darley told him? 'You wouldn't dare walk about in some of the quarters.'

A coolie hurried past them carrying two baskets full of frogs on a carrying-pole. The frogs were tied up in tight bundles, but their limbs struggled against the raffia bonds.

'Frog-eaters,' said Henderson, laughing, 'Like the French.' Samuel resented his confidence.

They walked uphill to Wellington Street, which was narrow and climbed across the contour of the slope: signs hung down over the shops and stalls, horizontal signs in English, perpendicular signs in Chinese characters. It made Samuel feel better that he could read the

Chinese. A woman was carrying on a loud conversation from a second-floor balcony with her neighbour on the other side of the street. The shop below her proclaimed itself the 'Exquisite Fragrance Mah Jong Maker'.

There *was* a distinctive smell; it caught at the back of an Englishman's nose, and yet there was something oddly familiar about it. Samuel thought fear might smell like that.

'Sort of food they eat,' said Henderson. 'Poison, to us, I should think.'

Samuel laughed. '*I'm* not afraid.'

'Who said I was?' asked Henderson. They eyed each other with dislike.

'All these cities smell awful,' said Samuel. 'Got to get used to it.'

There were the streetlamps, looking just like London, like old friends, but there were so many alien faces ahead of him, a river in smooth shades of light gold to bronze, running with black pigtails. Everything was dusty. It was dry in the cold season. Mrs Darley had told him that.

'You'll pant for the rain,' she had warned him.

Cattle, Samuel said to himself. They're cattle. He spied an English nanny shepherding a group of children. It should have been a relief. Hadn't the English the upper hand here? Wasn't he a lord, a master, and hadn't he learned the language? Only he didn't understand it on the streets, and though he might be the Queen's son, they'd never put flags up when *he* came into harbour.

'This is the road we want, ain't it?' said Henderson, grasping Samuel's arm: 'Lyndhurst Terrace. Takes us up to Hollywood Road.' They turned on to the steep, ladderlike street.

'Look at the fellow with the ducks,' said Henderson, nudging him. There was a coolie with two bundles of flapping brown ducks, who were tied by the feet, one bundle either end of the bamboo carrying-pole. It was difficult to keep them balanced, but the coolie managed it, always answering their movements with his: he was very graceful. Then a sedan carrying a heavy Englishman came downhill at the gallop and he swung too quickly out of the way. One bundle of ducks slithered off the carrying pole and lay in the road in a muddle of protesting feathers.

The coolie needed to get the fallen ducks back on the pole without losing the rest. The birds opened their bills and flapped their wings, while their yellow feet cramped together, straining against each other: it wouldn't be easy to get a purchase on them, and everyone was laughing at him. He bent down cautiously – but the ducks began to slide off the other end, so he had to straighten up. He looked hopelessly at his flapping wares: they were getting filthier by the minute. He didn't want to dirty the other ducks by putting them down on the street.

'Come on, Pink,' said Henderson.

'*No*,' said Samuel. He was dreadfully uncomfortable, and he had to watch.

The coolie manoeuvred for several more minutes, managed at last to crouch down with the single bundle of dun-coloured ducks carefully balanced at one end of the dingy yellow pole – and they slid off. He shouted what was obviously an obscenity, and kicked the protesting birds across to the gutter where they scrabbled with the others. The onlookers laughed yet more heartily.

'*Now* will you come, Pink?' demanded Henderson. 'Don't know why you're so interested.'

'This is one of *them*,' said Samuel, 'the people we've come out to govern.' But it was the man's failure that had held him. His back was covered in goosepimples.

'Not us,' Henderson reminded him, grinning, 'They say Hong-Kong's governed by Jardine's first, then the Jockey Club, and then the Bank.'

'And *then* the Governor,' said Samuel doggedly.

Suddenly, Henderson said: 'I don't like them. Did you see how they laughed at him?'

The government cadets were an élite even among other colonials, picked out for high office. They might govern colonies themselves one day – and who knew which parts of China might become new British colonies in the next twenty years? It was taken for granted that they would join the Hong-Kong Club. They went there that evening: their names were already in the book. There they met two other young men, Richards, a lawyer in his mid-twenties, and Caird from Jardine Matheson. They played billiards, they smoked. Richards had an enviable set of whiskers. Caird was dressed in well-tailored Scottish tweeds. Both were pleased to see them. There were few enough young gentlemen in the colony.

Samuel – not knowing why – asked Richards: 'Do you know a Mr Darley?'

'Certainly,' said Richards easily. 'The Surveyor-General. Do you know him?' He leaned over the green table and achieved a perfect cannon shot. The others applauded ruefully.

'I met his wife,' said Samuel, 'she was on the boat coming over.'

Henderson's aim slipped. The wrong ball went into the pocket, but he ignored it, looking apprehensively at Richards and Caird, who exchanged glances, winked, and laughed.

Richards took Samuel by the lapel. He said: 'You know Mrs Darley?' He shook his head. Quietly, he said: 'Oh, Pink, you're a dog. You know Mrs Darley! I'd never have believed it of you. I suppose you know her too, Henderson?'

Henderson grinned now, and nodded.

Richards said: 'Of course: she's back. It was in the newspaper. They get all the young men up to their house, you know, she likes to look us over.' He guffawed again, then turned away from the table to puff at his cigar.

Samuel thought he might have guessed that Mrs Darley was notorious – but that was apparently to his credit. It seemed he'd have to share her with more than Henderson on land – Richards and Caird almost without doubt. Dogs, all of them, and she was a bitch: his spaniel had been as shameless when she was on heat. He laughed with the rest, he helped debase Mrs Darley and washed shame away in brandy and soda.

The next day, he was invited to dine at Government House.

There was no invitation for Henderson. Samuel was pleased. It marked him out as special and it annoyed Henderson. He hoped Henderson would never get such an invitation. That would put him in his place.

Samuel had been invited because of who he was – did His Excellency know? Or had someone only asked him to be good to young Pink, reason unspecified? He imagined himself writing his memoirs:

So I set foot, for the first time, in Government House, little realizing that it was later to be my home, the scene of so much hard work and so many distinguished encounters.

His Excellency, it was said, practically ran a boarding house for visiting notables. Of course his memoirs would have to be highly edited, the Pinks would appear to be his parents, he would talk about their parents, his notional grandparents (he'd have to find out more about them). He thought he'd concentrate on his achievements.

He wondered if anything would be said to him. Supposing the Governor took him aside and talked about his mother? But of course, he wasn't supposed to know anything. Nothing would be said. All the same, he imagined a special talk, a particular look of interest in His Excellency's eye. Or would the Governor disapprove of him? He'd have good reason. He bolted back to his future memoirs.

Being eager to appear at my best and acquit myself well in company, I do believe I made myself quite odious to my servants. (And to Henderson, but that was intentional, and not to be set down on paper.) *I had hardly eaten for days* (he was anxious in case his trousers might fall down, and sent the servant out for braces, though they were bad for a man's shoulders). *I made the servant tie my bow-tie four times, and rejected one dress shirt for a minute crumple in the collar. And of course all my apprehension was groundless, since His Excellency showed great friendliness towards this insignificant cadet, and said* – He didn't dare think further.

He went by sedan: it was odd and slightly disagreeable to be carried by men, however much he might try to consider them cattle. He'd have to get used to it. They let him out at the main entrance, he went up the steps, across a verandah and into a hallway. It was quite small: 'intimate' said Samuel to himself. His meeting with the Governor, however, was far from intimate: Sir William asked him a few polite questions, didn't listen much to the answers, and greeted the next guest. Samuel walked off, not knowing where to go. He felt exposed, caught out. He should never have expected anything: now he'd been snubbed for his cheek. Mrs Darley walked past him with Richards and neither seemed to notice him. He couldn't see anything else. He wished he could leave.

Darley saw the youngster standing there, saw his wife ignore him and the look of distress on his face. He knew who Pink was: he'd been introduced to him at the Club.

'Pink,' he said, 'good to see you.'

Then he couldn't say anything else. He hoped Pink would continue the conversation but the lad only stood silent and scared.

Darley forced himself to go on: 'Crowded here,' he observed. 'I suppose you know a few people already.'

Like Richards, like Virginia. No wonder young Pink was scared of him: he couldn't know what was really in his head. Darley looked

89

him over: they were about the same height, but Pink was plump and fresh-faced – that wouldn't last, not in the tropics. His wide blue eyes had a short-sighted look about them, as if they were searching for something they couldn't quite see. Darley was made uncomfortable by a rush of affection. He stuck his hands in the pockets of his dress uniform.

'A few,' said Pink nervously.

'Come and meet some more,' said Darley, turning away and then twisting his face back with an awkward grin.

'There,' said Mr Jackson, pointing to the hazy Chinese hills, 'my destiny will accomplish itself.' He stood on the verandah of their new house on the Peak.

It had been built for an English family, who had never occupied it. The husband had died of brain-fever and the family had gone back to live in Yorkshire. The house was set well away from any others, which was why Mr Jackson had chosen it.

The exterior of the house was verandahed with classical columns in marble, but Mr Jackson had the inside walls panelled in wood and inlaid with scrolls and Chinese texts: all this work had been carried out while they were on the voyage. The wood was exquisitely carved in the Chinese style with symbols of good luck and long life, and the scrolls and texts were mainly stories and poems about the search for immortality. There was a particularly fine scroll picturing the Monkey-God stealing the Peaches of Immortality from the orchard of the Gods. This hung in the main reception room – but Mr Jackson received nobody except – very occasionally – the Registrar-General, Philips, whose scholarship he respected.

In the space behind the house, a Soochow garden was being made to Mr Jackson's design. There were many dwarf trees sitting ranked in their pots, waiting to be disposed about the verandah. Mr Jackson, in his Chinese robe, walked round and supervised everything. The Chinese workmen and servants were polite to him: they were pleased that he could speak to them in their own language. Their wrath fell the sharper on Lily: they didn't understand her Mandarin and they were outraged at her English.

If Mr Jackson was about, they were polite to her: otherwise they spat, called her a devil, a foreigner – she could understand that word, and guess at a few other insults – and had a thousand tiny ways of making her life uncomfortable. She pretended to be indifferent, but the pain inside her was so desperate she wanted, those first few weeks, to kill herself. She didn't. She asked Mr Jackson what he had been saying to them. He was in a very good mood these days, and so she managed to pick up a few words. She invested these in small exchanges with the servants, which yielded a fruit of more vocabulary. The insults became ever-so-slightly less frequent when they saw she was trying. She was relieved.

Mr Jackson performed his t'ai chi ch'uan, out on the coarse spiky grass in the garden – but carefully, because of the snakes. One day a bamboo snake fell out of a tree at his feet, but luckily the gardener was there and he killed it. Another time they found a king cobra underneath the marble-backed blackwood chairs in the reception room – it only hissed at them, spreading its hood, then slid away. Nobody dared try to catch it.

Mr Jackson had a use for ordinary cobras. Once a month the snake man came up to the house on the Peak. He came into the reception hall where Mr Jackson sat in one of the three chairs under the scroll of the Monkey-God. Lily sat beside him. The snake man pulled a cobra out from among the knot of others in his wriggling bag. Lily always shivered at the sight of the angry creature, but the snake man – to whom this was an everyday job – calmly pinned its head down with his bare foot. He ran his hand along the body, took up a knife, pierced the side of the body and pulled out the gall bladder with a blood-smeared hand. He teased the gall bladder away from the struggling snake – Lily usually hid her face at this part of the business – and held it out.

A servant took the gall bladder and placed it on a small Ming dynasty dish: it was dark, dark green against the blue-and-white. The servant handed the dish to Mr Jackson who tipped his head back and dropped the entire gall bladder down his throat. The snake man had stuffed the snake back into his bag and left: he would be paid by the Number One Boy. Mr Jackson sighed. He stood up and gave Lily his hand.

'I must go to lie down,' he said. 'Study hard.'

The gall bladder was essential for Mr Jackson's virility, and thus his life. Lily always had to vomit afterwards: that was another thing she did for him.

Mr Jackson lay on his curtained Chinese bed. The shutters of the room were closed: no one would disturb him. His thoughts flew round the ceiling like bats. He was pleased to think of them as bats. Bats were creatures of good omen in Chinese thought, another symbol of longevity.

He felt the snake's gall bladder dissipating strength throughout his body, and – yes – actually, as he lay there, he could feel himself becoming erect. He put his hand to his groin and began to grind his teeth. Not a drop of the precious fluid must escape. He thought of that golden body inside him, that immortal incarnation of the soul that would need no spurious Christian promises of resurrection.

He remembered the wandering monk who had sold him the Taoist text he was now following. He'd doubted the monk, all those years ago; had all but refused to buy the text. He had bought it, in the end, out of curiosity. It had been later on that same day that he had gone for a walk through Soochow and had heard the girl-child – always girl-children, never boys who were abandoned – wailing beside the ancient gate.

He had taken her because she was a Soochow girl, and girls from Soochow were usually beautiful. He'd been lucky. But of course it was meant: he could see that now.

Now too he remembered how the monk had come looking for him, 'the foreigner who is interested in Chinese scholarship.' The fellow had slipped out from a stinking alley between two houses, underneath a lattice of washing-poles trailing wet garments. They had stood by the bridge across the canal and haggled. When the price was agreed, the monk smiled and ran his fingers along his row of huge beads. He took the money and vanished. Mr Jackson remembered his face: a northern face with sharp high cheekbones and a thin moustache.

He'd been meant to have the scroll.

And Lily had stopped squalling when she lay in his arms. He had put his finger in her mouth and she had sucked it. He had taken her back with him and found a wet-nurse for her. He had watched her suck. She had turned her head away from the wet-nurse's breast and smiled at him.

She owed him everything. He was her life. So why this fear that she might learn to hate him?

He determined to be very careful with her.

All the time he had been grinding his teeth as the erection slowly subsided. Suddenly he felt a horrid twinge at the back of his mouth.

He mustn't wait too long. The first toothache of his life was a reminder that his time was limited.

Still he did everything very gradually.

He began to teach her t'ai chi, too: he said it would help her to help him, as well as benefiting her health. He would take hold of her to adjust her position in the movements, and when he did this, he would brush her breasts, her buttocks, or would put his hand on her belly beneath the navel, to show her where all the energy flowed from.

He would ask her: 'Does that feel nice?'

She would put her hands over her face, and laugh. It made her uncomfortable to feel pleasure when the servants were watching.

When he had the couch put in the room where she did her lessons, she felt as if the walls were closing in on her. Revulsion fought with desire: perhaps this was necessary, the counterflow of yin and yang.

She reminded herself that if she had remained in Soochow, even as the beloved daughter of a wealthy family, she would still have been sent away – and to a stranger's bed. She had read enough Chinese literature to understand this. Didn't she love Mr Jackson, who was kind to her, wasn't it better than a stranger? Yet she found herself longing for the undesirous, long-distant security of a woman's arms.

One day Mr Jackson gave her a lace dressing gown. Abruptly, he ordered her to put it on each day for her lessons. She was to wear nothing underneath. No one would see, he said, the door would be locked. He didn't touch her for another week, but he looked at her. Lily felt the butterfly again, fluttering over her bare skin. She wanted him to touch her.

Even when he did, he was patient, gradual. Till Lily was wet and groaning with desire for him. Then he smiled, and took her.

Mr Jackson kept his clothes on when he performed the exercises of Immortality with Lily. He didn't want her to see him naked.

Lily felt the silk against her skin, and his member rubbing against her, coming in at last. It hurt: he had warned her of that, but she was badly disappointed that all the pleasure she had felt withdrew, leaving her alone with awkwardness and pain. He withdrew after twenty trusts: she was used to his grinding teeth by now, but he did that more softly than before, or was that only her imagination?

'Stay still,' he said to Lily when his erection had subsided. He got a piece of white silk that he had lying on a rosewood table, and wiped Lily with it. Then he held it up to the light to see the blood.

Lily saw the joy on his face. She should have been pleased for him. She knew that. But he went away taking the silk with him.

She had never felt so desolate and cold as when he left her naked on the couch. And angry! The blood was hers: Mr Jackson had no right to steal it. She wanted to kill him. She was appalled at the strength of her hatred.

Then Mr Jackson came back. He sat beside her on the couch, stroked her hair and caressed her face.

'Oh, my child – ' he said. He drew the lace dressing gown over her. She curled round and put her head in his lap, on the thing that had pierced her and now lay soft and squirmy. She could never kill him, even if it were possible to escape punishment. It would be like killing herself.

Now Lily's studies became harder work than they had ever been before. The Taoist manual specified fifty different positions, each of which had to be perfected, each of which had to be achieved without ejaculation. Sometimes the positions made her legs ache. At least Mr Jackson was kind and gentle afterwards. He kissed her. He stroked her. That was her pleasure: the holding, afterwards.

He told her she must lie out in the moonlight, to feed her vitality.

In early March, Mr Jackson lay in his bed and dreamed he was undergoing one of the sixteen punishements of Hell. His head was being crushed between the turning stones of a mill, and all the knowledge was being ground out of it; everything he had laboriously and carefully learned throughout his life was trickling away to the sound of demonic laughter; he was drowning in it, or was it the womb he was drowning in? From whence he would presently be expelled, powerless, ignorant, with the sufferings of a lifetime ahead of him. He moved his hands in protest – they were no longer hands, they were paws. He was a puppy. He felt the other puppies wriggling round him. He opened his mouth to protest, and heard himself yelp.

He woke and was cold. He was in pain with the cold. He pulled the quilts back over him, but he couldn't get warm. His joints felt as if knives were at work inside them.

He sat up, wrapping himself in the silk-stuffed, silk-covered quilts. He tried to meditate. But his thoughts buzzed and cringed away from his dream, and he couldn't achieve an erection. He put his hand to the little futile thing between his legs. He thought he heard it yelp.

He shouted: 'Lily!' She didn't hear him. He got up, putting his feet into fur-lined silk boots, pulling a warm embroidered robe round himself. He walked through the dark house to where she lay asleep.

He shook her. She woke up and stared at him, her eyes wandering out of her dreams.

She said: 'Mr Jackson?'

'I want you in my bed,' he complained. 'I'm cold. I can't get an erection. I'll die, if you don't come into bed with me.'

Obediently, she got up and came in bare feet. She came into bed with him and lay against him.

'Your feet are cold,' he reproached her. 'You should have put your slippers on.'

She rubbed them with her hands till they were warm. She lay in the curve of Mr Jackson's body, and he was relieved to feel himself growing stiff against her. He carried out the necessary exercises, though his tooth was aching worse, and there was a hint of an ache on the other side now. He *would* carry it through, in spite of pain.

'Every night,' he commanded. 'You must sleep here every night, till it grows warm again.'

He was frail, he understood that now, his bodily strength was eggshell-thin, he needed her to enclose him like a quilted piece of silk, cushion against anything that might cause him to smash. Then the chrysalis of his failing body could enclose the growing immortal foetus who, at the moment of death, would take wing like a bright butterfly and leave the mortal shell behind. And his miraculous self would have limitless powers, having become magical, imperishable gold.

He took her into parts of the city where white men were afraid to go, to visit Chinese temples, where he taught her to get her fortune from the bamboo sticks. He himself only knelt and burned incense: he said he knew his destiny.

They went by sedan, but they were seen and gossiped about. Once, as they came out of an antique shop in Queen's Road, they came face to face with Henderson and Samuel. The sunset was colouring the sky among the islands: the energetic young English-men were strolling down to the quay, having sent their luggage on ahead of them. They were going to Canton to pursue their language studies.

They knew each other at once. Lily smiled briefly before she dropped her eyes, Samuel coloured and his heart thumped.

'That's Jackson,' said Henderson excitedly, 'flaunting his Chinese woman. I don't know what he sees in her, do you?'

'Come on,' said Samuel, 'or we'll miss the steamer.'

He hurried away.

8

1888, SPRING

THE Canton Steamer left in the evening, sailing out of Hong-Kong harbour among the hair-black Western Isles, apparently straight into the heart of a purple-and-gold sunset. Samuel stood on the deck and watched the sea turn to silk, lurid, sensuous, dangerous.

Henderson said: 'The rifles are over there, if we need them.'

Both young men had revolvers in their pockets. They were standard equipment in Hong-Kong. Samuel thought he'd shoot Henderson if he didn't stop talking.

'Wake up, Pink,' said Henderson. 'What'd you do if the rabble broke out from down there?' A horde of black-and-blue cotton-clad Chinese had been battened down in the steerage, where they would remain till Canton. The rifles were for protection against them as much as against pirates. 'What the devil are you thinking about?'

'That Chinese woman,' said Samuel and wished he hadn't.

'Jackson's woman?' Henderson was off. 'That sort of thing was all right forty years ago, when there weren't any white women, I'm as broadminded as the next man, but now –'

'Once a month with Mrs Darley is all right,' said Samuel nastily, 'or the prostitutes on Queen's Road.'

'Hold your tongue,' said Henderson. 'You know you were there, with Mrs Darley and me.'

Samuel blushed dark-red and couldn't answer. There were things it was better for a man to forget, if he ever wanted to be proud of himself again.

Grinning, Henderson said: 'Any moment, any boat – those fishing junks now –' he pointed to the fleet whose raggedy sails were picking up the evening wind ' – they could be pirates.'

'I'm saying my prayers,' said Samuel. Henderson laughed. They

97

hated each other because of their shared, inadmissible terrors.

The twilight was so short, out there, twenty minutes of exquisite grey-blue, a velvet-lined showcase for the jewelled lights of the city. And it was a small city, almost lost from sight now, a patch of home on a waste of darkness.

Henderson clenched his fists.

'I'd give a good account of myself,' he said.

The painter at West Burton claimed to have held a fleet of pirates at bay with only one revolver. Samuel had heard other stories like that at the Club, and he didn't believe them now. They were what men hoped other men would believe they had done. All the same, he couldn't think he'd die on this trip. He hadn't seen Canton yet.

Henderson said: 'I wonder what my sisters are doing now.' He began to talk about his home. Samuel had heard it plenty of times before, the old green water-butt, the apple-tree in the garden, the games Henderson had played with all those doting elder sisters.

Now it was Mrs Darley who was playing games with Henderson. Samuel had pulled out after that afternoon he didn't want to think about, but Henderson couldn't escape even when given the space to run free, he stayed yearning till Mrs Darley's claws came out and trapped him again. He had been doted on too much. He knew how to inflict cruelty but not to escape it: it was easy for her to make a fool of him.

It grew dark: they ate their dinner. Then they lay down in their shared stateroom, each with his loaded revolver under his pillow. Samuel read a letter from Reynolds. He was unhappy at the Manchester school, where he had to share a dormitory with the boys: he hated the sooty city.

There you are, he wrote, *living an exciting life, going out to dinner, seeing new sights, travelling to China. All I have is day after day of misery and hard labour. The boys smell and talk in their sleep. I never have any time for myself. I'm paid a pittance. I suppose I'm lucky to get my food, which is vile, but I'm not fussy about food. The poor of the world, needy ushers like me and those even further down, have to swallow whatever is served out to them. I think of you often, very affectionately, and wish I was still with you. Perhaps, when you've been out there a few years, you could recommend me for a post somewhere in Hong-Kong? I need something to look forward to. Do you remember how I used to bowl leg-breaks for you, under the old chestnut tree?*

He put the letter away and shut his eyes. He missed Reynolds, it hurt. He needed someone to show him his way through the world, as Reynolds had once done – but someone who was wiser than Reynolds, who wasn't sorry for himself and didn't need favours.

He wished he hadn't met Lily: the sight of her had been too disturbing. She wasn't a sublime visitation, as he'd thought. She was lonely and needy and disreputable, she'd been slapped and thrown off the steamer. She'd been found out. It scared him.

He fell asleep and dreamed he was in a schoolroom, stroking a silk-haired fox under his jacket. He'd saved the fox from the hunters, and now and again it bit him, not badly, but enough to make him want to yelp. It had Lily's eyes, or were they Reynolds's? He mustn't say a word about it, or the teacher – who was wearing a crown – would kill it and he would be to blame.

Canton was a low formless huddle of roofs, interrupted by high square towers: an English trader who was travelling on the steamer explained that they were pawnshops. Canton smelt. It shrieked, as well: as soon as they arrived they were deafened by river boatmen, sedan-chair bearers, and porters all yelling out together for custom. The English trader haggled for Samuel and Henderson in pidgin with the chairmen and warned them always to agree the fare before they set off.

They were borne away from the slapping brown water. The bearers laughed and shouted at their friends on the street. Samuel knew they were talking about the foreigners, calling them devils, he caught the word, *gweilo*.

The sound of pidgin was nauseating: English, mangled, made his stomach turn. He'd have to work hard at Cantonese, he'd always talk to them in their own language, and they wouldn't dare insult him then, because they'd know he understood.

The narrow streets reeked with a cacophony of smells, echoed with shouting and banging. It was a tenfold magnification of the noise and crowds in Hong-Hong. You couldn't even see the sky overhead: the street was closed in at the top with a network of bamboo poles and boards. And all the pointing and laughing of children and grown-ups alike!

Somewhere in Canton there was Mr Fawler, the Methodist missionary Samuel had promised his foster-father he'd visit. He had been there since September, standing in for a Canton missionary who was in England on furlough. It was an infernal nuisance; but Mr Pink had sent a letter to Hong-Kong demanding news of Mr Fawler. Besides, he was a Dorset man, from Abbotsport. Samuel even thought – bumping along past wooden tubs of live fish, past chickens being slaughtered on the street, past piled nameless vegetables and heaped embroideries and always the sounds and faces that had nothing familiar about them, that slid away from the attempts to grasp them, leaving him at best with a few wisps of comprehension in his head – that he'd like to see a Dorset man again.

They were taken to lodge in an old house that had once been a Chinese magistracy – a yamen – inside the city walls. It was furnished in a messy mixture of Chinese and European styles: it was oddly comfortable.

Every time old Master Feng came into the room in his dark-blue silk gown – fur-lined at this season – Henderson and Samuel had to stand. When he walked into the middle of the room and bowed, they had to bow in return, a couple of degrees lower. Whenever Master Feng was on his feet, they had to be on theirs. This was the proper way to treat a teacher, and reflected no shame on the pupils either.

Master Feng was a humble man: the respect he demanded was due to the Way, rather than himself. If his pupils didn't treat him as their superior, how could they hope to govern others? He explained this on the first day, in careful, excellent English.

They had come to learn Cantonese and Mandarin, but Master Feng also taught them the way of Master Confucius and Master Mencius. He'd taught a dozen cadets, he knew they had to learn – as much as they were capable – China as well as the language. He would even – with appropriate warnings – teach them to read the Taoist texts.

Master Feng, Samuel was told by other Europeans in Canton, had been an official in the Imperial Civil Serivce, but he was too honest, refused to take bribes, and made enemies. He had consider-ed suicide as a reproach to those above him, but decided the times were too corrupt for his suicide to have any effect. Now he lived simply and taught the young Englishmen.

'It makes sense,' said Samuel to Henderson, 'all this Confucian stuff: it's about doing your best where you've been put, responsi-bility for those below you, that sort of thing.'

'You're too excitable,' said Henderson, 'you go from one person to another, first Mrs Darley, now this Chinese, you don't stick things out. You think every new thing is going to open the gates of heaven to you.'

'You've written that character wrong,' said Samuel in retaliation, 'look, it ought to have the water radical.'

'What I really can't bear about you,' said Henderson, 'is that you're such a pompous little man.'

Samuel would have hit Henderson, except that Master Feng came back into the room, and they had to stand up.

They learned by rote, as every Chinese schoolboy must learn. He was straightforward with them: he expected a great deal of them.

'You must learn to be true to your heart,' he said. 'This is not given to everyone. The function of the heart is to discern and exercise morality. The gentleman has a heart, which tells him to act benevolently, for the good of all. The common people are ruled by their appetites, and it is therefore necessary for the gentleman to use his heart on their behalf. If the gentleman acts according to the rules of morality and the true heart, then the people will be virtuous in their turn. Unfortunately, many of those who call themselves gentlemen are no better than brute beasts in this generation, so how can they expect virtue of their subordinates? You must act differently: this is possible, even though you are foreigners. Bear that in mind.'

He had them reading simple sentences from Mencius at the same time as they translated: 'Ping and Hen received brushes from Feng.'

Samuel thought of Mrs Darley, of the biting fox under the desk in his dream. They represented confusions from which Master Feng, with his simplicity, was safe. There was nothing in Feng, it seemed, that wasn't working in accord with the proper forms of society. That was what he called the Way, and taught that when the outer forms were properly observed, the inner rightness would follow — so different, he added, from the anarchic confusion the Taoists called the Way. Samuel thought that if he was such a gentleman he would cancel out the shame of his bastardy. What did it matter if the Governor hadn't been interested in talking to him at a dinner? His modesty should accept it. He felt as if he was used to drinking muddy water, and had been shown a glass of water from a spring: though it wasn't the colour he was used to, something inside him recognized its desirability. It made him wish he didn't hate

Henderson: why should he, since he didn't want Mrs Darley any more?

And yet Master Feng wasn't a Christian, Master Feng walked in the dark of ignorance, didn't the glass contain, not spring water, but some dangerous narcotic? He remembered that he'd been sent here only in order that he might serve Her Majesty his mother better. His job was to civilize the East: he was unsettled and frightened to find it threatening to civilize him.

Master Feng said: 'I must tell you that I had rather Chinese were ruled by Chinese. But I had rather you ruled well than that you ruled badly.' Then he smiled at them: he had a remarkably sweet smile. What he was doing with them was merely to pursue the ancient wisdom of China: to overcome the invader absorbing him. He loved his own family more than strangers, his own people more than barbarians. But as teacher, he also cared for his pupils. No one could study with Master Feng and not appreciate his benevolence.

'Hold the Faith,' said Mr Fawler, the one-time Abbotsport draper. 'Here you are among heathens, even obliged to learn from a heathen. Your strength will need to be the greater.'

'Have you met Master Feng?' asked Samuel.

'I don't need to,' said Fawler. 'I've met plenty like him.'

There was little left of Abbotsport about Mr Fawler, only a slight hint of Dorset in his voice. And perhaps the excited air: he'd never in his life expected to become so important, to travel so far. He had brown eyes the colour of sweet sherry and tradesman's whiskers. He was an inch taller than Samuel, and knew it.

'I need hardly ask,' he said in a quiet, breathy voice, 'if you have made the decision for Christ?'

'Mr Fawler,' said Samuel (remembering that he was rather higher in the social scale than Mr Fawler was, though due to the lack of a regular clergyman at the English church, he'd be obliged to hear Fawler preach that very Sunday) 'I'm a Christian gentleman.'

'There's still a moment that comes to all of us,' he said in the same deliberately hushed voice, 'when we have to make that decision. Your father has entrusted you, as it were, to my protection – ' (and let him put that in his pipe and smoke it).

Samuel was appalled at the idea.

' – and I must warn you therefore,' said Mr Fawler, his voice growing louder (Mr Fawler spoke as he preached, under his feet was always the floor of the pulpit, there was never a minute to be wasted, when all about him he could see the extent of the work Christ had given him to do), 'I must warn you that China and the Chinese are a danger – yes a danger!' he cried out, 'to the souls of young men unused to the dangers of promiscuity.'

Samuel shuddered. He'd given Mrs Darley up, he didn't want to hear about her from this man.

'I mean!' exclaimed Mr Fawler. He waited a moment and looked about him. In the hushed voice, he said: 'I mean *religious* promiscuity.'

'I wouldn't dream of it,' said Samuel indignantly.

'Taoism,' he said darkly, 'demons masquerading as gods, idolatrous worship of ancestors long since lost in the flames of hell, oh, I don't deny that there is some glimmer of truth in the middle of all these mists that swirl before their sad misconceptions! Buddhism is probably the least objectionable of all, yet even there they fill their temples with idols, three figures of Buddha, Kwan Yin who is like a poor approximation of the Virgin Mary, hundreds of Arhats – it is our task to wean them. It is your task to show them the virtues of Christian government, Samuel.'

Having reached his peroration, his face wore an astonished look, as if he'd never expected to manage it.

Samuel wanted to protest at the wanton use of his Christian name. But Mr Fawler was older, and though not a gentleman, a friend of his foster-father, and a man of the cloth. Respect, fear, Master Feng's teachings even – they all shut him up.

'And what do they believe?' asked Mr Fawler softly, 'these teeming unconverted multitudes? They believe that they can worship many gods at once, that it doesn't matter how many temples they creep into to light their joss-sticks.'

He talks like an express train, thought Samuel. You hear it quietly, in the distance, it races up and almost deafens you, then it dies away. He stood in the path of the steaming black monster while Mr Fawler talked about *feng shui*.

'Lucky sites,' he exclaimed, and laughed. 'Lucky days. An obstruction to progress. They complain that a railway cutting is going to snip a dragon in half, yes, what do they believe, Samuel? They believe there are dragons in the hills. They say that the earth is composed of two opposing energies, male and female, hills are male, low-lying ground is female!' Again, he laughed. The train was almost on Samuel, Mr Fawler was going full steam ahead. He cried: 'The best sites are all occupied by graves as a result. The profits from the land go to maintain the graves. And look at the starvation, the poverty: does that justify their system?' The engine had passed Samuel, only the carriages were rattling through the station. 'They don't worship the Living God, but their own dead ancestors, who, by their own account, are being tormented in Hell – they're right in that respect.' The train vanished into the distance, with a brief snigger from Mr Fawler.

'Look,' said Samuel hastily, 'I'm all right. I'm not going to burn incense in a Chinese temple, I promise.' But there was another train on the tracks.

'I'll tell you,' said Mr Fawler, hushing his voice and looking about him, 'a shameful tale. There's a man in Hong-Kong who was once an English gentleman, a Christian gentleman. What did he do? He studied Chinese for years, and now he's become a heathen. He never goes to church, he visits temples, he lives openly with a young Chinese woman and – no, I won't tell you any more. You're still too young yourself. But be warned.'

Samuel didn't want to think about Mr Jackson and Lily.

He's corrupt, thought Mr Fawler, in some way I can't put my finger on.

He remembered how surprised everyone had been when Mrs Pink had born a baby after so many years – and no sign of pregnancy either. He remembered the housekeeper from the rectory buying linen in Abbotsport with a pleased expression on her face: I know what I know. A bastard, he thought, of some relative, brought up in the family to keep the scandal quiet. Bad blood.

He asked Samuel: 'Where did you go to school?'

'I was too delicate,' said Samuel, blushing. 'I was educated at home, by my tutor.'

Ah-ha! thought Mr Fawler. He looked down at Samuel.

Master Feng said the gentleman was always responsible for the crimes of the common people. Samuel wondered how much virtue the upper classes would need to redeem Nathaniel Fawler?

His birthday, in May, brought two letters: one from his mother as usual, one from Reynolds in Manchester.

You are learning a great deal, wrote Reynolds, *how to go to bed with a woman, how to rule the poor and feel virtuous about it. I see* your Chinese tutor has given up the attempt. Wise man! But not wise enough to give up the illusion that it is possible.

If the gentleman is responsible for the vices of the lower classes, surely he should be imprisoned for them: had you thought of that? Supposing you went into the prison in Hong-Kong, let out every prisoner and substituted a government official for each? It would be a nice sight. Would you volunteer to go? A joke, of course.

There is a small boy in my dormitory who cries for an hour every night after the lights go out. He has been sent here by an indigent family who have scraped together enough money to educate him: they expect him to rescue their fortunes. He is skinny and miserable and needs rescue himself. The other boys taunt him and he doesn't get boxes of food from home, so he can't buy popularity. I know how he feels. His situation was mine, once, yet there is nothing I can do to help him. I can prophesy that he'll come to no good.

The learned Doctor who heads this school read the other day from the prophet Ecclesiastes: 'All this have I seen, and applied my heart unto every work that is done under the sun, there is a time wherein one man ruleth over another to his own hurt.' He didn't even consider the message. Perhaps you should, Samuel, since you're thinking so hard about the philosophy of government. By the way, have you thought about recommending me for a post in Hong-Kong? I'd love to argue all this out with you in person, with a pipe and a glass of whisky.

His mother's letter was rather different.

Dear son, another year has passed, and what I hear about you pleases me and worries me. I am pleased that you are working so hard, both at your studies in Cantonese and in your work in the government in Hong-Kong. There you show yourself a dutiful son and worthy servant of Her Majesty. I cannot do anything but urge you to continue as you have begun. I have done everything I could to bring you foward in life: I long for your success and happiness.

Where I am not so content is in what I hear about your actions in your hours of leisure. I shan't beat about the bush: I am speaking of Mrs Darley. You may call me hypocrite if you like, but I loved your father, loved him as I have loved no man since. I cannot believe that you care about this woman. I know – don't ask me how – that she has ruined too many young men already. You may say that it is different for a man, perhaps you have been corrupted by the idea that a man can take his pleasure without love, that virtue is only for *women, but believe me, your actions are not without their effects. If you were following your true heart I would have more sympathy but the creature is incapable of love. Find yourself a woman you can be happy with, and marry her.*

Oh, dearest son, my own span of happiness was all too brief and was succeeded by deep sorrow. I don't wish you to repeat my experience. My bleak hours of duty and grief, my hours of longing that can never be assuaged but must be offered up in prayer, are comforted only by the hope that you will know a contentment that is denied me, that for you, at least, duty will bring satisfaction. Do not harm yourself.

Here in Scotland the heather is in bloom on the moors, and I drive about and see the bog-cotton dancing in the wind above peaty swamps. When it blows hard and bleak I find a strange content, as if it brings me something of those I love. Separation is terrible. You have indeed taken 'wings of the morning, and dwell in the uttermost parts of the earth.' May God, to whom all distances are nothing, hold you in the palm of His hand!

'No, that means fear,' said Samuel, explaining Chinese writing to Henderson in the yamen after dinner, 'look, there's the radical for "heart", and then the character for "white". White heart.'

'Lily-livered,' said Henderson brightly, and laughed.

Samuel said: 'This is anger, look, "slave", "heart", meaning that the angry man is slave to the dictates of the heart.'

'I thought the heart was supposed to be a good thing?' asked Henderson crossly. 'Why do they have to have such a complicated system of writing?'

'It must be the brute beast's heart,' said Samuel. 'Not the heart of morality. The writing isn't like our writing at all, you know that. It's a language in itself, isn't it? That's why it does for all the dialects. Learning it will help us to understand them.'

Henderson looked sceptically at Samuel, and asked: 'Are you telling me you understand them?'

'I don't understand anything,' said Samuel suddenly.

Henderson laughed.

The rain came down on the roof of the old yamen, streaming off the leaves and splashing on the stones of the courtyard. Samuel lay in bed and couldn't sleep. He wondered why his mother never mentioned her other children: perhaps she thought he'd be jealous? It hurt him, somehow, that she couldn't speak of them. He supposed she was hoping to preserve the secrecy he'd already penetrated. She didn't know Reynolds had seen the coat of arms on the letter.

She wanted him to love a woman, Master Feng wanted him to love a principle, he didn't know what Reynolds wanted, or how to fulfil it. Mencius had said it was a good thing for a man to be conscious of his own inferiority: it spurred him to improve himself. Samuel was afraid of improvement. His heart lay in the darkness of incomprehension, white because it hadn't been exposed to the light.

Nicodemus had come to visit Christ by night, fearing the daylight, St Paul had been so rooted in ignorance that it had taken a lightning bolt to show him the truth, and then he'd been blinded.

The light that couldn't reach his heart was moving on the stone wall, troubling, elusive patches of brightness. He was bewildered by a whiff of Lily's scent. Light and shadow, yin and yang, tormenting opposites that never reached equilibrium. As for himself, Henderson had described him, a shiftless enthusiast, fixed nowhere. And he wasn't allowed to write to his mother and assure her that he'd given up Mrs Darley! He hoped the person who was reporting on him was honest as well as observant.

In Hong-Kong, the winter passed, and it grew warm and damp. The clouds came to wrap the Peak in streaming moisture. Sometimes Lily and Mr Jackson could see nothing but cloud for days on end. Only the pavilion of the Soochow garden sometimes looked red out of the grey hopelessness. Their clothes and sheets were always wringing wet. Mr Jackson grew ill with rheumatism.

He couldn't hold the Taoist positions any longer. He couldn't get an erection. He fell down when he tried to do his t'ai chi exercises. He looked his age. He lost his temper with the servants, and sometimes hit them. Two of them left. He was shamed. He took to his bed.

He told Lily he was dying. She broke into desperate, frightened weeping. He was pleased to see how important he was to her. For a moment, he considered making a will in her favour: but that would be to despair more utterly than he really wanted to.

'It's the damp,' she said, wiping her eyes with a silk handkerchief. 'You have to get out of the damp, Mr Jackson. Is it like this everywhere in Hong-Kong now? Because if the whole city is wrapped in mist for months of the year, perhaps we should travel into China.'

'Travel,' he demanded, 'in my state of health? But it is better further down the hill.' He began to cough. 'Get me the spittoon,' he commanded. She brought it. 'There are too many people,' he said, 'further down the hill. The ancient Taoists always went to the mountains. They withdrew from the corruptions of everyday life.'

'Oh, Mr Jackson,' said Lily, 'you're so ill up here, perhaps when you're better we can come back to the mountain, or find a drier one, in China? Supposing we went halfway down the mountain, won't that be just as good?'

Mr Jackson had another coughing fit. Lily began to rub his aching back and shoulders. He lay back and let her do as she wanted. She rubbed his legs too. She found it easy to do. It was more straightforward work than the positions on the couch. She wanted so much to protect him.

'Not so stupid,' croaked Mr Jackson, 'we'll move to the Mid-Levels.'

She went with him to inspect the new house. He leaned on his cane and Lily's shoulder. It was a Chinese house, built for a very wealthy family in Robinson Road. It was still dark and humid down here: you could look up and see the cloud like a lid above your head, muffling the Peak: but the bedclothes would stay dry and Mr Jackson's rheumatism would have a chance to get better. Mr Jackson was grudgingly pleased. They walked in the Chinese garden that had been terraced down the hill, sat in the small green pavilion and watched a black swallowtail flutter between pots of chrysanthemums and azaleas.

'Well, I don't know – ' said Mr Jackson, hesitantly. He shook his head. Lily noticed that he wasn't quite as tall as he used to be.

'So much drier,' she cajoled him, 'and this flat space behind the house for your t'ai chi ch'uan.'

'Very well,' said Mr Jackson, 'we'll take it.' Again, he shook his head. He said: 'These houses are too much trouble. It's all dreadfully wearisome. But you're a clever girl.'

She really knew he'd never get to China.

Samuel and Henderson came back to Hong-Kong, and Mrs Darley invited them to dinner at 'Isola Bella'.

'I don't want to go,' said Samuel.

'Of course you have to go,' said Henderson, 'what do you think it'll look like if you refuse? You can go to dinner with her without – you know. And she'd ask me why. What would I say?'

'You could stay away,' said Samuel.

'You're a fool, Pink,' said Henderson angrily.

Samuel went to Mrs Darley's dinner party because Henderson needed him to go. Because Master Feng regarded Henderson with compassion, and so Samuel felt he had to keep an eye on him.

He hoped he was permitted to reverence Master Feng, Confucius, and Mencius. They could be ranked with those classical philosophers – Plato, Aristotle, Socrates – who had a part of the truth, though they didn't know Christ. And after all, his mother had urged him to work hard at his studies. The thought of her pleasure gave him a strange clutching feeling in his throat.

Mrs Darley asked Samuel to take Miss Roper in to dinner.

She was at the end of the line, here in Hong-Kong, and no one was going to marry her: certainly Samuel wasn't going to marry her, and he hated to take her arm and feel the limp hopelessness of it: Hong-Kong had knocked the life out of her. Samuel asked her questions and she answered chaotically, but he wasn't listening anyway: he saw Henderson staring at Mrs Darley's corseted breasts that were riding high under her wet silk gown at the top of the table.

The glasses ran with atmospheric humidity: you could have wrung gallons of water out of the curtains. The mossy velvet upholstery was soggy, everyone's clothes clung damply to their bodies, as if they were fully dressed inside a Turkish bath. And it was hot beyond surcease: your sweat couldn't evaporate when the air was so heavily laden. It coursed down you. Miss Roper's stained face was washed clean of powder: her eyes met Samuel's. They were a pretty grey but no one had ever noticed. She'd cried her eyelashes off.

He shifted on his velvet-seated chair: it squelched audibly.

'I'm so uncomfortable,' said Miss Roper suddenly, 'I can't breathe here, and people aren't nice, I wish I could go home, but I haven't the money.' Her eyes beseeched him.

'I'm sorry,' said Samuel. Why did she have to ask him, when he couldn't help her? The heroes of his boyhood's tales used to carry fainting maidens out of the dens of savages, but men didn't rescue women in real life: the things that threatened them were too nebulous.

The meal carried on relentless: sherry and rich soup made way for the cow, the sheep, the chicken, champagne, the pig salted, rice, curry, champagne, jelly, custard, blancmange, champagne, cheese, salad, bread and butter – and the ladies withdrew. Miss Roper withdrew. Samuel was relieved.

The gentlemen drank port and claret (Samuel added whisky to his) – they smoked cigars, talked: the taipans grumbled about the Legislative Council, wanted more share in the colony's running, the government servants took their point, then defended the status quo:

– 'My dear chap, you don't want the *Chinese* businessmen getting a majority, do you? They've *got* a couple of fellows on the Legislative Council, as it is, glad to have them, but – Here we sit, an important strategic base, with the Chinese Empire behind us – and the Russians – and the Germans – so important this place should be thoroughly – '

'But my dear Darley, *you're* sound to the core, it's just these new chaps who come out from England, even His Excellency, sometimes, look at all the trouble we had with Pope Hennessy – '

'Some of them are sound,' said Darley, 'Like Pink here.'

He smiled at Samuel, who jumped as if Darley had grabbed hold of him. He'd lubricated the evening with too much drink and its sense was slipping away from him. Darley's smile was staggeringly engaging. Oughtn't the man to hate him?

The conversation was off about tea: 'Chinese won't improve their conversation, won't learn from the experts – we're up against it here, they don't seem to understand there's *competition* now, the world is changing – '

'Frightful prospect for them.'

'Frightful prospect for *us*.'

More grim laughter. This was what the taipans were doing, the shape their money-making had taken: most of them had abandoned the opium trade to other operators and were peddling skills instead, engineering, science, hindered always by the folly of the home government and the pigheadedness of a Chinese nation that thought it knew better. The government servants had to work round the complex jigsawing needs of trade, the port, the coolies, of controversy over opium, of strategy. Pieces of knowledge spun round Samuel's tipsiness: he couldn't stop the motion, he had to live with its confusion or be injured, for all it was going too fast for him.

'Kidnapped coolies? A piece of nonsense. They agree to emigrate, are paid their bounty, then they jump ship and their friends pick them up, so they can start the game again.'

Listen, said Reynolds's voice in his head, *they're blaming the poor, suggesting their neediness is all deception, that's what they always do, their business is power and they rule over them to their own hurt. Why don't they want more representation? Be honest with yourself.*

'It'll stop,' said Darley drily. 'California will soon be refusing to take any more Chinese.'

They joined the ladies for coffee and small *petits fours*, their stomachs stretched and heaved in the heat, they smelt, smelt bad, pretended they didn't.

And Richards and Mrs Darley went out together on to the verandah to see the view, and everyone knew there wouldn't be a view, and everyone tried not to look at Darley. Samuel looked at Henderson who was laughing desperately. He remembered Mrs Darley turning from the spent Henderson to take him on in his turn. Her mouth had been open. She had an inexhaustible talent for pleasure: oh, Aphrodite, cruellest of all the gods!

Around him the conversation went on: 'and I said to old Lo – '

'The trouble is, these people don't seem to *understand* – '

'I briefed H.E. about it last week.'

A whisper, quite near by: 'Old Darley can't, so *she* . . .'

'telegraphed to Shanghai . . .'

'Tzu Hsi, the Dowager Empress, so graceful, so dignified, just like our own Queen . . .' and the whisper again:

'They say the Emperor's her own son, by her cousin Jung Lu, not her nephew as she pretends, and some of her eunuchs aren't really eunuchs, so she can – yes, quite insatiable, even at her age . . .'

Samuel thought of his mother, Queen Victoria, sitting naked astraddle John Brown's knee. John Brown had lifted his kilt up. Samuel sniggered in his drunkenness, and the lightning struck near the house.

It was blindingly bright: you could see it through the curtains. The thunder crashed a few minutes later. The ladies put their hands over their ears. There was a pouring sound outside: it was raining Hong-Kong rain, like a waterfall. It put an end to the dinner party. The servants appeared with wraps: the sedans were summoned to take the guests to the Peak Tram. Everyone wanted to get home.

By the time Samuel and Henderson got to their front door in

Caine Road the chairmen were wading knee-deep in torrents of water. The lightning flashed incessantly on the Peak, blue-white in the streets and inside the clouds. The chairmen refused to shelter inside the house, and hurried away to their families. Samuel wondered if they would ever get home alive.

Neither Samuel nor Henderson could sleep. They sat up smoking and playing whist till the gas failed in the small hours and water began to pour out of the gas burners. Then the Number One Boy brought an oil lamp. Samuel drank. It didn't seem to be having any effect on him now. He could hear the torrent of water rushing past the house, and now and again there was a distant roar that he couldn't identify.

It seemed to him that Heaven had spoken: he'd transgressed something vital. The water ran out of the gas burners and made lakes on the floor. Cockroaches paddled in them. He thought about Noah's flood.

'I say, Pink,' said Henderson, slapping his cards down on the table and standing up: 'don't you sometimes wish you were at home?'

Samuel looked up and saw that Henderson was crying. He was shocked. He tried to think that it wasn't tears, that it was the water that had got in everywhere. He came up behind Henderson and thumped him hard on the shoulder.

'I can't do it,' said Henderson, his voice struggling. 'I can't do it any more. I'm finished, Pink, aren't I?'

'Have some whisky,' said Samuel helplessly.

Henderson grabbed the bottle and drank it off. He rubbed the back of his hand across his eyes. He began to sag. Samuel caught him and helped him to lie down on the table so that he shouldn't splash down into the water. It was an inch deep by now.

Benevolence, he thought. I have to help Henderson. He needs me, poor fellow.

Reynolds said it wasn't possible to help another person, Reynolds said you couldn't reform anything. He stood up and fetched paper, pen and ink from the sideboard. There was just room to perch them alongside Henderson's prone figure, though he put the ink where any movement would throw it into the water, not over himself.

He wrote: *I need to believe in structure. Here I sit inside the house, while the unbridled forces of nature attack it and threaten everyone's lives.* He realized he was very tired.

He put his head down on Henderson's inert legs and dreamed he was adrift on a flat raft: the water lapped round his feet. Reynolds was telling him to drink seawater which would send him mad.

Henderson stirred and woke him. He was relieved to be awake.

He shook Henderson, 'Come on,' he said, 'if we go upstairs, we can get some sleep on our beds.'

9

1889:
MR JACKSON'S DESERTION

THE first man Lily fell in love with was Ah Kuen, the Pekingese noodle-chef. He could make the longest noodles in China.

Long noodles symbolized long life, and northern-style wheat noodles were stronger than Cantonese rice-sticks. Mr Jackson paid Ah Kuen an enormous wage to make them in his kitchen – and sometimes, when Mr Jackson was in the mood, in the dining room in front of Mr Jackson and Lily. He swung the dough, folded it, twisted it, let the noodles fall out of it. It was a beautiful sight, and Ah Kuen was a handsome man, smooth-skinned, bright-eyed and strong. Lily couldn't take her eyes off him.

He had to make a single noodle for Mr Jackson's every meal – except breakfast. The noodle was so long that it filled the whole of Mr Jackson's bowl, and it was the only dish Mr Jackson didn't eat tidily. He sucked it into his mouth, trying not to break it.

While Mr Jackson sucked and slurped, using his fingers to help because his chopsticks might break the noodle, Lily would sit holding her breath, willing it to remain entire. One day it broke.

Mr Jackson summoned the noodle-chef and picked up his cane to beat him, but Ah Kuen said he'd leave if Mr Jackson touched him. He said there were enough people longing to employ him, Chinese peope who didn't have crazy ideas about noodles. He'd be glad to go back to Peking and work for his own people, listen to proper Chinese instead of these barbaric screeching Cantonese.

Mr Jackson looked frightened: Mr Jackson backed down because he knew he'd never get such a good noodle-chef again. He'd overlook it this time, he said. Ah Kuen bowed to him and thanked him. He'd shown the troublesome old *gweilo* what was what.

Lily looked at Mr Jackson, hunched in his seat and she saw death sniffing round him like a hungry wild dog. He was pitiable, he was old, he was shrivelled. Was the immortal foetus within? How could anyone know?

It wouldn't be for want of effort. Every morning they had to apply themselves to one of the Taoist positions. They always worked on it for an hour every day, one position at a time. Mr Jackson was very strict. He said it was another form of meditation.

By now he had entered Lily standing, while she lay on the couch with her legs up in the air, had laid her on her front and entered her from behind, had made her sit on his lap and entered her from behind. He had pushed his member in deep, or lightly, or both, always the prescribed number of times.

'There is an infinite subtlety of variation in these exercises,' said Mr Jackson, pulling himself out of her and holding his groin fast while he ground his teeth. Then he shrieked. The tooth at the back of his mouth had burst apart.

He wouldn't have a dentist at first, till the pain became intolerable. Then it had to be a Chinese dentist. After the tooth had been pulled out, he had to lie quiet in bed for a week. He sent to the Chinese herbalist for remedies, and Lily stood in the kitchen making them up. She'd learned the remedies for his rheumatism, the potions that would preserve his virility. She was the only person he trusted to do it properly. Ah Kuen was watching her. He was a Mandarin speaker: his Cantonese was poor, too, but his position was good enough to intimidate the servants, who still paid no more than grudging respect to Lily.

And she thought: Mr Jackson is going to die, and he won't make a will because he won't let go of his hopes. I shall be destitute.

She knew there was no limit to how many wives a Chinese man could take. She thought Ah Kuen might take her north and instal her in a household where he would love her in the shadow of a flowering plum. The other wives would invite her to drink tea with them, calling her sister.

Mr Jackson always took a rest after his midday *dim sum*. The rest was getting longer every day. Now he lay in his big silk-curtained bed, and wondered if he'd made a vital mistake after all. A second back tooth was aching slightly: he'd have to get the dentist again.

The Taoist text mentioned virgins. He'd taken advantage of the material to hand: Lily could be trained to do exactly as he wanted –

and she had been what he wanted. But she was far from virgin now. At least she hadn't borne a child. She would have been useless to him if she had. Women lost *chi* with childbearing. Yet – why had his tooth disintegrated after the last exercise with her?

The problem was that he couldn't rely on virgins really being virgins. Nor would he be able to get hold of large numbers of Chinese women at all. The Kong-Kong brothels where Chinese women – certainly not virgins – were available to white men, were the very lowest sort and riddled with disease.

A new idea formed in his mind. It grew rapidly, eating all the ideas that had occupied space there before. Still he couldn't quite see the shape. He lay there, staring at the grey-blue bedcurtains with their design of stylized bats.

He'd had Lily taught how to play the *pi pa*, the Chinese lute. Now she sat playing it in a part of the garden that was nearer the kitchen than the rest, hoping Ah Kuen would hear her. Blossoms fell off the frangipani tree and nested in her hair. She stopped playing and sniffed the yellow heart of one of them. It was an almost unbearable sweetness.

'And whatever,' said the Colonial Surgeon, 'might have passed in the old days in Hong-Kong, nowadays it simply isn't acceptable – it's wholly unacceptable – to be so eccentric – to ape Chinese ways – and then there are so many respectable white women in the colony.' He put his glass down and lit his cigar. The gentlemen were alone after dinner at the Darley's house.

'When we're in the East to transfer the benefits of Western civilization – ' said the Dean of St John's Cathedral.

Darley said: 'Industry starting up in Hong-Kong – progress. You could almost say we're keeping pace with London.' He stopped, reluctant to commit himself too far.

'The sugar companies,' said the Colonial Surgeon, 'the gas – electricity, soon, even. The glass manufactury. And who makes the most popular ketchup in London? Hong-Kong, though the Londoners don't know it – you didn't know that, did you, young Pink, note it down, note it down, and you, Henderson!'

The Dean said, simply: 'Progress will convince them of the Bible.'

'I like Denniston's better myself,' said the Colonial Surgeon.

'I beg your pardon?' asked the Dean.

'The ketchup,' said the Colonial Surgeon. 'Denniston's ketchup. Superior brand.'

'The mob doesn't care,' said Richards, preening his moustaches. 'Let them have their Hong-Kong ketchup, disguised as England's own.'

Henderson laughed, and stared resentment at Richards.

Samuel poured whisky into his port. He didn't speak. He listened to Authority, conversing among itself.

He understood that the wound Mr Jackson had inflicted couldn't even be salved by the thought of progress, or the superiority of the Bible. The Dean said he'd been seen going into Chinese temples – filthy places with their smoke and dirty red paint and mysterious evil gods – 'Devil-worship!' said the Dean. 'And here we are almost in the twentieth century. We try to wean the Chinese off their superstitions, and here is one of our *own* indulging in it!'

The Colonial Surgeon said: 'But things are getting better, Smithers, you know there was far more of this sort of thing in the early days.'

'The number of virtuous families,' admitted the Dean, 'is on the increase. And has been for years.'

'The churches' task,' said MacVicary from Jardine's, 'the churches' achievement, to hold back vice! But these young men we get, out here on their own, drinking, getting into debt, you can hear them in the clubs, "Boy! Whisky and soda!" Deplorable.'

Darley watched Samuel blush and take his hand away from the whisky bottle. You could read his face like a book.

'The young griffins,' he said mildly, and smiled at Samuel who met his smile with endearing, bewildered gratitude, 'coming out here to Jardine's or Butterfield's. Silly young fools.'

'Has Jackson ever been seen in church?' asked MacVicary, lighting another cigar.

The Dean laughed bitterly. 'No, of course not. And here we are, trying to persuade the Chinese population – '

'And there'll be babies.' said the Colonial Surgeon. 'Haven't we enough Eurasians? Miscegenation,' he said, pouring himself more port, 'the curse of the white man in the East. It's only the lowest sort of Chinese who'll go with someone not of their own race – it's a matter of hygiene to keep them separate.'

The Dean said: 'Immorality is immorality whatever name you give it. And sexual immorality – the fabric of society is pulled apart.

Dangerous times as it is, women's heads turned with education, wishing to coarsen themselves, quit their homes, own their own property, work as men – what is to protect the sanctity of matrimony?'

'Nothing,' said Richards, puffing out insolent smoke. Everyone turned to look at him and tried not to look at Darley. There was a moment's unpleasant silence.

A flight of white ants saved the day, swarming into the room through the open windows, attracted to the light: the Chinese servants hurried to kill them and sweep them up.

Darley, still smarting, said: 'Shall we join the ladies?' The white ants poured in, catching in the gentlemen's hair, shedding their wings on the black jackets of their evening dress. The servants brushed them off. Some of the creatures would survive and gnaw the furniture in any case.

'You're a good man, Pink,' said Darley quietly to Samuel and there was desperation in his voice. He heard it himself.

Samuel blushed with confusion, but he was really thinking about Lily. He'd dreamed of her last night: he hadn't been to bed with Mrs Darley for a year now, and visions of naked women often milked his manhood on to the sheets, but it had never been Lily's slender body before. It made him ashamed of himself. Common soldiers and sailors went with Chinese women, and Jackson, who was an outcast.

He felt Darley wanted help from him, but he had no idea how to give it.

'I'm sorry, sir,' he said. 'I was wool-gathering.'

Henderson was in front of them, greeting Mrs Darley. She smiled at him impatiently, then turned away and set up a flirtation with Richards. Henderson stood, white-faced, staring at her crimson silken back. He was holding on by a thread she'd spun him: one copulation per spell in Hong-Kong. If she snipped that, he'd drop. Everyone knew he was going downhill.

Always the fearful forces of nature, engendering chaos and pain. If you didn't fight them, you were lost. Henderson was losing: the Chinese were destroying him.

He saw murderers on every corner. He looked through the daily papers for accounts of crime against the white population. He shouted at the servants when they came into the room too quietly in their cotton-soled shoes. Every night, before he would go to bed, he had to go into the kitchen and hide all the knives and choppers, shuddering as he touched them. He found a different place every night, and every morning the Number One Boy brought Henderson his shaving water and asked him where the choppers were, so that the cook could cut the bacon for breakfast. He did this in Hong-Kong, he did it when they were in Canton. Master Feng's virtue and benevolence frightened him more than anything else: he said they made the hair stand up on the back of his neck. He was frightened of the language, and of Master Feng's patience when he mangled it.

Mrs Darley kept her back turned to him.

Mr Jackson met the man in Hollywood Road: he was coming out of the Man Mo Temple with Lily. Lily never went there again.

The man was wearing Chinese dress: nothing like as rich as Mr Jackson's and his face was burned dark with the sun. It didn't occur to Lily that he might be another Englishman.

'Jackson,' he said, like a daily acquaintance. 'How are you, Jackson?'

'Wells!' said Mr Jackson. He put his hand out for a moment, then withdrew it, and bowed. Mr Wells laughed, and bowed back.

So he took Mr Jackson away, from that first moment.

Lily saw now that Wells moved like a Chinese. She remembered what the servants had made clear to her: that she moved like an Englishwoman, too free, her steps too large, the expressions on her face no more Chinese than the people on an English willow-pattern plate. It always frightened her: she'd rather not think it.

Mr Wells looked at Lily.

'Is this the baby?' he asked.

'The same,' said Mr Jackson.

Mr Wells laughed again.

'We've known each other since we were boys,' he said to Lily. 'I went out to China as a missionary – never had as much money as Jackson, but I wanted to travel. Lost my faith in a year. I was with him in Soochow – I can remember him coming back into our lodgings with you in his arms.'

It came to Lily that this man – Wells – had stolen her Chinese identity while she was still much too small to stop him, leaving her bereft and English, belonging nowhere. She stood beside Mr Jackson and hated what was happening.

'Outcast,' said Mr Wells to Mr Jackson. 'No one here wants to know me. Been in the trade' (Lily knew he meant the opium trade), 'teach English to progressive mandarins' sons. I don't like to leave China. Had to come because my brother's died: there are some papers I have to sign. Going back to China afterwards. Why don't you come?'

'No,' said Lily, patting Mr Jackson's arm. 'You've been too ill.'

'Come and stay in my house,' said Mr Jackson, 'and we'll talk it over.'

They shut Lily out and talked. It had happened. Lily knew she was lost now. She tried to summon up her love for Ah Kuen to comfort herself with, but it was too flimsy. When had she known life without Mr Jackson?

She should never have fallen in love with Ah Kuen. She'd betrayed Mr Jackson, and she was being rightly punished. He didn't see or hear her any more.

'I can go within a week,' he said cheerfully, coming out of his room to walk in the gardens with Mr Wells. Lily ran after him, trailing in their wake. They talked on. 'I can keep the household here going: my lawyers will pay the servants.'

'And the child?' asked Mr Wells.

'What would she do in China with me? She'd be in the way. She's safer here. She'll have plenty to eat, and I'll leave some money with her for clothing. She'll be provided for. I've got to see this t'ai chi Master in Soochow. I've got to learn chi kung. You have to go to the heart of things, to let go of whatever is inessential. I can see that I've been pursuing the wrong path.'

They left a week later.

'Goodbye, Lily,' said Mr Jackson. 'No tears, now. I can't have tears. Dry your eyes, there's a good girl. Here's a purse with a hundred dollars. Buy yourself something nice.' Lily remembered London: how he'd dismissed the cook, how he'd sent her nurse away.

At midnight – the night he left – she thought of killing herself. She looked at her earrings, but her mouth wouldn't open to swallow them. She searched for something to hang herself, but even when she found a long silk scarf, she couldn't bring herself to make a noose. A hundred dollars would have bought enough opium to kill her, but she knew she wouldn't buy it.

She couldn't understand how she could want so badly to die, and yet so stubbornly remain alive.

Samuel wrote to Reynolds: *The dust has settled at last and I am beginning to get a really clear picture of how the Government of Hong-Kong functions. May yet do my mother credit, albeit anonymously!*

I'm hoping to pass my examinations soon, and, as a Passed Cadet, take my place in Government Service. A useful and, I hope, happy life lies ahead of me.

I've just finished a spell in the Registrar-General's office, where I've found out a good deal about Chinese affairs – and also about the Sanitary Board which is dealing with good drainage and water, and good ventilation, sadly the Chinese property-owners aren't always so keen on that. We've been vaccinating Chinese children against smallpox, and regulating interest rates, weights and measures, and so on.

As you know, I'm keeping away from women – am enjoying the feeling of virtue! Playing a lot of cricket, walking every day before breakfast, studying hard. Looking over the nice young ladies here with a view to making a fool of myself in a few years' time – but not before I'm further on with my career. I've begun to collect Chinese porcelain and cloisonné, *think I've got quite an eye for them.*

You told me who I am, he continued, with a burst of affection – and yet he was nervous of his own confidingness – but hadn't Reynolds confided in him? *More and more I can see what a good thing it was that I was sent over here. I can fulfil my duties and be true to my blood – who needs glory and titles, when he can serve?*

He spent twelve weeks in Canton, leading an austere and studious life. He returned to Hong-Kong to find Reynolds's reply.

I wish I could see life with such rose-tinted spectacles as you do, Samuel, but I suppose you have your function. You've lived such a sheltered life. If you could walk some of the streets I'm walking now, see some of the sights I've seen, seen the maimed throwouts of the mills, the stench, the filth, then the world wouldn't seem such a cosy place to you. Oh, I know you're doing what you can. Don't tell me so again.

Forgive me if I laugh when you talk of doing your mother credit, as if she was a clerk's wife in Clapham. Isn't it rather commonplace? As for this continence you boast about, I think it's a sort of savings bank, only this one will do you no good, accrue no interest, though

*all of your sort believe it will. Why waste your life? Find yourself a
woman, a whore if need be. Have some fun.*

*I have a woman: she indulges me in rather a special way. I dress in
women's nightclothes and lie on my face while she sits astride me
and penetrates me with a leather dildo – if you don't know what
that means, ask for an explanation. The sensation is sublime: it
hurts excruciatingly. There's often blood on the tool afterwards.
And yet I feel refreshed when she's done – there are some mysteries
that don't require explanation. It would be sacrilege to try. I don't
expect you to follow me into such recondite pleasures, but do
something for yourself, for God's sake. Think of the relief. Don't
you shed it on your sheets anyway, and isn't there something rather
disgusting about treating sex as if it was money? Spend some on a
whore. Or are you still afraid of them?*

Samuel put the letter down on the dining table. Henderson said:
'Back again. Supposing they poison the breakfast rolls, Samuel?'

'They haven't yet,' said Samuel.

'They're biding their time,' said Henderson sourly. He resented
Samuel for trying to keep him sane. He'd rather have gone mad: it
was less effort.

Samuel was irritated with Reynolds for putting out an argument
and then refusing to fight it, shaken by the insurgent feelings he
had roused. Lust jostled hurt pride and an intolerable memory, a
panic between his buttocks. He swore to himself that he wouldn't
go near the Queen's Road prostitutes. He'd go to the Club instead.
He'd play cricket. He couldn't bear to be soiled.

'Continence,' he said aloud. What Reynolds was doing was
disgusting. He didn't want to think about it.

'What?' asked Henderson, pouring himself a glass of whisky.

'World's changing,' said Darley, letting his eyes open wide.

'Progress,' breathed the London engineer. 'Never have such
changes been seen as we're now – thanks to science – in a position
to bring about.'

Darley never got drunk, never talked. Tonight, at the Club –
'Boy! Another champagne cocktail' – he was doing both. He
didn't usually meet anyone who really shared his passion. Drains,
to the rest of them, were a means to an end.

And it wasn't only drains the two men dreamed of; there were gas mains, water mains, electrical cables one day – not to mention the London Underground system.

'Build one in Hong-Kong,' said Darley, hiccuping slightly. 'Under the Chater reclamation, when it's finished – did you know there were people who didn't want that? Can you imagine the short-sightedness, the folly?'

'You've wonderful possibilities, out here,' said the engineer, who had come out to consult on the reclamation and was thrilled with the colony, the Club, the shops, the hum of activity, the endless building.

'Plenty of bad buildings to get rid of,' said Darley. 'Gallons of carbolic needed,' he emptied his glass and called for another champagne cocktail. 'Never implemented the Chadwick Report –there'll be trouble, one of these days. Still, you do what you can.'

'They won't be able to hold on,' said the engineer. 'Out of date, all of them. We'll win. Think of this place all lit up with electricity! How long did you say it'd be?'

But Darley was too drunk to remember.

He said: 'I'll never let them name a road after me.' He chewed this thought with great satisfaction, relishing the thought of his anonymity. He would tunnel secret benisons under the buildings of the city.

He passed Samuel on the way out: he thought the lad had a hunted look, but couldn't hold on to his concern. He'd forgotten a few things, among them his wallet, and that he hated his wife. The London man took a chair back to his hotel, Darley to the High Level Tramway. They let him on even without his season ticket, because they knew him. He was pleased.

He saw the lights of Hong-Kong leaning away from him as he was drawn up the steep slope, saw the bay starred with man-made illumination where once there had been silence and scrub. The moon hung in the sky, enormous, asymmetric and pale. It would be Mid-Autumn Festival in two nights' time. The Chinese shops were full of ornamental lanterns. For the festival, they'd go into the open spaces of the city and light them in their hundreds among the trees. Darley thought the streetlamps were much more beautiful.

If he'd come home the old way, by sedan, it might not have happened. He'd have time to sober up, or at least to lose his exaltation. But he walked into the house and fell into his wife's arms.

Mrs Darley was a skilled tactician: she knew how to use the moment. She softened into her husband's embrace, moved against him, drew him, before he knew it, up the stairs and into her bedroom. She felt the stir inside his trousers. His mind, still frothy with champagne bubbles, muttered: Well, why not?

He let her undress him and pull him down on to her soft undulating contour, all ready to engulf him. Then he began to goosepimple with distaste, but his treacherous flesh wanted her, carried him away.

He couldn't let go. The horror grew on him gradually: he was locked inside her, his body had betrayed him, he was being drawn onwards down the tunnel that would lead him to destruction. And she lay beneath him caressing his face with her hands, kissing his neck, squealing, gasping –

He poured out, wastefully, into her spendthrift body, everything he'd been holding in for so long. She began to caress him. He pushed her away. There was a foul taste in his mouth. He'd have done better to spend himself in a drain.

He got up and ran out of the room, slamming the door and turning the key behind him. He heard her footsteps, he heard her fists on the door:

'No, John, no!' she shrieked, 'Come back! What have I done?'

The night was soft, the moon outshone the gaslamps – though the lamps were always darkened by mosquitoes at this time of the year. Samuel, looking over his shoulder from time to time, made his way to the little shop on Queen's Road, where the Russian Jewesses were supposed to be so adept and obliging.

It was Mr Fawler who saw him, and he took action at once. He was coming from a prayer meeting at his mission church, he ceased humming 'Oh happy day, when Jesus washed my sins away', saw Samuel, did not pass by on the other side, but caught him on the threshold.

'What?' he asked. 'Unable to stand strong?'

He was kindly: it made Samuel sick. He pitied Samuel and licked his lips over him.

There stood Mr Fawler, and there was Samuel at the entrance of the brothel, between the square pillars that supported the over-hanging first floor. The woman on duty had already come forward to greet him – but Mr Fawler plucked him away from the burning.

Mr Fawler said quietly: 'Come aside a moment, Samuel.' He sounded like the voice of the Lord in some edifying pamphlet. He asked: 'What would your father say if he knew where you are today?' He said again: 'What? Unable to stand strong?'

He stood in the open street and preached a sermon. He breathed: 'Are we not in these far-flung climes as standard bearers for the Light, have you not responsibilities, Samuel, responsibilities?' (*Mezzo piano*.) 'I have caught you about to desert the standard, it is hard, I know, Samuel. Is it not desperately hard to choose the straight path that leads to righteousness? But does not the reward make it all worthwhile? Who else are you endangering, Samuel – ' (*mezzo forte*) ' – have you thought of that? Have you thought of your namesake, called in the night to the service of the Living God, did he swerve away when he knew whose voice spoke to him in the dark watches?' (*Fortissimo*, sinking to the whisper again.) 'Speak, Lord, he said, for your servant heareth. Samuel, living among poor heathens as we are, every white man who enters that door – '

Several white men *had* considered the door while he was speaking, and had turned away with irritated expressions on their faces. The madam was tapping her high-heeled foot on the floor, calculating her losses.

' – every white man who traffics with these poor lost wicked creatures, what does he do?' Fawler paused and surveyed the impatient madam, the shrinking Samuel, and the ship's officer who was walking in, ignoring the missionary. Towards whom Mr Fawler directed his words, but the ship's officer was whisked inside by the madam. 'Does he not endanger, not only himself, but the hope of salvation for the whole world?' Turning his attention back to Samuel, he demanded: 'How should the heathen respect our faith if we conduct ourselves so? Go ye into all the world,' he cried, 'that is what our Saviour said, and make all men my disciples! Raised as you were, Samuel, you have a task. I do not ask if you have been here before. There is forgiveness, Samuel, for those who repent. There is salvation. There is life!'

He led Samuel all the way up the steep roads of Victoria to his house at the top of Kennedy Road. The fan-palms in the garden struck frozen dramatic attitudes in the gaslight.

'There is hope!' Fawler cried, ushering the strayed soul into the pen of his living room, dipping him in the unction of his forgiveness, marking him with the sense of his sin and sending him forth again subdued and dripping with piety.

He went home and drank himself silly. It was disgusting to have been saved from Reynolds by Fawler: he wanted to forget all about it.

He was working for Darley at the time, writing a report about the proposed land reclamation scheme: there was shortly to be a Praya Reclamation Ordinance. Three days later – the day after the Mid-Autumn Festival – they were saying at the Club that Mrs Darley had been taken badly ill and was on the P & O boat back to England for specialized medical attention. No one could imagine what was wrong with her, though a few suggestions were made, and a few young men looked nervously at their own symptoms: in Hong-Kong, you were never entirely without symptoms – a spot of malaria here, a little dysentery there. Visits were made to doctors, and most were reassured.

Darley behaved as if nothing had happened. He accepted good wishes for Mrs Darley's recovery, was kind and friendly towards Samuel – which he had always been, even when Samuel had been his wife's lover. Surely he must have known?

10

INFIDELITY

LILY sat, brush in hand, and wrote in Mandarin and her best calligraphy:

> I have played my lute under the autumn moon
> But there are no footfalls in the house.
> Who knows where your feet wander?
> I sing with the cicadas, and only the cicadas hear me,
> They have no pleasure in my voice.
> The scent of chrysanthemums is sorrow,
> My bedsheets are cold, white and uncreased.

She sat quite still, holding the brush properly as Mr Jackson had taught her. A few tears fell on the poem: they spoilt the writing, splashing filamented bumps on the rice paper. She stood up. She put her brush down.

She went to her bedroom and picked up her carefully wrapped, yellowing copy of *The Girls' Own Paper*. She turned to the article: 'Woman: A Man's Ideal', and read the passage that had been her bedtime prayer so many nights.

'The leading, guiding, and controlling impulse of women is to render themselves agreeable and helpful to men – ' She stopped. She heard Ah Kuen's footsteps walking past her bedroom door.

She gave the paper to one of the maids, to make shoe-soles. She'd never read it again.

'I *was* a good girl,' she said aloud, in English.

Mr Jackson was never going to come back. She wouldn't cry this time. She stuffed the pain away with all the others. If she couldn't kill herself it meant she was destined to live, so she must set to work at it.

She found a clean piece of rice-paper, and wrote: *When I yield is when I may gain advantage.* Then, on another piece of paper, she brushed:

> You fling noodles in the air as a dancer flings silk
> Ah, the sure touch of your hands, your body's grace!
> My face offers you plum-blossom and white jade,
> I am slender as dancing bamboo,
> Can you not dance with me?

But it would be no use to give the paper to Ah Kuen: he could hardly read.

'I,' said Ah Kuen to Lily, 'am the best noodle-chef in China. And if times weren't so hard I would never have come down here to waste my skill on a crazy *gweilo* – and then he hasn't even stayed here to appreciate me!'

Lily met his eyes for a moment, then cast hers down. She knew what that trick was about, she knew why Mr Jackson had taught her to do it. Some of his lessons could still be useful to her.

Ah Kuen wasn't proof against the look, or against the enticing fragrance of sandalwood and sensuality that hung round her. His face flushed: he took her in his arms.

He took Lily to bed: to her own bed, that was, which was wide and comfortable and sheeted in silk. She was delighted to discover how much pleasanter it was to love a young man. Her thighs ached, afterwards, only because she'd enjoyed herself so much: this was the pleasure she'd anticipated with Mr Jackson, but had never got from the twenty or thirty thrusts of his miserly member: he'd never got round to the exercises that required the woman's satisfaction.

Ah Kuen spent warmth into her not just once, but twice in an afternoon. Afterwards he held her close and let his hands run all over her body.

'Better than with the old *gweilo*?' he asked.

'I love you,' said Lily. 'Yes.'

'Of course,' said Ah Kuen, 'it's nice for you to have a Chinese man at last.'

Lily felt a momentary dart of pain when she remembered how much Mr Jackson had longed to be Chinese.

'He's dead to me,' she said.

Ah Kuen said: 'He'll be back.'

Lily said nothing. All she wanted was the warmth of Ah Kuen's body possessing hers, helping her to forget. She nestled into him as if he was her mother. It was a mistake, but it took her some time to find that out.

Ah Kuen had a house back in Peking – a good house, he told her, with a lovely garden in among the courts, and servants, and handsome furniture. Of course he had a wife. Lily didn't ask if he might take her back there as a concubine. She was waiting till she got pregnant.

Mr Jackson stayed away. He didn't write any letters. Lily put the hundred dollars he'd given her behind a loose brick in the wall of her bedroom.

Lily asked Ah Kuen about China; he told her things Mr Jackson could never have found out. He laughed at her ignorance. But he was tender with her. He called her Little White Flower.

He said: 'It falls to me to name you, since your family did not.'

Lily never doubted that she could conceive his baby. How could so much love and pleasure fail to bear fruit? She knew the moment it happened, was certain for the full two weeks before her body confirmed her knowledge; the second month came and went too, without so much as a speck of blood. All the time the baby nested under her heart: she could imagine its own small heart, beating in time to hers. It was winter, and the birds were eating the berries in the garden.

Ah Kuen lay in the bed with her, warming her limbs with his own, running his hand up and down her body. The night lay round them like thick dark fur. She asked him to take her back to Peking with him.

He laughed and refused. He took his hand away from her. Lily knew she'd said the wrong things first. She should have begun with the baby. Now she told him: 'Ah Kuen,' she said, 'I'm sure it's a boy.'

For a moment, she felt her mother's presence in the room: had her mother said the same thing to her father, above her own beating female heart?

He said nothing, but she'd used the right argument. His hand went looking for her belly between the navel and her sex: he held it there, as if he could test the truth with his clever fingers.

'If you have a son,' he said at last, 'I'll take you away with me. If it's a girl, you stay here.'

Lily said: 'I can't wait. The old *gweilo* is bound to come back before the child is born, and he'll know it's not his child.'

'He couldn't make a child,' agreed Ah Kuen.

Lily said: 'What if he kills me?' All the time she knew Mr Jackson would never come back. 'He has that sword, the one he uses for practice. He'd run it through me and your baby together.' She whimpered with fright: but it was abandonment, not death, she was afraid of.

'No,' said Ah Kuen, 'I can't take you away now. But if he writes to say that he's coming back, I'll pay for you to find yourself somewhere to live and wait for the child's birth. Then we'll see. If I was such a rich man that I could afford to bring more girl-children into my house, I wouldn't have to work here such a long way away from home.'

'But you have a good house,' insisted Lily.

'Good enough,' said Ah Kuen.

Later, Lily understood that his house was nothing like as good as he'd boasted to her. It was too late then, and for now, her eyes were shut by love and need. She began to cry.

He said: 'Don't cry, it won't do you any good. I like a woman to be cheerful.' He put his leg over hers and caressed her. She responded with a disharmony of pleasure and inward grief.

She said: 'I could find someone to do away with the child.'

'Destroy a life?' asked Ah Kuen, 'when it might be a boy? Don't let me hear such wickedness again.'

She lay awake while he slept, and shivered through the empty hours of the night.

Anyway, she thought, it has to be a boy. Her belly grew large, she felt the child kicking. She loved it. It was hers, the only thing she had ever been sure was her own. And everyone knew. All the servants knew.

Hong-Kong knew. Even the white community in Canton knew. Only no one took the trouble to count the months, so they supposed the child was Mr Jackson's.

The missionaries, the consuls and traders with whom Samuel and Henderson always dined in Canton wagged their heads and talked about gritting their teeth against the inevitable, but Samuel saw that they were satisfied: it had turned out as they had foretold. They chewed the matter more thoroughly than they chewed their dinners: probably, they decided, the woman was glad to be left alone with her own kind – 'where she should have been in the first place – but she's not a Cantonese, you know, he *brought her up*, he found her abandoned somewhere in the north when he was travelling there years ago, and took her home with him.'

'Irregularity,' they said, 'irresponsibility, such an offence to true Christian values.'

Samuel thought about Mr Jackson's age and Lily's helpless youth. He said: 'How could he do it to her?'

'Oh, my dear fellow,' said the French consul, 'don't suppose she wasn't more than willing.'

He thought how ugly they were with their self-satisfaction and their morality, smug and horrible. He thought he felt Reynolds nudge him in the ribs, heard his voice ask: 'You see?'

'She'll probably cut his throat one night,' said Henderson blurrily, 'and run off with all his money.' He was drunk as he usually was nowadays, and the missionaries disapproved of him, but tonight they nodded their agreement.

'Yes,' said the resident Wesleyan missionary, emptying his tumbler of lemonade, 'without the light of Christ, any bad thing can happen.'

The room felt very dark to Samuel. He wanted to leave but it wouldn't be polite. They were like slugs, he thought, soiling and spoiling.

'Regrettable,' agreed a German Lutheran missionary, 'but human nature, after all. Taking a rather strange shape in this instance, but the story is always the same. It must encourage us all in self-control.' He knocked the cold tobacco out of his pipe, and set about relighting it. It was carved with a grotesque face, and had a pewter lid. The face leered at Samuel: like the china dog at the fairground, it knew who he was, knew what he was feeling.

He remembered the bite of the night wind when you climbed out of the window, the thrill of his heart before it began to concern itself with morality. Maybe there was no salvation from corruption, maybe he might as well enjoy it? He wondered what they'd say if he told them he was the Queen's bastard. He imagined their recoiling faces. Then they wouldn't treat him as their accomplice. Whited sepulchres, he thought, full of dead men's bones. A shudder ran all the way up his spine.

I am hearing good reports of you, his mother had written this year. *I have no worries. Your progress warms my heart.* But it was all pretence: she had no idea.

Indifferent to the sensibilities of the Wesleyan, Henderson was busy getting even drunker.

Samuel got up, and said: 'We've got to go home. We have to start work at five, after all.'

'Good man,' they said, as they always did. And he wondered why he was so solicitous of Henderson? Hadn't Henderson made a fool of him in London? He ought to sit back and enjoy Henderson making a fool of himself.

In the morning, he asked Master Feng what he thought about Lily and Mr Jackson.

Master Feng's face lost all trace of expression, which was a sure sign of distress with him. He said: 'If we consider the right order of things, it becomes clear that the races should not be mingled. Where will the offspring belong? Nowhere. Each side loses honour. An Englishman cannot become Chinese, a Chinese cannot become an Englishman. They can learn about each other, but each must retain their own identity. This woman, of course, has no choice. He saved her from death when she was a baby. Perhaps one day she will think it would have been better to die than to endure the dishonour he has put on her.'

It was clear, implacable wisdom: it left Samuel with the muddiness of his own disturbed thoughts.

Mr Jackson and Wells were walking through the streets of Soochow, crossing the canals where early blossom trailed into the water. It was still cold: their clothes were lined with fur. Their breath steamed in the chilly air. Leaves of bamboo swayed in the sharp wind, brown and ragged with frost.

Wells was arguing with Mr Jackson.

'You're not really going to swallow that thing, are you, Jackson?'

'It was the same monk,' said Mr Jackson. 'The monk who sold me the Taoist text.'

'Monks,' said Wells, 'are cheats and liars – you know that, the dregs of society at the best of times, and this one is the worst specimen I've ever seen. And how could it be the same monk? That was eighteen years ago.'

'It doesn't matter,' said Mr Jackson.

'Why not?' asked his friend.

'Hot chestnuts,' said Mr Jackson. 'Let's have some.' He haggled with the seller, a ragged man with a rusty iron wok on top of a red-hot brazier: the nuts huddled blackened in the blacker womb of the metal pan. The man put the chestnuts inside a banana leaf and gave them to Mr Jackson.

The houses were interspersed with evergreen leaves: the sky was blue, streaked with faint cloud. The package of hot chestnuts steamed in Mr Jackson's hand. They turned towards the Twin Pagodas.

'I'm getting cold,' said Mr Jackson. 'This is the last hope I have left. You heard what the Master said. He won't teach me his skills. This may be nothing, or it may be the answer. Let's go home. I can't take it without drink.'

He walked along the street among the crowds of Chinese, eating the hot chestnuts and throwing the shells down on the smooth paving stones, going so fast he all but left Wells behind. When the chestnuts were gone, he put his hand in his pocket and fingered the Pill of Immortality he had there.

'Living for ever,' said Wells. 'Jackson, your nerves are disordered. You need a rest. Go back to Hong-Kong. Have a good life in your last years.'

Mr Jackson said: 'Lily would care for me.'

'Yes,' said Wells.

'I haven't been good to her,' said Mr Jackson. 'Or to anyone else, I suppose. But if this works, I can set all that right.'

'It'll kill you,' said Wells in despair.

'I don't know,' said Mr Jackson. 'There are records of men who've achieved the aim with pills – and it's very strange the way that monk turned up.'

'I can't do anything with you,' said Wells.

'No,' said Mr Jackson. 'So why bother to be angry?'

Lily thought about the little boy curled up in her womb, the boy with black eyes and black hair and gold skin, like Ah Kuen. As soon as he was born he'd smile at her. He'd give her a place in the world.

She went to the temples and burned incense to all the goddesses – she was sure they would be on her side – Tin Hau, Queen of Heaven who had her temple in Causeway Bay, and Kwan Yin, the Buddhist Goddess of Mercy, whose temple was nearer by in Cat Street. Lily loved Kwan Yin best. She went to the temple in Cat Street every day.

She offered also to the Kitchen God, to the Earth God, and to Ah Kuen's ancestors, whose shrine he had set up in the kitchen. She hoped they were pleased with her, even though her feet weren't bound.

She grew steadily fatter and every day was red-and-gold Chinese and auspicious. She never thought of Samuel now.

Ah Kuen bought candied lotus seeds and fed them to her: they were symbols of fertility. He was pleased with the child's kicking; it was so strong, he said, it was bound to be a boy.

It became summer, hot and steaming – the typhoons came near Hong-Kong and made it hotter still, shook rain over the colony, gusted wind and knocked branches and leaves off the trees before they bent away to spend their rage on some part of the mainland. Sometimes the rain would bring a hillside down, and people would be killed, usually poor Chinese people in huts, and so the authorities didn't worry too much.

Lily spoke no English now, only Mandarin to Ah Kuen and Cantonese with the other servants; now she was pregnant, they had forgiven her for her strangeness, for not being one of them. She learned Chinese movements and gestures: Ah Kuen told her to cover her mouth when she smiled, to look at the floor when he spoke to her.

He said: 'If you want to be my small wife, you mustn't behave shamelessly, like a foreigner.' He saw to it that she ate the sort of nourishing food that would make a boy.

She was so happy to be idle, to have no one but herself and the growing child to look after. There was always enough to eat. She had to spend her hundred dollars on loose clothes for herself, and a stock of clothing for the baby, when it came.

Ah Kuen was in the bed with her when she started the first pains. She had expected it to take a long time, but she was in agony from the beginning, doubled up and quite breathless. She hardly knew where she was any more.

He was afraid, he wanted to fetch the midwife, but she begged him not to leave her alone. Then she cried out. The baby was pushing at the gateway between her legs.

She couldn't speak. She could do nothing. She could only allow the birth to happen: it seemed in spite of her. Oh, the hurting and the tearing! All at once the baby shot out of her.

It was a girl.

II

LEGAL POWERS

————————

EVER since Mrs Darley had left Hong-Kong, Richards had been in a bad temper. He had grown a beard and curtailed his moustaches and claimed to be older than the rest of them. Though he wasn't too old to come to the Club and play billiards. Tonight he was as satisfied as it was possible for him to be.

'Old Jackson's dead,' he said, 'poisoned in China. I've just been winding up his affairs.'

'Poisoned,' said Henderson, glancing at Samuel.

'Some Chinese medicine,' said Richards, 'senile fool.'

'What about the woman, old boy?' asked Caird, 'That's what we all want to know.' He stepped back so that Henderson could shoot.

'I've got rid of her,' said Richards. 'I didn't want to leave her in the house a moment longer: God knows what she might have stolen.'

'Everything, probably,' said Henderson, hitting the wrong white.

Samuel asked: 'You turned her out?'

Henderson said: 'Pink's sweet on her. He saw her in the street once, and fell in love.'

'I know nothing about her,' said Samuel crossly. 'There are considerations of humanity.' He sounded priggish, and heard it.

Richards said: 'A second cousin's inheriting everything. I don't suppose he'd want her thrown in.'

Henderson sniggered.

Samuel said: 'She's having his baby.'

'Not she,' said Richards. 'It was born. It's dead. She told me so.'

'Did you give her any money?' asked Samuel.

His friends laughed.

'My own,' asked Richards, or out of the estate? Look, she's got a

135

career, Pink. She goes with white men. She can go to Wanchai and service the soldiers and sailors.'

Henderson said: 'I'm glad you threw her out.'

Samuel went home. The others decided he must have a touch of malaria coming on.

The first thing Lily did when she was out on the street was to pawn her clothes. She bought rags to wear instead.

There were eating places where she could buy a bowlful of rice. She had enough money for four days if she ate rice only once a day. She recognized the gnawing in her stomach, though it came from a long way back.

She didn't look for Ah Kuen to come and save her. He was going back to Peking. He said Lily was bad luck, she was a husband-killer, or why had Mr Jackson died? He said he'd saved her trouble by exposing the girl-child. Hadn't she wanted to get rid of it, when she first knew she was pregnant?

He had done the same as her father who'd thrown her away and if Mr Jackson hadn't found her then she would have died. Only no one had found her baby before it was too late.

She could feel nothing, could understand nothing. She knew as well as Richards that she could earn rice in Wanchai, but she was still bleeding from the baby – and she didn't want any man to touch her. She sat by the roadside and tried to sleep.

At the end of four days, she woke up and knew she had no more money to buy food. Well then, said the same inner voice that had told her to sell her clothes, you beg.

She held her hands in front of her, cupped suggestively. That was the way you did it. But all she wanted to do was sleep.

12

1889:
A DEATH IN THE HOUSE

Mrs Ellis, missionary widow, and Principal of the Hong-Kong Girls' Rescue and Educational Trust, had interrupted her busy day with a shopping trip. She'd had to buy some grey cotton for a new Sunday dress: it wasn't an extravagance, because she'd torn a hole in her old one, which would have to do for weekdays now. She took it as an opportunity for exercise.

Mrs Ellis had bought the cotton, and arranged for it to be delivered to the Refuge. Now she had to go back. She drew in a deep breath, and set off at a regular pace. She was a small plain wiry woman with no bust, strong and healthy. She exercised with weights. She would have chilled her baths with ice in the hot season, if ice wasn't a luxury. She was never ill.

She looked at the Chinese women about her, so many of them deplorably lamed by their bound feet – but it wasn't much better in the West, with woman corseted to within an inch of their lives. She let her breath swell out into her own moderate and comfortable corset. One didn't have to adopt the principles of the dress reformists, but –

Her hands itched to unbind the little girls' feet, though she knew she must not – but what the practice must do to their state of mind was nobody's business. Mrs Ellis didn't believe this: it would be her business as soon as she possessed the resources and the energy to make it so.

There had to be bounds, she reminded herself: her ambitions were no exception to that rule.

She was the relict of a missionary, whose burning ambition to work in the Field had matched her own passionate need to travel, to escape from the pettiness of life in England. Of course she'd also wanted to spread the word of the Lord. Christianity was so much better for women than other faiths. Her husband had died quickly, from one day to the other: she had stayed on. Now she rescued women from the slavery of heathenism and prostitution, and if they tried to slip back into it, she knew she had to keep them free, by using restraint if necessary.

There was a small jarring sensation at the back of her mind. She tried to still it. She didn't live in a perfect world. The women she worked with were like children, and children would die if they were allowed to do as they liked. Her mind slipped back into the proper position and she felt more comfortable.

Beggars. She hated to see the beggars on the roads, all in rags. She never gave them money. Many of them were opium smokers, anyway. One couldn't give opium smokers money to destroy themselves. They rented their space from Triad gangsters, and most of the money went to the Triads. To give money to beggars only perpetuated their dependency. You should give them work. She gave work to the women under her care.

I do my best, she said to herself, putting her hand up to smooth her hair. It was still the season for drying fish, and the smell permeated Hong-Kong, foetid, salty, creeping up nostrils and invading the stomach. Her luncheon would taste of dried fish. She was used to it.

A moment later she was shocked to the core. She heard an Englishwoman's voice. Begging.

After ten years in Hong-Kong, Mrs Ellis had forgotten the beggars of the London streets. Englishwomen didn't beg. Still less Englishwomen with delicate, cultivated voices, they should never whine and wheedle:

'Dear Lady, kind Lady, please give a little money to a poor beggar woman?'

Mrs Ellis turned, and saw a Chinese. Speaking like a gently brought up Englishwoman. Feet not bound, and the pale face was beautiful. The woman didn't wear her rags as if they belonged to her. Mrs Ellis's eyes grew large and fixed themselves on Lily, she looked, for a moment, exactly like a stalking cat.

She pounced on Lily, got hold of her hand, and raised her by force from the gutter. Lily cried out, but she was too weak to resist.

Now the sky darkened and the sudden rain of the typhoon season came pelting down on their heads and made it almost impossible to see or hear anything. It wet their hands, but Lily still couldn't slip out of Mrs Ellis's grasp. Mrs Ellis was frighteningly strong.

'Come,' she said to Lily, and tugged her onward, pulling her through sudden pools of water: hush, hush, hush, said the rain.

It stopped when they were fifty yards from the entrance to the Refuge. Mrs Ellis used every yard of them for instruction:

'Money, my dear child, I can't give you, but freedom, I can offer you freedom, which is better still. And sisters, child, loving sisters. Our Lord, who I will help you to know, our Lord healed the sick and forgave fallen women. He told them to sin no more. Dear child, I don't condemn you. I offer you the healing love of God.'

Freedom, thought Lily. What does that mean? I've never known freedom: I don't believe in it. But a home, and loving sisters! (And a bowl of rice, said her stomach.)

It was the stream of life: there was no sense in resistance. It pulled long-forgotten threads that had been woven into her by her nurse. Perhaps all these bad things had happened to her because she hadn't read her Bible? So she came willingly to the Refuge, and the doors closed behind her. She was locked in with her new family.

Henderson didn't pass his examinations in Chinese. Samuel passed, with distinction – though he'd have to keep working at his Cantonese. Samuel was going to remain in Hong-Kong – was about to start work as a Passed Cadet, but Henderson was going to have to go back to Canton and Master Feng in a month's time. Henderson didn't want to go alone.

The Rector wrote to tell Samuel that his dog had died.

Henderson was drinking too much: Henderson had been spoken to by the Colonial Secretary, was being given another chance. Henderson sat in their lodgings and got drunk.

The Number One Boy came in to inform them that the sideboard was full of white ants: 'More betta we take him away.'

'Don't talk pidgin to me,' said Samuel in Cantonese.

'You speak good, sir,' said the Number One boy, 'but Mr Henderson too muchee hurt my ear hear him speak Chinese.'

'Get out,' said Henderson.

'I just fetch other servant take sideboard,' said the Number One Boy, as to a child.

Henderson said: 'No.'

The punkah boy giggled silently. Samuel saw it.

'Henderson,' he said, 'you're making fools of us.'

The Number One Boy smiled and left.

Henderson looked at Samuel with the bloodshot melancholy eyes of Samuel's dead spaniel – only the spaniel had been a cheerful creature belied by her long face. Samuel remembered the nose against his leg on walks: always one nudge, to remind him she was still there.

Henderson went to the sideboard to get some more brandy, lost his balance, and fell against the sideboard. It collapsed in a powdery puff of dust.

The punkah boy laughed aloud, turning his face away. Henderson's face turned white and red in blotches: he stood up from the table, picking up the brandy bottle. He got hold of the punkah boy's jacket.

'You did it,' he said to the punkah boy in his bad Cantonese. 'You wanted to murder us.'

'No, sir,' said the punkah boy, looking frightened, but still giggling. 'I no want kill you, sir. White ants, sir. Eat furniture, furniture break.'

'Henderson,' said Samuel, 'control yourself.' It was all too much, he couldn't imagine why he had to be responsible for Henderson. He felt lonely and bruised.

'All right,' he said to the punkah boy. 'You get on with your work.'

Henderson let go of him and flopped back into his chair. The Number One Boy came in with the Number Two and they began to clear away the wreck of the sideboard, sorting out the white men's belongings and making a neat pile of them. As well as the white ants – which weren't white – there were shiny russet cockroaches scurrying fatly among the chewed and tunnelled woodpulp. The servants whacked them, but the cockroaches walked away. Only the huge poisonous spiders could kill cockroaches.

When Mrs Ellis brought Lily into the house, she sniffed what she hadn't noticed in the rain – the curiously alluring scent that hung round the girl. Of course she'd have to have a cold bath. Except that it couldn't be a cold bath, the water was lukewarm and Lily enjoyed it, which was not quite what Mrs Ellis intended.

It was meant to be a salubrious shock of hardiness on a soft body disgracefully held captive to the flesh. The soap was coal tar and bracing. Lily didn't use the soap, because she didn't like the smell, but she was glad of the chance to sponge the dirt off.

Mrs Ellis came in – Mrs Ellis had a habit of coming in to rooms without knocking since she believed nothing should be done that could not be done in front of a mother, and wasn't she in the place of mother to all her girls? They compensated for the children she hadn't had time to have with Mr Ellis. The scent was stronger than ever.

'What have you put in the water: what's the smell?' she demanded. 'Aren't you using the soap?'

'Oh, yes,' said Lily, quickly taking it in her hand and making it foam. She wanted to please Mrs Ellis, but she thought the soap would make her faint if she washed herself with it. 'It's the soap you can smell.'

'Aren't you ready yet?' asked Mrs Ellis, bewildered – perhaps by the scent. 'Hurry up, my dear, you have to learn regular habits in this house.'

'I'm used to regularity,' said Lily indignantly. She put her legs tightly together and held her arms over her breasts. She hated Mrs Ellis to see her naked.

Mrs Ellis opened her eyes wide. She put down a set of cotton clothes, white jacket, Chinese style, black trousers, white stockings and black cotton Chinese shoes.

'I'm bleeding,' said Lily, 'I had a baby.' She kept her face blank: she didn't want to drown in grief.

Mrs Ellis went out and came back without a word. She added some special paper to the pile, then told Lily to put her hair in a single plait at the back. She left the room and went to talk to her sister, who helped her in the work.

'The child says,' she said to Miss Atkinson, 'that she's used to regularity. What does that mean?'

Miss Atkinson carried on doing the accounts. There was no point in speculation. The permutations were limitless, but neither of them had much doubt about the essentials.

'He was an old man,' said Mrs Ellis. 'I suppose he kept early hours.'

Lily hated the clothes she had been given. She was going to have to dress like an amah – a common maidservant. But at least she was clean. And the ladies were going to feed her. That was worth staying for. Though she had no choice about staying, since she was locked in.

There was always someone telling her what to do, and talking about love. On the other hand, Mr Jackson hadn't ever said he loved her. He'd asked her if she loved him. Mrs Ellis had promised to love her. She decided that if the love was real, then cotton was better than silk. She dressed herself and made a long neat braid of her black hair.

They gave her a bowl of rice and some soup. She ate. In the middle of her relief she remembered the other empty place in her belly, the place that couldn't be filled with rice. She didn't want to show her grief, but she was weak, and the tears came in spite of her.

Miss Atkinson said: 'Dear child, if we were all to weep for our sins, we would never be done with weeping.' Proud of her saying, she smiled at Lily.

Miss Atkinson was taller and rounder than her sister and her face was soft and plump. She had soulful eyes, though they were small. She wrote religious poetry in her spare time: she didn't show it to anyone. It had piled up behind her underwear. Some of her woollen drawers were permanently marked with the ink.

It wasn't a scent, thought Mrs Ellis, it couldn't be. It was something harder to scrub off. She was always a little nervous of the new girls: they came with an aura of languorousness and sensuosity, seductions she herself had never been able to frighten away with the dumbbells and the work for Christ. Death, slavery, loss of self. No efforts could be too great to escape it.

'Now Lily,' she said, 'I'll tell you about our work here. We have prayers, three times a day. We believe in cleanliness. You're not used to clean living.'

'I bathed every day, where I lived before,' said Lily, wondering.

Mrs Ellis said: 'Child, I know where you lived before. You're huddling in darkness and ignorance. Have you ever heard of a man called Jesus?'

'Of course,' said Lily eagerly. 'I used to read the Bible with my nurse, in London.'

'You can read?' asked Mrs Ellis. 'You've read the Bible? Then how could you – '

'He fed me,' said Lily, as if she was explaining to her nurse. 'You must know I had to do as I was told. I wanted to do my duty to him.'

'Freedom,' said Mrs Ellis doggedly. 'I can offer you freedom, child. What's your name?' she asked: it hadn't occurred to her before.

'Lily Jackson,' said Lily. She smiled at Mrs Ellis.

'What,' asked Mrs Ellis, consumed with curiosity, 'what happened to your baby?'

'Dead,' said Lily, and found herself laughing so she wouldn't cry.

Mrs Ellis wanted to slap her face.

Lily knew. She shrank into herself. She put her hands in front of her mouth.

'Forgiveness,' said Miss Atkinson imploringly. 'Lily, there is forgiveness.'

Lily kept her hands in front of her mouth. They asked her more questions: she wouldn't answer.

Mrs Ellis sighed. 'Now Lily,' she said, picking up a brisk tone of voice. 'Your life with us here. There's more to clean living than washing the body. There's more to feeding than rice. We will feed you, but we must also feed you the Word of God that gives life to the world. We'll employ you in our laundry with other fallen sisters, and we'll lead you in prayer for the cleansing of your soul. You shall stay with us until we can see that you've learned the lessons. Then we'll find you employment. You will see no men.'

'I don't want to see men,' said Lily fiercely.

Mrs Ellis smiled. She said: 'You're safe from them here. You won't be allowed out on to the streets. We make this rule to keep the girls safe from men who might force them back into wicked ways.'

Mrs Ellis took Lily by the arm and led her down to the laundry. There nine young Chinese women were labouring among clouds of steam. Some of them were still pretty: all of them had been pretty once.

'Honest toil,' said Mrs Ellis. 'Rebecca!'

The tallest woman came forward, her arms all red and runcly with the water, her round face coarsening with exhaustion and steam.

'Your new sister, Rebecca,' said Mrs Ellis in Cantonese. 'You were nine sisters, now you are ten.' Her accent was poor and she pronounced nine in the wrong tone. The girls put their hands in front of their mouths to hide their giggles. Lily knew that if you pronounced 'gau' in that tone, it meant 'bum'.

Mrs Ellis knew. She tried not to show her annoyance. She understood the Cantonese street-jargon: couldn't do this work if she didn't. The girls came in speaking the coarsest language: they had to be taught better.

143

Lily thought: Ugly. And this laundry, dreadful. She calls me a horrible name, and this place is for common people.

Lily didn't want honest toil. She'd never imagined love could set her to work in a laundry.

Mrs Ellis bustled round, finding a place for Lily to work, telling her that she would have a biblical name chosen for her too presently. She wrapped an apron round her, gave her a huge bar of soap and a big linen sheet to rub and scrub. Lily tried to believe this wasn't happening. The soap-suds got up her nose and made her sneeze, and every time she sneezed, she could feel the blood gouting out of her womb. She wanted to cry again.

'Mrs Ellis,' she said in English, 'please let me out. You can have your clothes back. I think I'd rather beg.'

All the other girls were listening, distrust on their faces. Mrs Ellis shook her head at Lily and left her alone with them.

'You can guess why he made her have a bath every day,' said Mrs Ellis later to Miss Atkinson. 'What do you think happened to the baby? Do you think she killed it?'

'Oh, surely not,' said Miss Atkinson. Mrs Ellis usually thought the worse of people, and Miss Atkinson the better, though Miss Atkinson had more reason to be embittered, since she'd been sent out here to find a husband and no one had wanted her. Her parents had refused to have her back, so she had stayed on to work with her sister. She was racked with rheumatism and periodic attacks of malaria: she'd always been delicate.

Mrs Ellis was disappointed in her sister, though she hoped she never let it show (Miss Atkinson knew, and wasn't surprised). Mrs Ellis herself had decided, when she came out, to be immune to tropical disease, and immune she had been. She sometimes made calculations in pencil: the hours she worked against the hours Alicia was able to work. Then she tore them up and threw them on the kitchen fire. Disloyalty was a sin, as was unfairness.

Lily couldn't get the clothes clean. She could hardly even lift the heavy linen, all cumbersome with slopping water, let alone manoeuvre it on the ridged washing board and get the dirt out: it seemed to her that no matter how hard she rubbed, she made no impression at all. Her arms hurt and her knuckles bled.

And all the time she was carrying the baby she had been

pampered! Now she was weak and tired and the woman who had offered her a home and love left her alone with this impossible task and these other women who were looking at her askance.

They know about the city wall, thought Lily. They want me thrown out again. They know my own baby was put out to die. They want me to die too. This is no home. I have no home. And the lady is cruel: she knows I'm still bleeding – I asked her for the special paper. She isn't kind. She's hard.

Dragons of steam coiled round white mountains of laundry. As soon as she finished this sheet, there would be another one. And another: she began to distrust love, which always laid such dreadful burdens on you.

They were talking about her, quietly, so that she could only hear the odd word: 'Foreigner, speaks the devil language, doesn't speak our language, what's she doing here?'

Rebecca came round to see Lily's work, laughed, and slapped her. 'Lazy cow,' she said hardily, for the benefit of the other women. 'You think you can come here, eat our rice and do no work for it? You don't even speak our language.'

'I do,' protested Lily. I have learned to speak it. I speak Chinese, I am Chinese, except I learned Mandarin.'

'You speak Cantonese like a *gweilo*,' said Rebecca.

The other women said '*Gweilo, gweilo!*'

Rebecca said: 'She'll bring bad luck. The old foreign devil should have left her on the streets to starve.'

'She would starve,' said one of them then, giggling, 'No man would want her. Look at her big feet. But if *I* was let back on the streets – '

Rebecca turned on her. 'Shut up. You want to go back and get fucked twenty times a night, in your mouth, up your arse, get beaten and have all your money stolen?' She spat. 'Get on with your work.'

She slapped Lily in passing. Lily broke down in tears and they all laughed at her, but fell silent when they heard Mrs Ellis's feet coming downstairs.

Mrs Ellis said: 'It's time for midday rice. I hope you've been working hard, Lily?'

Rebecca said: 'She hasn't even got one sheet clean. She's lazy.' She twisted her pigtail as if it was Lily's neck.

'You'll have to learn, Lily,' said Mrs Ellis. 'Now come and eat. Rebecca, hold your tongue, you had to learn, too. You came in here

145

painted and stinking with scent – all you knew was how to lie on your back.' The women fell about with startled laughter – Ah ha! thought Mrs Ellis. They think I know nothing. It's good to catch them out. Rebecca's face lost all trace of expression. Mrs Ellis said: 'You knew no word of Scripture. Lily does. We'll see how you both compare in a year's time.'

Lily thought of a year spent scrubbing – and it would be the same sheet, all year – and fainted outright, on the floor among the suds and the heaps of dirty linen waiting to be washed. She came round to hear Rebecca say defiantly:

'Useless. She's useless.'

Mrs Ellis revived Lily with Miss Atkinson's smelling salts and dragooned her along to eat noon rice with a little salt fish and stir-fried *choi sum*: other women had made the food, in a brief respite from the laundry work. While they ate, Mrs Ellis told them a story from Scripture. She always made her way through the Bible, Genesis to Revelation: some passages needed a great deal of interpretation. It made her uncomfortable when she came to the Song of Songs, for example, or the story of David and Bathsheba, but she wouldn't leave out a jot or a tittle, she wouldn't defraud her wayward children. She was clear of the Old Testament now, with its concubines and lustful men, but the New Testament had its bad patches, and today she had to read the parable of the Dishonest Steward.

'There was a certain rich man,' said Mrs Ellis, casting her steel-grey eyes dubiously over her charges, wishing she could read their souls: 'who had a steward, and the steward was accused of wasting his master's goods. So the master called him, and said "What is this that I have heard about you? You are dismissed from my service, and must present the accounts for my scrutiny." '

Again, she looked – she hoped penetratingly – round at her girls.

He was thrown out, thought Lily. As I was.

'Then the steward said to himself: What shall I do if my lord takes the stewardship away from me: I cannot dig and I am ashamed to beg.'

Lily thought digging would be far easier than washing the huge linen sheets. She hoped the rice would make her stronger, but she found it difficult to get it down, and she felt very hot.

'The steward said: I am resolved what to do, so that when I have been dismissed, they will receive me into their houses. So he called every one of his lord's debtors to him, and said to the first, "How much do you owe my lord?" And he said: "A hundred measures of oil." And he said to him: "take your bill and sit down quickly, and write fifty." Then he said to another: "And how much do you owe?" And he said: "A hundred measures of wheat." And he said to him, "Take your bill, and write eighty."

'And the lord commended the unjust steward, because he had done wisely: for the children of this world are wiser in their generation than the children of light.'

Lily listened, and remembered: she'd heard the parable before.

'Dear girls,' said Mrs Ellis, 'this parable is not intended to encourage you to act dishonestly, that least of all,' she paused for a moment, irritated to find that the moral she had so carefully prepared had gone clean out of her head. It was all the fault of Lily's huge black eager eyes. What could she say to move Lily's heart?

Lily thought: I must do as the man in the story did, if I don't want the hard labour, I must find a way to make friends who will help me not to do it. Those two English ladies aren't as hard as the Cantonese women in the laundry – the second one is anything but hard.

'The man in the story,' said Mrs Ellis resolutely – oh, so beautiful, such a mouth! she thought, looking at Lily, 'this man is eager to gain friends with his dishonestly acquired money. What you should do, dear girls, is to make friends with God, using the means at your disposal, you should desire to be lovely in his eyes – ' she got up and went over to Rebecca, lifting her head. Rebecca looked down modestly. Mrs Ellis said: ' – these marks of labour are dearer to God than smooth skin and tawdry jewellery – '

Lily's head began to buzz, and a dark haze closed in on the room. It was as if something had taken her and was rushing her away from everything she'd ever known: she let go of herself and went with it.

Mrs Ellis just got to her in time. She laid her down gently on the floor.

'Poor child,' said Miss Atkinson, hurrying over to her. 'You've been too hard on her, Beatrice.'

Mrs Ellis wanted to cry.

Picture me in Manchester, wrote Reynolds, *walking between buildings furred black with soot – are there such buildings in*

Hong-Kong, Samuel? A thousand trails of smoke darken the sky, yet inside many houses in this city men, women and children shiver round a bare grate and eat cold food for dinner. The stink of smoke and bad drains fouls the streets, and you see the washing strung across side-alleys, greying rather than bleaching in the airborne filth.

Everywhere you hear the noises of industry, the producer of prosperity. Is it enough for a man only to earn his daily bread? I can't believe it. I must get out of here, Samuel. It makes me feel so hopeless. You've never answered my query about a post in Hong-Kong. Meanwhile, I tread my own mill as diligently as I can bring myself to do. In a year or so – oh, God, so long? No matter – in a year or so I shall try for another post. But I must work out my time here first.

I have criticized your work in the past – you know, don't you, that I only do it to keep you on your toes? You've responded with intelligence and interest. I do most heartily congratulate you on your new dignity, and wish you even more success in the future. But don't you long for the freedom of the past? I miss our fun. The world is so tame now, all the spark gone out of it. Samuel's stomach ached with nostalgia: it had been fun, and he'd been happy when the two of them had adventured on the sheeptracks of Dorset and the highroads of the imagination. *For my sake, Samuel, don't be the complete government servant all the time, I'm sure a little wildness does no harm.*

It was Saturday afternoon, and Henderson wanted to visit a fan-tan den in Kowloon City: 'But you know we couldn't possibly,' said Samuel.

'Don't be such a prig, Pink,' said Richards, who had dropped by with Caird, 'so you're a Passed Cadet, so you're working in the Colonial Secretary's office. What does it matter?' It had cheered him tremendously to throw Lily on to the street.

'But we asked the Chinese government to close all these hells down,' protested Samuel. He lit a cigar for protection.

'And they did,' said Richards, grinning, 'and so they're not open and our little jaunt has no legal status whatsoever. Look, think of Caird, he's a doomed man, his fiancée's on the boat already, she'll be here in six weeks. Do you want to stop him having a last fling?'

There was a biscuit-tin on the sideboard in Caine Road that had

Queen Victoria's Jubilee picture on it. Samuel looked over at it: the Queen looked angrily back at him, as she might at any stranger who came peeping in at her palace windows.

There are many temptations, his mother had written, *for young men in the East. I cannot keep you safe from them, can only beg you to respect yourself. You have no need to be ashamed of anything if your heart is pure.* He'd been moved by her acknowledgement that he might feel ashamed, shamed afresh because his heart was far from pure.

A man couldn't be a spoilsport, or a prig. Suddenly he hated to think that someone was watching him for her, making reports on his behaviour. It would be easier if he knew who, but he wasn't allowed to ask.

He remembered how she'd told him his father would watch over him. She might be communing with John Brown's ghost in spiritualistic seances, or perhaps she looked and heard through the hundred eyes and ears of her portraits throughout the colony. He turned the biscuit-tin round so she couldn't see him.

'You'll come, won't you?' asked Henderson.

'Yes,' said Samuel, 'damn it.' Kowloon City was in China: there'd be no portrait of Victoria anywhere within its walls.

Now hold your tongue, he said silently to Reynolds, and as for the post in Hong-Kong, I have no influence.

He'd write and tell him so.

When they got to the Chinese city, they found all the hells doing business as usual: they'd opened as soon as the imperial official had gone back to Canton. The Chinese liked to gamble even more than the British did.

They sat down to play, and Henderson lost money. Worse, Henderson wouldn't be a sportsman, didn't want to accept his losses.

Fan-tan was played by placing bets on buttons: a heap of them sat on a table in front of a croupier, who covered some of them with a porcelain cup and took the rest away, then you placed bets on the number under the cup. The croupier was supposed to rake them away four at a time: Henderson said he'd seen him take three instead.

A rat ran over the beam above them: you could hear its scuttering feet. Samuel noticed the characters for good fortune and long life hung on scrolls against the wall.

'Oh, nonsense,' said Richards, downing a brandy and soda and tidying his chestnut whiskers. He'd reverted to moustaches: he said the beard was too sticky in the heat.

'No,' said Caird, 'he's right. I saw it too.'

'Don't make trouble,' said Samuel, and immediately wished he hadn't spoken.

Henderson said: 'I want my money back. Your croupier,' he said loudly in Cantonese, beckoning the owner of the den from his desk. The man came, fanning himself. Richards and Caird waited: they couldn't understand Cantonese. 'He took three buttons out instead of four.' He said it like a child complaining to his parents that someone has been unfair to him. His accent was better than Samuel had ever heard it.

It was all horrid and filthy, not fun at all. There was always punishment for trespass: he should have remembered that. He felt ill.

Henderson said: 'I want my money back.' You could smell his nervousness, sharp and vinegary.

'Oh, of course, sir,' said the proprietor, smiling, and put all the silver dollars back on the table. The four men smiled at each other:

'You see?' said Henderson, 'it's just a question of being firm with them.' The Englishmen put their hands out for their coins: then Samuel looked up and saw that each of his three companions had two men with knives standing behind him. It looked unreal, posed, like an engraving in one of the boy's adventure stories he used to read. He knew there was someone behind him, too: he thought he felt the point digging into his flesh.

He had a revolver in his pocket: the four of them had each a revolver, and any of them could be knifed before they could even get their weapon out. Their hands stayed still, poised on the coins.

Nobody said anything for a moment. Then the proprietor laughed, and said: 'Chinese law here.'

A lizard ran halfway across the table, froze for a moment, then disappeared over the edge.

Henderson put his hand away from the silver: it shone in a tumbled heap on the grimy matting of the table-cover. Then Richards, then Caird. Samuel knew they were all waiting for him. He couldn't do it. He couldn't get his fingers to move: he was paralysed. You had to endure punishment, you couldn't defend yourself. He was going to die.

'For God's sake, man – ' said Henderson.

Samuel forced his fingers to move: he saw the knives vanish from behind his friends and felt the relief at his own back.

The proprietor offered them another game.

'No, thank you,' said Samuel, sweating.

'Oh – ' said the proprietor. 'Thank you very much, sirs. Goodbye.' He saw them out of the door as politely as if nothing had happened, bowing and wishing them health and prosperity. Samuel and Henderson returned the compliments. It was all very civil and proper.

They walked out of the narrow streets that echoed to the clatter of mah-jong, through the deep square gateway and out to the pier. A letter-writer was working for an old woman with a pipe, and touts for the gaming hells were sitting in the shade eating their lunch with chopsticks while they waited for the ferry to come in. It was desperately, frighteningly calm all of a sudden, though they could still hear the faint sound of mah-jong tiles coming from the walled city. It was very hot.

'Don't know how they can eat with those things,' said Henderson, waving irritably at the chopsticks. He hadn't put his pith helmet on.

'Henderson,' said Samuel, 'you'll get sunstroke.'

Henderson put the helmet on. Samuel wanted to tell him what a nuisance he was, but it had been his own hand that had hesitated over the money.

'It's a risk you take,' said Richards. 'Nine of them to four of us, we couldn't have fought them, not even with revolvers.'

'Silly thing to die for, really,' said Caird.

'Yes,' said Henderson, 'there are better reasons to die.'

Samuel thought: it happened. What he was afraid of. We're badly outnumbered, out here. If they really decided to get rid of us, our weapons, our knowledge of Cantonese – nothing we have would be any good.

And yet they all said: 'What an escape!', laughed, and poked each other in the ribs. Everything had to be a joke. Samuel thought he'd choke on so much laughter.

Henderson didn't come to the Club that evening. Samuel went alone. He drank and played billiards. Darley came past and watched for a moment, then grinned awkwardly and went off with the Colonial Surgeon.

When Samuel came home, he went straight to bed, so it wasn't till the next morning that the Number One Boy found Henderson hanging from a rafter.

Samuel heard him shout with terror, jumped out of bed and came running in his nightshirt. Henderson's face would never be handsome again. His body dangled at a horrid angle. He was dead as a brace of pheasants that the gamekeeper hooks casually over his arm.

If I'd gone to see him last night, thought Samuel. If I hadn't hesitated, in the hell. If I'd never hated him. If Mrs Darley had been kinder. No, I should have looked after him better. I'm his superior in the Service now. It must be my fault.

Henderson's corpse swung round and the blackened face leered pitiably. Samuel retched. 'Horrible,' he croaked aloud, 'horrible!'

He turned to say to the Number One Boy: 'A knife. Get a knife. We'll have to cut him down.' But the Number One Boy wasn't there.

The servant was frightened of Henderson's houseless spirit. Henderson had died violently, in despair. He was a white devil anyway: now he might be in the room, outside his corpse, reaching out to harm the living. The hairs went up on the back of Samuel's head.

'Get away from me,' he whispered.

But he had to be brave. He belonged to the Queen, her servant and her son. He had to cut the corpse down and carry out the proper formalities. Had Henderson hidden the knives as usual, or had he left them in the kitchen for the first time in three years?

Samuel went down there and saw the cook's retreating back. There wasn't a servant left in the house: for a moment, he did feel courageous by comparison. But he was going to have to go back into the bedroom with Henderson – his corpse, his possibly malignant spirit.

'I'm a Christian,' he said aloud. 'Christians aren't afraid of demons.' He hoped Henderson could hear him. The knives weren't in the kitchen.

Samuel opened boxes and chests, pulled drawers out, ransacked the house. He found no knives. He supposed he'd have to unknot the rope. He thought of his hands against that cold neck. He shuddered.

'I am a Christian,' he told himself again, and went into the room (no Christian burial for Henderson, only a suicide's outcast grave). There was a hump under Henderson's bedclothes. He pulled the bedclothes back, and there the knives were, Henderson had put them to bed in his place.

Samuel took the big, razor-sharp Chinese chopper, and slashed at the rope with it, strand by strand. The body swung and nudged him. Samuel tried not to look at it. Then the rope was cut. Henderson's body plopped on to the floor beside the chair he had kicked away to let himself drop. Samuel found a smaller knife and severed the rope round Henderson's neck. He made a little nick in the skin as he did so, but there was no bleeding.

He thought it couldn't be his fault after all: didn't a corpse always bleed in the presence of its murderer? He wasn't relieved.

He knelt and tried to straighten Henderson's neck, to give him some dignity, but it was impossible. The body was cold and stiff and the neck stayed crooked.

He'd have to notify the police. A crime had been committed: someone had taken his own life. But he couldn't fetch the Sikh policeman on the corner. The suicide belonged to the governing class, to the élite corps. He'd have to send the Sikh for the Commissioner.

He put his hand on Henderson's body again, and thought about dead foxes and dogs and cats. The body still smelt faintly of alcohol. It would decay fast, in this heat. The house was infested with ants, who'd come to scavenge Henderson if he wasn't coffined quickly. He couldn't move.

He thought Henderson had sat all alone, drinking till he reached the point where he dared get up on that chair, put his head in the noose, and let his legs swing free. And then what? A sudden jolt to the neck, and darkness. Or hell fire?

He thought he'd have to drink a great deal to forget this, then that he'd never drink again if this was what drink did to you. The body smelt of urine as well as of alcohol. Henderson had wet himself in his death.

'Lonely,' said Samuel. 'Dreadfully lonely.'

He wanted Reynolds, he thought Reynolds would have known what to do. Henderson had been a link with Reynolds.

'How could you?' he said to the corpse. 'How could you do it? And you've undermined us. You've betrayed us. What will they think of you?'

He thought Henderson looked helpless, apologetic, might open his blue lips any moment to make excuses, say he hadn't meant it. But he had. Samuel knew he had.

'They should never have let you come out here,' said Samuel. 'You're a failure. You're hateful. You don't deserve to be called a white man.'

Then he began to cry.

13

THE WRONG ROAD
TO DAMASCUS

———————

THE police came and took the body away, but the servants didn't come back all day Saturday and on Sunday morning there was no sign of them either. The house was getting dirty, there was nothing to eat and Samuel's clothes hadn't been washed or brushed or put away in specially heated cupboards. He supposed he could always go to live in the Club.

The clock tick-tacked steadily in the room and the warm rain came down outside, beating against the windows, seeping in and making little puddles on the polished wooden floor. There were black spots of mildew on the shirt he'd worn yesterday and his shoes were lined with furry mould: he'd got another pair out of the cupboard. He had no idea what you did with mildewed clothes. He'd been down to the kitchen and found it ascurry with more kinds of cockroach than he'd believed possible, so he'd had no breakfast. He was swallowing air to compensate, preparing himself a colic for later in the day.

He wrote to Reynolds about Henderson's suicide. As if possessed, he left out no horrid detail: it felt much better, when he'd got it all down.

He wrote: *The worst thing about it is the way it stops me doing anything at all, because nowhere feels safe any more. Nothing you taught me ever prepared me for this, and my dog is dead – can you tell me what to do with myself, because having fun isn't enough – I need to be told how to live my life.*

He stopped writing. He stuffed the letter into an envelope without signing it, before he should think better of it. He wrote to Master Feng, telling him what had happened. Then there was no one else to write to. He turned the biscuit-tin round: 'You were right,' he said to his mother, 'about the dangers out here, and it makes me feel so empty.'

There was no one he could hand his letters to: 'Take this to the post.' 'Yes, sir.'

A man could go himself, to the Post Office. It was quite possible. He could get up and go, now. Exercise would do him good. Instead he flopped across the rosewood dining table, letting his head fall on his arms and stretching his hands palms-up as if he was hoping a warm pair would comfort them. But no one would come. And it might be a cold pair. It might be Henderson's ghost.

He packed a bag and fled to the Club.

Lily was relieved to find herself running a fever. She might die of it, it was quite true, but she was certain she'd die in the laundry. She lay in an iron-framed bed (it was rusting from the humidity), and knew she was rambling. The picture opposite the bed reminded her to call on Jesus, though Jesus didn't come. The person who usually came was Miss Atkinson.

Once she dreamed of Ah Kuen taking the baby: she had heard the tiny girl's wails going away from her. Her parents were standing there in the white hemp of mourning, encouraging him to do it. She cried out in Mandarin: 'Murderers! Murderers without hearts. Why should you do this to us? I wanted my baby.' She woke up still sobbing: 'I wanted my baby.' She put her hand to her empty womb: it was flat, almost concave as she lay there.

Miss Atkinson wondered what Lily was saying. She took her hands and found them furnace-hot. She wrapped the child up warmer, to burn the fever out of her.

'Dear child,' she said, 'you're safe, with people who care for you.'

'You're boiling me,' said Lily, 'to wash my sin away. Like the sheets. You'll put me through the mangle and I'll die.'

'No,' said Miss Atkinson, 'you mustn't die, Lily. We – I – love you.'

It was true. Miss Atkinson had fallen in love with Lily and she couldn't lie: she'd never been able to do that. She scratched the prickly heat rash at the back of her neck, and went to get another hot drink for her darling patient.

Mrs Ellis, on the other hand, was precise, cool and efficient. She set the bed to rights and made sure Lily behaved herself even in her delirium.

'Hush,' she'd say. 'Hush,' when Lily rambled about Mr Jackson and his disgusting needs. She wouldn't allow that sort of talk in *this* house. Nor talk in Mandarin, when God alone knew what was being said – and God was jealous and quick to take offence.

Then she'd sit and think how disorderly the sick were, not to get better when you'd done everything that was proper. She wasn't a patient woman, and she regretted it.

Miss Atkinson made her backache worse by bending over Lily and spooning rice gruel into her mouth: she gave herself headaches sitting up with her all night, then, when her sister forbade this, she insisted that a truckle bed be brought into the room so that she could sleep alongside Lily.

'She'll have to go back to the laundry when she's better,' said Mrs Ellis sternly, 'your pet lamb.'

Miss Atkinson thought of mint sauce and dripping. 'Beatrice,' she asked, 'is that wise? She's *so* different from the rest of them, refined, educated. She's afraid they'll be cruel to her: she's been crying about it.'

'She must learn to get on with them,' said Mrs Ellis, not unkindly. 'Where else can she go? To be some white man's mistress again? And if we keep her here with us, how can she be useful if she's no sister to the other girls?'

She sighed. It had been a bad day. One of the girls had escaped to her pimp, and another had been found lighting incense-sticks – got from the Lord knew where – for the Kitchen God. Mrs Ellis had excluded her from kitchen work. She hoped this would do the trick. She wondered if there was a Laundry God?

'I must go to her,' said Miss Atkinson. 'I have to take her a drink.'

'Stay here,' said Mrs Ellis severely. 'I'll go. You spoil her.'

Miss Atkinson ran down to the kitchen, to see that Lily's beef-tea had been properly made.

Lily had pushed the hot bedclothes away from her and her face had lost its flush, was jasmine-white again except for the shadows that lay below her eyes, deepening to black where her long lashes lay. Mrs Ellis could see the sharp outline of her shoulder and the darkness of one nipple below the nightdress. She was breathing peacefully: the fever had left her.

Mrs Ellis stood in the doorway and felt the pull and push of contradictory emotions. There was an enormous gratitude to Lily for being a good girl and getting better at last, but this was laced with a sharp fearful longing that she couldn't quite trace. It tasted of the dream that sometimes plagued her: the flames in the house, her nightgowned shrieks of terror, the strong male arms lifting her up and carrying her away from the danger, the delicious, trustful helplessness.

She stretched her arm and felt its wiriness, but the sensation wouldn't go away: her stomach and lower limbs steeped themselves in a sort of sweet soup, and it was all connected with Lily's abandon as she lay sleeping away her illness. The scent came about her again and drugged the rest of her through her nostrils.

She knew then she'd never send Lily back to the laundry. Joy and love – unfamiliar emotions in spite of all her talk of them – had her hostage. It made no difference that they proceeded – apparently – from Vice.

Her busy mind tracked the new paths: I wonder if she can sew? My sister finds it hard to make her own clothes. My sister would find her assistance very timely. I could find one of the youngest girls to help. Or if she can embroider, she could do fine work for sale.

She wondered if she'd been too hard on all the girls? Were the marks of toil really such occasion for celebration? The laundry changed, in her mind, from prison to salvation, and back again.

Love, thought Lily, coming out of sleep. I could use up gallons of it. She opened her black eyes wide and saw Mrs Ellis's tender expression. It frightened her, after all. It looked like a trap.

'Have you seen her?' said Richards. 'She's wasted away.'

Caird said: 'Everyone said she'd gone mad.'

A young man from Butterfield and Swire said: 'Too much of – you know.'

Richards laughed ruefully, as if he'd been caught out at cricket: 'They say Darley had her doctored.' A brief look round to see who else was in the room.

'What do you mean,' said the man from Butterfield and Swire, 'doctored – you can't, you know. Not a woman!' Appalled laughter and a protective thought downwards.

Caird said: 'Yes, you can. If they're too lively – you know – you cut off part of their fanny and it steadies them.'

The balls huddled on the green baize table, span when the long wicked cue attacked them, scattered, ran for cover. The gaslights burned with a soft hissing sound. The young men sweated buckets in their waistcoats and shirt sleeves, smoked their cigars angrily, as if they were burning something to get rid of it. The hot season was at its end: and everyone was sick of it, waiting for the wind to change.

'She might just as well have died,' said Richards suddenly. He had been looking steadily down at the red ball, now his aim wavered just as he pushed his cue at it. 'He let her have the rope, then – '

'Oh,' said Caird with malicious pleasure: 'steady on, old chap. Medically recommended, you know. Old Darley didn't *ask* for it. He told the doctor to do what seemed best to him.'

Richards steadied his cue, and potted the white from a difficult angle.

'Oh, good shot!' exclaimed the man from Butterfield and Swire.

'By the way,' said Caird, 'have you heard? Jackson's woman never got as far as Wan Chai. She was rescued by Mrs Ellis who runs the reformatory in Pokfulam Road. She'll teach her to be a good woman. Seems a waste, really: they say she's a corker. Pink'll be pleased. He was quite worried about her, wasn't he?'

Richards shouted crossly: 'Boy! A brandy and soda here.'

They ordered drinks from the hurrying white-coated servant with his swinging black rope of hair, talking about the regatta, about cricket, about the lawn tennis tournament, about work.

Nobody mentioned Henderson.

Master Feng had written to Samuel about Henderson's death:

What is an especial tragedy is that he should be buried without rites, and no son to lay him in the earth. I have been examining my own thoughts and actions to see if I truly did my best for him: you can do the same. Should your heart absolve you from guilt, then believe yourself not guilty. In any case, the gentleman must continue to place himself, as far as possible, in the Way.

Not a stroke was out of place, not a character that wasn't a thing of beauty in itself. Samuel put a hand on his heart, then he laid down the sheet of soft rice-paper and picked up the letter from Reynolds that had come in the same post.

I've lost my job, wrote Reynolds, *they've dismissed me, Samuel, I don't know what I'm going to do with myself. And no references. I only spent my afternoon off with a few friends and got a little tipsy – not badly so, believe me. And we went to the house where that woman works – the one I told you about. We were seen. People can be so harsh, so merciless, a man has to have some compensations.*

At least I've left Manchester. I've found some cheap lodgings in Putney, and am looking for a post as a crammer somewhere. Now it's pointless for you to find me something, until I've rebuilt my credentials. I shan't write any more today. Do you think you could spare a little money to help tide me over? I'll pay it back, of course. For old times' sake. Noblesse oblige, you know, you're so fortunate, compared to me.

There would be neither help nor guidance from Reynolds.

The earth felt fragile under him, as if it couldn't hold itself up without his help. And how could he hold up the earth? Master Feng's way was praiseworthy, but he would never be able to walk in it. It was beyond him to achieve such singleness of purpose and purity of heart. He turned his eyes from the Way to Christ. Christ accepted repentant sinners, the ugly, the incapable, hearts as black as pitch.

He wrote to Reynolds: he'd enclose some money.

I don't feel like a fortunate man, I'm confused and unhappy. I hope you're not in too much need, here is as much as I can manage for the time being. I'm going to open my heart to God, Reynolds, I should have done it a long time ago. He said: Ask and you shall receive. It's difficult to believe it's as easy as that, but probably that's only false pride.

Write to me and tell me how you're getting on. I want to hear. I'm making a stand, I've refused to have my house exorcized. I've moved into the Club for the time being. Unfortunately, he added sadly, *they all think I'm mad.*

It was bad for his career to be so eccentric. His stand was exposing the inconsistencies of his Christian colleagues, and it seemed that the government of Hong-Kong by a Christian Queen depended on the continuance of such inconsistencies.

He glanced at Victoria on the biscuit-tin, and realized that his dreams for himself were implacably opposed to hers: she wanted him to be happy, he wanted to be great. He wanted more than to be Governor of Hong-Kong: he wanted sanctity. Surely that was an ambition worth striving for? So much the better if he had to suffer for it. He sat back in his chair and waited for the lightning bolt of conversion. It didn't come, so he went on writing to Reynolds.

My servants came back on Sunday night and asked me to have the house exorcized. They said otherwise they wouldn't dare work there. Because you know, he didn't have a Christian burial, because he was a suicide. They buried him over at Tai Tam, not in the cemetery at Happy Valley.

He thought how nice it would have been for Henderson, to be buried above the racecourse. Then he frowned: it was a frivolous thought and he must train his mind to work properly.

They wanted me to have the local Taoist priest in to exorcize the house. They said I could go out while it happened, I needn't know anything about it, they didn't want to offend me. I could see it was very good of them to offer to come back at all, but I couldn't accept. I want to bear witness to the Light, and those ceremonies are the work of darkness. Even my dear old tutor Feng, who writes me such kind letters, he's wandering in the dark, and it's because I was a lost soul too that all these things have happened. I have to stand firm. The fact that other men out here turn their backs on this sort of thing means nothing to me.

I'm different, you know that, and why. At least I can be different by following my conscience, and then – perhaps – I can do some good in the world. I owe it to the Chinese, too. What an example Henderson set them! They asked me if he'd had a moral reason for killing himself, to reproach his superiors for corruption, for example. They believe that would mean his ghost wasn't dangerous, and wouldn't need to be exorcized. You see what I mean, when I say it all comes from us, from the rulers? His lack of morals has laid us all wide open to this superstition.

I said to the servants: 'But he wasn't of your religion. He was a Christian. Now he's in the Christian hell, and no one gets let out of there. They're shut up there forever.' I was pleased with that argument, but it didn't work. The Number One asked – and his voice was gentle, believe me – 'Sir, so there are no ghosts in your country?' I wanted to say no, of course not. But then I remembered the bridge at West Burton, the one no one ever crossed after dark if they could help it. I couldn't say anything so they've all gone to look for other employers. I can only pray that God will guide me through.

'You're being moved next week,' announced the Colonial Secretary cheerfully. 'Good for you. Usual thing, you know that, get six weeks' grounding in this department, get an all-over picture of how the colony's run, shaping up nicely, made a brave showing, given the circumstances. Your bowling's come on well, too.' He grinned. 'Registrar-General's office for you now. That'll stretch you. Testing ground for cadets, Protectorate of the Chinese. They need your skills in Cantonese. Important job, after all, the Chinese are ninety-five per cent of the population, aren't they? Lifeblood, really, though we don't like to admit it.'

Doctor Philips, the Registrar-General and Protector of Chinese, was only faintly interested in cricket, though he played at the Cricket Club all the same.

He was in charge of a busy department whose functions stretched from the decennial census to constant liaison with all the Chinese community organizations. Registration of births, marriages and deaths was the least of it. He also had to represent Chinese views to the British rulers, and that was when the other administrators – especially Darley – sometimes felt he was on the Chinese side, rather than their own. Sometimes he was. He was quite happy to admit that they were the colony's lifeblood.

He was a plump man with spectacles, a formidable scholar with a harmless manner. He was the friend of Chinese and Jews, of Indian businessmen and Portuguese. He'd won tolerance for this eccentricity because he was honest and got results. His house was full of Chinese *objets d'art* and it was accepted even by his enemies that his taste was better and his finds more significant than anyone else's.

He led Samuel to a mountain of papers on a shabby desk. He asked: 'You were here in eighty-eight, for a month, weren't you?'

For a moment, Samuel wondered if these were papers he had left behind: they might have been breeding ever since. It wasn't so, of course. Mountains of paper were shifted in this department, efficiently and by the hour.

'These relate to the meeting I have this morning, with the District Watch Committee. Problems with the Buildings Ordinance – these inspections of premises, you know. You'll come with me. And here, transcripts of the session with the Tung Wah Hospital Group – and the Po Leung Kuk home for girls – vital that the Chinese community should look after the morals of its women itself, far better than the well-meaning efforts of missionaries – like that woman in Pokfulam Road – she's picked up Jackson's concubine, I suppose you know. Gossip travels like wildfire in this place. Well, I suppose the Jackson woman's a special case. Poor old Jackson. I used to know him well.

He went mad in the end, you know, but a wonderful scholar. Have a look through these documents before we go.'

Samuel knew that a small committee had been set up to report on housing in the westernmost part of Victoria, the teeming slums where white men never went. The Chinese organizations were all run by wealthy property-owners, and of course they didn't like to be criticized. They complained that there was no need to burst in on people's privacy. Had there been epidemics of illness? Why did they have to improve the buildings they rented out? The coolies would no longer be able to afford the rents.

'We listen,' said Philips. 'We listen thoroughly. You don't throw your weight around with the Chinese – I suppose old Feng taught you that. If you try to roll over them, you achieve nothing.' He looked hard at Samuel, sizing him up. Samuel sat upright at his desk, wishing he wasn't so ridiculously small: it might prove his descent from the tiny Queen, but he couldn't tell anyone else that when they looked down on him.

He thought of Lily Jackson in Pokfulam Road. Mrs Ellis was going to ruin her beauty by making her wash sheets. She might even wash his sheets. He couldn't decide if the thought was sweet or nauseating.

'Sir,' he asked, 'what do you think we're out here for?'

He really hoped Philips might give him an answer.

'Do you know,' said Philips, 'you're the first cadet who's ever asked me that question?'

'Am I?' asked Samuel.

Philips paused. Samuel met his eyes and knew he was naive, too open. Philips would surely tell him he was a fool.

'You have to find your own answer,' he said instead. 'No one else can give it to you.'

'No, of course,' said Samuel, ashamed.

'By the way,' said Philips, 'I gather you won't have your house exorcized.'

'No, sir,' said Samuel.

Philips said, quite gently: 'If I were you, I'd get it done.'

Samuel saw how lonely it was going to make him to follow his principles, and felt better. Again he saw the image of Lily losing her beauty among the soap-suds. God, he thought, God and God alone. Come, Lord Jesus.

Christ kept aloof.

Mrs Darley was carried to the shops in her sedan: she bought silk and cotton. She wrote letters to her children in England. She told them she was much better than she had been. She went to use the new sanitary flushing toilet they had had installed in the house on the Peak. It connected to the mains drainage system that had been installed to service the colonial houses. Mrs Darley pulled her drawers down reluctantly and sat on it. Presently she began to whimper and cry, her hands tight over her mouth for fear anyone should hear her. Afterwards, she had to lie down for ten minutes before she could do anything else.

'A polonaise would be nice,' said Lily cheerfully, 'don't you think? And I wish you would wear your hair differently, Miss Atkinson, it would be so much more becoming.' She looked at Miss Atkinson over the top of a huddle of brown linen, which she was making into a dress. She had never sewn before, but her fingers were quick to learn, and Miss Atkinson had a stock of paper patterns – all out of date, but neither Lily nor Miss Atkinson knew or cared. Lily crossed one trousered leg over the other and let her small foot dangle.

'Oh, dear child,' said Miss Atkinson, 'it doesn't matter what I look like.' She stood up with difficulty: the rheumatism was so bad. And she was only thirty! She'd never have a husband and children now.

England, thought Miss Atkinson, and the song of the thrush whistling 'pretty Dick' twice over in the freshness of a spring morning!

Outside, a water-seller cried his wares and a mynah screeched in a tree not far away. Miss Atkinson moved her bad shoulder backwards and forwards, to ease it. It made it worse. Every joint jarred on every other.

She felt Lily's hands on her shoulder.

Lily asked: 'You have pain, there?'

'Yes, Lily,' Miss Atkinson said. Tears sprang to her eyes with the admission. 'All the time.' Then she looked round to see if her sister had heard her. But Mrs Ellis was out.

Lily took hold of the aching shoulder. She began to rub it and knead it.

'Oh, dear, dear child,' said Miss Atkinson, 'indeed you mustn't – '

'Why not?' asked Lily. She smiled round at Miss Atkinson and carried on with the massage.

She smiles like an English girl, thought Miss Atkinson, not like a Chinese. She belongs to us.

She let her shoulder relax. The pain died under the warmth of Lily's hands.

'And where else?' asked Lily.

'What would my sister say?' asked Miss Atkinson, in a flutter.

'She's out,' said Lily, 'she's gone to talk to some ladies on the Peak.'

'But I shouldn't do things my sister doesn't know about,' said Miss Atkinson.

Lily saw her face twitch with conflict, coaxed her: 'Doesn't your shoulder feel better?'

'Yes,' confessed Miss Atkinson helplessly.

'Come to your bed,' said Lily, 'lie down, we can finish this sewing later, and I'll do your hair for you when you get up, you'll see how much better you'll look.' She put her hand on Miss Atkinson's arm and led her away from work, towards the room with the narrow little bed jutting out from the wall. Above it hung a text, the frame horned with black crosses at each corner:

'Blessed are the Meek, for they shall Inherit the Earth.'

There was no doubt about it that Miss Atkinson was meek, but Lily didn't think she'd inherit anything. The other sister, in England, would probably get hold of all the elder Atkinsons' money, for one thing. Miss Atkinson wasn't selfish enough.

'Now,' she said to Miss Atkinson, 'take off your clothes. I can hardly rub you with your stays on.' She laughed. 'Don't be afraid of anyone coming. I've locked the door.'

Mrs Ellis was more selfish than her sister, and Lily knew she respected her more. It was Miss Atkinson's helplessness that made Lily want to take care of her. It made her feel as if she was caring for her baby after all.

Miss Atkinson sat on the bed and slowly took off all her clothes except her drawers. Her body was plump and surprisingly pretty. She wrapped her arms round her breasts and said: 'But we're supposed to take up His Cross.'

Lily said: 'The Lord healed the sick, didn't he, Miss Atkinson? Dozens of them. I think He wants you to be well.'

'Are you playing with Scripture?' asked Miss Atkinson.

'Dear Miss Atkinson,' said Lily caressingly, 'come, lie down.'

Miss Atkinson lay down and felt the sweetness of Lily's fingers on her naked skin, pulling the pain out: she wanted to protest at the pleasure of it, but she couldn't have moved to save her life. Tears came out of her eyes and wet her pillow. Lily wiped them with her fingers.

Afterwards, Lily did Miss Atkinson's hair. She brushed it shiny, then drew it gently this way and that and found a curl in it. At last she took the cutting-out scissors and cut Miss Atkinson the sort of fringe that she'd seen on ladies in sedans. The short hair curled at once when Lily damped it. Miss Atkinson looked fearfully at her different face.

She said: 'I don't know what Beatrice will say.'

'It's not a sin to have a fringe,' said Lily, gathering up the cut hair. 'You look pretty.'

She was proud of herself for doing it.

'I almost think I do,' said Miss Atkinson shamefacedly. 'It's too late, though.'

'I don't think so,' said Lily. She wanted to carry on, testing a power she hadn't known she possessed. She wanted to encourage Miss Atkinson to be more selfish. 'I don't think you're too old to have a man fall in love with you. Not now you know you're pretty.'

'I'm not hurting any more,' said Miss Atkinson, in a wondering voice.

Lily smiled.

'Drains,' said Darley, 'ventilation, the mainspring of public health. Along with carbolic.'

His cheeks were just like leather: Samuel thought it was hardly surprising his wife had hankered for younger flesh. The wind blew the putrescent smell of drying fish in through the window.

'We're going to start entertaining again,' said Darley by the way, 'Mrs Darley told me to invite you to dinner.' Samuel understood that he was forgiven for working in Philips's department: even for the errand he was here on.

The Registrar-General sat on the Sanitary Board and was thus responsible for the inspections of Chinese tenements. But in his capacity of Protector of Chinese and receiver of complaints about the inspections he had promised to send a cadet from his department, to observe what was going on. The cadet he chose was Samuel, who had to arrange the visit with Darley's department. He ought to have been able to sort it all out with a Chinese clerk, but Darley had come out to ambush him and, surprisingly for him, to talk.

'When Pope-Hennessy was governor,' said Darley, 'he wouldn't let us interfere with the Chinese at all, liked them a good deal better than his own kind, well, we got rid of him. Wouldn't let us do a thing. The Taipingshan fire cleared a lot of the filth away, still, they will keep pigs in upstairs rooms, and earth closets work in Canton because they're linked to a system of drainage, which they aren't here. More people crammed in here, too.' He bit his words off suddenly, as if they were a cigar he was about to smoke. 'So,' he said, 'go out and see for yourself. Then you'll know what we're up against. All very well to talk about the coolie: if they all die of cholera, that won't help us, will it?'

'No,' said Samuel.

Darley inspected him, cocking his head to one side.

Samuel wondered why he liked Darley, why Darley seemed to like him. But maybe it was the first sign of God's grace, an involuntary love of your enemies? You had to begin somewhere.

'The Chinese,' said Darley unemotionally, 'have been fighting us for years on the question of buildings. Landlords wanting to make the most possible money out of their property, substandard unventilated housing with their lodgers crammed in like sardines and half a dozen hens and a pig thrown in, a cow walled up in the basement – believe me, I've seen it. Now at last we've got the Buildings Ordinance and the Crown Land Resumption Ordinance, which should give us the powers to have their shacks pulled down. They'll get compensation, and plenty of it. They're profiteering from it, throwing up as much as they can to get it in before the Buildings Ordinance becomes law – of course. Then we'll be paying them to pull it all down. But never mind that – we have to carry out the survey – we don't do it for pleasure, Pink. It's the devil of a job getting into their houses, God knows.' Again, he grinned at Samuel, who had wronged him. It must be the grace of God at work.

But when Samuel saw Taipingshan, where he'd never been before, he wondered if the job was a way of getting rid of him. Leaving aside the danger of cholera, of typhus, of plague, supposing a gang of Triads fell on them, would the Chinese policemen and the

Chinese official defend him? Had secret instructions been sent to Philips: *Pink is dispensable?*

It couldn't be: his mother sent him such affectionate letters.

He remembered Reynolds's criticisms of imperial power, his descriptions of the lot of the powerless. If the colony really needed such streets in order to prosper, it was easy to see Reynolds's point of view, and the concept of doing his best seemed punily insufficient. He prayed for guidance.

'Here,' said Kwok, stopping beneath the lean-to roof that sheltered the front of a hovel. There was no one sitting at the entrance to this one, no one mending shoes, remaking a bamboo basket, sewing, or gutting fish. But all the people who were busy with these tasks round about stared mistrustfully at Police Officer Wang when he knocked briskly on the decaying door with his truncheon.

There was washing on the bamboo poles that poked out from the wall. A gust of wind tried to slap a pair of trousers in Samuel's face. Flinching away, he almost trod in a large flat bamboo basket that held a foetid mess of pink shrimp paste: the last of the summer, he thought, left there especially for him.

He focused his eyes on the faded pair of red papers that had been put up either side of the door. They were peeling off. It was a long time since Chinese New Year. A joss-stick smouldered inside an old pickle jar for the Earth God, the only official who – in the coolies' eyes – had a right to report on the intimate detail of their lives. The Earth God reported to the District God, and so on up the divine hierarchy as far as the Jade Emperor himself. Master Feng had taught him this. It was exactly like the British Civil Service.

He saw half a dozen cockroaches erupt and scuttle away as the door shook under the impact of Wang's truncheon. From inside, a woman's voice demanded to know what they wanted.

'We have to come in!' shouted Wang. 'There are two officials here who need to see the inside of your house!'

'Anyone could say that,' retorted the woman – Samuel could just hear her, 'how do I know you're not robbers?'

Wang shouted: 'Government Service – open the door and you'll see.'

The woman asked: 'Open the door, and be robbed? My husband's going to be here soon, then you won't be so cheeky.'

Kwok nodded to Police Officer Ho who accosted a man mending

a pig-basket and forced him to come up to the door. The man shouted through the door that it was all right to open, that there were police officers and two officials on the other side. He added maliciously that one of the officials was a *gweilo*.

'A *gweilo*?' complained the woman. 'What's he want? We're good people here, no trouble, no stolen goods – '

Kwok shouted: 'We have to look at the state of your house. It's so that action can be taken to make your living conditions better. The foreign sir is here to make sure everything is done properly.'

'The landlord won't like it,' said the woman. 'He'll raise the rent if he has to get the house seen to. If we don't pay, he'll beat us. We came here because it's falling down: where else could we manage to live? Why does this *gweilo* have to come and make trouble for us?' There was a scuttle and cackle of poultry, and a baby wailed.

'If I were you,' recommended the basket-mender, 'I'd open up. It'll only make more trouble if you don't.'

Samuel felt horribly, dangerously sorry for the woman who was going to have to open her miserable dwelling for inspection: dear God, as long as he didn't cry! The poor had their pride, he thought, doggedly keeping his face stiff – though no one would think it. His stomach turned to see the door open. It churned when he smelt what was inside.

The place stank. It was a moment before he could see anything. Hens rans underfoot, and a pig grunted somewhere nearby. An old woman was feeding the baby with rice gruel.

The long room was divided into cubicles by bamboo mats hanging down from the low ceilings. Each would house one family: Kwok had told him on the way there.

Kwok said: 'The kitchen's certainly at the back, Mr Pink. There are probably pigs upstairs as well, that will be the reason for this dripping through the rafters.' Samuel sidestepped quickly. Kwok giggled. Samuel laughed at himself. He felt better.

Now that they were inside, the younger woman was nervously helpful. She flipped a partition up, and showed them a man sweating on a pallet underneath a bedshelf.

'He's ill,' she said. The man ignored them. 'He'll die soon,' she continued. Samuel shuddered. They walked through to the kitchen, where a murderous-looking chopper lay on a segment of tree-trunk in the middle of the room – if you could call it a room.

The woman laughed shrilly. She asked: 'Hasn't the *gweilo* seen enough? What did we do, to deserve this, devils in the house?'

'We'll go upstairs next,' said Kwok, unmoved. The dark upper floor was also divided into five separate spaces, all tiny, each home to a family. There were pigs as Kwok had predicted: two of them. There was an old grandfather who began to scream obscenities at them. Samuel's head ached. He remembered what Master Feng had taught him: When the Way prevails in the world, there is nothing for the ordinary people to argue about.

His pulse jumped, while the aggressive stench jarred, burned and fretted his senses. The question he'd asked Philips came back to him: What am I doing here? He remembered a sermon Mr Fawler had preached in Canton, taking as his text the Almighty's challenge: *What are you doing here, Elijah?* Mr Fawler had taken each word separately, emphasized them and given them ten minutes each of sermon time. Samuel couldn't remember what else Mr Fawler had said, only the confidence in his voice: could Samuel learn confidence from the missionary? Again, he appealed to God, but the usual silence greeted his prayer.

The building was a pattern of horror, exactly as Darley had described the tenements: no ventilation, no sanitation, no light, no space, pigs in the house – and his own intrusive presence the worst horror of all. He was sure Kwok and the policemen thought so too.

He thought: *What* am I doing here, what *am* I doing here, what am *I* doing here, what am I *doing* here, what am I doing *here*? The words sounded a chromatic series of discords inside his head. He thought how Jesus Christ had touched men with repulsive skin diseases, had wiped the encrusted eyes of the blind. That was holiness. He swallowed hard, and tasted pig muck and shrimp paste.

Darley was right, all these slums ought to come down and homes fit for people to live in should be built in their stead. Why should the rich squeeze profit out of the poor? The rents should remain low. No government could tolerate such conditions and retain its self-respect. There could be a fund, he could start it by making a generous donation from his salary. Then he remembered that he'd sent all his spare money to Reynolds, and he needed to buy himself a new suit. And still no word from God! He despaired.

Kwok came to him, shutting his little notebook. 'I think we've seen enough, sir,' he said.

The air in the street tasted fresh, like clear water. But he had to go into another street, into another house, and another, and another.

After a while, the stench was all through him, but he didn't get used to it. It was a miracle that he wasn't sick.

His head had become a belfry of pain by the time he got back to the office and his teeth were chattering: Philips saw him, realized he had malaria, and sent him back to his room at the Club, where he lay down. He was very ill indeed.

14

THE FALL
OF CITADELS

SAMUEL lay in bed suffering neck-breaking rigors. The mosquito-netting was a layered shroud spun round him by a monstrous female spider. Soon she'd come looking for him; she'd suck his blood out, drop by drop; he'd feel every minute of the death.

It was two in the morning, he couldn't move, and no one would come for hours. He couldn't reach the bell.

Pain ran over him: he thought it was a swarm of ants, nesting and breeding in his knees and elbow joints. Every few minutes his body locked and shivered. He could hear his teeth rattling.

It was his mother he was afraid of. He knew she'd done this to him. She hadn't forgiven him, she didn't love him. He'd gone to Taipingshan, and now he was ill. She must have intended it.

'Poor fly,' he said aloud. 'Poor fly.'

His head was splitting.

The door of the room opened, and she came in. She was dressed in flowing robes of cobweb silk, her crown was white and set with black pearls, but he couldn't see her face. Then he saw a smile – her teeth outlined it: she leaned over him.

'My dearest child,' she said. 'My dearest, precious child.'

He wanted to feel her arms round him, comforting him, but something drew her away.

A workday evening: Darley left the Club and strolled uphill through the dusk to the Garden Road terminus of the High Level Tramway, where he produced his season ticket and climbed into the angled open-sided car. By and by the Colonial Surgeon got in and sat beside him. The two men talked on and off as they waited for the tram to leave. They discussed the planned extension to Government House.

'A ballroom,' said Darley, and laughed. His mouth twisted into the laugh, as if he was biting a lemon.

The Colonial Surgeon said: 'We have to keep the ladies happy, don't we?' Then his eyes ran away from Darley's expression of leathern containment. He wished the driver would get in, but he was nowhere in sight: it wasn't time for the tram to leave yet.

Darley only said: 'Remember what it was like coming up here in a sedan chair?' and he still seemed to have the sour taste on his tongue. He bit his lip a little, imperceptibly, on the inside: it puckered his mouth.

The driver came in, sat down, and the little green tram began to move. Both men sat back in their seats with a sigh of content and let it draw them up the steep hillside among the clinging scrub. Neither admired the view: they were too used to it.

The tram came to a halt at Darley's stop. He nodded to the Colonial Surgeon and got out. His home was only a few steps away: it sat on the side of the hill, white, Doric-columned, red-roofed, a proud symbol of his status. Darley would far rather have lived in Robinson Road. Now his wife was cured, he was always meaning to tell her they were moving downhill, but he could never get the words out when it came to it.

Tonight, he thought. I might do it tonight. And I'll tell her Pink will come to dinner. Poor young fellows, he said to himself, what she did to them! At least Pink didn't hang himself. Got to keep an eye on him.

Tropical plants in pots were lined along the edge of the verandah – Mrs Darley was watering them. Her hand trembled when she saw her husband coming. He went straight up to her and pecked her on the cheek.

'Home, then?' she asked, smiling timidly. Her face was drained of colour. Her breasts seemed to have collapsed. Her gown enclosed her all the way up to her neck, as if it was the only thing that held her wounded flesh in place. She asked: 'And did you have a busy day?'

Now, he thought, she was safe. She moved slowly, like a cripple.

'Yes,' he said, adding, 'my dear,' to see how she'd react. She shrank. She was afraid. He could see it. He wanted to cry: You wanted my love. Now you can have it. There – I love you.

'Dinner almost ready?' he asked.

'Yes,' she whispered. She halted away from him. He didn't dare follow.

173

It would be another evening when he couldn't mention the move to Robinson Road.

'You've done your hair differently,' said Mrs Ellis to Miss Atkinson.

Miss Atkinson blushed. 'Yes. No – ' She admitted: 'Lily did it.'

Mrs Ellis inspected Miss Atkinson, her lips pursed. Miss Atkinson waited for her to order Lily back to the laundry. She wondered if she could leave the house with Lily. They could rent a little house together, and work as dressmakers. Lily could pretend to be her maid, but of course she'd be her companion, her best friend –

Mrs Ellis said: 'It looks very becoming. Do you think Lily could do something for my hair?'

Miss Atkinson stared.

Almost plaintively, Mrs Ellis said: 'Alicia, I don't believe God made us to be ugly.'

'No,' agreed Miss Atkinson, rather breathlessly.

'And another thing,' said Mrs Ellis. She took a deep breath and paused. Her sister held her breath and waited. 'The laundry work is very hard for the girls, with their bound feet – Mrs Darley on the Peak says she can find us as much embroidery work as we want for them, if they can learn. I think they can, don't you?'

Miss Atkinson was dreadfully, shamefully disappointed. She'd wanted the little house with Lily. And why was Beatrice looking at her like that, as if she was the one whose permission was needed?

'Oh, yes,' she said vaguely, 'you know best, Beatrice.'

Reynolds wrote: *Ironic that you choose this moment to ask me how you should live your life. I don't know, Samuel. I never have known, didn't you see that? I'm sitting in my lodgings, writing letters, visiting Register Offices, seeking out advertisements. I was interviewed for one post, but it turned out that the son, who needed a tutor, was an idiot. I may yet regret turning the father's offer down. I am sorry to hear that you have no influence in Hong-Kong – perhaps this may change?*

But to tell the truth, if I could knock the whole business to smithereens I would. A man tried to throw a bomb at the Prince of Wales last week, and I can see why. I can understand the despair and hatred that made him do it. He didn't succeed, he was killed himself. That's the way it usually turns out. I sit here in despair, unable to afford even a whore. I see nothing but misery all about me – like that idiot boy, writhing and slavering. My disgust wasn't his fault. But he has to endure it. How can man be just, when nature is so cruel? No wonder Henderson hanged himself. So why should I rail at you, out in Hong-Kong, possessing soil that belongs by rights to another people – they kill and torture their own race, no doubt. And here are the oppressed of this country, who don't care about anyone's sorrows but their own, and rejoice at the thought that their country – whatever that may mean – dominates others. The meaning of life is clear, Samuel – get yourself to the top of the heap, or as far up it as possible. At the bottom of the letter he'd scrawled: *I don't want to hear any more about Henderson. I can't bear it.*

Samuel smelt Taipingshan – there must have been a whiff of it lurking in his nostrils all this time. He couldn't contradict the substance of Reynolds's argument, but it was wrong of him to despair. Though there *was* no such thing as justice: the hope Master Feng had raised in him was illusory. The only hope lay in transformation, and that wasn't to be achieved by the efforts of man, but through God's grace. In which context, the consciousness of error was an advantage. Only he'd been waiting for transformation for a long time now, and it hadn't come. Again, he thought he needed a guide.

He couldn't go to the Dean, who was too diffident, too much of a gentleman. There was Fawler, of course, except that he didn't want to go to Fawler. Fawler was a vulgar fellow, and far too sure of himself. Then it came to him that Fawler had already saved him from vice. Perhaps he drew back from Fawler's enthusiasm because he was afraid of Christ, and that was why Christ hadn't visited him.

He threw himself on his knees and prayed for the cup to be taken away. It wasn't. He thought he felt the implacable will of God.

He must get back into his house, on God's terms. He must visit Fawler, who had been elected his proper penance.

'You're lucky to find me in,' remarked Mr Fawler, getting up from a rattan chair on his verandah and looking at Samuel with curiosity. 'I should be at the Men's Bible Class, but it had to be cancelled. The ceiling has most unfortunately come down in the Mission Church. Fortunately God has sent us the money for the repair. A wealthy Chinese convert.'

175

He knocked his pipe out into a small brass dish, and laid it down on the table at his elbow.

'Sit down, Samuel,' he said.

The wind rustled in the round-leaved banyan trees outside; their fibrous aerial roots stirred and groped towards the verandah, then fell back against the trunk. It was November, clear, blue and dry at last.

Now, thought Samuel, still standing up, I must make my sincerity obvious.

'I need Christ,' he said.

Mr Fawler said: 'I told you once before, Samuel, when I pulled you away from the promptings of base flesh: there is forgiveness. There is more joy in heaven over one sinner that repenteth – '

He put his arms round Samuel. Samuel tried not to breathe: Mr Fawler smelt strongly of mustard and his stomach was still weak after his illness.

'Be not afraid,' said Mr Fawler shortly. He stepped back from Samuel and surveyed him again. 'Oh!' he exclaimed, huskily – the dry air was affecting his throat – 'this shrinking flesh will be transformed, will become immortal on the latter day. I know!' he cried *mezzo forte*, building up for the crescendo, 'that my Redeemer liveth, and in my flesh I shall see God!' The Number One Boy looked in, thinking he might be needed, but he saw it was only the *gweilo* sir preaching and he went away again. Mr Fawler pointed to the sky: Samuel looked up and saw the blue enormous eye of God who saw everything. 'Plunge into His blood,' cried Mr Fawler, 'bathe in it, sink into its wondrous depths!'

'Servants,' said Samuel, recoiling before Mr Fawler could throw him into the flood, 'I have a problem with servants.'

Mr Fawler asked: 'You want my help with *servants?*'

'I need Christian servants,' explained Samuel.

'Convert them,' exclaimed Mr Fawler, 'my boy, convert them.'

'It's because of Henderson,' said Samuel. 'They want to bring a Taoist priest in to exorcize the house. I won't have it. But they won't work for me unless the house is exorcized. Surely you've heard.'

'You could move,' suggested Mr Fawler: he had a streak of realism about him. Samuel's heart sank. 'No,' decided Fawler. 'You mustn't show weakness. You must be an example to them.'

'There must be Christian Chinese,' said Samuel, 'you know them, don't you?' He was almost at the end of his tether. He wiped sweat off his forehead and into his fair hair.

Mr Fawler mused. Samuel watched his fleshy face with its full set of whiskers: it was even harder than he'd thought to consort with the godly. The mustard had permeated the air. He couldn't breathe.

'I shall ask my congregation,' said Mr Fawler finally. Samuel realized that the pause had only been for effect, and knew him for a charlatan, a dangerous pickpocket of men's souls. But it was too late to draw back, and there was nowhere else to go.

Lily had given Mrs Ellis a pretty haircut now, she had persuaded her to buy a few potted palms and a hibiscus for the yard at the back of the house.

'God's creation,' she'd cajoled, 'how could it fail to uplift our souls?'

When she'd first come to the Refuge, she'd been all but dead, desolate as the yard, but the ladies had tended her sickness and she was recovering. Now it was her turn to heal others. The white fields of laundry had blossomed into embroidered birds and leaves and flowers, and the other girls, who had hated her, were nice, if a little distant – they knew she'd done it. Only Rebecca looked at her askance.

She was still a servant, and the doors to the street kept her penned in.

But that was the way it had always been, it was the consequence of abandonment outside a city wall, of the terrible mortal crime of having been born a girl. The other girls in the Home were convicted of the same offence. They were abandoned women in every sense of the word, most of them sold into prostitution when they were still children. Some prisons were less disagreeable than others, Lily knew that, and yet there were so many times when she just wanted to run out on to the street. Especially when she saw the love in the English ladies' eyes.

Mrs Ellis stood in the small parlour and thought how heavy her heart had been all the years when the children she yearned after had failed to appreciate what she was doing, had escaped on to the streets, had lit incense-sticks to their heathen abominations after weeks, months, years of teaching. Even Rebecca, that very September, Rebecca had made paper money – out of tracts, of all materials. 'But Mrs Ellis, it is the Festival of Hungry Ghosts. Don't you want this house to be protected from demons?'

Lily would never have done such a thing: hadn't her nurse fed her on the milk and honey of Scripture? She caught herself thinking: I don't understand the Chinese. Lily is one of our own kind.

For a moment she wanted to open the doors: 'Get out,' she'd cry, 'if you want to go. I only want girls who really appreciate the good things in this house.' But where would her funding come from if she did that? The locks and bolts on the door represented – and guaranteed – the bindings of the cash box.

The sun came out and lit wet sparks on the pink hibiscus plant. The palms made explosions of green in the dim space between the back of the house and the steep hillside. The house had a verandah at the back only: this was why Mrs Ellis had bought it. It had been built by a Chinese family who valued privacy. The slope at the back, reinforced by a stout stone wall, was too much for girls with bound feet. Of course the door had to be opened to traders, which was how some of them got out. Or else the pimps smashed windows and came in to fetch the girls by force. Mrs Ellis slept with a revolver under her pillow, but if the abductors were well-armed themselves, she let the girls go. Then she felt ashamed, violated herself. It took her weeks to recover.

But Lily said she felt safe in the house. The softness in Lily's wide eyes warmed Mrs Ellis's heart. She had had an idea, just recently, that Lily's beauty of soul might warm other people's hearts as well. It was a tempting, seductive idea.

'Lily,' she said: 'I'd like you to testify to others, about what God has done for you. Do you feel able to do that?'

'Only if you'd come with me,' said Lily, 'and if they were kind to me.'

She was really frightened for a moment: Mrs Ellis took her hand firmly and patted it, pulled Lily to her and held her close. She stayed there, still, smelling the exquisite scent of Lily's hair, abandoned – she told herself quickly – to Divine Grace.

'I'd be with you all the time to protect you,' she said.

'I must do it,' whispered Lily, 'if you want me to.'

Mrs Ellis began to stroke Lily's hair, feeling how strong and smooth it was under her fingers. She let herself drift on that wave of sensuality, feeling every limb softening, sweetening, the child was so delicate, such a wonder!

Lily would have liked to enjoy Mrs Ellis's caresses, but they constricted her and frightened her. She was relieved when Mrs Ellis let go of her, and she had her body to herself again.

178

Samuel put on a silk hat and a black coat and went to church: there he listened to the Dean's sermons, the Bishop's sermons, the sermons of visiting clergymen from England. He'd leave no stone unturned to find God. After church, he went walking on the parade ground like everyone else. He met the wives of his colleagues: good morning Mrs Bradwell, good morning Mrs Philips – Mrs Philips was haggard and interesting – artistic was the word. Her hair was red and she wore long loose yellow shifts at the dinner parties where one met the Sassoons and the Kadoories as well as Mr Paul Chater and the members of Jardines. Good morning, new Mrs Caird: Scottish, small and dark and frightened of Mrs Philips who was too modern for her. Frightened too of Hong-Kong, where she had only just arrived – but not too recently to have got the malarial habit.

Mrs Darley didn't walk on the parade ground now. She could be seen – if she was well enough – in church, but she didn't stay.

There were young girls walking demurely with their families on the parade ground, with hats perched on top of their high-dressed hair and parasols to keep their faces white, and they smiled at Mr Pink, but guardedly. He wasn't earning enough to marry yet, and he was a little man. Some of their fathers said he was bumptious. He was making too much fuss about religion, he was too serious, he was only amusing as a butt, when he wasn't there.

Good morning Mrs Fawler, who came there with her husband after their own service was over. Mrs Fawler had a thin patient face and bright dark eyes: she agreed to everything her husband said. She did sterling work, said Mr Fawler on her behalf, among the Chinese convert women. She smiled, briefly, and Samuel caught a glimpse of irony on her face, of mocking faithlessness. He was frightened, then, of what was hidden under the stones.

He lifted his eyes up to the hills, as the psalmist had done – they'd sung the words that very morning. There were all the smart pillared houses, 'Isola Bella' among them, and, when he got back to the Club, he found a note from Mrs Darley, inviting him to dinner. He accepted.

For the first time for years, Miss Atkinson hardly noticed the onset of the dry season. Usually there was a morning when she woke up without pain and knew the wind had changed. Then she had three months of freedom before the damp set in again in spring.

This year Lily had taken her pain away already. Lily had done her hair and helped her make her clothes, had embroidered them with flowers – it was a wonder how quickly the child had learned. Lily had persuaded her to try Chinese herbs for her health and taken her out into the streets to find a herbalist's shop, Beatrice, astonishingly, having agreed to this when Miss Atkinson pointed out that there was no frustrated pimp on the lookout for Lily, Beatrice even more astonishingly having made no condemnation of the Chinese herbs.

The shop was frightening: jars of coiled snakes and gaping preserved lizards, strange white oval shapes, neat bundles of who-knew-what, trays of dulled deer antlers, rhinoceros horn. Miss Atkinson stood nervously at the end of the counter while Lily talked in Cantonese to the herbalist.

'I'll shut my eyes,' she said to Lily, 'when I swallow it. I know it'll make me better. I know you'll never do me any harm.'

'Let's go home,' said Lily, taking the parcel from the herbalist's assistant. 'It's so noisy out here on the street.'

It was an almost unendurable violence, when she'd been shut away so long, the yelled '*Maai!*' of the hawkers crying their wares, 'Pig's-blood congee, fish congee, chickens, ginger, rice, feather-dusters, pork . . .' Miss Atkinson's love and dependence shrieked still louder in her ears and she couldn't bear it. So she'd go back to prison and try to lose herself in her embroidery work.

She reminded herself that she loved the English ladies, she wanted so much to be nice to them, only Miss Atkinson seemed to want so much, so did Mrs Ellis sometimes, something Lily was afraid she'd never be able to give. And she couldn't stop trying to give it to them, though she didn't know what it was, and she was afraid the effort would kill her.

Samuel was all but lost to sin on the night of the Darley's dinner. It was the bow-tie that did it. The Number One Boy used to do it for him: Reynolds had been adept at it, now there was no one, and he was making a confounded mess of it as usual. Everyone would avert their eyes from his neck. He thought what a fool he was. It would be so easy to give in, and if he got the house exorcized, he'd find servants without any difficulty at all. He didn't think he'd lose face. It was now that he was losing face. He remembered Mrs Philips: 'And this is Mr Pink, the staunch opponent of idolatry.' She had smiled ironically, making him feel naive and clumsy. And he was going to be late at Mrs Darley's house. He tried again, and the whole thing fell apart.

He let his hands dangle. After all, he had a duty to the British community. Why should he care? He could move. He was sure it could be arranged. Or he could turn a blind eye. It could be argued that he owed it to his mother. And as for God, where was he?

There was a knock at the door.

He shouted: 'Come in!' and Mr Fawler entered the room.

Behind Mr Fawler was a Chinese man with a young boy at his heels: black clothes, trousers, tunic and hat, black queues hanging down from the back of their heads, their faces alert and interested, taking in every detail of the room.

The man had a hare lip: he was quite hideous. Samuel knew these were the new servants, sent at the double by God. The hare-lipped man was so unpleasant he could only be the gift of the Almighty. And now he'd never be able to backslide, never even be able to swear, not with Fawler's men in the house. It was a fearful thing to fall into the hands of the living God.

'My boy,' breathed Mr Fawler, 'I've found them.'

The man said something. Samuel made out that he was offering his help, and speaking pidgin. Automatically, he snapped: 'Don't talk pidgin to me. I speak Cantonese.'

'Yes, sir,' said the man in Cantonese: it was a little easier to understand him in his own language. He took hold of the trail of black silk wrinkling its way down from Samuel's collar, and the bow-tie was there in a minute. His hands brushed Samuel's neck: the bow-tie felt like a noose.

'Christian servants,' commentated Mr Fawler, as one arranging a revival meeting complete with testimony, 'safe, Samuel, godly, rescued from the mouth of the Juggernaut who would have swallowed them alive into eternal roasting!'

The manservant was picking at the rest of Samuel's outfit, looking to see if there was anything else that needed to be done.

'Sir,' he said in the horridly mangled voice, 'look, these creases, and this shirt, sir, if I look after you it will never be so badly cared for as this.'

Samuel felt he must smile at him, because he did represent salvation. He asked Mr Fawler: 'How did he learn to tie a bow-tie?'

'My wife trained him,' said Mr Fawler simply. 'And his soul,' he said severely to the Chinese, 'you will help tend his immortal soul, and he yours. You can see he's saved, Samuel. You can always tell a convert by the new light in his eyes.'

'My son,' said the man, indicating the boy. 'He will help you, too.' The son smiled, and said nothing.

Samuel was shocked at how much he disliked the man. On the other hand, you couldn't have both the satisfactions of morality and the full range of commercial choice granted to the careless. He was stuck with the satisfactions of morality. And growing later for Mrs Darley's dinner.

'His name is Paul Cheung,' said Mr Fawler.

Eagerly, Cheung said: 'You have trouble with superstitious Chinese servants, sir, if I come to work for you I have no fear of ghosts, Mr Fawler has given me Jesus and this keeps me safe. And my son, too.'

The son smiled and nodded. 'Oh happy day,' he said. 'Jesus washed my sins away.'

'The son,' said Mr Fawler sternly, 'has been baptized James.'

Sadly, Samuel arranged with Cheung that he should help him move out of the hotel in two days' time, should prepare the house for Samuel's re-entry:

'I'm strong,' said Cheung. 'I can do the work of three.'

Samuel knew that Chinese people were ignorantly prejudiced against the deformed: he couldn't quite remember why. Cheung was outcast, lonely: he ought to give him Christian love, it was dreadful that he was repelled by him. But he couldn't make himself believe in Cheung's conversion. By eating Christianity, Cheung had managed to improve his chances in life, to the point, now, of elbowing his way into Samuel's house. And everyone who visited would have to look at that lip, unless he served his guests their drinks himself, which he couldn't do. He wondered what would happen if the government assigned him another man to share his house, if that man came to him and said: 'Look, old boy, do we have to put up with the split lip?'

Yet the Cheungs wanted to get out of Taipingshan. How could he refuse to employ them?

'God bless you, my boy,' said Mr Fawler.

'God bless you, sir,' said Cheung.

And Samuel thought: how dare he? It's none of his business to tell God to bless a gentleman. Why wasn't his own religion good enough for him?

He was late for dinner with the Darleys.

'I'm ill,' said Mrs Darley weakly. 'Doctor Mackenzie said I oughtn't to be entertaining. I'm only doing it for you, John, I hope you understand that.'

The lady's maid had withdrawn from the room when the master came in. As soon as Mrs Darley was alone with her husband, her eyes grew darker, warier, watching his movements.

He had to say: 'It's very good of you, my dear.'

There were words and actions that hung between them, her words, her repeated: 'No!' echoing through the huge pompous bedroom with its dark-red velvet curtains dripping stained moisture, its palms with their knifelike fronds. 'No! No! No!'

His hand on the key in the lock, from the outside, her fists on the door. His steps, hurrying away.

His silence, while she screamed: 'No! John, no! Come back! What have I done?'

But she knew what she'd done. The fear of retribution had always given the edge to her pleasure, now retribution had come, and had removed pleasure altogether.

She shivered slightly, and wrapped her silk voile shawl round her. She had grown so thin now: she could hardly bear to eat.

Darley wanted to put a hand on her arm: but he knew she'd shrink away. He'd been equally afraid of her and of other men's pity. No one had ever had any sympathy with him. And his wife had won, surrounding herself with a façade of piety, taking to good works – that home for prostitutes she was supporting – now she had the sympathy. But that was the way it was, people liked women who were weak and damaged.

He caught the echo of many voices, whispering where he could just hear them:

'Poor Mrs Darley, how she has suffered!'

'We must go down,' said Mrs Darley, picking up the slim ebony cane she had to lean on nowadays.

Why was it she wouldn't understand? She'd wanted his love. Now, when she had it, she pulled away from him.

He's not a bad man, thought Mrs Darley. Only I can't bear to have him come near me.

They went downstairs, Mrs Darley supporting herself with the stair-rail and the stick. They sat down to wait for their guests, who were mostly deeply religious people. Mrs Darley had decided there wasn't room for the Colonial Surgeon and Darley hadn't dared protest. Mrs Darley was still a resourceful woman.

Samuel's lateness was another irritation: Darley was beginning to think he'd forgotten the dinner. He came at last, just as the newest member of the Fishing Fleet was wishing she could faint to escape the humiliation of going in to dinner unattended. But the sharp-elbowed girl had no skill in fainting and that was why she'd had to come halfway round the world in a bootless search for a husband. She was too honest. She could neither lie, flirt, nor faint, and Samuel wouldn't like her. She was doomed.

Mrs Darley had built up skills in all three activities – and now she was always on the edge of a faint. It was she who toppled over, at the moment that Samuel came into the room. She fell into the irresistible embrace of the dark, the waters rushed her over the edge of the world. Abandonment had brought delight once, now all she could get was a moment's freedom from pain.

She lay in a fuzz of hushed concerned female voices and a frou-frou of muslin and taffeta. One of the ladies pulled her skirts down to cover her legs, another pulled out smelling salts, another cradled her head till Darley brought a cushion.

The other men retreated, and stood in a huddle at the far side of the room. They fiddled with their bow-ties and eased their waistbands, though there was no food inside there yet. Samuel stood on the edge of this group, stealing glances at the huddle of silken women.

She lay as if wounded to death, and Darley knelt by her side, burning with a tenderness that could have no outlet. He stroked the wasted cheek, held the limp white hand, put his hand on her side and felt the grid of her ribs: or was it the whalebone of her corsets?

'She looks,' said the wife of a missionary, 'so spiritual.'

She came to herself. She tried to sit up: 'don't move,' the ladies said.

Gallantly, she whispered: 'No, it was a temporary fit, I don't need to lie down.'

She even said: 'Good evening, Mr Pink. I'm ashamed to have disgraced myself in front of you.'

'Oh, no,' protested Samuel, 'no disgrace – '

He was shaken to see her so changed. They'd sliced her plump deliciousness off, and she had no juice left. Yet at least she had found God. Whereas he was still in outer darkness.

It came to him that he hadn't sinned enough yet, but he hustled the thought away.

15

REVIVAL

'I feel myself shaken,' said Mr Fawler, 'at times like this.'

His wife nodded, and went on stitching little dresses for Chinese orphan girls.

'I've given a great deal, you know that, my dear,' he said, 'come so far from Abbotsport,' a beam of pleasure lightened his face for a moment at the thought of how far he had come, then vanished, 'even though they won't send me into China, I have been faithful, my dear, you know that. I'm prepared to give everything, as much as is asked of me. I'd endure any hardship, even martyrdom.' He paused to look into his soul's mirror, where he saw his head crowned with thorns. His eyes spoke God's triumph and the blood streamed down into his whiskers. He said, 'I can't understand why they won't send me.'

Mrs Fawler said: 'You have important work to do here.'

He let out his breath in annoyance. 'Mrs Darley doesn't think so. I always knew she was a vicious woman. Why Mrs Ellis chose her, I have no idea.'

Mrs Fawler licked her thread and slid it expertly through the needle's eye. 'She's repented,' she said.

'Good works,' said Fawler, 'oh, yes, she's never sent any money to *our* church. Any of the other ladies would have sent me an invitation. I suppose Mrs Ellis chose her because she's another interesting penitent – *she* should give her testimony as well as the Chinese girl.'

'Exactly,' said his wife. He felt better.

'Curiosity,' he said. 'They'll all be attending out of despicable curiosity. I don't suppose it would be worth going without an invitation – '

'No, my dear,' said Mrs Fawler. She held the dress up and inspected the seam. She wasn't quite satisfied with it and began to unpick it.

'There's joy in heaven over the repentant sinner – I don't question that – but whether the repentance is sincere, ah, that's the question.'

'Yes, my love,' said Mrs Fawler. 'Repentance must be sincere. Every feeling in the Christian breast must be sincere, untainted by self.' She shot a quick glance at him.

'To make a show of it – and not in any church – in a drawing room, and in front of gawpers – '

'Who,' asked Mrs Fawler, 'has been invited?'

'The Bishop,' said Mr Fawler. 'The Dean. The Minister of the Union Church. The Postmaster-General. The new young man at the German Lutheran mission – Marius. The Swiss Pastor. The Portuguese priest. The chairman of the Bank – ' His voice faltered. Everyone, in fact, who was anyone in the true Christian society of Hong-Kong. Except Mr Fawler. No one had even told him: he'd heard about it by accident. Had they hushed it up, like school-children trying to keep him out of a treat?

'I must pray about it,' said Mr Fawler.

'You are quite right,' his wife said. 'The Lord will know what to do for you. My love, I've made seven of these little dresses in two days.'

All the same, he wondered – falling on his knees in his study – why none of the other ministers had insisted he be invited, refused to come unless *every* important minister working in Hong-Kong were represented. Perhaps they didn't think he was important.

'He was despised,' he murmured, 'and rejected of men.'

He longed for China, but, failing that, Mrs Darley's drawing room would have done. He wanted so much to see what the young woman looked like. Everyone would talk about her testimony, about her interesting public repentance. They would say: 'Didn't you hear her, Fawler? Weren't you invited?'

Samuel hadn't expected an invitation to the prayer meeting, but Paul Cheung brought it in with his bacon and eggs at breakfast time. Paul Cheung was a good servant, unobtrusive, efficient. Samuel wished he could be more tolerant of the hare lip.

He didn't want to go. He was afraid he might find Lily coarsened by hard work – or decide that she had always been coarse – he was afraid of her altogether. Yet who was he to refuse an invitation that might be the mysterious work of Divine Grace?

He met Darley in the urinal at the office and opened his mouth to mention the meeting, but Darley got in first.

'Well, have you managed to stop the District Watch complaining about my people?' And laughed.

There were rumours – Samuel knew about them – that Kwok and his colleagues were bribed by the property-owners to inspect streets they wanted to pull down anyway. There was also gossip that Darley was taking his cut, but it was an axiom of the colony that the white man was above corruption. And in any case, the Celestial Kingdom was far more corrupt. Even Master Feng had admitted that. Nobody had ever tried to bribe Samuel and he was disappointed. He'd practised his dignified rejection often enough in his head. It would make the venial Chinese sense his royal breeding as well as the power of Christ.

'Why did they come here,' asked Darley, buttoning up his underpants, 'if they didn't want to comply with British law? Because they can make a better living here than they can in China. Well then, they take the consequences.' He began to do up his trousers. He was in a bad mood.

Samuel washed his hands, dried them, and pushed his hair back.

'How did you get that scar?' asked Darley, distracted. He ran water into the basin.

'I fell off a horse,' said Samuel.

'Ah!' said Darley.

There was spite in his voice. He washed his hands savagely. 'Where would all this water come from,' he asked, 'if it wasn't for my department? And so you're going to my wife's soirée this evening.'

Samuel said: 'I'm interested in the mission field, sir.'

Darley laughed. 'I imagine there'll be plenty of gentlemen coming to see this young Chinese girl – but whether she's really repented of her evil ways – I'll bet she's looking out for another gullible ass.'

It was a dangerous moment, something lay between them, something Samuel couldn't understand, but he feared it might engulf him. Darley saw his confusion, wanted to say: It's all right, lad. Don't be afraid of me. He said nothing. He moved his lips, chewing the invisible straw that always seemed to lie between them, and grinned suddenly. Samuel sighed, relieved and oddly warmed.

'I shan't see you there,' said Darley, grinning again. His face wore the careful helpless expression of an old dog playing with a young one. 'I'm going to the Club.'

It was meant as an apology, and Samuel understood.

Mrs Darley had the stage set for the repentant sinner. The Chinese staff decked the purple chairs and sofas with white lace antimacassars as crisp and clean as altar cloths, and washed the leaves of the palm trees in their pots. All the occasional tables had to be polished as well as the brassware that sat on them. The ornaments were dusted, the carpet cleaned with tealeaves. On the wall hung the picture Mrs Darley had ordered from England: it had arrived a fortnight ago and had just been framed by Ah Fong, of Wellington Street. The subject was: *The Repentant Harlot Washes the Feet of Christ.*

Her husband hated it.

Mrs Darley was suffering again today, so she sat on one of the sofas to await her guests. She needn't point the picture out: Ah Fong had made a small brass plate and engraved it with the subject and the name of the artist. This was the second brass plate: he'd engraved the first one: *The Repellant Harlot Washes the Feet of Christ.* Something she thought these people did on purpose.

The painting was in the style Mrs Darley liked: Christ was depicted as an emaciated blond with an intense angelic countenance, his hair and halo fusing brightly above his head: the harlot had a lot of black hair in a dense frizz and her clothing was attractively lacking in places. There was some ambiguity about the whole thing, and Mrs Darley saw it with secret pleasure.

Lily and Mrs Ellis were already in the house, discreetly awaiting the moment when they would be brought out for public view: a real harlot, unambiguously repentant. Lily was Chinese, after all.

Mrs Darley wore pale mauve, half-mourning, as everyone knew. The silk of her dress, though several shades lighter, was exactly the same tint as the deep purple velvet of the sofa: Mrs Darley had chosen the colour carefully. She wore a high white collar and a cap. She had a sweet small green bird caged in the room: its eye was ringed with white and it hopped and chimed like a bell. The cage was too close to the gaslight, and the bird was dying of the fumes, but Mrs Darley didn't know that.

The guests arrived. The servants moved among them, offering tea and cakes. The gentlemen stood balancing their cups and saucers, the ladies sat. The chiming of the bird's song was lost in their chatter, though one or two of the ladies went over to its cage and made kissing noises at it. The gaslights sizzled with a persistent high-pitched wheeze.

It was a mixed bag of well-off colonials and austerer missionaries, but no one was particularly elegant. No matter: the colony had its own standards of dress, solid, middle class. The ladies were rather smarter than the gentlemen, that was all. There was gossip; malice disguised as charity. There was even flirtation, even the possibility of something more. You couldn't get away from such things. Copulation could be carried out, if necessary, under a thick blanket of piety: Mrs Darley could tell, as she sat with her feet up on the sofa, which people were getting ready to go under the blanket together. Her memories brought an attempt at arousal: it was agony. She shuddered and bit her lip.

Paul Cheung was wonderfully clever at getting his master out of the house, and Samuel was punctual tonight. Mrs Darley wondered why she'd invited him. His wide-eyed hunger – she had no idea for what – irritated her and made her nervous. He didn't know enough, he didn't use people or circumstances. Mrs Darley knew that even suffering could be a means to an end: in her case a means of retaliation against her husband and all of Hong-Kong. Life was like that. You had to see the shape of things, and do what you could in the circumstances. Mrs Darley didn't believe in God, but she found him quite useful.

She whispered in the ear of the Minister of the Union Church, who begged the company for their attention. He prayed. The gentlemen stood, the ladies sat and all held their eyes shut. Mrs Darley cast hers down, rather than shutting them, and saw huge black polished ants running over the carpet. Borax, she thought. Again.

She thought of John, down at his club. He was uncomfortable because he couldn't come home. He was uncomfortable about her. She couldn't love him: he wasn't a bad man, but that didn't make any difference.

Lily waited in a side-room. She was frightened.

'You're going to do us credit,' insisted Mrs Ellis, trying not to show that she was nervous too. She'd thought she was bringing Lily to a group of ladies.

On the other hand, the men were all God-fearing. Virtuous men – Mrs Darley had shown her the list. Missionaries, ministers, government servants and taipans with large families to whom they were devoted, the young cadet who'd made such a brave stand against idolatry. There were even some among them who would listen to a woman's opinion.

They were men, all the same. Men who had come to listen to a penitent whore. Or just to a whore.

She wished she hadn't worn her white lace collar and little bit of blue ribbon. She ought to have left her dress plain grey: it would have been more appropriate, given the circumstances. She thought she looked frivolous. She was endangering everything she believed in by coming here.

She asked Lily: 'What – how do you feel – there are men here.' Her voice tailed off.

Lily said: 'Men have hurt me so much. But I shall speak, Mrs Ellis. For your sake.'

She hoped that was the right thing to say. She felt as if she was wearing a corset, fear had enclosed her chest so tightly. She was sure they'd hate her. She stretched her hand out to Mrs Ellis, but Mrs Ellis was too lost in her fearful thoughts to notice. Lily put her hand back carefully in her lap.

Mrs Ellis was thinking about the money, which would help her expand her work. There was really very little choice.

The Number One Boy came to fetch them.

There was a mass of faces, people sitting in front, standing behind, and Miss Atkinson's face smiling determinedly at one side. Lily looked down at the floor before she could see anything else. Her heart thudded: she was sure no sound would come out when she spoke.

'Dear friends,' said the Union Church minister, who was acting as Master of Ceremonies, 'now Lily will give you her testimony. You will hear how she was saved from Vice and found Christ. Lily!' He gestured at her, and sat down.

There was a silence, which she had to fill. They were waiting to hear her, but it couldn't be she who had to speak, surely someone else would come out and say the words for her? Then she could run away.

She'd rehearsed her speech with Mrs Ellis, she knew it off by heart. All she had to do was to open her mouth. Or her heart. She might as well take her clothes off in front of them.

She'd have to say it. The little bird sang: it felt like encouragement, since she didn't know the bird was dying.

'Dear ladies,' she said – the words came after all, but she tripped over them and had to take care with them, 'dear gentlemen, I was cast away before I could even speak, my father left me outside the walls of Soochow to die. That is all I know about my family. But I have found a heavenly Father, and a new family in Christ, through the kind and gracious merciful work of my dear friend Mrs Ellis – ' she felt the tears running down her face. She was shamed for ever.

They cooed and cleared their throats, they made sounds of sympathy. She could feel their warmth.

She was doing what was wanted: why did it hurt so much? She was a little girl again, feeling Mr Jackson's hands on her sore nipples. What would they say, if she told them about that?

'Oh,' she exclaimed – she'd practised the inflection – 'how I long for His love, and for the love of all my sisters and brothers in Christ! I would do anything to deserve the love of God, having mistakenly hoped to find happiness in the love of a man.'

Ah Kuen, she thought. I love you. I hate you. I hope all your sons die.

Mrs Ellis knew the bad bit was coming, the part she'd never have written for Lily if she hadn't been deluded about the guest list. She looked resentfully at Mrs Darley. She should have been told.

'I was used,' said Lily in her beautiful clear voice, 'by the man who found me abandoned, a little helpless baby, who picked me up and took me away, who should have protected me. I will say no more,' she said, with genuine bitterness. The audience were feeding off her distress, they were flesh-eaters, drinkers of blood.

Mrs Ellis had told her to look round at them. She hadn't done so yet. When she did, she saw Samuel. She'd forgotten his existence, but she recognized him at once.

How could he have been afraid when the grace of God was so sweet? It ran through Samuel's body, better than wine, Divine love washing his sins away. Lily was its mediator, the purified sinner, the outcast reclaimed, the stranger made familiar. His knees began to twitch: they wanted to be on the ground. He cleared his throat for fear he might open his mouth in praise. It was hard to do things decently and in good order when you were ecstatic with such joy. He was going to cry.

'But worse,' said Lily, remembering the words, 'the worst thing the Englishman did to me was to fail me in matters of religion, and tear me from the faith of Christ my English nurse had begun to teach me – but she was taken from me when I was still a child. I miss her so much!'

The ladies made more sniffing noises. The Postmaster-General was sobbing openly. Samuel let the tears run: he sat there, wet-faced, his eyes shining. She could bear *his* emotion, bear everything now, because she wanted to tell him what it had been like. But not in Mrs Ellis's words – she wished she could speak for herself.

While Mrs Ellis thought: We're there. She heard the sighs transform into the rustle of ten-dollar notes. The little bird chimed sadly in the pause. No one had noticed it was dying, but if they would only move it away from the gaslamp –

Lily said: 'I was forbidden to read the Bible. I was dragged into terrible heathen temples and removed from the dear consoling love of Christ.' She thought: I'll burn a few incense-sticks to Kwan Yin, if I'm ever allowed out on my own. Perhaps she'll persuade all the gods to forgive me. 'I was corrupted in the essential things of life,' she said, 'but God in his mercy sent hardship to me. Through sorrow, through being outcast, through beggary, He purified me. He sent my dear Mrs Ellis to find me and draw me away from evil. And I am so much happier with her and her dear sister and my other sisters. I cannot describe to you the perfect harmony and mutual strengthening of that house in Pokfulam Road, and the bliss of hearing the Bible read every day, and the prayers – dear ladies, dear gentlemen, I beg you to join me in prayer.'

It was over. She remembered that she was going to go back to the Refuge, back to prison. She felt wretched again, soiled, and she wasn't allowed to speak to the young man. She remembered his hands round hers.

There was a rustle and a sighing as all in the room bent their heads and clasped their hands. Lily led them in the Lord's Prayer.

They had just got to the trespasses when there was a disturbance at the door of the room. Mr Fawler stood there, waving his arms. He had thought of an urgent message for the Minister of the Union Church, and had arrived just in time to catch a glimpse of Lily. He looked for Samuel, and saw the expression on the puppy's face. Oh, wickedness, he thought with great pleasure. No good will come of this.

Lily took no notice of him. She said: 'for ever and ever, Amen.' She left.

Mrs Ellis, who was far less interesting, remained centre stage. But she was touched with Lily's patina, gilded with her charm. She had rescued this exquisite creature, arranged her as the chief flower in a bouquet presented to the guest of honour, God the Father. The audience was in raptures to have been invited to the presentation ceremony.

Samuel stepped back and leaned against a velvet curtain – dry, at this time of year, though delicately patterned with traces of black mildew. There was a heavenly fragrance in his nostrils.

He was sure he loved everyone now – he tried out a few people – Paul Cheung, Mr Fawler. Yet, blinded as he was at last by grace, he didn't see any of them. He cut the Dean dead, pushed straight past Harrison from Butterfield and Swire, and failed to pay his respects to Mrs Darley. All he could see was the collection plate: it was already full of money – money for Lily, money for God. He emptied his wallet into the plate. He wouldn't be able to take the tram. He didn't care. He'd walk home. There'd be neither thieves nor venomous serpents on his path. God would keep him safe.

'Good evening, Mr Fawler,' said Mrs Darley right behind him. 'I see you couldn't stay away.'

'An urgent message – ' said Mr Fawler uncomfortably, 'a matter of life and death – ' he slid away from her and took the Minister of the Union Church by the arm. 'My dear fellow – '

Samuel left, forgetting his hat.

The moon was full, larger than it had ever been in Dorset, turning the waves to gleaming fishscales far below. He could see sparks of light attached to a fleet of fishing junks. The little yellow points jumped among the white moongleams. The whole colony was blessed by the mild light, lit by blessing. God was working His purpose out.

A slight wind blew against his face: 'The wind,' he cried to the empty night, 'bloweth where it listeth, and thou hearest the sound thereof, but canst not tell whence it cometh and whither it goeth: so is every one that is born of the Spirit.'

He set out on the long and lonely road down to the Mid-Levels.

Back in Mrs Darley's drawing room, Mrs Ellis, her cheeks burning with excitement, was enrolling visitors to the Refuge. It was an idea that had come to her while she was answering questions, and she'd presented it as a carefully thought-out plan. All the ladies wanted to see Lily and it would increase the orders for embroidery and fine needlework if they were allowed to come. Of course Mrs Ellis would have to inspect the premises most carefully before each visit, to make sure there were no incense-sticks burning to the Earth God or the Kitchen God.

She had even conceded that certain carefully selected gentlemen might be allowed to visit. Under strictest supervision, of course. Ministers of religion, she thought, and very old gentlemen. Then she remembered that Mr Jackson had been a very old gentleman and wondered if it might be better to stick to the young. These were the complications of success, and there was still something hardy and stern in her that longed for the old days of the laundry.

All the same, the plate was filling up with ten-dollar notes and silver. Mrs Darley had sent the servants for a larger one. The laundry-wish withdrew to growl almost unnoticed in a fastness deep within her. Mrs Ellis kept enrolling visitors.

Paul Cheung recited the charm against evil spirits. Then he threw it on to the heap of paper he had stacked up in the room where Henderson had died. He burned paper models of everything Henderson could conceivably need in Hell, a smart suit, a top hat, a pretty concubine, a stack of money, a rickshaw complete with rickshaw boy, a bed, a table, a chair. He watched the blaze with satisfaction.

If anyone had questioned him, he would have told them he was a practical man, but it didn't occur to him to question himself. He did what was proper to do. To fail to propitiate dangerous spirits was as foolish as to forget your clothes and parade naked through the streets. Paul Cheung was no fool.

Afterwards, he tucked another charm into a crack in the wall. Then he opened the windows wide so that Samuel shouldn't smell any smoke when he came home.

I came home from my Wonderful Experience, wrote Samuel, *and went straight into the room where Henderson died. I felt a sense of heavenly peace. I noted a faint sweetness in the air, I believe. It's a beautiful thing to write. What a battle there has been!* He continued his letter to poor Reynolds. *It is laid on me by the Spirit to write this letter. I am now full of the joy of God and am strong enough to withstand all earthly temptations. Believe that there is nothing anyone could do to me – not even having me thrown in prison – that could disturb my happiness. There is hope, Reynolds, we must build, build with God behind us. If we love Him, our actions will be right. There is no need to agonize. As long as we practise true repentence. God offers Himself to you, too, my friend. You could feel that heavenly grace descending like a dove, smell the ineffable fragrance of its pinions.* He sniffed the air: he knew it was Lily's sweetness that permeated it. He must see her again. He'd go to the Refuge with a large donation: they'd have to let him in.

He wrote: *I can understand the despair that led you to think of destruction. Now I shall pray that you are vouchsafed the bliss that fills me at this moment.*

He was intensely relieved that he had been allowed to realize his ambition.

The ladies came. They came so often that Mrs Ellis had to ration the visits. Once a week only, and only two ladies at a time. They gave money. They kissed Lily, they brought her little presents of food, they gave her Bibles bound in white leather. They didn't offer her nicer clothes.

They wanted her to remain a picturesque penitent, in a penitent's coarse cotton. That was what they came to see. She hated the gleam of relish in their eyes.

Miss Atkinson didn't like it either. Miss Atkinson didn't want to share Lily. Lily heard her arguing about it with Mrs Ellis: the ladies had asked Mrs Ellis if Lily could come to massage their aching limbs, up on the Peak, Miss Atkinson said if that happened she'd leave the Refuge at once. She said Lily wouldn't have any time or energy left for her if she had to do the other ladies, and she'd fall ill, did Mrs Ellis realize, she scolded, what it was like to spend all her days in pain? Of course not.

Lily remembered that she'd wanted Miss Atkinson to grow more selfish: now – when she saw the hunger on their faces – she wondered if they'd pull her apart between them.

She thought of the little fair-haired man whose hands had been so gentle with her. She dreamed she found a red thread tied round her ankle: it stretched away from her and out of the door. When she reached down and tugged it lightly, he came running, his finger along the thread, his eyes full of joy as they had been when he'd seen her at Mrs Darley's. She laid her head in his lap and told him how unhappy she was. But afterwards she woke up on the hard bed in the room she shared with three other girls, and stared at the text hanging across the jagged crack in the limewashed wall: *Go and Sin No More.*

Then Miss Atkinson went down with a fever, and Lily persuaded Mrs Ellis to let her go out on her own to the Chinese herbalist's for medicine: Mrs Ellis agreed, rather helplessly. That was how it was, nowadays, she wasn't in control any more.

Mrs Ellis would never have believed that Alicia would rebel against her. She kept forgetting to exercise with weights.

She went to walk round the deserted laundry room, sniffing the waxy odour of dried-out soap. The Home sent its laundry out, now, while the girls did cutwork and appliqué on silk and fine muslin. She knew it was ruining their eyes.

Lily slipped into the Temple of Kwan Yin in Cat Street on her way back from the herbalist's, and bought three incense-sticks out of the change: Mrs Ellis wouldn't miss it because she didn't know how much Chinese medicine cost. It was only right: she'd offended the Chinese gods for the Refuge's sake, so the Refuge must pay for Kwan Yin's merciful intercession.

She knelt on the little red cushion and kowtowed three times to the remote figure of the goddess. When her head was down she felt more peace, more safety than she'd ever felt when praying to the Christian god, or reading the Bible. It was hard to drag herself away.

She stood up and saw Mr Wells standing behind her.

He knew her at once. He was embarrassed to see her. He asked her if she was working as a servant? She told him where she was living.

'I'm relieved,' he said, 'I wondered what had become of you.' He shifted from foot to foot. Lily hated him: he might have wondered, but he'd done nothing. But she wanted him to tell her how Mr Jackson had died. She had to know if he'd mentioned her.

'No,' said Mr Wells: he thought the lie was kinder to her. He looked at the floor and rubbed his hands against his Chinese robe. 'He was mad,' he said. 'I'd never have taken him with me if I'd known.'

But he'd been shaken by Jackson's death: now he shed a little of the burden on to her, since she was so eager to hear.

He said: 'I took him to the t'ai chi Master, the one he wanted to learn from. He was eager to learn the art of chi kung. The Master wouldn't teach him. He said he wasn't at the right stage. He told Jackson he hadn't learned how to live at all, let alone for ever.'

Lily wrapped her hands round her breast because her heart was aching.

'It was true,' said Mr Wells with difficulty. 'He didn't understand the Taoism he'd studied so long. He couldn't accept the law of change.'

'No,' said Lily. 'He couldn't.'

'Then he met the monk,' said Mr Wells, shaking his head. 'A crooked fellow, ragged and wall-eyed. He thought it was the same monk who'd sold him that scroll – you know – years ago. As soon as he mentioned the text, of course the fellow played up to him: yes, he said, he'd been looking for him.'

Lily's flesh crawled: she kept a tight hold on herself.

Mr Wells went on: 'So Jackson asked the monk what he had for him this time, and the monk fetched out a box and said he had a Pill of Immortality. He wouldn't take money for it: he had Jackson buy him a meal from a foodstall. If you ask me, the monk was mad as well. I even began to ask myself if I was mad. Jackson took the pill: I told him not to.'

Lily asked: 'Did he die quickly?'

'No,' said Mr Wells. He turned back to the monk who sold red altar candles and bought three. He stuck them in the huge sand-filled cauldron in front of Kwan Yin's image, lighting them from a candle that was already burning. The flame burst fatly from the enormous wicks, letting out black puffs of smoke. Lily thought Mr Wells wanted to get away from her, but he turned to her again.

His face was torn with grief. He said: 'Everything he did, in order to live forever, it was all false. I suppose you know that by now. I don't believe that text – the one the monk sold him – was genuine. I looked at it, after he died.'

He rubbed a hand against his cheek. He said: 'He died in agony. He screamed and vomited. I don't know what was in the pill. He wasn't able to mention you. Forget him, child. He had many delusions. You were part of one of them.'

Lily walked away from him. She couldn't have spoken. She didn't want Mr Wells to see her cry. She didn't want to cry at all for faithless Mr Jackson. She'd let him do everything he wanted with her and he'd suffered and died after all. It was quite unbearable.

There was a letter from Reynolds, postmarked Birmingham. He couldn't have got Samuel's own last letter: it was far too early.

I have a post at last, he wrote, without so much as a Dear Samuel to begin. *In Birmingham. It's not much of a post, I'm a tutor again. The sickly son of a rich tradesman, spoilt and foolish, but his father thinks he'll make a university man of him. As if it mattered! But I have plenty of free time, as the doctor won't let Master Clark study enough for it to come to anything. I can go out at nights and have a good room to myself.*

I have become part of a group of people – five all told – who share my feelings about society and its nature. Three men and two women. We have been studying the teachings of the Russian Nihilists, though we do not copy them slavishly – there wouldn't be any good in that! We have come to see that the existing order must be completely destroyed, in order that a new one can grow. It will come of itself, only chaos must be brought out of the cruel order that reigns at present. We are all – in everything we do – part of this process of breaking down, that is the sign of the times. We are considering what we can do to help it along. I have a purpose now – or rather I am a purpose. That is the way we think.

The women in the group are severe and prescribe free love. In submitting myself to their rule, I experience what the woman's lot has been through the centuries. It isn't easy, though I've engaged in similar practices before. I console myself that I am learning, and that it is better to lie beneath their lean and half-starved shanks than to feel the plump thighs of prostitutes. They beat me when I am bad. All the same, there is a maidservant in the house where I am – old habits die hard, and my punishments are sufficient to justify some transgressions.

You asked me for guidance. Here it is: keep your eyes open. Observe, as I have taught you, what is going on around you. Perhaps you too may have a part to play. The old world is rotten and decaying: expect the fresh air of the new. It is coming: it may come quicker than you think, like a thief in the night, Samuel. I shall be writing to you again.

He had made several large blots on the paper: Samuel pushed it away from him and blushed.

He'd been stupid to expect to convert Reynolds, but at least he was armoured against his horrible creed. He had his faith, and the affection he owed his mother. And there was Lily.

Against the image of Reynolds's flagellant Nihilist harridans, he set the image of Lily, standing in her redemptive cotton clothes and scented with holiness. He'd have to see her.

16

THE NEW YEAR

THE huge door echoed as Samuel knocked on it: for a moment he thought he was begging admittance to prison. Would he ever get away? Then he jeered at himself a little: the question was rather whether he'd be allowed in, though he'd sent a large donation and made an appointment.

He was afraid of Mrs Ellis.

The door opened and an old Chinese doorman waved a shotgun in Samuel's face. He dropped it as soon as his short-sighted eyes realized that Samuel was an Englishman, but he looked to right and left down the street, out of habit. Then he asked Samuel his name. Samuel gave it. He was admitted, and the door slammed shut behind him. Inside, the house was clean, but shabby, and it smelt of carbolic: he thought Darley would like it.

'Some of the pimps, sir,' explained the doorman to Samuel, 'they come with choppers or guns and try to fetch the women out. Ten years ago, the ladies had only begun their work, and the men came in and took every girl in the place. We know better now.' He fingered the shotgun: it was lace-patterned, rich with apricot rust. It disturbed Samuel: it didn't look as if it would ever go off. He hadn't realized how much danger Lily was in.

The doorman raised his voice and called: 'Taitai! The English gentleman is here.'

Mrs Ellis was wearing her grey dress, no ornaments, no ribbons. Her hands were nervously clenched into fists by her side. Samuel was the first male visitor who wasn't a Minister of religion – but he'd sent an enormous donation. And he had refused to have his house exorcized.

What she couldn't forget was that a man was a man, and there were other things in his trousers besides his pockets. It was a coarse thought, but she wasn't ashamed of it. After all, she'd learned it from the male sex themselves, and the white men were no better than the Chinese. There were too many little houses round Happy Valley where substantial men kept their mistresses, there were too many brothels she couldn't touch because European women worked them, and her money came from the wives of men who patronized them.

'This way, Mr Pink,' she said severely. She had her revolver in her pocket, and her eyes reminded Samuel of the cook at the rectory, whenever he came into the kitchen. 'Hands off, Master Samuel!'

Almost reproachfully, she showed him the dead laundry room, with the superannuated mangles standing about like a silent testimony, though Samuel wasn't quite certain to what. He was only glad that Lily didn't have to labour here, but Mrs Ellis knew the meaning of the laundry room. It was haunted by the faint sounds and movements of the past; she saw the girls' wraiths in front of her, washing, scrubbing, trying to remove the stains other people had made on the linen, on their souls. She was angry again. She took him into the next room.

Here were the girls now, doing their embroidery, their needles pecking into hooplike stands under gaslamps. Samuel bent to look at moonshapes of fine lawn being feathered and flowered, decorated with *petit point* and spaced with drawn-thread stitches, all white on white. Stainless work, like the sheets – no colours for Mrs Ellis's girls. She had to make some concessions to austerity.

Here was Rebecca, a skilled embroideress and overseer of the girls, loudly testifying to her salvation in the robust Cantonese of the streets. Samuel tried hard to see her beauty, 'the beauty of holiness', he said to himself. He made a good squint at it, but the beauty of holiness meant Lily to him: where was she?

Mrs Ellis knew what he was thinking, but this was the shape of the visit: she always left the best till last.

And all the while she felt the floor slipping under her feet. Suddenly, she remembered the end of her childhood, the day her big doll had been given to her youngest sister while she was out doing the shopping for her mother: they'd said she was too old for it. Now, though she'd come half a world away from her parents, she was still afraid the doll wasn't hers to keep.

'Here are our kitchens,' she said to Samuel, ushering him down stone stairs to the big smoke-stained room with its scrubbed wooden surfaces where two dainty girls dressed in white aprons were setting about a chicken with big choppers. In a moment the bird lay in neat sections on the board, each sliver of meat lying on a slender bow of bone. They giggled to see Samuel.

'Get on with your work,' said Mrs Ellis sternly.

Samuel asked them in Cantonese: 'Do you love God?'

They put their hands in front of their faces and looked at Samuel through their fingers. He smiled at them.

Mrs Ellis decided that his harmless expression was a ploy. What she wanted to do was to give him his money back, throw him out at gunpoint and tell him never to come near the house again, but she kept on with the tour, leading him towards Lily.

'Love and trust God,' said Samuel to the girls. Hypocrite, thought Mrs Ellis. She heard more giggles after the door shut.

She wanted to ask him: Cards on the table now, Mr Pink. What are you really after?

'Now,' she said to Samuel, 'we shall go to my parlour and drink tea and I shall answer any questions you have to put to me.'

Any of the lady visitors would have asked for Lily right from the beginning, would have chattered about Lily, would have given only spoilt, perfunctory attention to the other aspects of the establishment – like a child whining for dessert. But Mr Pink had munched his way diligently through every dull dish she'd handed him, which proved his calculating bad faith. She could feel his desire to see Lily. It must be burning his breeches out.

She brought him through to the sitting room: simply furnished, rattan and black cushions, white walls, and a framed print, *Christ Blessing the Children*. Both Christ and the children were blond and blue-eyed. Mrs Ellis knew this – though she had never done so before – for the incongruity it was, because Lily was sitting underneath it.

Lily had never heard Samuel's name, so she hadn't been expecting him. She raised her eyes from her embroidery and jumped, stabbing her finger with the long sharp needle. Blood spread over the white lawn. She cried out.

'Oh, Lily,' scolded Mrs Ellis, 'you've hurt yourself.'

'I'm so sorry,' she said. She was shaking. 'I'll fetch tea, I'll wash the work, please, dear Mrs Ellis – '

She ran away.

'Mr Pink,' said Mrs Ellis angrily, 'sit down.'

Each was as upset as the other. Mrs Ellis began to tell him the history of the place, twisting her strong fingers as if she'd like to throttle him with them: how she'd begun with the laundry, but how a few months ago she had changed to fine embroidery and dressmaking, and now so many ladies were getting work done here, which was a sign of God's grace, she was sure –

Samuel listened to Mrs Ellis talking about balance sheets and the need to extend the premises, about the unexpected vacancy of the house next door, and the possibility of obtaining more help from England, of the gratifying interest now shown in the work, and the increase in donations –

I hurt her, he thought. Why did it have to happen like that?

Lily came in with an English teaset, all roses and bits of gilt scrolling on a white background. She poured tea and added milk.

'From the new hygienic Dairy Farm herd,' explained Mrs Ellis at this point. She did this automatically, now.

Samuel enthused about the hygienic Dairy Farm herd. He mentioned his visits with Kwok. He said he'd seen cows chained in basements, who had to be butchered in there because they had been calves when they'd arrived and now there was no room to get them out. He heard his voice rambling on, and he couldn't really talk to Lily, he couldn't even say he was sorry she'd been hurt.

Cows, thought Mrs Ellis. This horrid little man gives time and energy to the misfortunes of cows, and look what men do to women!

'I want to start a hospital,' she said reproachfully, 'for poor fallen women who are dying of starvation and disease.' She had her speech off pat by now. Her purpose was the justification for all this anarchy, for her own infatuation with Lily. It wiped out guilt: at least she hoped so.

Lily offered Samuel a cucumber sandwich: you could make such things in the colony, though the cucumbers were tough-skinned, pimpled, and often spiny. This one had been peeled and sliced wafer-thin by the nimble choppers of the girls in the kitchen. Her hand brushed his, they both coloured, and Mrs Ellis saw them.

Samuel said: 'I'll give as much as I can to your project, Mrs Ellis, such a wonderful thing to do for these poor women.'

'Mrs Ellis is so kind,' said Lily, smiling at the Englishwoman and past her at Samuel. Mrs Ellis saw this and all she could think of was how much she loved Lily. She was lost. She knew it.

And Samuel's face was innocent, boyishly sweet. Her sister had been a sweet girl, but she'd had the doll all the same.

Mrs Ellis wanted – now as then – to throw herself down on the floor, tear her hair out of its bonds, scream and shout. She'd resisted the desire then, and she would now.

'I'm sorry you hurt yourself,' Samuel at last managed to say to Lily.

'It doesn't hurt any more,' said Lily. She smiled at him: her soft black eyes met his, then looked down. He reeled with the delight of her presence, that exquisite fragrance –

'Can I visit again?' he asked Mrs Ellis.

'There is a rota,' said Mrs Ellis. 'As it now stands, your name will come up in three months' time.'

She was glad to get rid of him.

He couldn't admit that he was unhappy, because religion had come to fill his heart. He prayed diligently, he kept off drink, he read the Bible instead of playing billiards at the Club. He began to look out for a Christian young woman to court: the Dean's daughters were anything but devout, but the Postmaster-General had a child who was serious and quite pretty. He began to visit the house. He couldn't help noticing, though, that her skin was coarse by comparison with Lily's. Also, she giggled when she saw him.

A young cadet called Higgs arrived in Hong-Kong and was assigned to share Samuel's quarters. He seemed a good-natured fellow – religious, even – and Samuel liked him. Higgs was standing in the street watching his stuff being delivered to the house, when a trunk fell off the cart and killed him.

A day or so later, Bradwell offered Samuel the opportunity to take a different house. Not – Bradwell said hastily – that he was worried about ill-luck. He just thought the house in Caine Road might have unhappy associations for Samuel.

'It's very kind of you, sir,' said Samuel respectfully, 'but who else would take the house? You wouldn't be able to sell it to a Chinese.'

Bradwell said: 'I don't think you should be constrained by that kind of worry.' He hesitated, then said: 'We've made quite an investment in you, Pink. Your welfare isn't only your own concern.'

'I don't think the house is insanitary, sir,' said Samuel, as politely as he could manage, 'and for the other thing, I have my faith to sustain me.' He was intensely aware of how little a man he was as he said it, and yet, at the same time, he had a sense of soaring royal height, transcending Bradwell's fearfulness.

It was one of the great moments of his life.

'Very well,' said Bradwell, a little crossly, 'as long as you're happy to live alone.'

'Thank you, sir,' said Samuel. He went back to his work.

He had a letter from Reynolds to spoil his breakfast:

So you've been converted. The other drug the British are trying to force on the Chinese, along with opium, which you wouldn't take for yourself, would you? But now you turn your back on knowledge, and lull yourself to sleep with the nursery-tale of heaven. Can't you see how much better it is for a man to dedicate his life without hope of anything but the betterment of the future?

The religious salvation of the few is built on the torment of many. Only one hundred and forty-four thousand are to be taken up into heaven. Whereas what we are talking about, here in Birmingham, is the salvation – through revolution – of the entire earth. I am making great strides, I am becoming a new man, which is the most important thing of all.

I suppose you have your own road to tread, perhaps this religious conversion is part of it.

Samuel poured himself out a cup of tea – Paul Cheung made a perfect pot of tea – and thought about the one hundred and forty-four thousand. That was less than the population of Hong-Kong at the last census. But surely Reynolds had got it wrong, he must read Revelation again. He was sure that there were to be many more saved and living happily on earth: only the élite went to heaven. That was a disturbing thought though – he might be destined for a second-class salvation. He tried to bow his head – even while eating bacon and kedgeree – and accept what God had in mind for him. It wasn't easy. He understood his own hope: though he was barred from the palace in this life, in the next he might be on the right hand of the King.

The foundation of all things, wrote Reynolds, *is chaos. Forests rise on the earth, house millions of tiny creatures, flower and fruit – and a fire starts and burns them all down. When the fire had passed, new growth sprouts.*

To overturn the specious certainties of the ruling classes – to break down the oppressive structures of authority – to spread awareness – that is what we are about here in Birmingham. We have constructed a printing press and are distributing a newspaper. We are studying chemistry so that we have at least the theoretical knowledge of how to make a bomb. Greetings, Reynolds.

Samuel didn't like to think about Reynolds making bombs, but he didn't believe it, though they had grown a long way away from each other and he supposed Reynolds might be capable of more than he could believe. It made his head ache: he escaped to work. He sat at his desk, tried to concentrate and fell asleep.

He dreamed that a dragon had come out of the hillside underneath the offices because workmen digging in the road had disturbed it. It was poking its scaly brilliant head out of the floor and trying to bite Samuel's leg, but it couldn't quite reach. Its dotted eyes glared with frustration: it cursed Samuel, in pidgin, while its neck worked at the floor, splintering the boards, its teeth came nearer and nearer and Samuel could neither move nor speak: he was transfixed by the dragon's bulging eyes. He knew, any minute now, that the teeth would snap his leg: then the monster would go for his belly and scoop his entrails out.

He woke to find Philips' hand on his shoulder. He started guiltily. He tried to apologize, but the words wouldn't come because his teeth were chattering too much. He could feel the dragon's hot breath burning them both up.

'You've got a touch of malaria again, old man,' said Philips kindly, 'no shame in it, happens to all of us. I'll have them get you a chair home. Your new servants'll know what to do for you, will they? I'll send for Doctor Mackenzie, too. Shall I have someone go home with you?'

'No,' said Samuel, 'I'll be fine.'

He managed to get out of the sedan that had brought him unaided: he felt quite pleased with himself. Then he heard the noise that was going on.

Brain-fever, he thought. I'm a dead man.

He thought he was outside his own self, seeking admittance. Nobody answered the door.

There was a clanging and cracking inside the house: it was like his nightmare of the dragon, like Reynolds's letter about chaos, and he was very frightened of it. Yet where else could he go? His things were all here.

He fumbled his key out of his pocket, found the keyhole and unlocked the door, resting his hand on the doorpost for a moment. Paper crackled under his hand, there was a piece of paper pinned there. He inspected it and was bewildered to see the paper head of a cock.

The noise came out and whacked his head when he opened the door.

He walked up the stairs towards it, fascinated, mesmerized, no longer at all master of himself. It was coming from the room that had been Henderson's. There was a stench of gunpowder made sickly with whiffs of sandalwood smoke, and when he opened the door of the room, it was full of devils.

They had red bodies and black heads. The air was fuzzed with smoke and shook with the frightful noise. He saw shuddering, smoking flames: then the red backs moved across his line of vision and cut him off. The only thing that surprised him was that they hadn't seized him yet. He knew what they'd do then.

I was converted, he cried silently to God, how could you forsake me?

It was when he saw the Cheungs that he understood. They were sitting in a corner of the room, drinking the whisky he'd left in the cupboard for medicinal purposes, and smoking his cigars. It didn't trouble them to be in hell, because this wasn't hell, it was an exorcism, and the devils were Taoist priests who were banishing evil spirits. He could even understand the words one of them was chanting: the azure spirits were sent off to the East, the red to the South, the white spirits to the West. At those last words the priest faced Samuel and spat some liquid towards him.

He *was* a white devil in their eyes, a *gweilo*.

He backed away, slamming the door shut: the gongs clanged louder still as he retreated, and a salvo of triumphant crackers sent his hands to his ears. He went into his bedroom and took hold of his arms, his legs, put his hands round his stomach to make sure he hadn't evaporated. He lay down – but was afraid that any minute now he'd find himself whizzing through the air – in straight lines, which was the only way a devil could travel. He put his hands round the edge of the mattress now and held on tight.

The noise stopped abruptly, as if his brain wouldn't admit it any longer.

Then it was as if nothing had happened.

Paul Cheung came tiptoe into the room, and began to help Samuel out of his clothes. His hands – to Samuel's surprise – were kind as he turned his master and eased off his trousers, his shirt, his

208

socks. Samuel was in his nightshirt in no time. Cheung pulled the sheet over him and folded the blanket back. He said nothing about the exorcism.

He fetched Samuel a jug of iced lemonade and a glass and held him up while he drank, then laid him gently on his back. He wiped Samuel's brow with a damp sponge. He said he'd sent James for the doctor and showed no irritation when Samuel said it had already been done.

The room was so quiet now, quiet and uncomplicated as the thoughtless time before birth. Only the sunlight came in slits through the shutters and danced with the dust.

When he got better he reflected that it was, in many ways, the worst of both worlds. He'd had a nasty experience. He'd been cheated out of his integrity, and saddled with a harelipped servant to boot – who was admittedly very good at his job – but a swindler and a drinker of the master's medicinal whisky. In the light of all this, he couldn't understand his odd sense of relief. He hadn't liked to go into Henderson's room: now he had bookshelves and a desk put into it, bought pictures to hang on the walls, and made it into a study.

He sat down in the room and wrote to Master Feng about his conversion, and how happy it had made him.

'Progress,' said the Dean, 'is undoubtedly part of the Divine Plan. Even Science – though not when it claims we are descended from apes. Pass the port, Darley.'

If Darwin's right, thought Samuel, and we're all descended from gorillas, what price royal blood? But then, if Darwin's right, some humans might have evolved to a higher stage than others, becoming the aristocracy and monarchy. And naturally they pass their qualities on to their descendants. But does the marriage tie affect that?

His Christmas goose rumbled in his stomach with all the other things that had gone down after it.

'Electric streetlighting,' said the Postmaster-General, 'what's wrong with gas? When the first rainstorm puts the electric lights out.'

'Defeated by God?' asked Darley. 'What do you think, Pink?'

Samuel said: 'The lights haven't gone out since, and they've been burning for over a fortnight.'

The Postmaster-General said: 'It hasn't rained.' There was laughter. He said: 'Electric streetlights are an expensive luxury for the better-to-do. Have they installed electric lighting in Taiping-shan? Of course not.'

'It'll spread,' said Darley.

'It'll break the lamplighters' rice bowls,' said the Postmaster.

Darley said: 'Plenty of other work for them. Don't you mean it'll be bad for the Gas Company's shares?'

Darley had invested in the Hong-Kong Electric Company.

MacVicary from Jardines said: 'You're a bold man, Darley, upsetting dragons, I hear.'

Darley shrugged his shoulders.

'What's this?' asked the Dean.

Darley said: 'I'm planning a new water main. The Chinese have put a dragon in the way of the excavations.'

'Going to cause deaths,' said MacVicary, 'bad business.'

'So they say,' said Darley.

He didn't join the ladies with the other men. There were going to be prayers. He left the house.

He walked along the road, turned on to a rough track and scrambled up the hill between bushes of red and black berries, all inedible if not poisonous, and the pippy little kumquats that the Chinese dug up and brought down to decorate their homes at New Year. He climbed for half an hour, right up to the top of the hill, a little way away from where the Governor's decrepit Mountain Lodge sat in the lap between two higher peaks.

Forty thousand dollars to repair it, thought Darley. The Legislative Council voted it, but H.E. doesn't like the damp. Neither do I. We ought to move downhill. I hate the Peak. I'll never dare ask her. She knows that. She's ill on purpose. She's doing it to get back at me. And as for all this Jesus stuff: she doesn't believe in it any more than I do.

He couldn't defeat her. Even if he murdered her, she'd have won.

They were building a new ballroom at Government House. *She* would never dance there. The English doctor had diagnosed hysteria and Darley had written the words that cut her dancing days off.

I give my consent to whatever measures are necessary.

He'd thought it washed his hands for him. But he'd known, all along, what the doctor would do. Hadn't the Colonial Surgeon told him?

'A radical practitioner, I don't know – ' Darley remembered his friend's hesitation, his frown. 'He gets results, but – '

Darley watched the junks sailing far below, looked over the water – sapphire-blue from this height – and over to the hills of China. The air was so clear that he could see people moving on the Kowloon peninsula.

It was 1890, and about to be 1891, which was to be Hong-Kong's Jubilee year. People would dance in the ballroom at Government House, but his wife wouldn't dance. She probably wouldn't even attend. She'd be praying with her new friends.

He thought about young Pink, so diligent, so eager, so intelligent, so foolish somehow, sitting dreaming at dinner. What was going to become of the lad? He ought to marry in a few years' time: but that wouldn't necessarily make him happy.

He thought that he loved his wife: needed her to love him. It was a very different feeling from some he'd had years ago, when he was Pink's age. It was appropriate now, when feeling had stopped burning wastefully, like a torch. He'd made enough of a fool of himself. Tenderness, now, that was all that was left, if you could give it, if you could get it. He'd never understood, back in those days, how soon you got older.

The few thin clouds moved across the blue behind the Chinese mountains: it was as if the whole landscape was moving through history and towards the twentieth century and they were all passengers, even the cobra that slithered quietly past him with its hood down. The Postmaster-General could sneer at electricity as much as he liked: he'd be using it in his house in ten years' time.

He thought if they must remain on the Peak, he'd have electric lighting brought up to the house as soon as possible.

There was a ball to celebrate the Jubilee and the opening of the new ballroom: Samuel was there and danced with plenty of pretty young women. But they weren't interested in him: he could see that, and he didn't know what to say to them. He left the ball early and went to bed. There he dreamed of Lily. It was more than three months now since he'd seen her at the Refuge, but somehow the list of visitors had lengthened, and he hadn't been invited again.

Mrs Ellis kept Lily in the Refuge. She didn't forbid her to leave, but found excuses to stop her going. If Miss Atkinson sent Lily out to buy embroidery floss, Mrs Ellis discovered an errand she had to run herself: 'So I can get the floss, too.' She smiled and brushed her hair back: she kept doing this nowadays, and though it always started off tidy, it soon flew out from her head in wisps like loose straws from a haystack. She ruined the fringe Lily had cut her, too, so it dangled instead of curling, and then she stuck pins in it to hold it flat.

There were the Chinese herbs, of course: Miss Atkinson said Lily had to get those, till Mrs Ellis pointed out that Lily could brush the prescription on paper, and Miss Atkinson could go herself. She said the exercise would do her sister good in the wintertime.

Miss Atkinson complained that she'd never find the shop.

'All right, then,' said Mrs Ellis, running her hands into her hair and bringing the whole mass of it down, 'take her with you, if you must.'

She was desperately afraid of letting Lily out alone. She was sure Samuel was waiting out there. He'd be walking up and down the streets round about the Refuge, though he was clever enough to get away when she patrolled them. When she came back, she'd pull Lily into her arms and kiss her fervently. Lily was obedient and let herself be kissed: Lily said she loved Mrs Ellis, and Miss Atkinson, of course. Lily kissed Mrs Ellis's cheek and offered to make her fringe right again.

Mrs Ellis thought Lily was a child, irresponsible, careless. Children needed to be shut up somewhere safe where no one could ruin them.

And Miss Atkinson, forever demanding too much of Lily – she was foolish, self-indulgent! She wanted to be massaged, she wanted to be pampered. Lily had hardly any time to do embroidery – who was Alicia to expect a personal maid, didn't she know they were out here to lead a hardy, God-serving life?

Lily didn't know where to hide. There was nowhere you could be alone at the Refuge: you worked, ate, slept, dressed and bathed with the other girls. Miss Atkinson and Mrs Ellis walked in everywhere. At least she'd been able to spend time alone at Mr Jackson's house: she'd had hours on her own, while he was busy with other things. She wished she could crawl under beds or shut herself in cupboards, but even there she was sure the ladies would come calling her, peering in at her. She felt as if the life was being slowly crushed inside her, smaller and smaller it crumpled and hurt.

Rebecca watched her and smiled. She knew Lily was in distress and it pleased her. And all the time there were the ladies' voices, telling Lily how much they loved her. The only reason Mrs Ellis was keeping her in was because she loved her. Miss Atkinson was so demanding because she loved her.

So she had to be nice to them: she couldn't bear it, and still there was no way out. When the other ladies visited, petted her, fussed her, she had to do her duty too. She had to say the words, the ones about salvation and love, and she was so tired of saying them she believed she wouldn't be able to get them out any longer.

She began to dream of men's embraces, wild, shameless dreams, a different man in every one, Chinese, English, it didn't matter. She dreamed she killed Mrs Ellis and Miss Atkinson and ran through the streets afterwards, naked and covered in blood. She dreamed of Mr Pink, again she tugged the red thread round her ankle, and again he came.

Then at last, one Saturday afternoon in February, she got out. They ran out of embroidery floss – Miss Atkinson couldn't imagine how it had happened – when Mr Fawler was bringing an English missionary to visit in half an hour. It wouldn't do for the girls to be sitting idle when he came. Miss Atkinson couldn't go to buy it because Mr Fawler had been known to come as much as twenty minutes early, and Mrs Ellis, who should have been home, was out. Miss Atkinson couldn't imagine what was keeping her.

Miss Atkinson sent Lily.

'Come back quickly,' she said, 'because of course he wants to hear you.'

It was ten minutes walk to the shop: Lily all-but skipped it, she was so glad to be released.

Samuel had spent the morning dealing with correspondence about the Po Leung Kuk, who had asked the Registrar-General's office for help. They had little money, and were forced to carry on their job of keeping young Chinese women from vice in a few cramped rooms above the Tung Wah Hospital. Samuel didn't approve of the Po Leung Kuk: he thought the young women should be saved from vice by converting them to Christianity. The Postmaster-General was convinced they were actually a Triad organization, and should be banned like all the other Triad organizations: he had had a row with Philips about it. There was gossip that its main function was to provide concubines for the members of the committee. It all proved that only the light of Christ could enlighten the world. He was glad he'd written his testimony to Master Feng.

However, a man had to do his duty, even if it involved the legitimation of the Po Leung Kuk. And the ordinance Philips was drafting might not pass the Legislative Council. He hoped it wouldn't. He decided to walk home to get the bad taste out of his mouth.

It was a cold grey afternoon, easy to walk. He was almost home when he thought he'd go down to the Cricket Club instead: he'd get something to eat there and probably find someone to practise with him. He turned downhill towards the harbour, walking rather aimlessly, because he wasn't sure what he really wanted to do. The dry wind prickled his ears with dust. He met Lily on the corner of Wellington Street and Wyndham Street.

She was carrying a square black bamboo shopping basket on her arm and wore a quilted black coat swinging over her black cotton trousers. The first shop had been out of white floss, so she'd come to Wellington Street to get it. There were a dozen other shops in between, but she didn't care, even though Mr Fawler had probably arrived at the Refuge by now. She'd have liked to walk for ever.

'Miss Lily!' he exclaimed.

'Oh! Mr Pink,' said Lily. She looked down at her ankle but she couldn't see the red thread.

They stood and looked at each other and neither knew what to say. Only Samuel thought how exquisite she was, it was a crime to dress her in those servant's clothes, they could have made a distinction between her and the other girls. And Lily thought she must pass on. She'd have to go back to Pokfulam Road.

She began to cry. It happened, as it had happened to her before, without her consent and without sobs, only the tears coming out of her eyes.

'Please,' she said, as she had on the ship. 'Please.'

'I don't understand,' said Samuel. 'You're unhappy – but it's not like *that* time – on the ship – when you were still with Mr Jackson. You have Christ, now.'

He was frightened. He was in danger.

It was as if a little vixen had run into his house and told him he alone could shelter her from the hunt. And the huntsman was God, God was sitting astride a huge horse and whipping His hounds after

214

Lily, after Samuel if he dared help her. He didn't want to think God so vindictive: yet hadn't He required the death of His own son, hadn't Christ begged for mercy, in Gethsemane?

'Is Mrs Ellis with you?' he asked.

'No,' whispered Lily, and began to sob. Her sobs killed his resistance.

He asked: 'What can I do?' She couldn't answer. He said: 'Come to my house, and we'll talk.' Then he remembered what people would say, if they were seen walking together.

'I don't know if you can do anything,' said Lily, wiping her nose with a cotton handkerchief, 'I shouldn't go to your house.'

With some difficulty, he said: 'No, you must come.'

'I'd better go a different way, Mr Pink,' said Lily. 'Hadn't I? Then I'll knock on your door as if I was a servant.'

She *was* a vixen, or how else would she know what to do? Only she was such a distressed, pretty little vixen, he had to help her. He told her to go by the longer way: he'd be waiting by the door to let her in.

He was sinning again, he knew it, this was far worse than Mrs Darley. Both he and Lily would be ruined if anyone knew. He didn't think anyone would – Lily looked like any amah about her household duties. All the same, when the knock came on the door, he opened it as quickly as he could, and shut it as hurriedly behind her. He shut her in his study, called Paul Cheung and told him he didn't want to be disturbed. Then he went to her.

'It's a nice room,' she said. She smiled at him, but her face was still damp.

He asked: 'What's wrong?' Before he knew what he was doing, he had her hands in his.

He began to shiver.

'Mrs Ellis,' she said, 'Miss Atkinson. I don't love them, they don't love me, not really, they're cruel to me.'

He said: 'I love you.'

It was quite true, irrevocable and frightful. He really hadn't known.

Lily felt the wonderful tenderness of his hands round hers, and her mind showed her a little house, food in her mouth she could choose herself, and hours to herself while he was at work. He'd be good to her. She'd never need to go back to Pokfulam Road.

Thinking of the Refuge, she began to cry again. He put his arms around her.

He said: 'Don't cry.'

She wiped her eyes on her sleeve: she had to do as she was told. She told herself she didn't want to cry.

He took her on to his lap, as Mr Jackson had once done, but she'd learned too much since then: that innocence couldn't be taken back. She felt him grow hard.

She begged: 'Don't ever be cruel to me.'

'No,' he said, 'how could I?' But he glanced at the door: he kept imagining someone was trying to force it open.

He was wondering how he'd get her to his bedroom unseen – it wouldn't be possible – till he felt her fingers on his trouser buttons. She was a little clumsy with them, clumsier certainly than Mrs Darley, but when she had them open, she knew what to do. She slipped off his knee for a moment and dropped her own trousers, unbuttoned her coat and her jacket – it happened admirably quickly and he was excited by the slenderness of her body, the ivory texture of her skin. He couldn't wait to have her: it had been so long. Only how? On the carpet? He didn't want to crush her on the floor.

She came back on to his knee and enclosed his eager member, which spent itself inside her at once. She cooed, and stayed where she was, smiling down at him and moving delicately. He grew again, and this time the pleasure was almost unbearable. It was like hanging on the edge of a steep, endless waterfall. It was she who was holding him there and fright grew on him: he panted and cried out and she didn't recognize the fear.

His brain talked to him all the time: he didn't take any notice but he remembered it afterwards: you're betraying your caste, Samuel, you're doing the worst thing, you'll have to keep this secret, why don't you find a nice girl to marry, this is chaos breaking out, Reynolds's dangerous delusion, what would Master Feng say, what about an ordered world, what about Christ and his law?

Lily let him go, and he fell down the waterfall. He thought he'd die. He imagined his body, pierced by sharp rocks: he'd always know ecstasy felt like pain. Lily kissed him tenderly, rather anxiously, mapping out his face with her lips.

Then he felt such love as he'd never experienced before, her lips were so gentle, so comforting! Rather wildly, he thought: God is Love, Love is God. He relished the frisson of outrage that ran through him.

His faith was ebbing away: it had been a piece of folly after all, a fraud. Mrs Ellis was a fraud, Mr Fawler was a fraud, and he was quite sure, now, that Mrs Darley was a fraud. He'd seen through them all. He would keep Lily, he would be wicked, he *would* cock a snook at all of them.

17

A CHANGE OF CAGES

ABOUT an hour before Samuel and Lily had carnal knowledge of each other, Mrs Darley said to her husband: 'John, this house tires me. Could you find somewhere in Mid-Levels – Robinson Road, perhaps, or Conduit Road? It's the damp, in summer. It makes me feel so ill.'

Darley looked at his wife. Her face was half-turned away from him, her eyes on the floor. She was beaten after all: and he hadn't even had to mention Robinson Road.

He had no idea what to say.

She said: 'So you'll look for another house, will you, my dear?'

And this was the first time she'd used the endearment since – since –

He wanted to ask her to forgive him, and he couldn't. He mustn't admit he'd done wrong, because how could it ever be put right?

Outside, the wind blew up dust-devils on the verandah, and the servant came in and brought tea.

At the same time, Mr Fawler stood on the doorstep of the Pokfulam Road house and exclaimed to the visiting Wesleyan missionary, Mr Webster:

'My dear fellow, what is happening here in Hong-Kong – ' his voice grew louder, he spread his hands and smiled at Mr Webster as if a rabbit was about to jump out from between them – 'this place is a pool of Bethesda to the poor strayed females of this city, and there is one, especially' (and yet he still had doubts about Lily) 'you will go a long way through China before you find the Spirit working more powerfully. This colony is far from Christian, you know.'

Mr Webster drew back a step. Mr Fawler stepped nearer to him. Mr Webster was pinned against the door.

Mr Fawler thought: let him dare imply that I have an easy task here, only because this is a British possession. He was waiting for Mr Webster to imply it, his raw soul expected another assault of the lash. I don't care, he thought. I shall speak the truth as I see it.

At the same time, a heavy green tile slipped off the roof of a rich Chinese house close to the spot where the Public Works Department's contractors were digging the new water main and bisecting the spine of the dragon. The tile fell on the head of the merchant's Number Three Wife, the favourite Tai-Tai who had borne him two sons and was pregnant again. She was killed at once. The merchant knew it was the dragon's revenge. Hadn't his neighbour's eldest son just died of fever? Hadn't representations been made to the Public Works Department? Why had no action been taken? He was grieved and angered. He and his neighbour prepared a dignified scroll of complaints for the Registrar-General.

'And now,' said Mr Fawler to Mr Webster, steering him away from the two pretty girls in the kitchen, 'we will see Miss Lily.'

'Oh, I'm sorry,' said Miss Atkinson, blushing. 'Lily's out. I sent her to do some shopping for me.'

'You trust her so much!' wondered Mr Fawler. He couldn't get the note of disapproval out of his voice.

'Lily,' said Miss Atkinson fearfully, 'is a good girl. Come and talk to my sister.'

There's something wrong here, thought Fawler. She's run away. She's made fools of them, but I mustn't let my missionary guess, or I'd be a laughing stock, too. I *will* be a laughing stock: I visit here. I've been betrayed.

Mrs Ellis got rid of them as quickly as she could. Though it hardly mattered if they were suspicious. If the suspicion was true, then everyone would soon know.

Lily, she cried silently, come back.

The visitors left.

'I'm going out now,' said Mrs Ellis, 'I'm going to search the streets.' She put on her bonnet and ulster, and pulled her revolver out of the drawer where it lived in the daytime. Miss Atkinson looked away from the revolver. She hated to think why it was in her sister's hand.

Inside Mrs Ellis, an adolescent girl complained: 'I want my doll back. They *shan't* take my doll away from me.'

The youngest sister had given Beatrice's doll to her younger son, who'd broken it. She'd actually written the story to Beatrice, in a sentimental letter full of sighings, bad spelling and worse handwriting. Beatrice's parents were pleased with her: she'd married a lawyer in Aylesbury and lived in a house with an orchard just outside the town.

Mrs Ellis marched out of the door of the Hong-Kong Girls' Rescue and Educational Trust, with a sidelong glance at the disused laundry. She must have the bars on the windows renewed.

She walked through the streets of Hong-Kong, staring at everyone, Queen's Road West, Queen's Road Central, Wyndham Street, Wellington Street, Lyndhurst Terrace. She even walked along Caine Road and stood outside Samuel's house. Her nostrils twitched like a searching dog's, but her sense of smell had none of a dog's sensitivity. It had been vitiated by years of dried fish, bad drains and the vapours of the laundry. She walked all the way back to Queen's Road and through the crowded streets she'd already searched: it was none of it any good.

She went back to Pokfulam Road in case Lily had come back after all, but the doorman waved his hands from side to side, and laughed.

'She's not here,' he said.

Mrs Ellis knew he was laughing with distress: it didn't stop her wanting to slap his face. She put her hands together in front of her and clasped them tightly.

Her doll had been smashed in the orchard by little Claud, a bright lad who wanted to go into the army: now Lily was gone too. She'd never get enough money to buy the building next door and make it into a hospital and if she cried about it everyone would tell her she was a great girl now and should be ashamed of herself.

She went up to the parlour. Her sister was there. When Miss Atkinson saw Mrs Ellis coming, *she* began to cry.

'Don't cry,' said Mrs Ellis. 'It's my fault. Entirely my fault. I'm in charge here, not you. We had rules, we relaxed them. I allowed them to be relaxed. I should never have let her out of the laundry. Now she's ruined us.'

She hated herself. She would have liked to do away with herself: coldly, unemotionally, she felt she deserved it.

'Where do you think she is?' asked Miss Atkinson miserably, 'poor Lily, kidnapped by a brothel-keeper, probably, and here we are thinking of ourselves.'

'No,' said Mrs Ellis, a little contemptuously, 'no brothel-keeper would want her. You know what Chinese men are like about bound feet. And the white brothels are full of white women.'

'She could have had an accident,' suggested Miss Atkinson.

Mrs Ellis laughed harshly. 'Stop inventing excuses, Alicia. She's too clever to have an accident. She's found a white man to keep her. One of the men we've let in here, who knows? Don't try to believe it will turn out well. I've wanted to believe so many things,' she began to cry herself at last, 'only to be snubbed again with the truth.'

Dear Miss Atkinson, wrote Lily, *dear Mrs Ellis, I will never come back to live with you again.'*

Her handwriting and spelling were perfect, but she wrote too hurriedly to give complete attention to punctuation or grammar. She was afraid that if she stopped to think, or read over what she had written, she would never be able to finish, and she wanted to do this, to let them know she was unharmed. Though she needed to escape from them.

I will be perfectly safe, I assure you. And shall live a virtuous life and read the Bible every day. I love you both. But I couldn't bear to live longer in a house where there were bars on the windows. And the girls were cruel to me. I never told you this. But they used to put bamboo splinters in my bed. – it was a lie, but better than the truth – *And of course I shall be always grateful for what you did for me and love you dearly. And I hope I will see you again some day and perhaps make tea for you in my own house. You see, I have met Mr Wells, who went with Mr Jackson to China. Mr Jackson gave Mr Wells quite a lot of money for me, and with that I can live respectably on my own, and hope to find work as an embroiderer – perhaps you will tell the Peak ladies about it? I hope we'll always be friends, but I can't come back to your house because the other girls will pinch me again and call me a devil.*

She'd written as much as she could bear. She signed it: *All my love, Lily.* She took one of Samuel's wax sticks, sealed it, and gave it to Paul Cheung to take.

Paul Cheung was going to find her somewhere to live: until which time she was to stay at the house in Caine Road. Paul Cheung didn't think she was very pretty, and she knew it. Her feet were too big. Nor did he approve of her going with a white man.

She wouldn't care.

I am very glad, wrote Master Feng to Samuel, *that you have found such happiness in your religion. It is characteristic of a gentleman that he observes the rites, and I see a praiseworthy modesty in your awareness of your own shortcomings, as well as in your determination to turn to your religion to help yourself. Whereas a Chinese must find help in his own religion, it is clear that your Way – that of Christ – is what Heaven ordains that you should follow. It always gives me great pleasure to receive letters from you.*

Samuel thought it was just as well his proselytizing fervour had come to an end.

Samuel dreamed he was at the office, working on the ordinance for the Po Leung Kuk. Lily was sitting against his knee, huddling under his desk. Philips came in and he was terrified she'd be discovered: he couldn't imagine how she'd got there. She was stroking his legs while Philips was telling him how important it was for young Chinese girls to be found marriage partners by their own people. Then Reynolds came into the office, carrying a bomb. He threw it and darkness fell.

Samuel found himself in bed at West Burton. He heard Victoria's voice, saying, once again:

'My dearest child. My dearest, precious child.'

He asked: 'So may I have her?'

'Of course, my dear,' said the Queen. 'You shall have whatever you want, as long as you stay away from me.'

18

1891–1892:
THE GAMBLE

———————

THE move to Robinson Road put Darley in a very bad mood. He hadn't realized that Mrs Darley would want so much new furniture: she sold all the purple velvet *chaises-longues* and armchairs and replaced them with midnight blue. New curtains had to be made, new ornaments bought. It was terribly expensive.

All the time he was being bothered about the water main and the excavations into the dragon's spine: he knew quite well you had to take such things into account when you were working in Hong-Kong, and every time he looked at the bills for his new house he grew angrier about the water main. Then – deliberately to annoy him, of course – one of the workmen died of a sudden fever and another disappeared without trace. The other workmen refused to carry on.

'Dragons,' he said to Samuel, whose unwelcome job it was to plead the dragon's case, 'hate 'em all.'

It was all pointless, and they both really knew it. The dragon would have to be appeased, which would be best done in the form of hard silver dollars. Then the people affected would be able to have the Taoist priests and geomancers in to conduct the necessary ceremonies. Also, the route of the water main was going to have to change. This was Darley's sticking point, because it would be more expensive and would exceed a budget in which he was already being asked to include compensation to the dragon. London, who were notoriously lacking in local knowledge, wouldn't like it at all.

Samuel knew this, and Darley knew he knew, and was well aware that Samuel had no choice but to play the role he was appointed to play. But he'd been almost unreasonably kind to Samuel in the past, so he felt empowered to kick him a little now.

Samuel was tired: he'd been having bad dreams. Last night the dragon had chased him for hours, angry about its backache, blaming everything on him. He'd woken up, relaxed in the warmth of Lily's body beside him, but as soon as he fell asleep again the dragon was waiting for him: 'Where have you been?' it demanded in archaic Cantonese, 'whoring about, I suppose.'

'You're spending my money for me like water,' said Darley irritably, 'don't blame me if there's an outbreak of cholera.'

'It's all very unfortunate,' said Samuel wearily.

'Hills are full of dragons.' said Darley, 'damned creatures, interfering in my department.' He grinned, suddenly. 'And you having to plead for them, with your Christian principles.'

Samuel thought of Lily and the elaborate ways she knew how to make love. He was already quite addicted to them. Hastily, he said: 'It would all be so easy, if they weren't so superstitious. And of course we're trying to avert a greater danger to them. They don't understand that.'

'Idiots,' said Darley. 'Pigtailed dunces. Look at the mess they've made in their own country.'

'The Manchu *are* an alien dynasty,' said Samuel.

Darley said: 'Not that much difference, is there? Look, Pink, the trouble is quite simply that they haven't made the advances we've made.'

'They come here,' said Samuel, 'and the place prospers, dragons and all.'

Darley laughed. 'They should never have sent you to Canton, should they? I know what you're saying, Pink. No need to spell it out. But remember: they do good business under a British administration.' He stood up straight, almost to attention.

Samuel nodded, but he felt more guilt than patriotic emotion. Paul Cheung was renting a house for Lily today, and buying second-hand furniture for it as well.

He hurried back to his own office: he had plenty to get on with. An ordinance had been drafted that appeared to brand the entire Chinese population as potential criminals: the Department had seen at once that it wouldn't do. Samuel sat down to compose a suggested redraft. It was going to take a long time.

Two days later Paul Cheung took Samuel to see the house, in which he had already installed some furniture. It seemed appropriate that he'd bought Mrs Darley's purple velvet armchairs and one of her *chaises-longues*, just when Samuel had been remembering the old Mrs Darley and drafting a few reflections in his head: a new autobiography, the story of an unrepentant lover of women. He wished he was allowed to write to his mother. *Your Majesty, you do not have a monopoly on illicit love, I am your son, I too have been carried away by something too powerful for me to resist. I too shall have secrets I will share with no one.*

Only there must be no children. He'd told Lily so.

Lily found Samuel prettier than Mr Jackson, though a little too fat. But he needed help, just as Mr Jackson had done – perhaps all white men needed help? She enclosed him gently, made her gateway silk-satiny for him, stroked him and petted him.

He didn't give her pleasure: he made use of her body and nothing flowed back to her. Still, she was glad to help him. It was nice to use the skills Mr Jackson had taught her, and he was very grateful. Afterwards, his face would be flushed and childishly satisfied, and his body so heavy and relaxed she was drawn into his relief: she felt it, and was almost content.

She couldn't explain her hurts to him. He wouldn't understand, and what would she say to him? When he explained to her that she mustn't have children, he pointed out to her how difficult it would have been if she'd had Mr Jackson's half-Chinese child. She didn't tell him the baby had been Ah Kuen's daughter. She'd die if she told: she'd never realized that before.

She thought he'd change his mind if she got pregnant: he never did anything to prevent it anyway, he seemed to think she knew what to do. But she didn't, and she couldn't abort her child when it came. She saw Chinese people about her, laughing, squabbling, chattering: they all had families, except her. She had to have a baby.

The house was an old-fashioned place at the Bonham Road end of Caine Road, convenient yet not suspiciously close, and pleasant: it had a nice little garden at the back. Lily bought herself a white-eyed bird in a cage – she kept it well away from the gas-mantel. She draped the windows with lace and had Paul Cheung buy her a potted palm in the market. He got her a small dining table and four chairs, a dressing table, a wardrobe, a grandfather clock made by a Chinese workman in the exact style of the Old Country, and a large bed. The bed had also been Mrs Darley's, but neither of them knew that.

225

Samuel bought a set of engravings for her walls. The subjects were: *The Maiden's Prayer, An Elizabethan Wedding,* and *Little Nell.* Lily hung them alongside a painting of bamboo she had done herself: she bought the ink and brushes the first day, as well as a *pi pa*, so she could play to him. She told Samuel that the white porcelain figure of Kwan Yin in her bedroom was an ornament, and he didn't ask about the flowers she put by the figure, and the occasional smell of incense.

Paul Cheung hired an amah, Ah Ling: she was a scrawny little thing – older than Lily – with protruding teeth and tremendous energy. There was also a shaky doorkeeper, Uncle Liu, who – Paul Cheung told Samuel – was far stronger than he looked. Samuel wanted him old and unattractive. It felt safer.

It was nice to be taller than Lily – Mrs Darley was the same height as him. All the same, he sat at work and worried who Lily might be seeing while he wasn't there. She said she loved him, he tried to remember that, but he kept remembering what it had been like to watch Henderson making love to Mrs Darley. Lily would insist on going out into the streets, though Ah Ling could have done all the shopping, though tradesmen could have called to show her merchandise at the house. At least she took Ah Ling with her, and the amah was his ally: she wanted to keep Lily indoors. There was Mrs Ellis, too, who might kidnap Lily back again. Uncle Liu had a detailed description of Mrs Ellis, and instructions to keep her out if she came to the house.

'Samuel,' asked Lily – he'd asked her to call him Samuel. No one else did except Reynolds. 'Would you like me to dress like an Englishwoman?'

'Of course not,' said Samuel, quite shocked. He'd only seen her in European dress once, and then she'd been Jackson's property.

'I'm glad,' said Lily cheerfully, 'corsets are so uncomfortable.'

So Lily gave her cotton servant's clothes to Ah Ling, and bought instead silk satin in rose-colour, leaf-colour, night-blue and patterned moon-white: she embroidered them herself with intricate designs in Peking-knot stitch and they lay sleek and smooth against her skin.

She asked Samuel for pearls to put in her hair: he met Mrs Philips in the shop and had to invent a cousin in England he was sending them to. She was very interested and helped him buy the earrings and ring to match. She teased him about his intentions towards his cousin, but he said they were a wedding present: he said his cousin was marrying a gentleman-farmer in Berkshire. He hoped his lies were convincing.

When Lily went out, she drew her hair back in a bun and dressed in black silk – cheap silk, just good enough for a servant. With Ah Ling beside her she melted into the Chinese crowds and was anonymous. Ladies passed her who had visited her at the Refuge and they didn't so much as notice her. But she kept a sharp eye out for Miss Atkinson or Mrs Ellis.

She saw the elder sister now and again, striding round the Hong-Kong streets in her grey clothing – cool season, hot season, dry season, wet season – Mrs Ellis always wore grey, and her hair was turning to match. It was easy enough for Lily to drag Ah Ling down a side-street and disappear into a Chinese shop.

She didn't see Miss Atkinson, and wondered if she was ill – though Samuel said she wasn't. She never went down Pokfulam Road.

She wished they'd both go back to England now. She'd feel so much safer if they left Hong-Kong. But they stayed. Samuel told her Mrs Ellis had sent all the girls back to the laundry. That meant there'd be embroidery business to be picked up: if she could remember which ladies used to have work done at the Refuge, she could send Ah Ling round to their doors, inviting orders.

She didn't think Samuel would want her to earn her living, but she didn't care. She wanted to have her own money at last. She didn't ever want to be a beggar again.

A new routine developed: Samuel ate with her on the evenings he wasn't dining out, and stayed the night. He always left just before dawn and Paul Cheung made him breakfast in his own house. During the daytime he went about his pursuits as if nothing had changed. Everything had changed, of course. He was living a lie, pretending to be a responsible government servant while he did the one thing a white man must never do.

A generation ago, it had been possible: some of them had even married their mistresses. It would have been possible if he'd been the same age as the Prince of Wales. Now, discovery would bring his career to an end.

He cared about that. He wanted to rise in his profession, to be cool and impenetrable. No one should guess what he was up to. He didn't tell Reynolds about Lily, though he did admit to a mistress. Why should Reynolds be allowed to think he was the only one who could seduce women?

Reynolds had made a fool of himself again: he had got the maidservant pregnant. Luckily for him, she'd had a miscarriage and managed to hide it from her employers. He claimed to have learned exactly how to make a bomb, but hadn't yet – thank God – been able to obtain the ingredients.

It was May, and Samuel's mother's letter arrived.

You are a good boy, she wrote, *you've worked hard and passed your exams, and now a bright future lies before you. Soon you'll be earning enough money to get married. For my sake as well as your own, choose someone who'll make you a careful wife, someone who can give you the love that I can only give you at a distance. What a horrible experience you had when Mr Henderson hanged himself! My heart grieved for you, you must miss him so much, as well as having had to discover the body, my poor dear son. But be of good courage, and learn by his death that shirking and dissipation do no one any good. Be a loyal servant of the Queen. You have a duty out there, Samuel, to show those in darkness what true Christianity is, and I was glad to hear of your stand on this matter, though I wouldn't have you go too far to extremes. I'm glad you are capable of passion, but uncontrolled passion – I have to admit it – can lead to pain. You know I – I walk round this comfortable Scottish castle – I hardly ever get to London, since – no, I can't say, I mustn't say. Too much depends on it, for you, as well as for me. But – oh, Samuel, if it hadn't been for the cruelty of others whom I may not name, you would have been my legitimate son and I would be happily married to your father. I have given away more than I ought already. I send my affectionate wishes across the sea. Your loving mother.*

Samuel thought: My father's dead. They prevented him from marrying my mother. Did someone's cruelty hasten his death, was he murdered even? His heart raced. He thought: she'd never have kept me with her, she's fooling me there.

If they'd killed his father, they might try to murder him. He preferred not to think it. A man mustn't think too much, if he was to make something of his life.

A year passed, the dragon was pacified, the new water main built. People noticed that his evangelical fervour had worn off, but they only teased him about it. They would order him Watson's Aerated Water, in the Club, so that they could mock him when he said he wanted whisky. It only troubled him a little.

He really began to think he'd get away with it.

Mr Fawler observed Samuel and thought it was suspicious that he showed so little interest in young ladies. He reflected on the complete disappearance of Lily, who would certainly have turned up begging somewhere, if she hadn't put herself under someone's protection. He argued this through with himself at least once a month and especially on the first anniversary of Lily's disappearance, which this year fell at the Chinese New Year Holiday.

The only person he had told about it was his wife: it was hardly surprising, he remarked, when the young men were taken off to Canton and taught by the heathen.

'And what have the Chinese ever done for their own people?' he demanded of his wife. 'Have they built hospitals? He remembered the Tung Wah Hospital in Hong-Kong: but dismissed it as proof of benign English influence. He cried: 'If a man is ill, they stick needles in him – needles, I have been told by my own congregation. It makes him better, they say, to be treated as a pincushion. Superstition! Or they dose him with noxious potions. Have they cared for the orphan – no, they make them into slaves and prostitutes. Have they preached the Gospel?' He drew breath.

'You're quite right,' said Mrs Fawler, darning his black socks over a wooden mushroom. 'They don't preach the Gospel. They're heathens.'

Mr Fawler started, and looked at his wife. Her face was bland and harmless.

'Did you hear what I said?' he demanded.

'Of course, my dear,' she said. For the first time, he noticed the faint hint of malice in her voice.

'Do you love me?' he asked, though he felt ashamed of the question.

She said, 'Of course I love you, my dear. You're my husband.' She dropped a mended sock on to a table, and took another one out of the basket. He'd used to approve of her domestic carefulness. Now he worried in case she was stitching lumps into his socks.

'I'm going to the races,' he said, hoping for mercy. 'I have to be seen there, you understand. My flock may be there, gambling. They must know that my eye is upon them.'

She said: 'You'll enjoy the races, my dear.'

Oh, now, he knew. How long had this been going on in his own household, she'd been mocking him for years, for years dangerous anarchy had been sprouting under the floorboards, atheism, feminism, nihilism, sexual libertarianism, and God knew what else. And sitting there so docile, sabotaging his socks! They'd knobble under his feet while he went about his business. They'd trip him up and hinder him.

Mrs Fawler, the sceptic, was one of the few people in Hong-Kong who didn't go to the races. It was the only social event that united the entire colony. Here were Parsees and Sikhs, Muslims and Jews, white men and women from the New World and the Old, as well as crowds of Chinese: but not intermingled. The ordinary Chinese milled in the middle of the track: the more well-to-do were placed with the Europeans round the outside, and the Government, the Bank, Jardines and the other great merchants were represented in the wrought-iron grandstand. The brand-new Governor was enthroned there in his white ostrich-feathered hat and two seats away from him sat Darley, wearing a cocked hat and a uniform with gold braid and buttons. It didn't matter that the outfit didn't suit him. Even Mrs Darley was there, sitting on a soft cushion. The Jockey Club was a more accurate index of power than the Hong-Kong Club: Parsees and Jews, Kadoories and Sassoons, were allowed into the Jockey Club though never the Hong-Kong Club even if they were friends of the Prince of Wales. Mr David Sassoon was one of many gentleman jockeys racing today.

It was a day of patchy bright sunlight, cold and dry. Samuel perched on the railings that fenced the track and watched the horses running. He'd have to be careful, he'd placed a couple of bad bets and was losing money. Lily was nothing like as expensive as a wife would have been, but he didn't have the stuff to burn. He'd bet on MacVicary in this race: everyone said he was bound to come in first. A cloud came over and all the colours dulled at once.

The new Governor was just behind him and he looked like the Prince of Wales too – or like Samuel's elder, taller brother. People had commented on it. It worried Samuel. He supposed Prince Albert might have misbehaved: he was the Queen's cousin after all.

It was unsettling to think about chance resemblances. Only – in

Samuel's case – there was more to it than that. Hadn't Reynolds given him proof?

The horses ran past. MacVicary was in the lead, but then the sun came out again and dazzled MacVicary's horse. She shied, and lost ground. Samuel saw his money being trodden into the racetrack. He wished he could be more reckless. Only he was leading a life of vice, so he had to be prudent.

He loved Lily. She was so sweet to him, and he desired her, no doubt about that. Only this time last year he'd seen her image everywhere, felt her whenever he touched anything, heard her soft voice whenever he was quiet. He looked across the racetrack and caught sight of her exactly opposite him. For a moment he thought the magic had come back, but it was really Lily, taking a stupid risk. Now he was angry, and afraid. His heart went pale.

Lily had decided to come to the races – rather to Ah Ling's dismay – because Mrs Ellis and Miss Atkinson never went to the races either. Ah Ling had a good tip for the first race, and Lily had put some of her embroidery money on it.

The gentlemen jockeys lined up in their stalls, the starting pistols sounded, and the gates opened. Lily and Ah Ling leaned up against the rails, and Ah Ling showed Lily the horse they were backing. The Postmaster-General was riding it: Lily remembered his emotion when she had given her testimony at Mrs Darley's house. Then the blur of horses cleared and she saw Samuel staring at her. She tugged Ah Ling away in case she lost her invisibility after all. It would be dreadful if anyone else recognized her, and Samuel looked angry. But she had to stay at the races and win some money.

The Postmaster-General came in first.

They hurried off to the bookmaker and collected their winnings. Ah Ling advised Lily to put some money on Sir Paul Chater's horse: Lily took a chance on an outsider instead.

'You'll lose all your money,' said Ah Ling, shaking her head. 'Then you'll be sorry.'

Lily refused to go back to the place opposite the grandstand, but she didn't tell Ah Ling that Samuel had spotted her. She remembered how she'd sneaked out of her stateroom on the boat: she had the same feeling now, it was escape, intoxication. It was the pleasure she'd enjoyed in Ah Kuen's arms, because he'd been so dangerous, so unreliable, and she'd always known it.

The horses set off and pelted away from her down the track. The dust made her cough, but she didn't care. The speed, the excitement held her. She thought: sixty dollars if I win. If I lose, nothing. She loved the horses, because they might run away with everything she had.

She caught a glimpse of Paul Cheung a little distance away – his hare lip was unmistakable – but she was safe from him. Men didn't speak to women in public, not even to coarse women who went out in the streets.

The outsider won. Lily collected sixty dollars in addition to the ten she had already won. She laughed. Ah Ling, who had lost, laughed too, with vexation.

'But don't try it again,' she said to Lily. 'Next time, you'll lose.' She tapped Lily's arm with her fan.

'I'll bet one more time, and then no more,' said Lily. 'Lucky three. Three times again tomorrow, and each day I come.'

'Tomorrow, again!' scolded Ah Ling. But she didn't argue with the third bet. It made sense. Three was an auspicious number.

Lily bet on her third horse, owned by Mr Kadoorie. It won again. Now she had ninety-nine dollars: she was going to invest them on the stock market.

Lily and Ah Ling bought sesame seed candies to eat: they stuck all over their teeth, so that they had to lick and lick till the sticky came off. Lily fingered the money in her pocket. The horses drummed past in a blaze of colour.

Samuel had bet on Sir Paul's horse, and lost money. He guessed that Lily was betting too, and assumed she must have lost – his money, too! And to stand about opposite so many people who knew her – it was unforgivable, she must want to ruin both of them.

Now the very air and the smell of it were hostile to him, everything getting out of control, as if he were back on the fairground gallopers and they were spinning faster and faster, throwing all the riders off to lie in a swathe of corpses.

From a vantage point in the corner of the stand, Mr Fawler put up his field-glasses to observe Lily with Ah Ling. He had recognized her. What was she doing? She might be a prostitute: they came to the races like everyone else. But she was with only one other woman, an amah, identifiable by the long black plait down her white cotton back, black trousers and black cotton shoes. If she had a maid, it meant she was a kept woman, as he'd always thought.

He put his field-glasses down, and looked for Samuel. He shouted: Bull's-eye! to himself. Samuel was coming down from the stand and walking all the way round and across the track to where Lily was. It took five minutes, but Mr Fawler watched patiently. He's a fool, thought Mr Fawler.

'What are you doing here?' demanded Samuel.

'Sir?' asked Lily, looking down at the trampled coarse tropical grass. Ah Ling put a hand over her mouth and shook her head from side to side.

'Have you been betting?' demanded Samuel.

'No, sir, no,' said Lily eagerly, (mightn't she be thought his wife's baby-amah, or personal maid?) 'I only come watch races.'

But she put her fan up between them.

'Liar,' said Samuel hotly: the pidgin grated worse than ever on Lily's lips. 'I'll speak to you later. I suppose you lost?'

'No,' said Lily indignantly.

'You won?' demanded Samuel, even more angrily. 'How could you win? I lost.'

Lily laughed: she was furious and frightened.

She lied to me, thought Samuel. She lied to me. Disgustedly, he turned his back on Lily, and went back to his own kind.

Mr Fawler stood by his wrought-iron pillar and praised the Lord. He was the only person in Hong-Kong who knew the secret of Lily's flight and he was going to keep it to himself for the time being. That would teach them to leave his name off lists of invitations.

Samuel stood on his own proper side of the racetrack, leaning angrily against a pillar. He felt verse come upon him: he'd never tried that before, but he had to vent his passions. He pulled out his pocket-book and wrote in it:

> Behind that lily face there lurks
> a loathesome serpent, venom-fang'd
> where vice and cunning go to work –

The first rhyme he could find for fang'd was hanged, and he didn't want to use that: it made him shudder.

Mr Fawler came up unseen behind him and smote him hard on the back. Samuel stood quite still, breathless and terrified. He was sure he'd been stabbed, perhaps by the same agency that had killed his father. He even saw the headlines in the newspaper: TRAGEDY AT THE RACES: PROMISING CADET ASSASSINATED.

'The vice of modern literature, Samuel,' said Mr Fawler, 'beware of it. How few images do we find there of good true womanhood? How little to inspirit and inspire!'

Samuel invited Mr Fawler to come for a whisky and soda.

'I don't drink, Samuel,' said Mr Fawler warningly.

'Don't you?' asked Samuel, beginning to enjoy himself. 'Then you can watch me get drunk.'

Mr Fawler shook his head. He breathed in Samuel's ear: 'What a waste of promise, Samuel, and are you sure that you have not incurred still deeper moral degradation?'

'I don't know what you mean,' said Samuel.

'Oh, you do, Samuel,' said Fawler. 'You do, you do.'

Damn him, thought Samuel. I *am* lost now. He saw me talking to Lily and he'll never keep his mouth shut. Why did I lose my temper? Oh, now, he thought, I am certainly going to get drunk.

Caird came past with his wife. Mary Caird had scrunched her curly dark hair back into a chignon and she looked at Samuel with enormous scared eyes.

'So noisy here,' she whispered.

'I'm done for,' said Samuel, 'and it's all your fault. Mr Fawler saw me talking to you on the racecourse. He'll tell everyone, and I'll lose my job.'

'You can tell him lies,' said Lily. She put her lips together and looked away from him.

'Don't sulk,' said Samuel. He didn't mind her sulking for his amusement, but this was different. He said: 'Not everyone can lie as easily as you can.'

He wished she'd had an accident on the way home. If she'd been killed he could have found himself a white mistress and set her up in Happy Valley. Then the tears came to his eyes to think of her lying dead. How could he want to hurt her?

'Give me some whisky,' he muttered. He was drunk already, now he'd drink himself silly.

Lily got up, fetched the whisky from where it was kept on a shelf, and poured it into one of the cheap cut-glass tumblers that stood beside it. He looked round the room and thought how makeshift and sordid it was, in spite of the lace curtains and the caged bird. He could have had a real home, with a real wife, and had everyone's approval into the bargain. Tears ran down his face and into his moustaches where they nested like raindrops in hay.

'What have you done to me?' he demanded, adding, 'Viper.' He found himself searching for rhymes to Viper. 'Griper,' he muttered, 'piper, riper.'

'I haven't done anything,' said Lily. 'I was luckier than you with the horses, but it doesn't matter, truly Samuel, tomorrow you'll win.'

'Give me the money,' he said, 'it's mine.'

'No,' said Lily. 'Please.'

'You made it out of my money,' said Samuel.

'No,' said Lily, 'dear Samuel, listen, one day I met Mr Wells on the street, the man Mr Jackson went to China with, and he was sorry for what had happened to me, and he gave me ten dollars. You can see my housekeeping book if you like, I'll show you what I have left. It's all accounted for.'

'What do you think I am,' demanded Samuel, 'a shopkeeper?'

He made to slap Lily, but she slid out of the way and began to laugh with consternation. They stood on opposite sides of the room and he watched her laughing: he'd never known her, so how could he truly love her?

'Please don't be cruel,' said Lily, still gasping with laughter. 'Don't be heartless.'

'You,' he said, 'you care about money more than you care about me.'

'Oh, no,' said Lily, 'I love you, I do Samuel, you give me so much pleasure – '

He didn't know what to say now, so he drank more whisky. Lily came up behind him and began to stroke his neck. He felt her slim fingers, shivered, and wanted her. He drew her round to sit on his knee. She giggled again, and he took her clothes off. They made love, but he didn't enjoy it much. He kept imagining Fawler's face watching them.

Lily went to the races the next day, and the next after that. Samuel pretended not to notice her. Nor did he ask her advice about his bets, and so he lost more money. Lily risked her money again and again and won two hundred dollars altogether. It would have kept her in comfort for a year, but she used it to buy herself a small portfolio of Chinese joint-stock investments. They were all sound businesses, and her money grew.

She didn't tell Samuel about her investments. He didn't ask.

'H.E. needs his head examined,' said Darley to Samuel. 'This new accounting system means we're going into debt just because he's changed the way we do the books. Settling all the accounts in the year they arise in: no one's ever complained before, when we stood them over. You know what it's really about. They think we're getting above ourselves. They didn't like it when we had the electric lighting system put in. We're not meant to be prosperous. We're supposed to channel the money back to the Mother Country.' He chewed his invisible straw. The water hissed in the government urinal. 'It'll mean staff cuts, and worse,' he said, 'mark my words. Why do we get new governors?'

It occurred to Samuel that if cuts were made they'd begin with anyone whose reputation had been blown on, be it never so slightly. He was always expecting to be brought in to the Colonial Secretary's office and exposed: he'd see Fawler, the informer, hurrying away as he went in.

'Due for a move soon, aren't you, young fellow?' asked Darley.

Samuel extended his penis over the running seawater, but he couldn't urinate. He hoped Darley hadn't noticed.

'I should think so,' he said, 'I don't know.'

'You've been doing a good job,' said Darley, 'protecting the Chinese. I mean it!'

'Am I protecting them?' asked Samuel.

'We're out here to do our job,' said Darley. He looked lovingly down at the gushing stream of seawater in the urinal: it was the clear colour of health.

'What is our job?' asked Samuel.

'Don't you know by now?' asked Darley. 'What the government tells us to do.' He laughed. Then he said very seriously: 'And to hold the fort out here, whatever the cost.'

Samuel asked: 'Doesn't Jardines do that better than we do?'

'Jardines,' said Darley, 'need us to install a drainage system. They'd be pirates without a Governor. Listen, Pink: Anything, *anything*, I say, that upholds the prestige of the white man in this colony is of use: anything that undermines it must be quashed.'

Samuel wondered if he was being warned.

236

'It isn't easy,' said Darley, peeling off a section of his fingernail. 'It isn't always agreeable, sometimes it's damned painful. But law, order, system – are they worth it? Ask yourself that question.'

Samuel walked along the Praya in the evening and listened to the water slapping against the quayside. The breathless spring mists had swallowed the nine dragon hills of Kowloon: he couldn't see the Peak when he turned round, or anything beyond the dark arches of ranked godowns. The lights were coming up in a fuzz against the hanging warm vapour.

A sampan came up past him: the woman at the oar brought it to a halt with an expert twist, and the child with her jumped out and made it fast. They began to unload baskets of some struggling seafood: Samuel couldn't see what it was, only that it was a mass that moved in an ugly way. Formlessness, he thought, is the most frightening thing of all. The muddle of the half-finished face, leering out from the mist to devour me. The hungry ghost.

He thought of Darley: no equivocations in *his* head. Whatever undermines the prestige of the white man must be quashed, however painful it might be. Darley was a strong man: he hadn't stopped short at destroying his wife.

All at once, the mist lifted: or was it only in his head? He saw the ranked white buildings on the hill, mansions for the white man and the rich Chinese, cramped tenements for the coolies. Here, where he stood, the godowns: stuffed full of opium, some of them. Trade to determine the future, the government offices to legitimate the operations with clean water and a constant flow of ordinances, the navy as guard dog. The Chinese, lured into a world where money could be made more swiftly, and all the while that same world leeched the blood out of a Celestial Kingdom drugged drowsy with British-supplied opium. Hong-Kong itself was a life-sapping parasite: it had been put there for that purpose.

The cathedral reminded him of God (who was white, and, when it came down to it, English). He understood what he had known for years. That was what the mission hymns had been about. ('Oh, happy day,' sang the convert Chinese, 'when Jesus washed my wits away.')

This was form, this was the meaning of Darley's 'law, order, system'. He'd seen it now, the way Reynolds wanted him to. He the illegitimate, the unpermitted child, he was bound to have such visions, this had always been in store for him. If it hadn't been for the cruelty of others – if it wasn't for the cruelty of a system that refused to allow the alliance of a Queen and a servant – it was unbearable. And his mother suffered as much as he did!

And could this pattern of misery come right, after revolution, or after death? It seemed more likely that it would continue for ever, that, if there was any stronger reality outside the cave of this life, it contained worse injustices, greater loneliness, more hideous pain. He couldn't bear it. He began to walk uphill, towards the Mid-Levels, towards Lily. He wanted to see if he'd feel better with his head between her breasts.

It was at the end of Caine Road, just above Taipingshan, that he encountered Mrs Ellis. She accosted him just under one of the new electric lamps.

'Mr Pink,' she said, 'do you know where Lily Jackson is?'

'No, I don't,' he said quickly. Did his voice give him away?

'I'm ruined,' said Mrs Ellis, searching his face. 'I've lost all credibility. Some man has ruined me. I shall never be happy till I know who he is. She wrote me a letter, full of lies.' She put her hand to her hip. There was a bulge there that Samuel knew was her revolver.

'How do you know they were lies?' he asked.

Mrs Ellis asked: 'Do you think she was a truthful girl?'

'I thought so,' said Samuel.

Mrs Ellis said: 'She told me she loved me. She was lying. She is a liar. I'm warning you, Mr Pink.'

She nodded at him and turned away down a steep ladder street. He walked on, trying to believe that she was so mad no one would take any notice of her.

There was a large sack lying in Lily's front doorway. He wondered what it was doing there, and what was inside. He bent to examine it.

There was a hiss. He backed instinctively. A cobra's head shot up out of the sack: the snake spread its hood and hissed again.

He was at the other side of the street, his eyes on the indistinct clump of the sack. He was cold with fright. The street itself was a snake's body; the yawning mouth with its fangs all ready to strike him was bigger than the house, inescapable, ineffably powerful. There was nothing left in the world but that hideous gateway: he cowered against the wall like a panicked mouse.

Then a coolie in a conical hat came walking up the street, stepped into the doorway, grasped the neck of the sack, and walked away carrying it. As if there was no deadly snake inside. As if the snake knew him and was tame enough not to bite him.

Samuel looked up and saw streetlights, not fangs, above his head, a street, not the dreadful tunnel of the snake's digestive tract, running ahead of him. After a moment he crossed the road again. He inspected the doorway. There was nothing there now.

'Virginia,' asked Darley, 'did they chloroform you?'

She turned away from him, and walked slowly out of the room.

19

SPRING 1892:
THE INTRUDERS

SAMUEL knocked on the door, Uncle Liu answered it sleepily, and he went straight to Lily's parlour. She was hooding the little bird's cage in black velvet.

He couldn't speak. She ran to him, smiling, and put her arms round his neck. Everything was perfect, the movements of her full, pouting lips, the arousing glance, the light twin greeting of her small breasts. He could see how well she did it. It left him cold.

'Samuel dear,' she said, 'what's wrong?'

'Someone tried to kill me,' he said. 'Someone left a cobra in a bag, on your front doorstep.'

'But Samuel,' said Lily, 'it was an accident. People have snakes for sale, it's the time of year for eating snake. It warms you up in the cold season.'

'Who'd carry snakes round at this time of night?' demanded Samuel. 'And the cold season's ending.'

'Oh,' said Lily, 'who'd want to kill you?'

He pushed her away and poured himself a glass of whisky. She wished he didn't drink so much whisky. She wished he would take soda with it.

He said: 'You don't understand.'

She said: 'Tell me,' though she was frightened of what she might hear.

'No,' he said, 'we'll go to bed.'

Then he couldn't do anything. Lily tried to pretend he had, and he went along with the pretence, but who did it fool? He thought he'd never be happy again.

'Samuel,' said Lily, 'dear Samuel?'

'Leave me alone,' he said.

She rolled away from him and lay beside him, clutching the edge of the silk sheet in her fingers.

Whichever way his mind ran, it came up against something dreadful: the snake in the doorway, the fear of disgrace if Fawler denounced him, the dreadful cynicism that had come over him down on the Praya and spoilt everything. The terror that God was evil, so evil that anyone's wickedness and rebellion were, by comparison, but a small and slightly soiled pocket-handkerchief.

'Samuel,' said Lily, 'you must be ill.'

She was afraid he'd die, Mr Jackson had said a man who couldn't get an erection was as good as dead. If she lost him, she'd have no choice but to go back to Mrs Ellis who would forgive her and force her back to the laundry. She'd never have her baby. She pulled the edge of the sheet to her mouth and stroked it against her lips. She wished she was allowed to cling to Samuel. She might be able to give him an erection after all.

'I want to tell you something,' he said, 'but you must never tell anyone else. I'm Queen Victoria's son.'

'What?' said Lily.

'Don't you believe me?' he asked.

She thought he was definitely ill, probably with the early stages of brain-fever.

Carefully, she said: 'Of course I believe you, Samuel. Please tell me more.' She touched his face, but he didn't seem to be hot. He might be mad, of course, as Mr Jackson had been. She wondered why she was always the lover of madmen and murderers.

He explained to her how he'd always known that the Pinks weren't his real parents, how Reynolds had told him who he was on his sixteenth birthday. He told her about his mother's yearly letter, about John Brown, whom she'd never heard of, though she knew all about the Empress Dowager's lover, Jung Lu.

She asked: 'You're sure your tutor wasn't lying to you? What sort of a man is he?'

'He never lies to me,' said Samuel angrily. 'He still writes me everything he does. He's my oldest friend.'

'I'm sorry,' said Lily hastily, 'I'm sorry, Samuel.'

He said: 'You don't believe me.'

'Oh, I do,' said Lily, 'I do believe you, dearest Samuel.' She wished she could pluck the delusion out of his head, shut it up in a jar, seal it and hide it away from him, away from her.

'I should never have told you,' he said.

'Oh, no,' said Lily desperately, 'I'm so glad you told me, please, Samuel, tell me anything you like.'

She couldn't convince him.

He woke with a headache the next morning, just as Ah Ling knocked on the bedroom door as usual. Ah Ling lit the gas, but Lily slept on.

Ah Ling put a pot of tea down for him, and a few slices of toast. He got out of bed, ate and drank.

Lily stirred, opened her eyes, and looked drowsily at him.

He said: 'Don't tell anyone what I told you last night.'

She shook her head.

He kissed her red lips, the cheeks that were still pink and warm with sleep, and her eyes with their long black eyelashes. He felt a sad, bereaved tenderness.

'Go back to sleep,' he whispered.

She turned over and lay on her side. He glanced at her from time to time as he dressed, lying defenceless, her mouth a little open, her slim knuckle against her lips. She was such a child!

He had loved her, did still care what happened to her, but none of it made up for the time when she'd mediated divine love to him, no physical pleasure had been able to translate that ecstasy. Now even physical pleasure had been withdrawn.

He had to go: his sedan would be waiting for him.

Mr Fawler was also beset with the desire to tell secrets, but he didn't want to tell his wife, not any more. She'd betrayed him, had been betraying him for years, more comprehensively and cruelly than if she'd had – heaven forbid – a lover.

When the Minister of the Union Church mentioned Mrs Ellis one afternoon after an orphanage committee meeting, Mr Fawler reminded himself that the man snubbed him about the urgent message he'd brought to Mrs Darley's. The desire to keep him in the dark fought the desire to show him how little he knew.

'Regrettable,' said Mr Briggs, 'she is still doing such wonderful work, yet I do feel a certain loss of balance – ' he stopped, and left the rest to Mr Fawler's imagination.

'She grew infatuated with the Jackson girl,' said Mr Fawler sternly.

'She walks the streets, looking for her,' said Mr Briggs, 'like Christ searching for the lost sheep. I expect the girl's left Hong-Kong.'

'No,' said Mr Fawler smugly, and then bit his lip.

'You've seen her!' exclaimed Mr Briggs. 'What's she doing, then?'

'What do you think?' asked Mr Fawler, 'selling her body, of course.'

'In a brothel?' asked his brother clergyman. Then Mr Fawler had to tell him more, for fear he might be suspected of going to Wan Chai himself and entering a brothel.

'No, a white man.'

'Oh, no,' breathed Mr Briggs. 'The girl's a walking contagion. Who has she infected now?'

'I believe I know,' said Mr Fawler, puffing his chest out, 'I don't yet know for sure. Not an old man, not this time. Not a madman like Jackson. The contagion is far closer to the heart of our little society here.'

'A clergyman?'

'No,' said Mr Fawler, 'not a clergyman.'

'Married or single?'

'No,' exclaimed Mr Fawler in his pulpit voice, 'I have said enough. When the culprit is exposed, he shall be exposed with justice. And not a word, my dear fellow, not a word till I know.'

He took his hat and left. He hoped he'd done the right thing. Later, he realized that Mr Briggs hadn't promised to keep the secret. The more essential that he should find out the truth himself.

Reynold wrote: *I have been dismissed again, but this time I am glad. Old Clark found me in bed with the maidservant, so we both flew out of the door. My main problem is that she wants me to marry her. I have explained to her that the concept of an honest woman is only a piece of oppression, but she's very hard to teach. The women in our little circle are attempting to instruct her. We have decided to form an ideal community. We are renting a house together and sharing everything, including our bodies. Poor Dolly doesn't want to share me, but she knows she must, if she is to be fed.*

We get what work we can: I am doing the accounts for a semi-literate grocer round the corner. At the same time I am working on a book, which we will publish privately and sell to those who have ears to hear. We have decided that books are better weapons than bombs – they reach more people. The women are improving the printing press to deal with it. I am to be the first, but we shall all write books – there is no privilege among us. The women are teaching Dolly to read and write better, so that she will also have the opportunity. Thus we work, slowly, from the bottom up, maid-servants write books, women sit on top of men in bed, marriage is renounced in favour of free choice, and the fabric of society is shaken – you may not think it's shaken hard, but thrown stones can bring a hillside down. There is you, for example. I detect a falling-off in your naive chatter of religion and grace. There are other ideals, Samuel, learn them. I believe our influence will spread out to you. And of course we are short of money, and I know you have plenty to spare. Five pounds would buy us a great deal of paper and ink, or food, or coal, or whatever you like, except a Bible.

Samuel tore the letter to pieces and threw it down behind his chest-of-drawers where the cockroaches, who were just coming out of hibernation, ate it as they ate every piece of paper that wasn't varnished. He sent the money, all the same.

That night he dreamed he was at the rectory, in an attic he had never seen before, and he had to spend the night there. The room was haunted, there was something terrible behind the plastered walls, a ghost he'd known once, and it was creeping out to get him. He fought to wake up: every time he thought he'd managed it, he was back in the attic, ectoplasm misting across the room towards him and the taste of blood in his mouth. When he did wake up, he lay awake for two hours. He didn't dare go back to sleep again. Lily woke, and they made love.

She was wonderfully relieved that he could do it again.

Mr Fawler was a busy man, but he walked the streets when he could, looking for Lily. It was weeks before he saw her: then he followed her home.

He waited for several minutes before he knocked on her front door. There were no doubts in his mind at this stage. It was only when Uncle Liu peered at him through the crack of the door that he began to wonder what he would say to her.

'My name is Mr Fawler,' he said in Cantonese – his Cantonese was good, he was proud of it – 'I am a friend of Miss Lily.'

The best friend, he thought, encouraging himself, that she could have.

Uncle Liu shut the door again. Mr Fawler wasn't deterred. He was used to this sort of thing. He heard Uncle Liu yelling for Ah Ling (the amah, thought Mr Fawler, with the satisfaction of the detective on the scent), could hear Ah Ling answering something or other: the Spirit will guide me, thought Mr Fawler.

Lily was very frightened when she heard who it was, but she thought it wouldn't be a good idea to send him away. And she didn't have the scruples about lying that Samuel had. It didn't do, if you wanted to avoid beggary. 'I shall see him,' she said to Ah Ling.

She said: 'Make him tea, the way the English like it, we have milk, haven't we, and Mr Pink's biscuits?'

She took the whisky off the shelf and hid it in her bedroom, under the bed. She removed the ashtray that Samuel used for his cigars, the hat he had forgotten that morning. She put her embroidery on top of the sideboard instead, and arranged a pile of folded cotton lawn beside it. She was still wearing black, from the street: good. And no ornaments in her hair. She looked like a virtuous widow.

'Bring him up,' she said to Ah Ling.

'Watch out for him,' warned Ah Ling, 'you know what priests are like with pretty women.'

'Not English priests,' said Lily. 'He's married.'

Ah Ling clucked with her tongue but she marched downstairs and let Mr Fawler in.

'Come up,' she said. 'Missee got tea in parlour. She see you now.'

Mr Fawler asked her, in Cantonese: 'Do you know that Jesus loves you?'

Ah Ling didn't answer.

'Mr Fawler,' said Lily, springing up from one of her purple velvet armchairs, 'I am so glad you have come.'

Mr Fawler winced at the sight of the chairs, which he recognized: was Mrs Darley in this conspiracy?

Ah Ling remained in the room, watching every move Mr Fawler made.

'Salvation,' breathed Mr Fawler courageously, 'salvation is still possible.'

'Yes,' said Lily eagerly, breathlessly, 'and I need a Bible. I want your spiritual help, Mr Fawler – you will drink tea?' She poured out tea, milk, added sugar. 'Please, Mr Fawler,' she said, 'sit down.'

He sat. His legs bent without asking his permission first. He found himself on the *chaise-longue*: the velvet was soft as sin to his hardy behind. He looked at Lily. No, he thought, her appeal wasn't to the eye – he was no admirer of Chinese women – it was her voice, so sweet, so caressing. It hypnotized him: he remembered the sound of a running stream, in his boyhood. He used to sit beside it for hours, that was where he first became aware of the grace of God. Her movements, too –

'If you want help from me,' he said, attempting sternness, 'you must be prepared to practise true Christianity.'

'I have forgiven Mrs Ellis,' said Lily. Gracefully, she put a cup of tea in front of Mr Fawler and felt the process of change within herself: courage, cleverness were growing there.

'Forgiven her?' demanded Mr Fawler. He felt as if Lily had pulled the *chaise-longue* from under him, and let him fall on to the carpet.

'Miss Lily – ' he protested. Feebly, he said: 'I thought, that is, Mrs Ellis is angry with *you.*'

Lily said: 'I wrote to her about the money Mr Jackson sent me.' She sat in an armchair and put her face in her hands. 'Has she told anyone that? Or is she spreading malicious rumours about me? I can't bear it.'

Mr Fawler pulled himself together. He reminded himself what he'd seen with his own eyes.

He said: 'Aren't you Samuel Pink's mistress? He spoke to you at the racecourse.'

Lily said at once: 'Yes, he also blamed me for leaving Mrs Ellis. He wanted me to go back. You don't understand, Mr Fawler.' She wondered if she could tell Mr Fawler that Mrs Ellis had threatened to sell her to a brothel? She decided he wouldn't believe it.

The little white-eyed bird chimed its fairy bell in the corner of the room like some exquisite watchmaker's toy. She leaned towards him: his head and body swam with her nearness and the scent of sandalwood. He couldn't breathe: he recognized danger.

'Miss Lily,' he said with an effort, 'Miss Lily, go back to Mrs Ellis, and *she* will give you your Bible.'

'If you say I must,' said Lily sadly. 'Then she'll send me back to work in the laundry, and I'll fall ill again. You don't know – no one ever saw – the heavy work she made me do. And the doctor said I should take care of my health. He said I might die of tuberculosis if I didn't.' Lily coughed a little, carefully, putting her handkerchief in front of her mouth. She said: 'Since I had the legacy from

Mr Jackson, and came to live here, my dear Ah Ling has been looking after me so well, I've hardly coughed blood at all.'

'Which doctor?' enquired Mr Fawler.

'A Chinese doctor,' said Lily. 'Doctor Kwok. He lived in East Point: he was trained in America. Only he's gone to Singapore. Don't ask Mrs Ellis about it. She never believed I was ill.'

Lily sat there and looked – he could see it now – fragile and delicate. He imagined her coughing blood on to the wet white sheets, watercolour flowers of blood blossoming there, and Mrs Ellis angry with her for dirtying the linen. He imagined himself, putting his arms round Lily, lifting her tenderly away from the cruelty, taking her to a hospital – but it was too late.

And Mrs Ellis hadn't insisted that he be invited to Mrs Darley's soirée.

Lily said: 'I'll go back to Mrs Ellis if you say I must, Mr Fawler. I'll be guided by you.'

The voice of reason protested somewhere at the back of his mind, but it was swept away by a mob of emotions.

He said: 'I will send you a Bible, Lily, but you must promise me to read it every day, and abide by its teachings: all its teachings. You will read the story of the woman taken in adultery – I will mark it for you – go, and sin no more. You must ask yourself if your present conduct is in accord with the teachings of the Master. And I hope that virtue will gain and maintain a hold over your heart.'

Lily put her hands over her face. She said: 'I will take courage from the virtuous woman Susanna who was accused by the wicked and lascivious Elders. She was justified, as I shall be. I will remind myself that God always protects the innocent and the poor. Will you come to see me again, Mr Fawler, will you pray with me and explain the Bible to me?'

It would be nice if he came. She liked company. And he was lonely – she could see that. There was no harm in protecting him from the hurtful knowledge that she was Samuel's mistress, and that Christianity was not the only religion she took comfort from. There was no need to mention it at all.

Mr Fawler met her wide eyes, and he *saw* the light of the Gospel in them: but she dropped them almost at once. He liked her modesty.

He asked: 'Is there anything else I can do for you?'

'I need work,' said Lily. 'I need to save money for medical help, in case I fall ill again. Could you get me dressmaking work from the English ladies?'

'I will try,' he said eagerly. 'I will try.'

He'd proclaim her innocence to the whole of Hong-Kong. He was the only man to know the truth of the situation. Though they *had* excluded him from the meeting at Mrs Darley's.

Samuel played billiards at the Club, with Richards and Caird. He thought neither of work, nor of Lily, nor of his unhappiness. He concentrated on the simple arrangement of three balls on green baize, lining his whole attention up and down the smooth diminishing cue, shooting himself across the green: finished, done. Aim achieved. He thought about nothing else.

'Good shot, old fellow,' said Caird.

'Tolerable,' conceded Samuel.

A club servant came up to him and handed him a note. He opened it. It read:

Samuel, I see that I have misjudged you. But do not try to persuade Miss Lily to return to Mrs Ellis. I have made myself master of the situation. I will make sure Miss Lily is kept safe. She is a virtuous child of God and has been misjudged in her turn. Nathaniel Fawler.

'Boy,' shouted Samuel, 'whisky here!'

Caird said: 'I heard a rumour about Miss Lily – Jackson's mistress – you know. They say she's living with a white man.'

Samuel drank his whisky, and demanded more.

'So I wondered who it might be,' said Caird, 'Richards, it's not you, is it? You met her before, after all.'

'No,' said Richards, 'I've got Elise, why should I spend money on a Chinese whore? Why don't you ask Pink, he's a dark horse, you never hear anything about him.'

Samuel said: 'I like the simple life, old boy. Queen's Road does for me.'

He thought he saw Caird's eye on him, measuring him up.

'Tell him to stay away,' said Samuel to Lily.

'Dearest Samuel,' said Lily, stroking his face – he thought, like a cat, rubbing against me – 'I did it for your sake. He won't tell anyone about us now, after all.'

Samuel said: 'You've decided to let him trot in and out of the house: all you have to do is leave the whisky bottle out once, and we're done for. And supposing he comes while I'm here?'

She said: 'Then Ah Ling can tell him I'm asleep. But he won't come in the evening. It wouldn't be virtuous. He's got his own reputation to think of.'

'And if I wanted to come in the daytime, and he's here?'

Lily said: 'But you never do come in the daytime.'

Samuel said: 'I can see I'll end up kicking my heels in the street while you read the Bible with the old fool. I suppose it's our only chance – they're beginning to talk, at the Club.' Then he said: 'You were lying to him. How can I ever believe anything you say, when you lied to him like that?'

Lily said: 'Don't you tell people you're glad to see them, when you're not, only to be polite? I didn't lie to him. There were just a few things I didn't say.'

My dear Samuel, wrote his mother, *you are such a comfort to me, you can never guess how much it means to me. I have a photograph of you in my desk, but you were very young then, and it is rather blurred: please have your photograph taken in Hong-Kong and send it to Mr Pink: he will make sure that it reaches me. But no messages, Samuel, no writing on the photograph, it must not be, I dare not risk exposure. Your face will be message enough.*

Another year has passed and I grow older, and quite infirm from time to time, more so than I would expect at my age. It must be the life I am obliged to lead. Scotland is very damp, you know, and the cold winds blow in and make my bones ache. I think, rheumatism, already! and hesitate to greet the unwelcome visitor. What can I do? He comes whether I want him or not. Alas!

Goodbye, my son, I shall write to you next year. Sometimes I dream that circumstances alter, that I am able to travel to Hong-Kong, and there we are brought together at last. But I fear it will never be. You have my dearest love, never forget that. Your affectionate Mother.

Samuel calculated the Queen's age. She must be seventy-three, which was old enough for rheumatism, surely? What an indomitable spirit, not to resign herself to it! He wondered what circumstances could prevent her from coming to Hong-Kong: there could be a state visit. Then he knew that he didn't want her to come. She might find out about Lily.

249

Mr Fawler went to see Mrs Ellis and Miss Atkinson. Mrs Ellis told him – through the doorkeeper – to go away. Mr Fawler said he would knock, as prescribed in Holy Scripture, till the door was opened to him. Mrs Ellis grew tired and let him in.

He begged them to be reconciled with her.

'Never,' said Mrs Ellis, and went out of the room.

Samuel felt as if everyone was watching him. He wouldn't get out of his sedan at Lily's house unless the bearers had assured him that the street was empty. He began to be morbidly aware of everything he was saying, so that sometimes he stopped in mid-sentence and couldn't get anything out.

In addition to this, he didn't like what was happening to him at work. He found himself looking at every ordinance, every minute, every piece of correspondence, in an unwelcome new light: or rather darkness. He blamed Reynolds. His tutor had always been happiest at night.

A Chinese criminal, apprehended in Hong-Kong, was returned to the Celestial Kingdom as laid down in the Treaty of Tientsin. This was quite routine and worried no one except, suddenly, Samuel, who had to go to the water-closet and shed tears at the thought of the man's horrible end: he had killed his father and would probably die by slow slicing. Christ had said the merciful would obtain mercy, but that didn't seem to trouble the Christian Governor. His sole concern was the letter of the law.

The coolies, thought Samuel mercilessly, were cattle to white man and wealthy Chinese alike. A wise man made sure his cattle were healthy, so that he got the best work out of them, but they were meant for slaughter, and the farmer mustn't care about them too much. He remembered the accusing face of the woman in Taiping-shan.

And again he was frightened of the shadowy person who might want to kill him. Though it would have been easier to kill him in his boyhood, if anyone wanted him dead. Had the Queen been forced to send him to Hong-Kong because the climate was so unhealthy? And there had been the snake on Lily's doorstep. Sometimes, he thought he saw a pleading expression on his mother's face, on the walls of the Government Offices, of the Hong-Kong Club, on the biscuit-tin. She was a hostage: her letters made it clear.

Mr Fawler had vouched for Lily, but the men at the Club were still talking about her, wondering whether Fawler was to be trusted, and what he was getting in return for his championship. That was the most galling thing of all.

It *was* Reynolds's world, it was dangerous and unreliable, and he didn't like the adventures.

Miss Atkinson came to see Lily on a Sunday evening, when she ought to have been at church, dressed in dark clothing and a close bonnet. Mrs Ellis wouldn't have the Refuge left unattended nowadays, so they had to go to the cathedral turn and turn about. It was Mrs Ellis's week to go to Matins. She told Uncle Liu she'd come about dressmaking, so Lily had no warning. Uncle Liu knew what Mrs Ellis looked like, but not Miss Atkinson: Lily had never expected Miss Atkinson. Ah Ling – pleased to help more money come in to the house – brought her straight up.

Miss Atkinson was distressed to see how frightened Lily was. The blood drained out of her face, even her lips: Miss Atkinson thought for a moment that Lily's hair would whiten too.

Lily felt as if she was going to faint. Then Mrs Ellis would come in off the street, pick her resistless body up, and carry her off to work in the laundry.

'Please –' she said, 'please – '

Ah Ling ran to her side and made her sit down. She stared angrily at Miss Atkinson: Lily felt better.

'Oh, please,' said Miss Atkinson, 'don't be afraid, Lily, I haven't come to take you back.'

'But Mrs Ellis – ' said Lily.

'Oh, Lily,' said Miss Atkinson, 'my sister would never have you. She says you've betrayed her. She's closed down the embroidery business and sent all the girls back to the laundry, didn't you know? Except that four of them have escaped. They don't like the laundry, and they don't like us. It's dreadful to live in Pokfulam Road now, Lily. It's like living in a prison.' Her voice wavered and tears came into her eyes. 'Then Mr Fawler told us where you live, and – I had to see you.'

Lily saw her look round the room and notice the whisky bottle. And there was Samuel's hat – which he'd left behind the night before. There was no room left to be clever. There was no room at all: Lily shrank against her chair, crowded by the weight of

Miss Atkinson's love and her need. If only Miss Atkinson wouldn't cry.

'He said you weren't living with a man,' said Miss Atkinson. She put her hands to her streaming eyes. 'I – I don't blame you for running away. I wish I could, too. I've missed you so much. I won't tell anyone, Lily. Not my sister, or Mr Fawler – are you happy?'

Her face was wistful: she wanted Lily to be happy, Lily could see that. She wiped her face which was as wet now as if she'd been out in the rain, blew her nose, dried her chin.

Lily thought she wouldn't tell Miss Atkinson who the man was.

Miss Atkinson said: 'It's Mr Pink, isn't it? I hope it's Mr Pink, because my sister said he was in love with you. I want you to have someone who loves you, Lily.'

Lily said: 'Yes.' She felt defeated. She had nowhere left to hide. She was out in the open now, meat to be eaten. But she'd help herself still: if Miss Atkinson *would* pull her so ruthlessly out of her cover, then she'd get something out of Miss Atkinson in return. Nicely, of course: she couldn't be nasty.

Miss Atkinson put her arms round Lily and kissed her. She said: 'You smell so sweet, Lily.'

'Sandalwood,' said Lily. 'He lets me buy sandalwood for myself, and my hair, and my clothes.'

'Oh,' said Miss Atkinson, and blushed all over her body, at the images this conjured up.

So simple, thought Lily. Innocent, truly innocent and good. And a little foolish: she's not so much of a threat. She'll go away – and come back – and I need friends.

'Lily,' said Miss Atkinson, 'do you love him?'

'Yes,' said Lily. It was the only answer that would do for Miss Atkinson, she knew that.

I can be water, she thought. I can be strong because I take the easiest way. I can be like Cook Ting, who kept his knife sharp and saved himself effort because he knew every space in an animal's carcass and directed his knife towards those spaces. And the animals he slaughtered didn't even know they'd been killed.

Then she wished she hadn't thought that, in case the knife in her mind cut Miss Atkinson.

She said: 'You've come to visit me, and I haven't even offered you tea. Please sit down.'

'Is it all right?' asked Ah Ling in Cantonese.

'Yes,' Lily said, 'don't worry. She's a friend. Bring tea, Ah Ling, please.'

Crossly, Ah Ling said: 'Too many *gweilos*.'

Lily smiled and shook her head.

Ah Ling went away and came back with the tray, the silver teapot, the silver cream jug, the sugar bowl, the spoons, the cups and saucers, white with gold rims. Miss Atkinson sat, feeling the familiar sweet lassitude.

'And your rheumatism,' Lily coaxed, 'how is it, dear Miss Atkinson?'

'Not good, I am afraid, Lily,' said Miss Atkinson, 'but I mustn't complain. She gave a little sigh.

'Oh – ' said Lily. 'Before you go, you must let me massage you. And the Chinese herbs that helped you so much – I could get them for you again.' She knelt beside Miss Atkinson and took her sad aching hands in her own – Miss Atkinson felt the pain slip away from her.

Lily said: 'Could you do a little thing to help me, Miss Atkinson?'

'I will try,' faltered Miss Atkinson, wary after all of what Lily might want.

Lily poured out tea for her, adding milk and sugar.

She said: 'You know, I need to save a little money in case – to safeguard myself – men are so fickle!' She put her hands in front of her mouth. 'Now if I could do a little dressmaking work, I could earn something – honestly.'

'But the ladies won't employ you,' said Miss Atkinson.

Lily said: 'Mr Fawler will tell them I'm a good woman. If you tell them as well – '

'But Lily,' said Miss Atkinson sadly, 'I'd have to tell a lie.'

'I'm sorry, Miss Atkinson,' said Lily at once. 'Forget I asked you: it was wrong of me. So now I'll massage you.'

Miss Atkinson followed Lily into the bedroom, churning with guilt, but too needy to refuse the treat – which she knew she should, if only because she mustn't pay for it.

The guilt intensified when she lay down on the wicked bed: Lily took the deep crimson counterpane off it and revealed a light silk quilt and silken sheets embroidered with phoenixes in bright Chinese colours. (Like Samuel, Miss Atkinson turned her attention away from the white porcelain goddess with her tribute of chrysanthemums. Sin was more comprehensible than idolatry.)

Once again Miss Atkinson took off her skirt and blouse, her corsets and liberty bodice and stockings and lay down in her drawers under Lily's strong yet gentle hands. It was heaven to feel them over every part of her body – except her breasts – Lily knew quite well that Miss Atkinson wouldn't be able to bear her to touch her breasts. Miss Atkinson let herself drift into a gentle state between sleep and waking, into pleasure: she felt pleasure again! Lily covered the parts she wasn't working on carefully with a quilt: Miss Atkinson felt how sweet, how safe it was to be covered up.

Lily, for her part, felt safe because she was in charge. And Miss Atkinson would have to go home again soon.

'Oh, Lily – ' said Miss Atkinson, getting dressed. 'How can I repay you?'

'No need,' said Lily, with her back turned. 'No need at all.'

But Miss Atkinson knew Lily was only being polite. Now she felt pressure, pushing into her dishonesty – no, not pushing, luring, enticing.

She fell.

'I *shall* get you embroidery work, Lily,' she said. She felt a strange excitement – she'd pull Hong-Kong's nose for it – and Mr Fawler's – and her sister's – 'I'll tell the ladies you're living off your own work and Mr Jackson's legacy. I'll tell my sister, too.'

Lily embraced Miss Atkinson and kissed her cheek. For a moment there was all the deliciousness of her delicate body close to Miss Atkinson, her scent, the soft touch of her lips, her pliability. Miss Atkinson held her close and her own body melted with love.

The grandfather clock struck seven, and she knew she'd have to let go.

Just after the clock struck twelve the same night, the door was beaten down: smash. Samuel heard it at once, and at once knew what it was. This was Henderson's nightmare. Robbers. And the knives were all in the kitchen, easy for anyone to lay their hands on.

Lily, he thought. I must protect Lily.

He couldn't move.

He heard the feet on the stairs, the Chinese voices, a laugh. He imagined the chopper gashing into the back of his neck: for some reason, he was particularly fearful for the back of his neck. It was an outrage that Lily was still fast asleep, when the house was filling up with terrifying noises. My revolver, he thought. I have a revolver.

He'd left it in Lily's parlour, and the robbers were there.

'Lily,' he whispered, tugging at her arm. 'Wake up and don't make a sound. There are robbers in the house.'

Lily woke immediately, heard the voices and the feet. She knew without taking his words in. The darkness was peopled all about them. Any moment now it would explode with violence.

'Samuel,' she asked, 'where's your revolver?'

'In the parlour,' said Samuel. He ought to have had the revolver on him, then he could have used it to chase the robbers out of the house. He took his hand off Lily's arm so she wouldn't feel it shaking.

There was a noise of drawers being pulled out, of furniture being tumbled, a clang on the floor that must be the silver teapot.

'Ah Ling,' said Lily. 'Do you think they've killed her?'

'I don't know,' said Samuel. He wondered if they could climb out of the bedroom window, but it was barred, to keep robbers out. He raged at the uselessness of it.

'What's happened to Ah Ling?' asked Lily again, shivering. 'And Uncle Liu? And my bird, Samuel, I don't want them to have my bird.'

'What would they want with your bird?' asked Samuel.

'Do you know how much I paid for it?' demanded Lily in a whisper.

She wondered why she was worrying about her bird's value. The men would come to the bedroom, and they'd be prepared to kill.

'We'll have to get under the bed,' said Samuel. His hand curled for his absent gun.

'They'd look there,' said Lily.

'Don't argue!' whispered Samuel angrily.

Reluctantly, she climbed out of bed and squeezed herself in under the springs. He had a job to follow her: his round stomach grazed the underside of the bed. It was dusty in there, and a cockroach ran away.

Lily said: 'I don't want them to kill Ah Ling.'

'Stop talking,' commanded Samuel, hoarsely. 'You'll be heard.'

It was more frightening under the bed. They were trapped in a small trap inside a larger trap. Nor was it as easy to hear the robbers moving about the house. The sounds seemed to have ceased altogether. For a moment, Samuel wondered if he'd imagined the whole thing.

'Have they gone?' asked Lily.

At that moment, the door opened, and lamplight shone across the floor.

Now, thought Samuel, now I'm found out. If it's the robbers, they'll kill me, and if Uncle Liu has called the police, I'll be found out and ruined. His merciless vision clicked on like an electric light and showed him the figure he would present, in his nightclothes, huddled up to Lily, under her bed. And covered in the dried-out carcasses of insects and dust: their dust, the filthy detritus of their own bodies.

He heard the robbers talking to each other in the rough and ribald Cantonese of the streets. Of course he'd be dead and wouldn't have to hear the comments, the censure. Only his mother would know – but she'd arranged for him to come here. It was all her fault. He thought of the chopper-blade, the pain, the fear – and then what?

I won't die, thought Lily. I don't want to.

'Look where?' asked a voice.

'Savings, under the pillow or under the bed.'

Samuel wished he'd never hidden: at least he might have died on his feet. Then he felt he was going to cough. His stomach froze in terror, while his mind yammered at Lily and Ah Ling for their slatternliness: they ought to sweep under the bed, it was quite disgusting.

Lily knew they wouldn't find her savings, but money wouldn't be much good to her when she was dead. She'd sit in hell, with no one to pray her out of it or send her comforts while she was there. Parentless, childless, she came from nowhere and had no confidence in where she was going.

She could hear the intruders tossing the bedding about. It was probably Mr Jackson's revenge: she'd never made offerings for him at the Festival of Hungry Ghosts.

Please Mr Jackson, she mouthed in the fusty darkness, I will, if I live. Every year.

The quilt, the sheets landed on the floor beside her. Then the robbers set their hands to the bed. They sent it across the floor with a hideous squeaking and cracking of wood. Another cockroach ran for cover, but Samuel and Lily were helplessly exposed.

The robbers looked at the dusty night-clad pair, and laughed. There were five of them. They were Cantonese of the streets and the boats, dark with sun, wearing blue cotton and had their queues wound round their heads so they wouldn't interfere with action. They were pitiless and strange. One of them carried a crowbar for breaking open safes and doors, two had knives, and two carried choppers: they'd be razor-sharp.

Samuel looked away from the derision in their faces and thought what a fool he'd been to let himself be shipped out here. He'd haunt his mother, when he was dead. She wouldn't be able to send him away then.

'Kill them?' asked one of them of the others.

'Please don't kill us,' begged Samuel, getting on to his knees and talking English, 'please leave us alive, we promise we won't tell the police about this, we'll say nothing at all – '

'They saw our faces,' said one of them. 'Better to kill them.'

'Oh, no,' blubbered Samuel, still in English, 'you see all Chinese look alike to us, I'd never know you again – '

Then there were more voices, more footsteps in the house. The robbers looked at each other: one made a grab towards Lily, but the new set of voices came closer.

The robbers turned and ran out of the door. There were shouts, and shots; you could see the shadow-play of their struggle on the wall of the room, and a man fell, wounded or dead. They must be Sikh policemen: the Chinese weren't armed.

'Uncle Liu,' said Lily, beginning to cry and laugh together. 'He must have called the police. Now you must always sleep with your revolver, Samuel.' She sat on the floor with her hands over her face.

Still kneeling, Samuel said to her: 'Why do you never sweep under your bed?' They were both grey with dust. Samuel began to brush himself down.

'They musn't find me here,' he said.

Lily wanted to be angry with Samuel, but she didn't know how to do it.

'You can't get out,' she said. 'Supposing the police come here? You'll have to hide again. You'll have to go back under the bed.'

'I won't,' he said, 'you go out and talk to the policemen. Keep them out of here.'

'Please, Samuel,' said Lily, 'I don't want to go out there because one of the robbers might kill me, or the policemen might shoot me dead.'

'And my reputation?' asked Samuel, 'you don't care about that?'

He was a coward, after all, that was what his reputation was worth.

Lily remembered that she'd been sleeping with him for more than a year and still she wasn't pregnant. And he told her he was of royal birth!

'Please,' she said, 'please go under the bed, Samuel.'

In the passage, the policemen fought it out with the robbers. Samuel stood up, and sneezed.

If only he could stride out to the battle, the British lion, undaunted, draw his revolver and shoot a Chinese dead – he'd see the man fall, his arms out wide, bending backwards. Samuel would stand – and it wouldn't matter that he was in his nightshirt – holding his revolver, frozen for a moment in the picture: The heroic white man defends his home against the invasion of cowardly robbers.

There was fluff all over his face and in his beard. He thought he felt an insect crawling over his leg.

It wasn't like that. He had neither royal courage nor daredevilry. And the robbers had been poor men, probably acting out of desperation. He wondered if he'd ever achieve proper insensitivity.

The shots died away, and footsteps came towards the doorway.

'Please, Samuel,' whispered Lily, 'there's still time to get under the bed.'

There wasn't. A Sikh policeman stood there, holding a smoking gun.

He said: 'Good morning, sir, the robbers have gone.'

'Keep the other men out of here,' said Samuel at once, 'and keep your mouth shut. I'll make it worth your while.'

The policeman said: 'Thank you, Mr Pink.'

Samuel was appalled that the man knew who he was. He remembered how grandly he'd imagined refusing bribes. Now he was offering one, and covered in fluff and filth into the bargain. And there *was* an insect crawling up his leg.

Lily cleaned him off, and fetched his money to pay Constable Singh. Uncle Liu and Ah Ling came back into the house. Ah Ling chased Lily away, so that she shouldn't have to speak to the strange men.

20

DECEMBER 1893:
THE TYPHOON

IT was the first of the month: Constable Singh called at the house in Caine Road and received his money: for keeping his mouth shut, three dollars. He was a humane man, and though he never failed to collect his money, he was moderate in his demands. He had already accrued sixty-three dollars, twenty-one months' worth of dividends from the information he had acquired.

Paul Cheung was envious of the constable. He knew he was hostage to his employer's fortunes. No one else would employ him as a house-servant, and Mr Pink would point that out to him, if he tried blackmail: if Mr Pink was dismissed, so would he be.

When he had made the payment, he went into the sitting room, helped himself to a large crystal glassful of whisky, and drank it in one swallow.

Samuel had just been moved to work under Darley in the Public Works Department – the new name for the Surveyor-General's office. He'd been in the Registrar-General's office far longer than a cadet would normally expect. It was an ominous sign for his career, and sometimes he worried about it. He always worked harder than he need, for fear someone might notice that his heart wasn't in it.

Certainly someone knew, or suspected, about Lily: the person who was watching him had written to his mother.

Samuel, she had written, *for your sake I hope that the suspicion which has fallen on you is not true. You can have no idea of the loneliness, the misery that would result. Mrs Darley was bad enough, but if you have taken this young Chinese girl as your mistress – I sent you out to Hong Kong so that you could do useful, important work. The people out there would tolerate a liaison with a European women, but not a Chinese. You know that, Samuel, you know that you'd never be promoted. If it is true, I beg you to bring it to an end. Marry, Samuel, please marry a nice girl.*

He had considered it, but, when it came to the point, he couldn't. When he thought what it would be like never to see Lily again, never to kiss those full red lips or smell the fragrance of her naked skin, his good intentions died. There'd be nothing left. The only English-women who wanted him were the members of the Fishing Fleet, and he wasn't going to settle down with one of *them*.

Oh when I think of what a happy life I could have led, if it were not for the ruthless ambition of a parent – but I have said too much –

Every time he picked the letter up to reread it, he came to this passage and stuck. He supposed it might be an oblique reference to her royal ancestry. Unless Lily was right, unless Reynolds had lied to him.

If he admitted the possibility, it set the whole world reeling. He couldn't bear it. And Reynolds *was* a truthful man, almost in spite of himself. He had reason to know that. It was his mother who was trying to mislead him. He wished he could write to her and ask her not to put these little falsehoods into her letters. His stomach ached.

I have almost finished my book, had written Reynolds at the same time, *and it seems our printing press won't suffice for the task of production. After all our work, too. You can imagine the effect on our spirits. I have approached a private printer, and he is prepared to take the work on, but it will cost a substantial sum: if you could send another five pounds, that would go a long way towards that figure, as well as helping us to survive the cold weather.*

Dolly has left us: run off God knows where. I am afraid I grew a little too impatient one day – to tell the truth, Samuel, the woman was a fool, vicious and addicted to property. I believe she's gone to work in a public house. I suppose she hasn't really much to reproach me with – there is only so much a man can stand. There was a gap in the letter here, and the writing grew scrawly and hardly legible.

I do sometimes have a rage within me that frightens me – I think of the straitjacket and shudder. Images rise in my mind – something drives me – I am beside myself and desire insanely – yes, that is the true word – to be free of the thing that possesses me while at the same time I cannot help but do what it dictates. Few people are strong enough to control it, certainly poor Dolly wasn't.

'I won't,' Samuel said when he read this, 'I don't want to – ' He didn't know why. He read on quickly.

Samuel I will admit the truth. I don't need money to finish my book. I need it for myself. They drove me out of the house and I am in London, searching for a post again. I don't know what to do. I need help. Please give it to me.

No, Reynolds wasn't the man to sustain such a lie for years on end. Of course he'd sent him money, and was still sending it. It was lucky that his salary had been increased. Reynolds had forged references for himself and got jobs clerking here and tutoring there: he described them with savage humour, and he never lasted long in any of them. Samuel wrote to him at a post office in Willesden. He didn't know where he lived.

He dreamed repeatedly that he was playing cricket with Reynolds on the rectory lawn, in the shade of the huge Spanish chestnut tree. His dog rose from her grave to chase the red ball again: it was fun until the tutor grabbed him by the scruff of his neck, dragged him upstairs, and shut him up in the strange unknown attic where the ghost came at him to drive him out of his mind.

He didn't let himelf brood on the dream. He'd get up in the morning and go to work: it was a dreary, everyday sameness.

'Tai Tam Valley for us tomorrow,' said Darley to Samuel. 'There's been a report of seepage from the reservoir.' Darley liked to inspect the facilities for himself from time to time. 'Pleasant weather, we'll have tiffin at Tai Tam Chuk and go back by steam-launch.' He grinned. 'All work and no play – ' He bit the words off, looking alarmed, as if something really dangerous had been about to escape, but Samuel was used to this mannerism. The sun was shining outside, though there was an odd discomfort in the air, a hint of clamminess, of summer.

Lily received a blouse from one of her five outworkers: Ah Ling brought her in. Lily employed two women to do embroidery, and three to make up finished garments, while she herself, thanks to the approval of Mr Fawler and Miss Atkinsom, went to ladies' houses, took orders and gave fittings.

She knew she was profiting from the same fascination that had brought them down to Pokfulam Road, but it was less unpleasant when she offered them a service and was paid for it. They would look her over, wondering whether she was truly repentant: there was an air of recklessness about them, as they went near Sin for the sake of the best tailoring in the colony.

Lily inspected the finished garment, going carefully over every inch: the inside was as well finished as the outside.

'Good,' she said. Her Cantonese was excellent now, but not quite perfect: a foreigner, local people guessed. She admitted to Soochow birth. 'As long as the fit is right.' She smiled. 'Thank you,' she said. She was always courteous to her workers. The woman smiled back, but Lily didn't trust her. The only Cantonese she trusted was Ah Ling.

She had the women's money all ready, so she didn't have to show where she kept it.

The blouse was for Mrs Darley. Accompanied by Ah Ling, Lily went up to Robinson Road herself to deliver it and make sure the fit was right. It would take a long time, because she always had to stay for prayers: today that was going to be uncomfortable, because she was bleeding. Her bleeds were dreadfully painful nowadays. She'd consulted the herbalist, but none of his potions made any difference. The blood poured out of her and she doubled up in pain. She knew why: it was her body weeping for the child she couldn't conceive.

They got to Mrs Darley's house, and were taken inside to wait for the lady. They waited for a quarter of an hour, for half an hour. Then at last the Number One Boy came in and told them Mrs Darley didn't want the blouse after all. They were to leave, he said, as quickly as possible.

Lily thought she was going to faint. Then she thought how humiliating it would be to lose consciousness here. The Number One Boy would rake her out of the house like rubbish. She put her lips tightly together, smiled, and went. All the time she could remember Richards throwing her out of Mr Jackson's house.

She thought: 'Now no one will employ me,' but she walked gracefully and smiling out of the Darley's pillared mansion. She knew the Number One Boy thought her feet were too big.

Ah Ling said: 'What have they found out?'

'I have my money,' said Lily, 'I have it invested in my Chinese companies, I can make it work for me.'

'And if *he* stops keeping you?'

'I don't know, Ah Ling.' She laughed, and bit her lip. She still felt dizzy. 'Let's go to Kwan Yin and ask her.'

The temple of Kwan Yin, Goddess of Mercy, was in Taiping-shan. They walked there: usually Ah Ling wanted Lily to take a rickshaw or a sedan, but today she didn't insist. It would have cost a least ten cents, and Lily might need every cent she had.

Lile did spend money on a packet of incense-sticks, which she set to burn in a large bronze vessel full of sand in front of Kwan Yin's image. She threw the carved yin-yang cups which told her whether she could proceed to the divination with fortune-sticks: it took a little time before they fell favourably.

Her womb was hurting with its emptiness: she'd been disappointed month after month, year after year, till her desire threatened to overpower everything else. And now her business was going to be destroyed. She wondered if she ought to leave Samuel. Another man would surely be able to give her a baby, a Chinese man, a less complicated liaison. She could join Mr Fawler's church and find a Christian husband, a good man, who wouldn't mind that her feet weren't bound. A man who suffered from no delusions about immortality or royal birth.

The Goddess's kind face looked earnestly at Lily in the unstable, smoky light of the red altar candles. Lily shook the fortune-sticks hard, rattling them against each other and the side of the container. Gradually, four or five of the flat sticks began to rise up from among the rest: she watched them with some fear, but kept shaking, and one of them jumped out from among its fellows and fell on to the floor. She picked it up and read the number: Forty-six.

She brought it to the fortune-teller for the interpretation: he was sitting at the side of the dark temple, dressed in grey, waiting for customers. She asked him if she should leave her present employment: it was an oblique question, but she was sure the Goddess would understand. The fortune-teller sorted through the printed messages to find Number Forty-six. Then he gazed at it in silence, glancing at Lily's face from time to time: she dropped her eyes. She could hear Ah Ling rattling the sticks now, a small steady noise like the wind in a grove of bamboo. Again, her head swam and she grasped the table to steady herself.

The fortune-teller said: 'The advice that is given is to remain and not to initiate any move. Be careful neither to plan action or any new move.'

Lily put her hands together in resignation.

Ah Ling got up and came to stand beside Lily, holding her own stick in readiness. The fortune-teller glanced at her sidelong and continued: 'Have patience, for a man will soon come who will help you. At that time the withered tree will come to life again.'

Then he looked Lily up and down: Ah Ling shook her head at him.

Lily kept her eyes on the floor, but she knew he was looking at her, stripping her in his mind. She blushed angrily – and yet part of her was pleased, because he was a Chinese. Was he suggesting that he might be the man who could help her? My baby, she thought, my dead baby was all Chinese.

Then she remembered what a Chinese man had done to her baby, and pain ran right through her body. She clutched the edge of the table again.

Ah Ling was too plain for the fortune-teller to eye her up, and she didn't care. She belonged to the sisterhood of amahs, vowed to celibacy.

'Come, Taitai,' she said to Lily. She scowled at the fortune-teller as Lily paid him. 'Let's go home,' she said sternly.

Lily did as she was told. The life had gone from her. She wanted her home: she wanted Ah Ling to order her about.

Ah Ling said: 'That filthy man must have seen you came on foot, that's why he was so cheeky. Now look how grubby you are. You'll need clean clothes when you get in, and a bath.'

As soon as they got home, she chivvied Lily into the little bathroom, filled the porcelain bath-jar and made Lily get into it.

'No, don't wash yourself,' she said, almost sharply. 'I'll do it.'

The warm water was gentle to Lily's pain. She felt the amah's little hands running over her back, her breasts, her buttocks, her feet –

'They're small, aren't they?' she said to Ah Ling.

'What are?' asked Ah Ling.

'My feet,' said Lily. 'Even if they're not bound.'

'There's nothing wrong with you,' said Ah Ling. 'Now out with you, you'll get cold.'

Ah Ling patted her dry, dealing skilfully with the blood. 'You're lovely,' she said, 'you don't need me to tell you that. I'll look after you, whatever happens. Now what are you crying about?'

'I'm not crying,' said Lily. 'Ah Ling, I love you.'

The shutters rattled outside the windows. Ah Ling said: 'It's getting warmer again, Taitai. The wind must have changed.'

At noon that day Mr Fawler called on Mrs Ellis about a Christian amah for a devout family of Methodists. Mrs Ellis saw him, grudgingly, only to tell him none of her girls were ready to face the world. Mr Fawler tried hard to persuade her, and the more he coaxed, the harder she stuck her heels in and refused. She interrupted him when he tried to preach to her about Trust.

Miss Atkinson watched her sister frustrating him: her embittered, twisted sister. She comforted herself that she'd visit Lily in the afternoon, and have half an hour of happiness, at least. Sometimes in the last two years she'd even wished she had the courage to rob the cash-box and buy herself a passage back to England, only to get away from the Refuge and the harsh smell of white laundry soap and despair.

The sky darkened outside and the light drained out of the room. The wind came down on Hong-Kong, throwing handfuls of rain at everything in sight.

'If it wasn't December,' said Mr Fawler, 'I'd say that was a typhoon squall.'

'Far too late in the year,' snapped Mrs Ellis. Mr Fawler looked pained.

Miss Atkinson noticed the damp in her armpits, and looked at the thermometer they kept in the sitting room. It had shot up and was registering eighty-two degrees. The barometer, on the other hand, had plunged.

'Mrs Ellis, I must go,' said Mr Fawler, shaking himself into a decisive pose. 'I'll just look in on your workers in the vineyard.'

He smiled at her with Christian forbearance: Mrs Ellis scowled back and reminded him that he couldn't speak to the girls unchaperoned.

'I'll take you down,' said Miss Atkinson.

'No, I shall,' said Mrs Ellis.

The workers were at the mangles, not at the vinepress: steam rose round them, their arms were reddened to the elbows. The juice that ran out from between the rollers was a vintage of dirt, sweat, and soap-suds, and there was no light in the girls' faces as they looked at their visitor.

'You like the sight?' Mrs Ellis demanded of Mr Fawler. 'Or do you like Miss Lily better?' She laughed.

Mr Fawler swallowed hard.

'Go on,' she said, 'get out of here.' She pushed him out of the laundry, out of the home, and the door shut noisily behind him.

Miss Atkinson had gone back to her room. She was taking the Chinese herbs against her rheumatism again. Lily had got them for her, had been massaging her all the way through the hot season. She had never been so well.

She did her hair the way Lily had shown her. She felt so much prettier! It was as if some of Lily's beauty had come off on her with her touch, had pollinated her with an allure she had never had before. There was a young German pastor with the Lutheran Mission who was showing an interest in her. He was tall, fair, gentle and handsome. Pastor Marius: her body trembled at the thought of his name.

She was still only thirty-four, and skilled in missionary work. She wouldn't be afraid to accompany him to China, or anywhere else in the world.

Lily had bought her sandalwood chips and she'd slipped them in among her clothing. Sometimes Mrs Ellis sniffed her and looked askance. She didn't care.

She knew what a married woman had to do: she could hardly work here and not know what men and women did together. She also knew Beatrice thought women were better off without it. Beatrice hated men. She tried to stop her sister going to the prayer meetings where she'd meet Herr Marius.

I'm sick of Beatrice, thought Miss Atkinson. She imagined the bars being wrenched off her bedroom window – but it was the wind rattling them, not her lover. She wanted to be in his arms.

She was writing love poetry now: layers and layers of love poetry sat on top of the religious poetry in her drawers. She checked it daily to make sure there were no insects in it.

She got her pen and inkpot and tried to find a metaphor for his eyes. All she could think of was that they were China-blue – hadn't he been destined to come here, and didn't it follow that he had been meant to meet her?

She wrote: *He kissed my hand.* The wind gusted savagely, and there was a thump. Miss Atkinson looked out at the little courtyard to see that the hibiscus had fallen over and broken its pot. Soil spilled all over the paving stones, and a triumphant whirlwind danced over the mess, picking up dust and dead leaves and flying them in circles before it dropped them. It was the bush Lily had got them to buy, Miss Atkinson's pet and her pride – she'd stopped Mrs Ellis getting rid of it when she'd sent the potted palms away. Now it needed more help.

Miss Atkinson went down to the kitchen and fetched a sack that had held rice. She went outside with it and put the hibiscus into the sack. Then she carried it up the stairs to her room. The rootball was heavy, even without the pot, but she struggled on.

'What are you doing, Alicia?' Mrs Ellis demanded.

'The pot broke, Beatrice,' said Miss Atkinson. She put the sack down on her bedroom floor. 'I want to save it, I'm sure there's a typhoon coming.'

'It's too late in the year for a typhoon,' said Mrs Ellis.

Miss Atkinson laughed.

'Don't argue with me, Alicia,' said Mrs Ellis in a sharp brittle voice. 'I'm stronger than you. You know that.'

'No, Beatrice,' said Miss Atkinson to her own surprise. 'You're not stronger than I am, not at all.'

'There will be no typhoon,' said Mrs Ellis to the world outside the window. 'And that man,' she said to her sister, 'that man won't ask you to marry him, so why do you let him flirt with you? Even if he did ask you,' she said cruelly, 'I wouldn't permit it.'

Miss Atkinson itched to tell her that Pastor Marius had asked for her parents' postal address. Why else would he have wanted it? And of course they'd give their consent. They'd be relieved that she was getting married after all. They'd talk about their three married daughters. As long as Beatrice didn't write to them and tell them the Pastor was a bad character: which she might well. So she mustn't tell Beatrice anything.

A handful of leaves thwacked in to lodge among the window bars.

'There isn't going to be a typhoon,' said Mrs Ellis again.

The wind tore through the spaces between the house and the hillside, howling derision at them both. Mrs Ellis wasn't surprised. She already knew that there was someone out there, laughing at her.

The monsoon had turned round in its tracks, and the typhoon was whirling in along the warm airstream. The watchman who stood on the lawn of the Royal Observatory saw the clouds race from the south-east, pewter overpowering light grey and not a trace of blue to be seen. The red ball went up for the little junks and sampans to return to the Causeway Bay typhoon shelter, but most of them were fishing too far out to get back in time.

The typhoon had been racing up towards the island of Formosa, but it had turned, drawn as if by a magnet towards the Pearl river estuary, then had bent north again towards Hong-Kong. It was a scourge of roaring air, merciless and immensely powerful.

Lily had never experienced a typhoon, but she knew what you had to think about. She asked Ah Ling: 'Is there enough to eat in the house?'

'Rice, meat, yes,' she said, 'but I haven't bought fresh vegetables. I'll go and see if there are any hawkers on the street.'

'Don't stay out too long,' said Lily anxiously.

'Bad time,' said Uncle Liu, putting the heavy shutters across the windows.

They might all be dead before morning.

Lily saw the chrysanthemums Samuel had brought her last night, wintry purple-pink, standing in a blue-and-white vase on her sideboard. She wondered if he'd come to her, and if she wanted him.

She asked Uncle Liu if there was enough water for the household. The water mains often broke, in the typhoon, so it was a good idea to store as much water as possible in large jars and cooking pots. He set about filling them from the single tap in the kitchen. Lily herself began to move the furniture away from the windows in case one of them flew open, letting rain flood into the room. She made sure she had a full bottle of whisky in case Samuel came. She was glad to work, to forget what had happened earlier on in the day. She'd put Mrs Darley's blouse away in tissue paper: maybe she could alter it for sale to somebody else. She might try to work among the kept women of Happy Valley – but they might resent her as a Chinese. And if she died it wouldn't matter, but she didn't want to die. She wanted to live, and have her baby.

She found herself expecting Samuel: when the wind rattled the shutters she thought he'd arrived. She heard the door, but it was only Ah Ling coming back with carrots and cabbage. Then Lily remembered where he was. He wasn't in his office: he'd gone to Tai Tam with Mr Darley.

Lily thought of the trek back across the island's hilly spine, fully exposed to the worst the wind could do. Of course they'd never attempt it. They'd take cover, over the other side, in some Chinese hut that would be swept away by the wind. She would never see him again. Once again, she'd be left behind – with more money than last time, sure enough, but alone.

The good Chinese man from Mr Fawler's church grew a harelip and jeered at her for her big feet. There was that cold painful emptiness in her stomach, and she felt sick.

She didn't want Samuel to die. She really loved him, more than the house, more than the money, even as much as the hope of a baby.

She was caught.

Samuel and Darley stood in the treeless Tai Tam Valley and saw the leaden sky, felt the increasing power of the gusts. The scrubby bushes bent and showed their bare-stemmed undersides: everything was on the move except for the rocks and they stood up like watchful gravestones in a disordered cemetery, ugly in the sullen light.

'Typhoons do come in December,' said Darley, 'only it doesn't happen very often. You can't rely on this climate, that's the trouble. Now how do we get out of this?' He put his moustache in his mouth and chewed it. 'If we try to get back to Victoria, climb up that ridge to Wongneichung Gap, down that road to Happy Valley – exposed, every inch of the way. We'd be dead. We'll have to stay here.'

He explained it all over again to the bearers, in his perfectly comprehensible yet oddly British Cantonese. They nodded. He was the senior government servant, it was his business to come to conclusions: their business and Samuel's was to act on them, especially when their lives were in danger. It was the wisdom of Confucius, and of the Service.

The wind was scouring the bald hillside, searching them out. There was no shelter from it. It was already difficult for them to stay on their feet.

'The tunnel?' Darley asked Samuel. 'Could we shelter in the tunnel?'

The tunnel took the water from the Tai Tam reservoir through to filter beds and a service reservoir just above Garden Road. It went right through the mountain.

'No,' said Darley, arguing with himself. 'That's no good. Might get a sudden rush of water, be drowned in there like rats.'

'It's a bad business,' said Samuel, trying to keep his voice cool, like Darley's. He knew that the older man's matter-of-factness was admirable. He remembered how he'd read stories about situations like this, lying on his stomach on the rectory lawn. The heroes had always behaved like Darley. What was missing was the heroine, not Lily, but the angelic blonde he'd once dreamed of, courageous, yet apt to faint and become an extra piece of baggage at significant moments. He feared they were better off without her.

'We'll have to go down into the village,' said Darley. 'It's our best chance. I know it's a long way down, but it's sheltered on both sides. And we'd better move quickly.' He grinned, though the wind tried to brush the amusement off his face. 'Our skills are too valuable to Her Majesty to be smashed all over this valley.'

There was no argument about the sedans: they had to be left behind. The typhoon dealt with any doubts anyone might have about that by picking them up and hurling them down the hillside: the baskets of food went with them. The men ducked and swayed and managed to stay upright. When the wind dropped, they started walking.

The track followed the stream that trickled down from the reservoir. Pieces of the sedans lay across it now, and they had to step over the smashed wood.

Eternal Father, thought Samuel, strong to save. He hadn't prayed for months, except officially, in church. Now his mind sniggered: Who helps the strong the weak to enslave. He tried to think about his soul, and saw a dark indeterminate blob rather like a tadpole.

A burst of rain pelted their faces, laden with leaves and dirt, stinging like gravel. Again they all rocked on their feet, fighting the wind for purchase: this time they had to fall on all fours and cling to the ground. Samuel saw a bush beside him straining at its roots as if it was trying to get loose and fly off to China. He couldn't look to see what his colleagues were doing.

The wind dropped slightly. They got up and hurried on. The stream beside them was already thick with debris, and now the clouds plunged down, fogging their vision so that they had only the path ahead of them to go by and could barely see each others' soiled and frightened faces. The wind was gaining strength every minute. It pushed them sideways into each other as they walked during the lull between gusts, then forced them to their knees when it blasted the hillside. It pressed them into a tiny moving space where they could only think about their own actions.

He felt an overmastering desire to urinate, but he didn't dare fall back. They had to keep moving. His bladder was bursting and his distress was hampering his movements. He wondered if it would be worse to wet himself? He wished he'd never come here, wished he'd spent his life as a bank clerk in London, reading adventure stories in his spare time.

The wind was shockingly powerful. He remembered the fight with Reynolds on the clifftop and the moment when he knew he was defeated. He remembered the other thing – the nightmare – it must have been a nightmare. He'd fallen asleep and Hell had hideously ravished his poor squirming tadpole-soul.

They came to an enormous boulder: the shelter and the quiet were so startling they hurt.

'We'll take a break here for a moment,' said Darley. 'I've got to – '

'So have I,' said Samuel. He all-but laughed with relief.

They stood in a line, Chinese and English, pissing against the rock: the wind was so low here that they made arcs of urine as perfect as they would have made in the urinals at the office. Then, while they were buttoning themselves up, the wind changed direction and came in behind the rock like a hunting snake. The next moment Samuel felt himself picked up – he hung in the air for a moment – he was dropped.

He lay winded on the ground, he thought he was at the fairground and Reynolds was bending over him: No, he wanted to cry out, take him away.

'My God,' said Darley, 'are you all right, lad? I thought you were dead then.' Darley was beside him and his face was quite grey: he helped him up and guided him back into the lee of the wind.

'I think I'm all right,' said Samuel. He wanted to weep, but he was afraid to: *anything* that undermined the prestige of the white man in this country – and what would do that as surely as a white man's tears of pain? He felt very cold.

'Here,' said Darley, and passed him a silver flask of whisky. 'Take a pull. You need it.'

'Thanks,' said Samuel, trying not to shiver. He was glad of Darley's hand on his shoulder.

'Nasty fix,' said Darley, and chewed his invisible straw. 'We'd better go on. It'll get worse. Hours yet before the eye comes, though this one is moving fast.'

They were struggling on: it should have been easier as they came downhill and the shelter of the hillside rose around them, but the wind speed was rising all the time. When a particularly strong gust flattened them on to the ground, Samuel saw a small rodent blow past him: the tail whipped against his face. He wondered what it had been doing above ground: it might have been forced to flee from a predator, a snake perhaps, and had been caught by the typhoon instead. It was time to get up and go on.

'Come on, lad,' said Darley. 'We'll get there.'

Lily sat at home and felt the wind trying the strength of the house. The shutters rattled and complained. Lily was trying to work, while Ah Ling was cooking a midday meal of rice, cabbage and pork in the kitchen.

The fierce *yang* energy of the wind was stripping her of protection. It would listen to neither excuses nor pleas for mercy, but went ruthlessly about the business of change, shrieking its rude music through the streets of the city.

Lily found herself crying for Mr Jackson: I really loved him, she thought, and he died in so much pain. He used to take me on his knee and tell me stories. He was father and mother to me. Oh don't, she begged the storm, don't take another man away from me. I don't want to be a husband-killer!

The typhoon yelled derisively: 'Didn't you betray Mr Jackson? Then you're disappointed he didn't mention you on his deathbed? What man mentions a faithless concubine?

I didn't betray him, protested Lily, it was only when he went away – I was always afraid he would die, so how could I fail to do something to protect myself?

There was a clattering noise as a tile came off the roof. The wind had made a way into the house: now it could take the whole roof off if it wanted to. Lily sat tense and terrified, waiting for it to happen. It didn't.

Lily thought it was playing with her, giving her a respite before it hurt her worse. She knew it intended her death.

'You can't look after them properly,' it screamed and chattered, 'that's why they die. Then you blame me.'

Lily said aloud: 'It wasn't my fault that I had a girl baby.'

The typhoon smashed something against the wall of the house. She thought it was tired of her.

Oh, she thought, I'm nothing. I'm rubbish, fit only to be left out for the dogs to eat. And I gave birth to more rubbish, how could I have expected to bear a boy?

But why had Ah Kuen exposed the baby, why hadn't he let her go out on the streets with her? Mrs Ellis would have taken the baby from her and sent her to an orphan asylum, she'd done that to Rachel's little girl, but even that would have been better than the child's death. He'd left her near a watercourse on the Peak: he hadn't wanted to say, but Lily had screamed and threatened to kill herself if he didn't. Then she'd got up, weak as she was, to find the baby. But the rain had come, swelling the stream. Lily found the small sodden body half a mile downhill.

Lily scored her wrist with her nails.

I should have protected her, she thought.

It was so gloomy outside it felt like night. The wind took the house and rocked it: flakes of plaster fell off the walls and lay like snow on the floor.

'Ah Ling!' shrieked Lily. 'Ah Ling!'

Ah Ling came up from the kitchen with her blue apron on:

'What's happened?' she demanded.

'We're going to die,' said Lily. 'Mr Pink's probably dead already, and I love him, Ah Ling. And the wind's going to break the house down. I'm so frightened.'

'Let's pray to Kwan Yin,' said Ah Ling. Her little frame shivered but stood firm like a scrubby well-rooted bamboo plant. 'Then we can eat, we'll all feel better with some food inside us.'

'Food,' whimpered Lily, 'we're going to die.'

'Not for sure,' said Ah Ling, 'it always feels like this, in the typhoon.'

It was Ah Ling who lit the incense-sticks in front of the Goddess. The smoke was pulled here and there about the room: little threads of the typhoon were hissing in through the cracks around the windows. Lily remembered Samuel's face in bed, his smiling excited face. He had always been gentle to her, as he'd promised. Surely Kwan Yin could help him to give her a child, surely he'd be pleased to father one?

Another huge blast of air hit the house. The window cracked, and a few splinters of glass fell into the room.

'If I die,' said Lily, holding on to Ah Ling, 'I'd like to be reborn as a Mandarin, or a man anyway, a rich man, and I shall never kill a girl baby. I'd like to live in a house with red pillars and green tiles, a

273

reception room with scrolls of my ancestors, with mother and father, sisters and brothers, aunts and uncles, and children, dozens of children.' She began to cry. 'But I don't want to die at all, I don't want to be hurt. And I don't want Samuel to die. I'm hungry, Ah Ling, can we eat?'

'Why not?' said Ah Ling, 'It's high time you thought about that.'

The movement was far worse up in Robinson Road, though the Darleys' house was more recently built than Lily's, stoutly bedded in granite and designed to withstand the typhoon. It rocked all the same. Mrs Darley felt sick.

I could face it far better if I wasn't so ill all the time, she thought.

She felt breathlesss, as if the turmoil outside had sucked all the air out of the house. She remembered the chloroform sponge over her face, the nurse saying severely: 'You'll be better when this is over.' She remembered the strange ugly dreams, and then the awakening: she'd felt suffocated, had snatched at the air and got no satisfaction. And the pain, the horrible pain between her legs.

'There,' the nurse had said. 'You're better now.'

John was out in the typhoon. John wasn't a bad man. She'd adored him once, she *had* given him pleasure in bed. Till she'd gone home to have her fourth baby and come back to find him no longer interested. Now it was too late for him to care.

No one could ever restore what he had done to her. She'd been well, now she was ill, and she'd be ill for the rest of her life.

'I hope he dies,' she said aloud.

A gust rocked the house again.

'Take him away,' she begged the typhoon.

'Thing is,' yelled Darley against the racket, 'this valley's sheltered. Or else we'd already be dead. If you have to be caught in a typhoon, this is the place to be. But whether we ought to keep going towards Tai Tam Chuk — what do you think? he shouted to the bearers, repeating the question in Cantonese. The men huddled together and discussed the issue.

One of them remembered an abandoned house not far from here: now that he'd been asked for his opinion he thought it would be a good idea to shelter there. The typhoon would get worse yet before the eye of the storm gave the island an hour or so of calm.

The wind combed the valley brutally, without mercy. The rain came in their faces and soaked them to the skin. They struggled into the blinding harsh rain. When it cleared a little, they saw the house: it was lacking a door, but solid enough otherwise, with a thick tiled roof and pointed gable end. It seemed a long time before they got to it, it seemed they would never reach it, and the wind raved round them, leaned against them and jerked them off-balance. At last they arrived and entered, frightening a snake. Darley lit a match to see if there were any more, but it was all right. Their eyes got used to the dimness. You could see the old cooking stove with the hollow where the wok usually sat.

'So,' said Darley, 'we sit down and wait it out. Have a smoke?'

He had cigars in his pocket: the two officials smoked them, while the bearers lit pipes. The house shook when the wind hit it: it might collapse round them, but that seemed better than the fight in the open. All of the men sat heavy on the floor, too tired to speak for at least half an hour.

'Pink,' said Darley, 'another cigar?'

'Thanks,' said Samuel, 'don't mind if I do.'

He'd been dropping off to sleep, but he was glad to wake up. He'd been having the nightmare about the attic again, the voice of the typhoon had transformed too easily into the howling madness emanating from the walls. Now he wondered why this house was abandoned, perhaps it was haunted. Darley's voice drove such thoughts away.

'Nothing to do but smoke,' said Darley, 'and talk. Here, have some whisky.'

Each drank out of the flask.

'I should have brought some,' said Samuel, feeling guilty.

'It doesn't matter,' said Darley, 'we'll just have to ration it.' The bearers smoked their pipes and looked away from the drink. There wasn't enough for everyone, and they wouldn't have drunk out of the same flask as the *gweilo* if he'd offered it.

'D'you know,' said Darley, 'back in London, the waterworks are palaces. Ornamental tilings, fountains of clean water – wonderful, really.' His voice was tender. Samuel wished he could feel as much love for anything. 'We might die today,' Darley went on, holding his cigar tight, 'but at least I've left something behind me, sewerage, main drainage here. Justifies a man's life.' He didn't seem to want an answer, and Samuel said nothing. Five minutes later, he asked with a sort of anxious kindness: 'What does it make you think about, lad?'

Samuel couldn't tell Darley he was frightened, that was one of the things you didn't mention. He said: 'When I was a boy, I used to dream of things like this. They seemed so exciting. Of course, I was always the hero.' He laughed aloud at himself.

'What was it like,' asked Darley, 'when you were a boy?'

The cigar-scent filled the mouldery interior of the house with incongruous luxury.

'I was wild,' said Samuel, 'I was supposed to be delicate – I had a tutor, but he was a great gun, we used to have larks – climbing out of my bedroom window at night to get out into the countryside.'

'Boys will be boys,' said Darley.

'We went to the fairground once,' said Samuel, 'but it wasn't really much fun and I fell off the gallopers.'

'Ah!' said Darley, amused. 'The scar you got falling off a horse.'

Samuel was embarrassed. He said: 'Such a silly way to get a scar.'

Darley only said: 'Was your tutor a good fellow? You got a good degree, didn't you, he must have taught you well in spite of all those larks.' There was the anxiety in his voice again. He began to chew one side of his moustaches.

'He was a clever man,' said Samuel, 'I liked him. I still write to him. But he's gone off the rails a bit since.'

'Orderliness,' said Darley, 'you have to have it. Have some more whisky.' They sat in silence. Samuel felt uncomfortable, as if he'd betrayed Reynolds.

'Place like this,' said Darley, 'small place, full of Chinese, what a man does matters more than it would at home, even. Represent our country.'

Samuel didn't answer. His heart thumped. But Darley was right, surely? He thought of Feng's concept of the gentleman and, this time, the cynical voice had nothing to attack it with. At the same time, he had a vision of Reynolds, out in the typhoon, on the run from it, tumbling head over heels in confusion.

'A man has to think,' said Darley, 'what he owes to himself, what he owes to Her Majesty. People talk.'

'I know,' said Samuel. He was barely able to get the words out.

'Look at Miss Lily Jackson,' said Darley. 'MacVicary was in China, and he met that fellow Wells, the one Miss Lily said sent her money from Jackson. Wells didn't know anything about it.'

Samuel held his breath.

Darley said: 'My wife was supposed to be having a blouse from her. She said she wasn't going to pay for it. Of course, she lost the material. Miss Lily's lost her income, though,' there was a vindictive note in his voice, 'she should have thought of a cleverer lie. People are talking about her and Fawler, but she can't have run to Fawler, because he told Briggs at the Union Church that he'd found out who was keeping her. Mrs Ellis says it's you. Have some more whisky.'

Samuel was glad to.

'Give her up, lad,' said Darley, very quietly. 'She's not worth it.'

'What is?' asked Samuel, and desperately wished he hadn't.

'I don't know anything,' said Darley, 'I haven't said anything. I won't say anything. You're a sound fellow.' He passed the whisky flask to Samuel once again. He said: 'You know, when a man's young, he loses a woman, it's so easy to think the world's come to an end. He thinks he'll never recover. Then he learns there are other things that matter, things outside himself. The Service.' He bit his words off suddenly, and chewed his moustache again.

Samuel remembered how once he'd seen beauty in the forms of words of the Service: now they were part of his mind, used unnoticed. A man dulled, as he got older. It was a long time since he'd minded being carried by other men in a sedan. He remembered a passage of Ecclesiastes that Reynolds had quoted in one of his letters: 'For what hath man of all his labour, and of the vexation of his heart? Whoso removeth stones shall be hurt therewith, and he that cleaveth wood shall be endangered thereby.'

The wind fell silent outside. There was an enormous, breathless hush and no fresh gusts came to smash it.

'The eye,' said Darley, getting to his feet. 'Now we can go down to Tai Tam Chuk.'

With no wind to hinder them, it should have been easy to get down to the village, if only they hadn't been so tired. The air had a solid quality, as if they were wading through water, and the grubby sky weighed on their heads. The feeling of breathlessness persisted. They walked slowly, feeling the weight of each step.

Duty, thought Samuel, this is what duty feels like. You make slow and difficult progress. But you get to a different place in the end. He thought it reluctantly, he seemed to hear Reynolds pleading with him not to deny wildness. But what did Reynolds get out of his life, after all? He thought of Lily – but she didn't believe in his birth, she didn't believe in *him*. And he'd gone to bed with her and everything was going wrong. He could give her money, he could help her, so that she wouldn't be destitute. And she did have her savings.

Darley cared about him. He was almost shocked to understand it. It roused warmth in him. It made him want to live, to strive, to encounter difficulty. He wanted to be a man approved by men. He didn't want to be ostracized.

It came to him that he didn't have much choice.

They came down to Tai Tam Chuk and they negotiated with the fisherfolk for shelter and a meal: they were very hungry. They didn't like the food, rice with strong-tasting fish, but since it was all there was they ate it, dousing it with the rest of the whisky. They sat out the rest of the typhoon in the village, hindered from the sleep they wanted by the bearers and the family playing mah-jong. When the wind dropped, they hired an undamaged boat to take them, for an enormous fee, to the barracks at Stanley, from whence they were returned by steam-launch to the other side of the island.

Both Samuel and Darley were ill with dysentery by the time they got home. Samuel was far worse affected than Darley, probably because he wasn't so used to the climate.

21

ESCAPES

_____

As soon as the typhoon had passed, Lily wanted Ah Ling to go to Samuel's house to ask if he was safe.

'You don't think they'll know anything yet, do you?' asked Ah Ling. 'But I'll go anyway. I've got two houses in Taipingshan: I want to see if they're still standing.'

'Two houses?' asked Lily, surprised out of her anxiety for a moment.

'Thrifty living,' said Ah Ling, modestly.

'Not taking sedans,' said Lily, and made a face at Ah Ling. Then she said: 'Please, go quickly, Ah Ling.'

'And again, and again,' said Ah Ling, 'when I find he's not there. And there's work to be done here, you know, the window in your room, there's that lake of water where the tile came off the roof, all the furniture to put back, the mess to clean off the windows, not to mention what I'll have to arrange for my own houses – '

'It doesn't matter,' said Lily, 'Uncle Liu will see to it. The landlord will send someone round.'

'In two weeks,' said Ah Ling, and left.

She came and went three times, shocked and excited by the damage she'd seen, relieved to find her own houses almost untouched, scolding Lily for her impatience. It wasn't till the evening, by which time Lily was white and exhausted with worry, that an irritated Paul Cheung told her Samuel had come home, and that he was ill.

'So now, I suppose,' said Ah Ling, 'I'll have to keep trotting back and forth to his house.' She looked at Lily's hair, and clicked her tongue. 'You've been making a fright of yourself, running your hands through it.'

'It doesn't matter,' said Lily.

'You shouldn't care so much,' said Ah Ling.

'Why,' asked Lily, 'do you think he doesn't love me?'

'I thought you were a sensible girl,' said Ah Ling, 'love comes and goes.'

Lily shut her mouth tight, pushing her red lips out.

'You're a baby,' said Ah Ling, and bit her own lip with her two protruberant front teeth so that she looked like a hungry mouse.

'No, I'm not,' said Lily.

The doctor came to Samuel, shook his head over him, advised him to rest, and fed him laudanum: Samuel spent the bulk of two days asleep, only getting up to use the pot. He had a high fever.

Doctor Mackenzie had a nurse sent for the first few days: Paul Cheung disliked her and made her life a misery. She left as soon as possible. Paul Cheung was in a bad mood. He too had a house in Taipingshan – he had just bought it – and it had been smashed to pieces by the typhoon. He'd have liked to take it out on Samuel, but he was afraid of losing his job.

He compensated by giving short snappy reports to Ah Ling, and exaggerating Samuel's illness when he was already getting better. He wanted to torment Lily. She was a low woman who went with the *gweilo* and her feet were too big.

Lily sent notes to Samuel, telling him she loved him. Paul Cheung said the doctor had forbidden Samuel to read anything and sent them back.

'Then I'll go to see him,' said Lily, 'if you say that nurse has gone.'

'You're crazy,' said Ah Ling.

'Don't try to stop me, please, Ah Ling,' said Lily. 'I'll take a sedan.'

Ah Ling was not impressed. She said: 'You'd better take me with you.'

'Does it make any difference?' asked Lily.

Ah Ling said, 'I've got more wits than you have at the moment. I could think of something to say – that we were Mr Cheung's cousins, for example, though I'd hate to be related to that ugly thing from the gutter. You should stay away from him – they must have found out about you anyway, or else the Big Man's wife would have taken the blouse. The best thing you can do is to hope they stop talking. How much money have you got saved up?'

Why?'

'Because if he loses his job because they find out about you, you'll have to keep him as well as yourself.'

Lily began to cry. Ah Ling shook her head.

'You're a child,' she said.

'No one will see me, really, Ah Ling,' said Lily.

'Get ready, then,' said the amah, 'if you're determined to go.'

The sedan took them through past innumerable workmen busily repairing the buildings the typhoon had damaged: Lily could hear hammering and scraping and shouts through the curtains. Now and again she peered out and saw bamboo scaffolding round battered buildings. The damage was quite arbitrary: at one part of Bonham Road the lampposts had all been blown down, a few paces further they were standing. The house next to Samuel's had lost half its roof.

'You,' said Paul Cheung, 'what are you doing, coming here?'

'I have to see him,' said Lily.

'He's too ill,' said Cheung.

Lily thought how hideous his flapping cleft lip was, and his mangled speech: Ah Ling wondered what unspeakable sin he'd committed in a past life, to be visited with that deformity. She was quite sure the younger man wasn't really his son. What woman would have married him?

Lily said: 'Mr Cheung, he can't be too ill to see me.'

Contemptuously, Ah Ling demanded: 'What'll he say to you, when he's better, and she tells him you kept her away?'

'Come in, then,' said Cheung, looking away from them both and letting his face go blank to hide his rage.

Samuel was in bed, and running a slight fever, since it was the afternoon. His eyes were smudged and his features drawn: he was living on beef-tea and gruel, made for him with imported oats by Paul Cheung. He didn't much like either, but he could get them down. He liked the quiet, the complete absence of events. He had a blue-and-white jar in his bedroon, that he'd bought in Canton. Its delicate brushwork represented lotus flowers and clouds, all stylized: life metamorphosed into pure form, or rather, the formal essence of life captured on silk-luminescent porcelain. He'd described it as 'a nice piece', when he bought it, now he was amazed that he hadn't seen its sublimity. It soothed him, took him beyond thought or emotion. In spite of the pain in his bowels, he was at peace. Only the sunlight, moving over the walls, the light made him want to cry, and he had to call Paul Cheung to close the shutters. He didn't want to think about what was outside the room.

When Paul Cheung came to tell him Lily was there, he wanted to have her sent away: then he thought he'd better tell her now, it would be kinder, he felt, than to leave her hanging on. It occurred to him for a moment that he could write her a letter, but he knew that would be cowardly, utterly despicable.

Lily made soft, cooing exclamations of distress when she saw him, plumped his pillows up, knelt down beside the bed, and stroked his face. He found her fragrance unpleasant. He sneezed.

Lily picked his hand up and kissed it.

'I love you,' she said, 'I was desperate with worry about you, during the typhoon, I wanted so much to tell you how important you are to me.'

He was upset by the softness of her lips on his hot hand. He was too close to her: he'd been to bed with her and his flesh wasn't quite distinct from hers. He pulled his hand away.

'I love you too,' he said, 'but love isn't everything.'

Lily put her hand on his cheek and stroked it, but he flinched from her touch. His face, which looked so young and fragile, was stubborn against her.

He said: 'They know, they're talking, it'll have to stop. Lily – if I gave you some money? You could stay in the house. I mean, a man has to do what's right. The government invested a lot of money in my training. I'm sorry, I know it seems hard.'

His words were quite inadequate, but maybe it was better so.

'Don't,' said Lily, 'don't stop seeing me.' Again, she realized that she was caught. And he had his job, and his prospects, what did she have? At the back of her mind, she began to calculate the income from her shares. She'd been reinvesting it all up till now, but if she used it – if only she could be sure she'd find work! She said: 'We could go away together, somewhere where they don't mind so much about white men and Chinese women, Malaya perhaps, I've got money – '

'I can't,' said Samuel, 'you don't understand, how should you? I'm an Englishman, I have loyalties, I'm the Queen's son – '

'I know,' said Lily, 'but she doesn't care so much about you, she's never seen you, she can't love you the way I do, dear – '

'Go away,' said Samuel, 'please, Lily, I can't bear it, go away.' It was as if he was the one who feared destitution.

Downstairs, Paul Cheung, so angry he couldn't think straight, saw Doctor Mackenzie coming and let him in before he had time to knock on the door. Ah Ling was in the kitchen talking to James, and she didn't even hear the doctor coming.

Cheung warned the doctor to go quietly up the stairs, in case Samuel was asleep. He tiptoed up himself to open the door for the *gweilo* physician, and hoped spitefully that he'd find Samuel and Lily in bed together.

It was bad enough, though they weren't. Lily was still kneeling on the floor by Samuel, a position that made it impossible for her to pretend she was Paul Cheung's cousin. She saw Cheung pull his mouth apart in a grotesque grin and make a rude gesture at her behind the doctor's back. She knew Ah Ling had been right. It was a dreadful feeling, when it was already too late.

Doctor Mackenzie was a tallish man just turned fifty: he had a fine head of unruly grey hair, a moustache to be proud of, and bright dark eyes that were cynically kind. He liked women of all races, and had encountered a fair selection since he left Edinburgh at the age of twenty-five and took a job as a ship's doctor in order to get out to the East. He was interested to see that Pink really was Miss Lily's lover, but all he said was: 'Well, my dear, you'd better go now, while I look at Mr Pink.'

Lily got to her feet and slid out of the room.

He remembered the Chinese mistress he'd kept himself, once, in his early days in Malaya. She'd gone on to a rubber-planter when he left for China. He'd married late, in the interests of respectability, and his wife had died with her baby in childbirth: it was his status as inconsolable widower that gave him such credibility with Hong-Kong wives and daughters. In Hong-Kong he visited the respectable white man's brothels, but now and again he thought it would be nice to go to bed with a Chinese woman again.

He was wool-gathering, but it didn't trouble him. Why should he hurry, since the end of all haste was the open grave? He'd been described as stately, recently. That had tickled him.

He examined Samuel.

'You're doing fine,' he said. 'Just don't get excited – or worried.' He grinned. 'I'm not going to give you away.'

283

'I'm pensioning her off,' said Samuel. 'She doesn't like it, but I'm prepared to be generous. I made a mistake, anyone can, but I've got duties, I can see that now.'

His eyes begged for comprehension, but Doctor Mackenzie only thought he was either dishonest, or a coward: bumptious little fool of a priggish official. He asked Samuel personal questions about his bowels, and prescribed an aperient, though he didn't tell his patient what it was. He said he'd send it round presently and it would get the poisons out of Samuel's system.

Maliciously satisfied, he left the room, and found Lily leaning against the door of the study opposite. She was crying.

'Oh, my dear,' he said, going to her, 'you mustn't do that.'

Lily felt as if he'd known her – and cared about her – for a long time.

'I'm so unhappy,' she said. 'I've ruined him – unless you're kind to him.'

Paul Cheung stood still halfway up the stairs and listened with great pleasure to Lily making things worse for herself and Samuel.

Doctor Mackenzie wondered if Samuel really was going to give her up. 'I shan't tell anyone,' he said. He put his arm round her and noticed the subtle, alluring scent – was it sandalwood? It occurred to Lily that the doctor could hardly expose her liaison with Samuel if he was in a position to be exposed himself. He might even be persuaded to vouch for her, since all her clients were his patients – he had the reputation of being such a clever man. And it was so nice, so comfortable, in his arms.

Paul Cheung, hearing only Lily's sobs, waited for something more interesting. Then his son yelled for him to come and talk to the meat man. He slapped James for disturbing him, because he didn't dare come up the stairs again. They creaked.

'You're too kind,' said Lily to the doctor, and dried her eyes on her little silk handkerchief, taking care to stay inside his arm and touch a breast lightly against it. His warmth soothed her fear and upset.

It was agreeable to feel his hand gently caressing her bottom. Unlike Samuel and Mr Jackson, he didn't seem to need any help at all. And there was the hope the Goddess of Mercy had given her: a man who was going to help her, a withered tree coming to life.

She whispered: 'Would you like to come to my house, for tea?'

'Where do you live?' asked Doctor Mackenzie softly.

He knew he had dropped into the trap that Pink was trying to escape from. But she was in distress, and he wanted to be nice to her. Also, he was just a little bored with his well-thought-of life and the admiration of his patients, and the Club and dinner-parties and the prostitutes in Queen's Road.

After Lily and the doctor had both gone, Samuel lay in his bedroom and tried to get back to the peace he'd been enjoying. He couldn't. The blue-and-white jar was a beautiful Chinese thing, like Lily, and what he now saw in its lines was not form, but movement: the flowers and clouds were moving – away from him, he now saw – with grief-stricken fluidity and grace.

But he'd pay her a generous sum, he wouldn't let her beg, and she had her own money, she knew how to place winning bets on the horses, she knew how to change and move with circumstances. She read the Bible, her favourite deity was the Buddhist Kwan Yin, but she was a Taoist, she was like water, she knew how to absorb change and move with it, while he held fast to one idea of himself after another, and was always thrown off reeling. He was sure Lily never troubled to define herself. Of the two of them, she was the better off.

And yet – to lose himself, to be nothing more than the office he fulfilled, to be true to a heart that neither lusted nor searched for affection – to sacrifice his body and his soul on the altar of duty – wasn't that worth doing? He was back to Master Feng's Confucian philosophy: the outer forms, properly carried out, redeemed what was within. There was no conflict with the Christian duties of a government servant. Feng himself had said so. But as for the wild enthusiasms of an evangelical – they were too disorderly, too unreliable, too treacherous. They'd delivered Lily straight on to his lap.

He'd tell Darley, but it wasn't Darley's approval he wanted. He knew what he really wanted. If he was never to have Lily again, he'd write to his mother. He'd send the letter enclosed in a letter to his foster-father, he'd admit that Reynolds had told him the truth, and beg him to send it on.

He rang for Cheung.

'I want pen, ink, and paper,' he said, 'sealing-wax and an envelope.'

'The doctor's medicine has arrived for you,' said Cheung.

'I'll write the letter before I take it,' said Samuel.

Deliberately calm, he wrote the first letter, to the Rector, then passed on to the difficult one.

'*Madam,* he wrote, then threw the paper away, and started again. *My dearest Mother, you have always forbidden me to write to you and I never shall again, but I want to assure you that* – he paused for a moment, dropping blots of ink on to his sheet. He smelt Lily, her sweetness was all through the room, he felt her nakedness against his fingers, she might have been in the room with him, begging him not to let go of her. He wrote determinedly: *I have told the Chinese girl that I shall never see her again. I don't want to distress you, nor do I wish to throw away the great opportunities you have given me. I am so grateful for all your care of me, and for the letters, and what has by chance been made known to me, I shall never betray to anyone. I am glad of the knowledge, because I can see your portraits everywhere, your dear eyes watching over me. Your dutiful loving son, Samuel.*

He told Cheung to post it at once, and took the medicine. It drove him to the water-closet where he sat and groaned, then staggered back to bed, considerably weakened. There he lay while his thoughts ran to seed, yielding a crop of nonsense: he thought of the form on the inside of things, and the shadow of reality coming from outside them altogether, then that idea turned itself inside out and he thought he was held inside a stiff form, an image of himself, yet he was trying to make himself smaller, because if he got into the tiny tadpole-soul that was wriggling somewhere in the depths of his being, he might understand everything: if only he could move, he cried within the case, or could stop struggling!

He woke up and remembered his mother's words: *I dare not risk exposure.* She wouldn't be pleased with him, she'd be angry, perhaps, even afraid. He rang for Paul Cheung, but of course the letter had already gone in the post. He felt miserable again, trapped inside his own folly.

Doctor Mackenzie came to tea with Lily a few days later. She took him straight to her bedroom. Doctor Mackenzie had attended Mrs Darley, and was startled to recognize her old bed. He found it very comfortable, all the same.

Lily lay beside the doctor under the quilts, while his hands roved over her body, cataloguing her perfections, her lovely femur, her exquisite gluteus maximus, her sweet vulva and –

'Doctor Mackenzie,' she said, 'you know I'm not a rich woman.'

'And?' he asked, gently pulling at her labia.

'And,' said Lily, a little distracted by his pursuit of anatomy, 'I'll have to bribe my little amah, and Uncle Liu who let you in to make sure they don't tell Mr Pink anything, because he musn't find out, you know – '

Doctor Mackenzie wasn't surprised she was trying to get money out of him: he guessed she needed it, and he'd never been particularly interested in pure women. When he was younger he'd have tried to beat her down, but now he was softer, flattered, he supposed, that a young woman could still enjoy him.

'I wouldn't want you to be out of pocket, my dear,' he said. Lily liked the endearment.

'And you'll come again?' she asked. 'Mr Pink won't know. He always comes in the evenings.'

He came, and every time he gave her money. It came cheaper than the cost of her maintenance, though no cheaper than a high-class prostitute. He thought it was probably healthier.

Lily gave ten per cent to Ah Ling, and, since the rent was still being paid and Paul Cheung still bringing her housekeeping money, she invested the rest.

'You'll end up in prison,' said Ah Ling, bringing tea to Lily and the doctor in bed. She knew Doctor Mackenzie didn't speak Cantonese.

'I'll be rich,' said Lily.

The amah said: 'Uncle Liu has had to send that priest away, and Tai-Tai Atkinson. He told them you were ill.'

'Good,' said Lily.

'Two *gweilo* lovers, now!' complained Ah Ling. 'Which one are you going to keep on?'

'I don't know,' said Lily. 'Ah Ling, go away, please.'

'If you were younger,' said Ah Ling, 'I'd smack your behind.'

Lily knew she didn't quite mean it. Ah Ling knew the value of money as well as Lily did.

Lily was expecting not to bleed in a fortnight's time: she trusted the fortune-sticks. Doctor Mackenzie would give her a baby: pleasure always brought conception. And yet she couldn't help wanting Samuel. She wished she didn't.

She fixed her thoughts on her investments, and the baby. All her dressmaking clients were cancelling their orders, apart from the

287

work for Miss Atkinson, which wasn't very lucrative. She had to let her outworkers find other employment.

'Quite disgusting,' said Mr Fawler, 'Miss Lily is pure as driven snow, and that anyone should suspect me of immorality – it is only proof of the degeneracy of these times.'

'You'd do well to stop visiting her,' said the missionary from Canton. 'You don't want to bring the Society into disrepute.'

'Christ,' cried Mr Fawler, 'Christ ministered to the outcast. My work is among the Chinese in Hong-Kong, am I to neglect this lamb?'

'Does she come to your church?' enquired Mr Lawley.

'She will,' said Mr Fawler with hushed confidence, 'she will.'

'I hope so,' said Mr Lawley, and looked Mr Fawler up and down as if he might detect traces of lasciviousness hanging like dust on his black clerical suit.

Samuel got better, and MacVicary cut him dead at the Club. The ladies weren't inviting him to dinner: he hoped he'd be able to live the scandal down.

In January, there was a spell of freak cold and frost. The white population were delighted: they lit fires and huddled round them, they put mufflers on and exposed their cheeks to the biting wind so that they could feel them fire up. It was so refreshing, so bracing, so easy to think straight, to get work done: so comforting to come in from the cold!

Lily bought flannel and made a warm nightshirt for Samuel. She sent Ah Ling to Caine Road with it and Samuel sent it back.

'Well,' said Ah Ling, 'that's it. You'd better make do with this doctor. At least it'll save you money, if you fall ill.'

Lily wouldn't answer.

Samuel came home after work and read Confucius and Mencius: he set up a correspondence with Feng about some points that he felt needed elucidation. At night he shivered in a cotton nightshirt, and sometimes regretted Lily's warmth. He dreamed he was in a corner with his mother. Everyone was pointing at them and throwing eggs at them: her crown dripped yellow fluid. He woke feeling sick.

He was startled to get a letter from her just after Christmas, though she couldn't possibly have got his own letter yet.

My dear Samuel, she wrote, *I am disobeying instructions to write to you now* — he wondered whose instructions? Somebody might harm him for writing to her? — *but I feel so wretchedly ill sometimes that though the doctor assures me I shall get better, I am quite certain that I shan't be long for this world. I cannot tell if I shall be able to write to you on your birthday. There are things I must say to you.* Her handwriting was shakier than usual: the Queen, he thought, the Queen is ill and might die and no one here knows but I, except perhaps the Governor. *I hope that you have done as I begged you and given the Chinese girl up: if only I could hear that you were engaged before I die.* He wished he could make the effort, but you had to go to dinner-parties to meet girls. *You cannot imagine, dear son, how much guilt I am beginning to feel: every spasm of pain I suffer reminds me that I have sinned. Not in the act, not that, I shall never accept that, but in bringing you into the world, that I cannot but now think was irresponsible. If I'd only known I wouldn't be able to care for you myself! Yet how cruel it is of me to write to you and regret that you were born! I long to hear of your happiness.*

I grow daily weaker and have nothing to do but brood. I lie in this castle and the possessions I have surrounded myself with jangle my brain and make me feel sick. They remind me how much falseness there is in the world, yet we must accommodate ourselves to it. Fashion, rank, money, how much is not sacrificed on those cruel altars? May God bless you, my son, and lead you on the right paths. For my sake, if not for your own, strive to be happy. Farewell, perhaps for ever, on bad days I even desire it, but shall watch over you from beyond the grave. Your loving Mother.

It might be the Prince of Wales who had such a hold over her, and when she was dead, what would become of him? He might be dismissed, just like that, killed even. He began to cry for his mother: he'd never really had her, now he was going to lose her. He wanted some comfort: he wanted Lily, whom he couldn't have.

He fell ill with a cold and Doctor Mackenzie sent him back to bed again.

The houses at the top of the Peak dripped icicles, and the Chinese made parties to admire the hoar frost on the trees. They brought silvered branches home with them: 'How stupid,' said the colonists smugly, 'don't they know the frost will melt?'

At the Refuge on Pokfulam Road, the old doorkeeper also went down with a feverish cold, and had to go to bed, drink infusions of ginger, which he felt were the right thing for him, and wear a mustard plaster, which Mrs Ellis brought him and he didn't like at all.

'Now we must take care of the door,' said Mrs Ellis to her sister. 'It will have to be kept bolted – no dreaming when you go in and out!'

'I'll do my best, Beatrice,' said Alicia: but she went on dreaming with the love poetry in her bedroom.

And on Bowen Road, Pastor Marius of the German Lutheran Mission made a slide and used it, again and again. He slid like a boy, he was a boy for twenty minutes or so, and other colonists came past and tutted at him indulgently or joined him, depending on their age and state of health. He laughed.

He was beside himself with joy. He'd got a reply from Mr and Mrs Atkinson in England: they'd given him their consent to marry his daughter, and he was going to ask her, today.

He didn't ask her in that house with the bars on the windows. He asked her to come for a walk with him, to admire the frost.

Mrs Ellis tried to obstruct. Miss Atkinson insisted. Her cheeks were bright with the cold and with delight. She went.

Mrs Ellis watched her sister go and knew that she was beaten. She went to her bedroom and prayed, but the dust remained in her mouth. They were all going away from her. Then she went down to see the girls in the laundry. There was no one in the room.

The mangle was sitting with a white sheet halfway through its rollers, the tubs were still full of steaming water. Herr Marius and Miss Atkinson had left the door open behind them and all the girls had escaped. Back to heathenism, back to their pimps, back to exploitation and degradation and misery and disease.

Mrs Ellis got her revolver, and set out into the streets.

She thought now she'd do anything to reclaim the girls, she'd promise them embroidery work, husbands in due course, anything. She was so lonely she couldn't think clearly. Excited, laughing, talking Chinese hurried past her, wrapped in layer upon layer of dark quilted garments and carrying branches exquisite with frost.

She understood, then. The beauty was the sweeter because it was just about to melt. It was the melting that mattered, the one sweet melting. She stared at the bobbing crystals of winter edging a kumquat's leathery leaves, and remembered the moment that she'd met Lily — at this place, where she now stood bereft. She put her hands over her mouth and felt her heart eat itself out.

Pastor Marius walked Miss Atkinson to the Botanical Gardens. He asked her the question as they walked round the ornamental fountain with its flowerbeds now all stricken by the frost. He said his life had been in the frost without her, and now she had brought him the springtime. If she said yes, his happiness would bring him into full summer.

She didn't know what to say, she didn't want to say anything yet, wanted to remain inside this moment: couldn't she nestle there forever?

He put his ring on her finger: it was a plain band, German-style, which would be moved to her wedding hand when they were married. He produced another for her to put on his hand. She felt wonderfully generous as she slipped it on him. Her own fingers were prettier now, they were an engaged woman's fingers, the ring changed the world to gold around her.

From Causeway Bay, the noonday gun snapped a sharp report through the frost air. Miss Atkinson turned to her lover. They kissed, bumpily, incompetently. He had kept himself pure for her.

Lily wasn't thinking about Samuel, and certainly not about Mrs Ellis. She was lying under the doctor, laughing with pleasure. She was glad she'd invited him to tea.

Mrs Ellis had seen none of her girls on the streets: but she hadn't really expected to. Instead, still clutching the revolver, she was walking up the steep hill to Lily's house. She tripped over chickens who were running about complaining of the cold, and walked into hawkers, almost upsetting their bamboo baskets. She was muttering to herself. And of course, she knew, it was quite obvious, that she'd always meant to go to Lily's house. There was nowhere else for her to go.

Samuel had been lying in bed with nothing to do but read, and he was tired of his book. His eyes refused to take the words in, and he thought about Lily. His hands stretched for her white smooth skin, mimicked her sinuous movements. His longing became intolerable.

He asked Paul Cheung for his clothes: Cheung was pleased to see him get out of bed, even to visit Lily. He wanted some whisky.

'Get me the sedan, and help me dress,' said Samuel. 'I'm going to visit Miss Lily.'

Lily would give him hot tea and would rub his limbs, she would get Ah Ling to make him his dinner and fuss with the amah about the ingredients – he would scold her for Chinese superstition – look what happened to Mr Jackson, he would say, and she would laugh.

He forgot to care about reputation or duty.

He was amazed, enchanted at the cold when he got outside, it was as if England had suddenly drawn far closer to Hong-Kong. He thought he'd hear the thrush call any moment, the brown-headed Indian tree-sparrows would turn their caps round and the tops of their heads become English grey.

Paul Cheung – who hadn't turned into an Englishman – handed him into the sedan. Reluctantly, Samuel admitted that this was Hong-Kong after all. But if it had been England, he wouldn't be visiting Lily. Cheung drew the curtains of the sedan and Samuel was born along the road to Lily's house, anonymous and agreeably warm.

He met Mrs Ellis on the threshold of Lily's house.

The doctor knew it was time to go. He had to call on Mrs Darley, who was lying in her new bed with an ailment he couldn't diagnose. He didn't want to. He knew what was to blame for all her illnesses. It came to this, that Darley was a brutal madman, and as for the doctor who had operated on her –

She'd been a fine woman. She'd always preferred younger men, but there had been an afternoon –

He stroked Lily's thigh, so different, so slight, so fragile! He slipped a finger back inside Lily's vulva to assure himself that everything was still present there. Lily lay back and allowed him to stroke her, sighing with gentle pleasure: like good food, she thought, good Chinese food, duck stuffed with taro or fresh silky beancurd in oyster sauce. She sighed deeply. The doctor was so nice, so restful, and if he asked her to marry him, she might even – but then there was Samuel – if only not Samuel –

Her thoughts confused and lost themselves.

'Oh, Doctor Mackenzie,' she whispered, 'you are such a clever man.'

'You're a sweet thing,' said the doctor tenderly.

'Taitai,' shouted Ah Ling, bolting into the room, 'get up,

quickly, Mr Pink's come and another lady, they're arguing at the door – I told you no good would come of this, but you never take any notice of me, do you, you bad girl!'

Lily could hear them. She could hear now Samuel, now Mrs Ellis –

'How dare you come here?' demanded Samuel.

'It's you,' shrieked Mrs Ellis, 'I always knew it was you, it's all your fault, you lured her away, and now all the others – '

'I'm a sick man,' shouted Samuel, 'I need to rest and restore myself and you come here making me responsible for the fate of your whorehouse – '

'Don't use that language to me!' Mrs Ellis snapped. 'You're a hypocrite, like all the rest of them, you pretend you can make a woman happy, no man can make a woman happy. I've seen too much to fall into that trap. You're wicked. Utterly wicked, all of you, and why did you have to take her away from me? Did you know my sister is getting engaged at this very moment?'

'Why aren't you at home, then,' demanded Samuel, 'you unnatural harridan? You should be waiting to congratulate her.'

'How can anyone be natural,' demanded Mrs Ellis, 'when nature has been bent and tortured and exploited? Bound feet, corsets – '

Lily said quickly: 'Get dressed. We'll pretend I'm ill, I asked you here to attend to me – '

She began to put Doctor Mackenzie's clothes on him, but she was in too much of a hurry: his shirt went on back to front, and she had to turn it round, his tie wouldn't tie, she couldn't put his trouser buttons into the holes, and Mrs Ellis burst into the room, her revolver out at the ready, with Samuel on her heels scolding her and complaining about his health.

Samuel thought he was going to lose consciousness.

Mrs Ellis gasped. She raised her revolver and pointed it, first, wavering, at the doctor, then at Samuel.

'Whore,' said Samuel. He leaned against the wall. 'How many other men have you been entertaining at my expense?'

'The doctor came because I was ill,' said Lily.

'Surely,' said Samuel, 'you can think of something better than that. Why didn't you put him under the bed?' He laughed, lunged at Lily and tried to slap her face, but she slid out of his reach. Mrs Ellis fired the revolver. She was a good shot, but her hand shook: the bullet missed Samuel and smashed the porcelain figure of Kwan Yin. Lily shrieked.

'Idolatry, too!' wept Mrs Ellis. 'You took her away from me,' she cried again, and pointed her revolver at the doctor.

Doctor Mackenzie had managed to get his trousers done up by this time, and was clutching his tie around his neck as if it might ward off the bullet. Once he'd disarmed an English seaman suddenly gone raving mad on a hot afternoon on the dockside in Singapore. He tried to use the same voice for Mrs Ellis: but it would have felt better if he had his tie on.

'Come on, ma'am,' he said – but his voice sounded ingratiating rather than soothing, 'you don't want to fire that thing, do you?'

'You think I'll pay your rent after this?' demanded Samuel of Lily.

'I told you,' said Doctor Mackenzie to Samuel, 'I told you to stay in bed.'

'So that you could come here,' said Samuel.

Mrs Ellis loosed the second chamber of the revolver at the doctor, and just missed his ear. She fell back against the wall of the room, her hand shaking, holding the weapon in front of her.

'Calm,' pleaded the doctor, 'is what we all need.'

'You dare say that,' shouted Samuel, 'with the smell of her on your fingers.'

Lily sank in a heap against the opposite wall and clutched her knees to her breast, sinking her black head on to them.

'I want to be dead,' she said, 'but I don't want her to kill me. I only want never to have been born.' Her teeth began to chatter.

Her hair swung round her and clothed her nakedness. Ah Ling ran over to her and put her silk dressing gown round her shoulders. She put her arms into the sleeves and huddled up again. Ah Ling crouched protectively by her.

'She's so unhappy,' said the doctor to Samuel, 'don't be too hard on the little thing.'

'She's a little animal,' said Samuel. Lily raised her head and stared at him.

'An animal,' said Mrs Ellis to Lily, 'is what you are to both of them. A hole,' she said, 'for them to poke.'

'She's a vixen,' said Samuel, 'pretending to be human, a monster, a murderer.'

The ruins of his trust and his repentance were cluttering his ankles: Mrs Ellis would tell everyone now.

'Mrs Ellis,' said the doctor, 'put the revolver down.'

'No,' said Mrs Ellis, 'I *shan't* put the revolver down. My sister is going to get married. My girls have all run away and are lost. It's all *his* fault –' she pointed the barrel at Samuel, who ducked automatically, 'and *yours* too,' she added, moving her gun towards the doctor, who faced it, staring her down.

'Please, Mrs Ellis,' said Lily, 'don't fire the gun.'

Mrs Ellis said: 'I should shoot both those men, and take you away. It's only when women live together that they can be happy, why don't any of you understand? But I've fought enough. I know when I'm defeated.'

She turned the gun round and put the barrel in her mouth.

'Oh, no,' whispered the doctor. 'No, Mrs Ellis,' he pleaded, 'you don't want to do that.'

'I do,' said Mrs Ellis, mumbling round the barrel of the revolver. Then a poisonous spider came out of the crack where it had been hibernating and stung her on the back of the neck. The shock made her drop the gun. She swooned.

It was all right then. An unconscious woman on the floor, that was familiar, that could be dealt with. The men sprang to help her.

Only Lily sat hunched, and Ah Ling beside her, stroking her cold hands.

The doctor said to Samuel: 'See to Lily, if you really care about her.'

Samuel knelt down beside her, hating himself.

'Lily,' he said, 'I love you, Lily. I forgive you.'

She *was* a little vixen, bedraggled and miserable, and she belonged to him – he couldn't rid himself of her. He said: 'Only you must never again – not with him or anyone else.'

'Fool,' said the doctor, undoing Mrs Ellis's stays with an expert hand.

'You think I'm a whore, too,' said Lily to Doctor Mackenzie. 'Then I'll be a whore. I'll leave Hong-Kong, and get on a ship. I'll go to San Francisco, and become a prostitute there.'

'San Francisco,' said Samuel automatically, 'has refused to accept any more Chinese.'

'Singapore, then,' said Lily, 'or Bangkok.'

'No,' said Samuel, 'I don't want to lose you. Please stay, Lily, and I won't ask anything of you.'

He was so tired. His head buzzed. Doctor Mackenzie had been right, he should have stayed in bed, and then the doctor would have had to handle Mrs Ellis all by himself. He didn't feel strong enough to look after Lily – hadn't he wanted her to look after him?

Mrs Ellis stirred and groaned. Doctor Mackenzie spoke kindly to her: 'Now, ma'am,' he said, 'you've been bitten by a spider, but they're not deadly. You're going to have an uncomfortable day or so but you'll soon be well again.' For a moment, he wished the spider had been deadly – but how would they have got her corpse out of the house? He patted the revolver, which he now had in his own pocket.

'I shall die,' said Mrs Ellis. 'I've got nothing to live for.'

Soothingly, the doctor said: 'There are plenty more prostitutes for you to save. Now we'll get you back to Pokfulam Road and I'll have a remedy fetched from my surgery. You're not such a coward that you'll let one setback destroy you – not the way I know you.'

'It's such a nightmare,' she said miserably. She began to cry.

'A nightmare is what it is,' he said with all the authority he could muster. 'You must forget all about it.'

'Oh,' said Mrs Ellis, 'do you think I want to remember this disgusting scene? I shan't tell a soul. I'm washing my hands of her. I never want to see her again. Or any of you.'

Samuel hoped she meant it.

Doctor Mackenzie pulled his greatcoat on over his disarranged clothing, and sent Ah Ling for a sedan. His own chairmen took him back to Pokfulum Road behind Mrs Ellis.

Rebecca was standing in the doorway of the house.

She said: 'I came back. I remembered how much I hated the men, all the things they wanted me to do. I remembered being beaten. I wanted to stay with you.'

She took Mrs Ellis, laid her down, and tended her. The doctor went himself for the remedy.

Ah Ling delivered the doctor's tie and other particulars of his clothing to him in a parcel that evening. There was a message from Lily in the parcel:

Dear Doctor Mackenzie,
You have been very good to me, but I musn't see you again. I still love you, but I love Samuel best. Lily.

He was sorry, but he wasn't young enough to fight a hopeless cause. He poured himself a glass of whisky and reflected on some of the gossip in the Club: he still thought he could have ridden it, if he could have had Lily. However much a fool she'd made of him.

The month came and went and Lily knew she was pregnant.

22

APRIL 1894:
THE BEREAVEMENT

'MY dear – ' said Mrs MacVicary, ' – and quite shameless.'

Mrs Darley said: 'Fawler, and Pink. And a Chinese! And to think she stood in this very room – it's not the sort of thing one can condone.'

She felt a twinge of pain, but no embarrassment. There *were* things one could condone, she stood by that.

'I didn't think,' said Mrs Caird, shivering a little. 'No one ever told me, when I came out here. And I keep a baby-amah: I wish I could afford a good Scotch nanny.' She looked dubiously at the Number One Boy, who was bringing tea.

'Send the creature away, I told the boy, at once,' said Mrs Darley. 'I'd like to have seen her face.'

'I've invited him to dinner,' said Mrs MacVicary, 'allowed him to dance with my daughter, lay hands on my daughter – Never again.'

They shivered.

'Nothing is safe,' said the Postmaster-General's wife, 'none of our husbands are safe, my dears, with that sort of bad example. We have responsibilities to them. Men,' she said stoutly, 'have their weaknesses. We are out here to make homes that keep them safe. Women like Miss Lily prowl round like wolves, out to devour us all.'

'Amen,' said Mrs MacVicary devoutly, just as she did at Matins, at the cathedral.

Samuel was in a box lined with purple silk. A moment later, he was looking into it from the outside, and it was six foot deep at least, a growing chasm at the bottom of which he could see a face. He peered down, expecting to recognize his own mirrored image, but it

297

was Reynolds down there: he could see him clear and tiny, as at the wrong end of a telescope. There was a look of reproach on his face, though his eyes were closed: as if he knew Samuel was up there.

He found he had a shovel in his hand and was dropping clods of earth on Reynolds, who began to wail, like a baby, and he tried to stop what he was doing, but the last shovelful was on its way down and fell on Reynolds's face, filling his mouth.

He woke thinking: 'The Victorian Age is dying, and only I know.' At once he realized what nonsense that was. The Queen's doctors must know, if no one else. He turned over in bed and his hand touched the strange warm moon-curve of Lily's growing belly. She sighed in her sleep and stretched with pleasure. She was happy to be bearing the baby, who wasn't his.

He put his hand away and lay on his back, staring at the bright lines the streetlighting made between the dark shutters. Between them he read judgement, written in letters of fire.

Item: Everybody knows about your liaison. Mrs Ellis's silence has only protected the doctor. You are in disgrace.

Item: You have let yourself be snared by lust and tenderness, defying morality, faithfulness and decency.

Item: You have disappointed Darley, you have disappointed Master Feng.

Item: The Colonial Secretary has spoken to you, and didn't believe your lies.

Item: You have been weighed in the balance, and found wanting.

He thought of Reynolds again: hated him with a vehemence he didn't understand. He imagined himself hitting Reynolds in the face, screaming that it was all his fault. It wasn't. He often blamed Lily, too, he was nasty to her. But it was he himself, Samuel Pink, who was despicable. His own weakness was the origin of his disgrace and probable failure of his career. He had learned this much from Master Feng: if other men insulted him, it was because he deserved it. The disasters inflicted by Heaven, had said Mencius, could be survived. From those a man inflicted upon himself, he couldn't expect to escape.

He felt the to and fro of life in Lily's body: She didn't seem to feel that the dishonour she had incurred was worse than death, as Master Feng had once prophesied. He thought that she had neither shame nor morality, and perhaps that was why he needed her.

There was the black-bordered envelope addressed in Burrows's handwriting. The postmark showed that it had been put in the wrong postbag and had gone to Singapore before anyone noticed and forwarded it to Hong-Kong. Samuel thought his mother must be dead. That was nonsense, he'd already have heard. At last he tore the envelope open. His own letter to the Rector tumbled out with its seal intact.

It was the Pinks who were dead, both husband and wife. Samuel hunted words out of the crowded text: 'tragedy', 'your poor parents', 'who would have thought it?'

The words were so well worn, he'd heard them from her lips so many times before, but that didn't rob them of force. He said to himself: 'It went to Singapore, I might have known three weeks ago if they'd put it in the proper postbag.'

He was guiltily relieved to know his letter had never been forwarded to his mother, at the same time his heart ached. And ached, after all, for the Rector and his wife. They'd brought him up, they'd been there in his childhood. He wondered if Reynolds knew. He'd better write to tell him.

Just a little piece of the cliff must have crumbled off, wrote Burrows, *sure Gods ways are not our ways, just that little piece where poor Mr and Mrs Pink was standing and so generous left me an annuity forty pound a year what with my savings Im all right Mr Samuel so no need to worry, the lawyer says he means to write to you about the will, takes time all the same, Mrs James from the village come in and lay them out battered as they were.*

He wished he'd never laughed at the Rector blowing his nose. He wished he was leading a better life.

'Poor Samuel,' said Lily, 'to be orphaned and never to be able to visit the grave.'

'Why should you care?' he asked. 'All you can think about is your baby.' Then he was ashamed of himself.

Few people condoled with him on the loss of his parents, because people talked about him now, they didn't talk to him. He still attended the cathedral on Sundays, and saw a prospect of turning backs when he came out, so he hurried home so as not to embarrass them further. He'd stopped going to the Club: instead he went to Lily's house. But as her pregnancy advanced, she didn't really want to make love any more. For three weeks now, all he'd been allowed to do was to sleep beside her.

Darley was speaking to him: he had to, at work. He was forbearing towards Samuel, affectionate even. He never mentioned Lily. Samuel supposed Darley was sorry for him, and was grateful and a little resentful in return.

Lily didn't know who the baby's father was. There was a chance that it was Samuel's, but what really mattered was that it was hers.

There was only one baby. She had been driven away the last time she had tried to come to Lily, but now she was returning. Lily stitched at Miss Atkinson's wedding dress – she embroidered it with white birds on a silver-grey background – and talked to the baby inside her womb.

'I wish it was all white,' she said, giving a little pat to her lap, 'dear Miss Atkinson deserves a white dress – she's the only person who gives me work, so that I can earn money for you – but at least the embroidery is white, and the dress is made of good silk. I shall ask her to be your godmother.'

She talked to the baby in Cantonese, though the little girl would have to learn English too.

'I don't know why you're so happy,' said Ah Ling, bringing her tea, 'it's only a matter of time before the *gweilo* loses his job.'

'We'll manage,' said Lily, 'I've got enough money to keep myself, or else we can go away somewhere and he can get a different job. And my baby girl is coming.'

'What,' asked Ah Ling, so startled that she spilled the pale scented tea, 'don't you want a boy?'

'Why shouldn't I want a girl?' demanded Lily crossly.

'Would you have wanted to be born a woman?' asked the little amah.

Lily snapped off a thread and held out the dress: there was a day's work left in it, at most. Miss Atkinson would wear it to dinner-parties in her first year as a bride. It was so well-cut that all the other ladies would wish she was still making for them. Lily felt a pang of loss.

For a moment she thought she saw Mr Jackson's ghost, standing at the side of the room.

'Is it you?' she asked, 'who is trying to bring misfortune on me? But you were buried in Soochow, with all the proper ceremonies. We were never married, so you can't call me a faithless widow, can you, Mr Jackson? And I *do* burn offerings for you at Hungry Ghosts, lots of money, plenty of books, and give you sucking pig to eat. You won't harm my baby, will you, Mr Jackson? Please go away.'

He vanished. If he came again she'd have to get a medium to deal with him. He'd looked very unhappy: she wondered if he was comfortable enough in Hell? She could burn a paper concubine for him, he'd surely like that. A virgin: she wondered if the shops that made paper goods for the dead could manage virgins. She'd have to find out.

She heard a knock at the door, voices, footsteps on the stairs: Mr Fawler, Bible in hand. Lily began to recite the Lord's Prayer. Mr Fawler stood on the threshold and joined in. They said the 'Amen' together. Then he entered the room.

'You see me,' said Lily sweetly, 'working on a very special dress.' She folded it up and put it away.

'Ah-ha!' exclaimed Mr Fawler. 'I won't try to look, Miss Lily. I know. What is the text?'

'A man shall leave his mother and father,' said Lily, 'and cleave to his wife, and they shall be one flesh.'

'The wedding at Cana,' said Mr Fawler earnestly, 'must never be interpreted as some celestial conjuring trick. It is a sign of the transformation of all our lives when we allow ourselves to be washed, bathed in the redeeming blood of Christ. Sacrifice, Miss Lily, pain, suffering, everything we are going through, we must welcome them as blessings.'

His face was marked, nevertheless, with the inglorious martyrdom Hong-Kong had bestowed on him: attendances at his church had shrivelled, and so had the monetary contributions from the English community. They despised him as a lecher or laughed him to scorn as a gullible idiot.

'As I welcome you,' said Lily, 'dear Mr Fawler. And would you like some tea?'

Ah Ling had come in with it already. Lily poured it for Mr Fawler, sweetened his cup with one spoonful of sugar: she knew his tastes.

'Not as I will,' breathed Mr Fawler, drinking, 'but as Thou wilt. Our Lord's words in Gethsemane, Miss Lily. Don't fear, I shan't abandon you.'

Lily thought: Unto me a child is given. I shall endure the blood and the pain to bring her into the world. She didn't put her hand over her womb, because Mr Fawler had no idea that she was pregnant and she didn't want to upset him: he had enough troubles.

He said: 'If only – Miss Lily, if only you'd come to my church – '

'Oh, Mr Fawler,' said Lily, 'I can't come to your church, Doctor Kwok told me to stay away from large gatherings of people. Perhaps it would be easier for you if you didn't come to see me any more?'

'My wife,' he said, 'my wife begged me to abandon you. She wept.'

He was grieving, Lily could see that. She didn't want him to be so unhappy. She said: 'I have my Bible, and perhaps I can convert Ah Ling.'

'No,' said Mr Fawler with determination. 'I must do what seems right to me. Or how could I face my Saviour on the last day?'

Lily said: 'I do admire you, Mr Fawler.'

For a moment, she wanted to tell him the truth, but no, she couldn't. She must lie, in case she could do some good to Samuel. When the baby was born, she could pretend she'd adopted her.

Samuel, at his desk, was supposed to be reading documents about the drainage system of Hong-Kong when a cramp of grief made him clutch his stomach. He sat quite still and endured it for a moment. Then he pulled out a piece of blank paper and wrote on it:

They knew who I am. Now they've been smashed to pieces.

That was it, that was what hurt so badly.

A Chinese clerk came into the office and left him a note from Darley.

'Mr Darley would like an answer soonest,' said the clerk.

'Thank you,' said Samuel. He scribbled hurriedly: *Lily doesn't believe that I am who I say I am. Only Reynolds is left.*

He wondered what it was like to die such a violent death. He tried to read the note from Darley and could take nothing in. All he could think about was that long fall, the air whistling in their ears as they tumbled helter-skelter on to the rocks, and his foster-mother's skirts disarranged. Then he seemed to hear a child crying.

Babies, he thought, children, they're the product of desire, they scream and shout, they can't even stand upright, for God's sake. They come from chaos.

Again, he felt furiously angry with Reynolds. He wanted to fight him, smash him into the ground this time. Then he wanted to cry.

He went to the door and asked the clerk: 'Has someone brought a baby into the building?'

'No, sir,' said the clerk, looking surprised. But for all Samuel knew he'd smuggled it in himself, and was covering up. He went back to this desk and saw the cliff again. But now *he* was the bloody huddle among the rocks, and a crowd of respectable people stared down at his ruin, baying like hounds. One of them held a baby, whom he understood had been born to replace him.

The Colonial Surgeon walked straight through the office without greeting him. The baying rang in his ears: he felt hunting dogs' teeth meet in his stomach, and writhed. He was surrounded. Hadn't Reynolds been right after all, didn't the imposition of power destroy both ruler and ruled?

He must read Darley's note through: he managed it this time, though the cliff was still in his mind, the cliff where he'd been soiled, had soiled himself, the cliff that had thrown his foster-parents down, he was sure it was exactly the same spot.

He was eating with Lily: he arrived in a temper. He hadn't been able to get on with his work. He complained about the food: he accused her of putting ginger in it.

'Poor Samuel,' said Lily, nervously, 'poor Samuel.'

The bird chimed from its cage.

'It makes too much noise,' he said. 'For God's sake, put the cover on it, I can't stand the racket.'

'No,' said Lily suddenly. 'It doesn't want to be covered up yet, why should I cover it up?'

Samuel dropped his knife and fork loudly on his plate. 'You don't care, you haven't any feelings yourself, don't pretend. You don't love me.' He knew he was being unkind to her, but it was her fault that so many other people were being cruel to him. And she had her baby – which wasn't his.

She turned her face away from him: he thought how foreign she was – and yet so damnably familiar.

She said: 'I can't speak about my feelings, so you pretend I have none. You make me very tired.'

He said: 'I'll go home, then.'

Very quietly, she said: 'Go home if you like.'

He was shaken to find her turning against him too.

'You've never loved me,' he said, 'you never believed I'm the

303

Queen's son, you think I'm a liar like you, you think I'm nobody. I suppose you've been sleeping with the doctor again, have you, that's why you want to get rid of me. I can expose the pair of you, no one will speak to him either – '

Lily said: 'I don't want to sleep with anyone.'

He found himself in tears. 'There's no one for me,' he said, 'no one.'

'You could get yourself a white mistress,' said Lily 'and set her up in Happy Valley, since you hate me so much.'

'But I want you,' he complained, 'I don't know what you've done to me, I don't want anyone but you. I want you now. Don't I have any rights?'

He saw her shiver. Then she got up from the table and went to her bedroom without a word. He followed her.

'It won't harm the baby,' he said uneasily.

'No,' she said.

He wished she'd smile, talk, caress him, even if it was all a lie. Because she wouldn't, he said: 'If it's my child it won't be hurt. Only if it's the doctor's child.'

He heard the bird chime triumphantly next door, but it was in a cage, after all. Everyone was in a cage. He began to cry again. 'You went to bed with the doctor. You won at the races. You're a whore. A decent woman wouldn't even know what horse to back.'

She lay there and let him do what he liked: he knew she was only waiting for him to finish. He wondered if she'd ever enjoyed him. He rolled off her and fell asleep.

After a little while she got out of bed gently, softly, and went through to the little room next door, where Ah Ling had left a large pot full of scented water. It was cool now, but she washed herself carefully, smoothing her belly and the breasts that would feed the baby: oh, the pain of that unwanted milk when her baby had died! She had bound her breasts tight and at last it had gone away. It had gone away inside her like her tears.

Now she sang quietly to the baby, relieved herself in the pot, and went back to bed. She slept.

She dreamed a tall Englishman: she couldn't see his face, could it be Mr Jackson? He put his thumb on her belly: the pressure went straight through her skin and down into her womb. The pain was the worst she had ever experienced. She thought he was killing her. She knew she was asleep, but the death was real.

She lay awake, by Samuel's side. The room was empty. There was a stickiness between her legs, and yet she'd washed herself off. It was blood, she put her hand there and brought it away wet with blood. And then the pain came, and, though she wanted to cry aloud, she couldn't make a sound. She got out of bed and crouched silent on the floor, cradling the pain in her arms.

Samuel woke and called her. She didn't answer. He got out of bed and lit the gas, then he saw her. Her lower garments were soaked in blood. He called Ah Ling in a panic.

Ah Ling nodded grimly. He watched while she got Lily's clothes off, cleaned her up, and padded her. He saw the tiny fruit of conception halfway down the leg of Lily's trousers:

'What are you going to do with it?' he asked.

'Burn it,' said the amah.

He thought for a mad moment that he'd inspect it, to see if it looked like the doctor.

Lily didn't talk or groan, only moved to help Ah Ling tend her, and her face was so expressionless it was frighteningly beautiful, like that of the dead.

There was a strange peace about the next day: it was clear and shiny and when he got to the government offices he could see the hills of China quite clearly across the harbour. You could get days like this in April, unexpected scraps of blessing between the stifling fogs of spring and the fierce sodden heat of summer. He hated the beauty.

Darley said something kind to him: but he deserved everything he was getting. He tried not to notice the expression of concern on Darley's face. He hunched over his desk and applied himself.

Nightsoil collection outside houses, he wrote, *though not ill-organized* – he changed this to 'though well-organized', in case it was read by the Chinese. There was big money in the collection and sale of nightsoil: not much agriculture on Hong-Kong Island, but it was easily shipped across the harbour to the rich rice-fields of San On. He continued – *is a system that is flawed of its own nature.* He stopped to look at this sentence. He'd have to reword the last clause, or else Darley, who was a stickler for good writing, would do it for him. He let it stand for a moment because it illustrated a point he wanted to make to himself: his own nature was flawed. Then he crossed it out and wrote instead, *is a system which cannot be improved to a satisfactory level. It is essential that the whole of the city should be served by proper main-drainage and sewerage, or else we may expect to be punished for our inaction through the arrival of some major pestilence –*

Again, he looked back at his text. 'Punished' was too strong. But he knew why he'd written it. He altered it and went on working.

Lily lay in bed, weak and ill, her face powder-white, but she wasn't wearing powder.

He'd felt he must come, but she didn't seem to want him. She didn't seem to want anyone.

Samuel's mouth dried up and he cleared his throat. He was afraid of her. He glanced away, but the whiteness was still there on the edge of his field of vision. He blinked, and it fell into pieces, like Mrs Darley's lace petticoats as she lay in a swoon on her drawing-room floor, like the white porcelain fragments of the Kwan Yin that Mrs Ellis had smashed with her revolver, or like jasmine flowers, except that these flowers had a red heart and smelt threatening.

'I'm sorry,' he said.

'Don't think about it,' said Lily, gasping for pain, 'it's fate. Men destroy girl-children. It was my baby. She keeps trying to get back into the world to be with me, and always her father makes her die.'

Samuel said: 'I didn't want to destroy her.' He didn't like to say that he wasn't the baby's father.

'No,' said Lily, 'but you did, just like Ah Kuen, you're all the same, Chinese or English, you destroy girl-children.'

Her voice was so indifferent that it took him a few moments to understand what she was saying. 'It can't be helped,' she added.

'Ah Kuen?' he asked, and suddenly he was furious. 'You went to bed with a Chinese man?'

'The best lover I ever had,' said Lily, 'he gave me pleasure, and destroyed my baby.'

He got on to the bed beside Lily: he sat there and seized her thin shoulders, while something inside him shrieked with horror at his actions. He shook her all the same and put his hot angry face into hers: 'Who was he?'

'Ah Kuen,' said Lily, 'the Pekingese noodle-chef.'

A Chinese, a low fellow, a cook, practically a coolie, had been *there*, where his own unsuspecting penis had been.

'His hands were so clever, so clever.'

Lily's voice faded. She lay unconscious on the bed, and Samuel gave her a few more shakes before he realized what had happened.

'Have I killed you?' he asked her foolishly. He put his hand on her wrist: he thought he felt a fluttering there.

He wanted to see what state she was in, dead or alive: he pulled the thin silk coverlet off her and saw how the blood was seeping out into her nightgown: she had thick padding between her legs and it was soaked. He looked at it, fascinated that so much blood could come out without killing her. If she was alive. He thought of his mother, who might soon be dead too. He thought he might have killed her off by writing to her. He was terrified.

He put his hand on her heart, and felt motion. He was relieved. But he didn't want to look at the blood any longer. He put the coverlet back on the bed. The raw smell of it stayed in his nostrils.

He must get a doctor. He could call Ah Ling and get her to go, but then he'd have to stay with Lily and all that blood. He'd go himself. He went out of the room and shouted for Ah Ling: she came.

'She's been fainting like this all day,' said Ah Ling, biting her lip with her front teeth.

Samuel thought he saw accusation in her face too.

'Losing too much blood,' said Ah Ling anxiously.

'I'm going for a doctor,' said Samuel.

Ah Ling said: 'No need, tell Uncle Liu to run for a Chinese doctor.'

'No,' said Samuel, 'Chinese doctors are quacks.'

Ah Ling shook her head.

Samuel didn't wait, but hurried down the stairs to where his chairmen waited as he'd instructed them. Then he realized what he was doing. The only white doctor who'd come to Lily was Doctor Mackenzie.

'No,' said the doctor's Number One Boy, 'he's at the Club. Shall I send to fetch him?'

'Yes,' said Samuel. 'I'll wait here.' The servant looked at him strangely, though he didn't argue. But Samuel was afraid he'd go back to Lily's house and find her dead. If she was dead, he needed someone – another white man – at his side. Someone who knew how to deal with the situation. He felt sick and weak.

'Please,' he said, 'ask him to come home.'

The Number One Boy showed him into the doctor's sitting room.

It was like many others of its type: green velvet on the chairs, photographs of his dead wife and of friends on the wall, sporting trophies. But the doctor was a collector: there were pieces of coral on shelves, nautilus shells of all kinds, one halved to show the intricate coil of chambers inside, one in *statu naturae*, patterned in cream and brown, one, facing it, stripped to the mother of pearl within. Samuel wondered if the sea-creature's ghost had lingered round the shell, if it had suffered when its coating was stripped off, screamed when its home was sawn in half? Would anyone have heard?

Lily was lying at her house, shell-white in the face, and all the colour leaking out of her below. Why was the doctor taking so long to come? And he was in Hell. The corals on their shelves looked like brains that demons had excised: the sepia photographs were ghosts, the oars on the wall were flails with which the guilty were to be flogged. He put his head into his hands and acknowledged the rightness of it all.

Then Doctor Mackenzie came home.

'You?' he asked, raising his wiry eyebrows.

'It's Lily,' said Samuel, 'she's had a miscarriage and she's very ill, she won't stop fainting. I'm afraid she'll die.' He couldn't bring himself to speak of the blood.

'I'll come,' said the doctor at once. 'Who's with her?' he asked, going for his bag, opening it and checking the contents.

'Ah Ling,' said Samuel.

The doctor ran down the stairs: Samuel followed him. The doctor's chairmen were still there: he told them to run.

Samuel stood on the street.

'Where, sir?' asked his own chairman.

He couldn't go back to Lily after all. He didn't know where to go. Finally, he went back to his own house, where he sat smoking cigars, one after another, and drinking whisky.

Lily lay in pain, black cindery specks veiling her eyes, and thickening now and again to cut her off altogether. She could hear the doctor talking to Ah Ling in pidgin English.

'Now, Lily,' he said, bending down to her, 'I'm going to wash you out with warm water. It's going to stop the bleeding: you've got some bad stuff in there that we need to get rid of, and your womb isn't doing its job properly, so I'm going to help it.' He said to Ah Ling: 'Hold Missee hands.'

Lily felt a pair of little Chinese hands round hers, like to like, and in the bewilderment of her pain she thought she was being born. She murmured 'Mother', in Mandarin, but neither the doctor nor Ah Ling understood. She thought her father was outside there, helping, but would he let her live when he saw she was a girl? She was desperately frightened.

'Ah-ha!' said Doctor Mackenzie. 'We're getting somewhere.'

'I don't want to die,' said Lily in English.

Doctor Mackenzie said: 'You're not going to die, Lily.'

Lily sighed, and went under for a long time.

When she regained consciousness, she muttered in Cantonese to Ah Ling: 'Mr Pink, did he come back?'

'No, Taitai,' said Ah Ling. 'He'll send later, perhaps.'

'That's much better,' said Doctor Mackenzie to Lily. 'The bleeding ought to stop now. I'll come back in a hour or so to make sure, and then tomorrow. Beefee tea,' he said to Ah Ling. 'You know how make beefee tea?'

'I know,' said Ah Ling.

'You must have beef-tea,' he said to Lily. 'Strong good beef-tea. Build you up. I'll be back later.' He patted her leg. 'You'll do, never fear.'

Ah Ling changed the sheets, gently edging Lily from one side of the bed to the other. It was such a comfort to lie on clean sheets! Ah Ling put clean cotton wadding in between Lily's legs. Again, Lily thought she was a newborn baby, till she remembered what had really happened.

'The baby went away,' she said. She was too weak to sob, but large tears came out of her eyes and ran down her cheeks. Ah Ling put her hand on Lily's head.

'Cry now,' she said, 'then you have to get better.'

'Oh yes,' said Lily, 'I must get better so that I can finish Miss Atkinson's wedding dress.'

'Rest yourself,' scolded Ah Ling.

Lily said: 'I want to make the dress for her, I want to earn the money so the baby will come back. I can find a medium and tell the baby what a good home I have waiting for her.' She couldn't stop crying.

'Yes, yes,' said Ah Ling, stroking her hair, 'but first you must get better.'

'It's my fault,' said Lily, 'I said bad things to Mr Pink.'

'The doctor's a kind man,' said Ah Ling.

'Yes,' said Lily.

Ah Ling said: 'If you've got to go to bed with a *gweilo*, or a man at all' – she looked as if she was about to spit – 'you might as well get a kind one.' Then she said: 'Who's going to pay him?'

'I can,' said Lily. 'But Mr Pink sent for him. I suppose Mr Pink will pay.'

Ah Ling pulled her upper lip down over her teeth and shut her mouth tight. She opened it only to say: 'The doctor said I was to give you this medicine, but I've sent Uncle Liu to buy you Chinese medicine. I'll make Chinese soup to strengthen you, with ginger in it. I must get some ginseng root.'

'But I shall have beef soup,' said Lily, 'then we can tell him we're doing as he said.'

Ah Ling said: 'Drink the medicine, Taitai.'

The medicine had laudanum in it, and Lily fell asleep.

The doctor went straight to Samuel's house, and told him what he had done.

'Thank God,' said Samuel. 'How much do I owe you?'

'Don't be a fool, said Doctor Mackenzie, leaning against the sideboard. 'Nobody's going to pay me. You can give me a glass of whisky.'

'If I can't pay you,' said Samuel, 'you'll have done her a favour, not me.'

'And?' asked Doctor Mackenzie, reaching out to pour himself some whisky. He'd saved Lily's life: he thought he deserved it.

'You know,' said Samuel, and yet he handed Doctor Mackenzie a cigar.

The doctor grinned. 'Nice cigar,' he said. 'You know you'll have to leave her alone for a month or so anyway? She mustn't get pregnant again till I've built her up. We could call it a truce.'

After all, he *had* looked a fool when he was caught with Lily: perhaps he had withdrawn from the situation to heal his wounded *amour-propre*. Now he was the saviour, the man with authority, the man whom it was foolhardy to disobey. He looked down, agreeably, at Samuel.

Samuel gulped the rest of his own spirit. He realized, for the first time, that he couldn't ever make love to Lily again. He'd been so bad to her, he thought the touch of her flesh would burn him to ashes.

'Thank you,' he said feelingly. 'Thank you.'

Doctor Mackenzie pulled his moustache. He was amused and a little embarrassed by Samuel's gratitude.

Samuel sent Lily orchids, sprays of yellow orchids that hung like tiny bright moths on their stems, sandalwood perfume, pearls, jade trees in *cloisonné* pots, red carved lacquer: he even had Paul Cheung buy her a Kwan Yin of ivory to worship. He sent her an eggshell thin porcelain bowl, painted with white cranes. He bought her a sideboard and silk brocade curtains for her bedroom. He stayed away.

She and Ah Ling arranged all these things in her house, in case Samuel ever came again. She didn't know if she loved him now. She did as the doctor and Ah Ling told her, obedient as a good child to her parents. She rested. She sat at home and played her *pi pa*, painted bamboo, that bends to the storm and springs up afterwards. Her investments throve.

Only she cried when she wondered where her little girl might be wandering between rebirths.

It's strange, thought Mrs Darley on the thirtieth of April, that I never get used to pain. There's always that moment – just after waking – when I feel nothing at all. I could get up and be just as I was. And then I stir, and it comes back. It comes to me every day as a new and unexpected guest, a brutal stranger.

Her maid brought her her tea.

'Is it a fine day?' she asked.

'It's raining, madam,' said the maid. Mrs Darley sighed. The damp heat was back, and it always made everything far worse.

They had explained to her that it was necessary, that the small piece of flesh was diseased, making her ill.

Oh, she thought, I enjoyed it so much! Can that be bad? I must be a bad woman.

It had been so easy and pleasant to be a bad woman, and now it was so hard and painful to be good. But that was what the Bible said, that it was the steep difficult path that led to Heaven. And if there was a cross to be borne, she had been laden with it. She thought on the whole that Jesus had got off lightly: only nine hours of agony, after all.

She considered killing herself, ran through the means in her head, poison, the rope, slashed wrists. She'd arrange it so that John would find her. But she wouldn't see his horror: even that satisfaction would be denied her. And they said suicide led infallibly to Hell. She didn't really believe in Hell, or Heaven either, but she was afraid to put her unbelief to the test, in case it failed her.

At dinner-time, Darley came home early, instead of going to his club. He sat at the end of the table and looked at her anxiously.

'How are you?' he asked.

'I'm well,' she said dully. She thought even if he had died in the typhoon, it would make no difference. Nothing would make any difference. Only she'd like to be spared the burden of his guilt and rightness.

'There seems,' said Darley casually, 'to be some kind of outbreak of sickness in Taipingshan.'

'It's getting hot again,' she said, 'and damp. We ought to be used to it by now.'

'It's been so dry,' said Darley, 'and the rains coming now, brings sickness out of the soil. Taipingshan's a disgrace to the colony, and they won't let me get to work on it. The coolies want their miserable accommodation to stay miserable. And what would we do without coolies? And so it goes on, the same old story. I only hope we're not in for a bad go of cholera.'

She shrank, and fiddled with the food on her plate. She didn't like to hear about illness. She thought she might get the cholera. He stared at her, and she could see he was puzzled. He had never understood her, never really loved her.

He said: 'Couldn't you put in a good word for Pink, the poor fellow's suffering. If you spoke for him — '

She couldn't understand his concern for Pink, she didn't like it, just as she didn't like him. Why should she be the only one to suffer? She shook her head, and left the table.

Doctor Mackenzie visited Lily at the end of his day's work. He inspected her tongue, looked at her eyes to see if she was making enough blood to replace what she'd lost, felt her pulse and listened to her chest with his stethoscope. He handled her as her doctor, not her lover, only she made him tea afterwards and he dropped a little kiss on the top of her head when he left. She smiled up at him.

He was intrigued with the situation, as well as with her. He had no idea where it was leading him. He was taking a risk. It made him feel young.

He went straight from her house to the Club. He got out of his sedan and admired the sun setting in its usual flamboyant purples and crimsons over the black bulk of the Western islands. He smiled. He walked up the stairs and met the Colonial Surgeon.

'You look grim' he said lightly. 'Got a hangover?'

'Worse than that, my dear fellow,' said the Colonial Surgeon. 'There's an outbreak of plague in Taipingshan.'

Doctor Mackenzie thought about his practice. He knew most of the women would go back to England. Fortunately, he had a good nest-egg to tide him over.

Darley came up behind them: 'Drains,' he said, 'if we'd been allowed to install drains there this would never have happened.'

'I hope it doesn't spread,' said the Colonial Surgeon.

'It's the rains,' said Darley, 'on top of the drought.'

Doctor Mackenzie thought: Words. We all make words to hide our fear. Plague. Cholera. Words that turn your liver yellow. You lose your appetite for food. Only drink, drink makes it tolerable. Only that turns your liver yellow too.

He said: 'Some fellow in Japan says it's to do with rats and fleas. Plenty of them in Taipingshan.'

'Nonsense,' said the Colonial Surgeon. 'What can a Japanese know about it? Eastern medicine, all superstition. Probably because he thinks rats are evil spirits.'

The three men laughed. But:

'It's serious science,' said Doctor Mackenzie.

'Nightsoil jars,' said Darley, 'encouraging rats. This'll show those Chinese. Why have buildings reform, they said. No plague in Taipingshan, they said.' Angrily, he went at his invisible straw.

'I don't believe it,' said the Colonial Surgeon. 'Plague is caused by bad air and there's plenty of that in Taipingshan too.'

Doctor Mackenzie asked: 'Bad air migrating from the epidemic in Canton? Rats come here by boat from Canton all the time.'

The Colonial Surgeon made an irritable gesture. He said: 'It's going to be a damned filthy business.'

23

THE PLAGUE SUMMER

AND yet the plague became Samuel's lifeline, though it was a little while before he knew it.

By the middle of May, six hundred people had already died. More ran away, the Portuguese to Macao, Chinese to Canton, though the disease had been there before it came to Hong-Kong. Most of the Englishwomen left: many, like Mrs Darley, were going home for the hot season as they always did, off to see their children in England. Only this year, the P & O steamship was crowded with mothers whose children were too young for school.

Darley had brought his wife out to the boat and taken her down to her stateroom. He kissed her goodbye, briskly, distastefully, touched her on the shoulder, and left. She felt ill, she lay down on her bed with an open bottle of eau-de-Cologne.

The boat was full of noise: children screaming and being hushed, people finding their berths, the trundle of luggage trolleys along the passageways. It was full of memories. The stateroom was the very one in which she had lain with Pink, with Henderson, with other young men. She recognized a stain on the globe round the electric light-bulb: so little time had passed! There was the other journey she'd made in this boat, the dreadful journey with the young doctor in charge of her, the gaoler, who had different business with what lay between her legs.

Mrs Darley tried to decide if she wanted her husband to die of plague. A quiet wickedness inside her needed him to die, needed him to suffer – he who had always been so fanatical about his drains and the public's health. Not hers. She laughed aloud when she thought that. She'd been wanting to think it for months. Still she didn't want to live with the contagion of such an ugly, medieval death: people

314

wouldn't know what to say about it, back in England when she was a widow. After all, it *was* almost the twentieth century. Brain-fever would have been acceptable. Everyone knew that people died of brain-fever, in the tropics.

Or he should have died in the typhoon.

Henderson was dead now, Pink was in disgrace – and she was glad – Richards was married to a lush young woman who reminded him – she supposed – of her. He was still kind to poor Mrs Darley.

She didn't want him to be kind.

There was nothing she could wish on Darley that would pay him back for her loss of pleasure, her lifetime of pain.

Samuel noticed the black butterflies dancing in the streets: there seemed to be more of them, this year, and they looked larger than ever in the emptiness between the buildings, their long tails like points of lace on a widow's mourning veil.

The city smelt different: less fish was set out to dry, there were fewer cooked-food merchants; less charcoal-roast peanuts; less yellow blobs on skewers came sizzling out of streetside cooking pans. There was less smell of humanity, of ordure and excrement. There was still the rankness of wet foliage after rain.

There was an increasing faint smell of carbolic: he twitched his nostrils when he smelt it. It meant officialdom was out there, making war on uncleanliness. And all the time the hibiscus, the bougainvillea, the yellow-and-white frangipani sent sweet signals to the butterflies in mourning: the flowers didn't care about the humans who tended them, they were interested only in their fertility, beautiful, irresponsible things.

Pastor Marius and his new wife remained: they couldn't have born to be parted. The German Lutheran Mission was high in the Mid-Levels after all, probably safe from the bad air that caused the plague. Mrs Ellis was still in Pokfulam Road with Rebecca and two prostitutes who had come to Mrs Ellis of their own accord: both were very ill with venereal disease. Mrs Ellis and Rebecca nursed the two sick ones, and Mrs Ellis taught them all to read and write English: she didn't know why, especially since the sick women were certainly going to die, and surely they wouldn't be faced, on the steps of Heaven, with an examination in written English?

Mr Fawler was shaving himself. He didn't do this particularly well: he usually had a manservant to do it for him, but now he was all alone in the house, except for an elderly shaky-handed amah, and he didn't trust her with his throat. The other servants had fled, his wife had gone on the boat with Mrs Darley. Most of the rooms had been shut up and left to the jaws of white ants and cockroaches.

Mrs Fawler must now be negotiating the Suez Canal. Her letters had come to him from Singapore, from Georgetown, from Colombo, from Aden. She was going further and further away from him. A tear ran out of his left eye: he watched it in the mirror as it tracked through his whiskers and lost itself in the white froth underneath.

After he'd left his wife on the boat, he'd got straight off the launch and gone to visit Lily. He'd told her how difficult it was for him to be parted from Mrs Fawler: she had listened and told him – in that sweet voice – that he was a brave man. He didn't want to be brave, he wanted to get out, on the boat with his wife. He needed her sceptical presence. He'd never known how much her malice had anchored him. If only he hadn't let her go!

He should never have championed Lily: her charm was wearing thin now. Why had he sacrificed the lambs from the fold for the one who was straying? So many had been filched by other shepherds or had run out to wander afresh, while Lily had never set foot in his church.

He wanted only to know if Mrs Fawler loved him. He'd given her so much to put up with. Wouldn't she have stayed, if he'd cast Lily off? It made it worse that he'd acted in good faith.

Shaving up underneath the overhang of his whiskered cheek, Mr Fawler cut himself. He swore – there was no one listening. Then he called himself to order: 'No one except God, Nathaniel?'

He dabbed at the blood with his shaving-cloth and went on more cautiously.

The world was harsh, always ready to scourge the faithful. But didn't that only prove the truth of the gospel? Misjudged he might be, calumniated, heartsore, and yet: 'The stone that the builders rejected is become the head of the corner.'

The sky darkened outside and the rain poured down. Mr Fawler had electric light in his house. He went to the wall and pulled a switch. The room was flooded with light. It reminded him of the City of God where the sun never went down. What power under his hands, Christian power demonstrated! And his courage *must* bear fruit, Chinese converts, their eyes electrified with saving grace.

As if he were arguing with someone, he said: 'While my church has *one* faithful member still to attend it, while there is *one* Chinese soul to be saved, Nathaniel Fawler will labour in the field. However hard it may be.'

On Sunday he went to take the service, and there were three people there, three reasons for him to remain. He strove hard to find them convincing.

I am growing used to my hand-to-mouth existence, wrote Reynolds, *and am learning to enjoy its small consolations, a meat pie when I can afford one, a woman when I can persuade her, a drink of beer or something stronger when I feel I can stretch to it. Life isn't so bad among the dregs of society, when you have given up all aspirations to anything better. I may even, from time to time, be happier than you.*

Samuel didn't doubt it.

Now the flow of letters into the colony petered out, the husbands left behind received nothing from their wives because the yellow flag was up at the harbour mouth, warning ships away from the plague port. There was no letter from Samuel's mother to mark his birthday. The colony was under siege.

Junks appeared in the harbour, but they had been sent by a Chinese charitable organization in Canton, to take the victims away. The Governor refused to release the corpses.

'Got to grasp the nettle,' said Darley to Samuel, 'this is going to be a damned difficult business. The Chinese are going to hate us, so many measures we're going to have to pass that they won't like.' He hesitated for a moment, then said: 'It's a chance for you, though, hardly any women to gossip, work to do – '

'I'm not seeing her,' said Samuel sadly. 'I haven't seen her for a month. I've really given her up.'

'And not paying her any more money, I hope,' said Darley, 'scheming little whore.'

'I can't let her starve,' said Samuel. He felt besieged himself, holding a lonely fort against government colleagues.

'You're a fool,' said Darley. 'This special committee of the Sanitary Board we're setting up to deal with the plague – I've got you on to it. That'll help, you'll see.'

'Thank you,' said Samuel, and looked away from him.

Darley was on the committee, and Philips, and the Colonial

Surgeon among others. The men let Samuel sit down at the table with them, they talked to him as if nothing was wrong. Bewildered, he fell in with what they wanted. Work to do, he thought, work to do.

The Colonial Surgeon said: 'We have to get into those houses in Taipingshan and make sure they're not full of corpses. Or the air down there will be even fuller of disease.'

'Who are we going to use?' asked Darley.

'Soldiers,' said the Colonial Surgeon. 'And coolies.'

The clerk Tsang, who was taking minutes, raised his head for a moment, but none of the white men noticed.

'About the bodies we've already got,' said Philips.

'Mass grave,' said the Colonial Surgeon. 'It's the only way.'

Philips said: 'I've received several complaints about the Governor's refusal to release them. The difficulty is that we're trampling over their sensibilities. We all know what the Chinese feel about burial on auspicious days. If we ignore that – '

'If we allow the bodies to lie around,' said Darley sharply, 'shrouded, I admit, but what use is a shroud – '

Philips said: 'They can't imagine what we want with them. It's dangerous ground, gentlemen. They suspect the worst.'

Even more irritably, Darley said: 'You're the man to explain it to them, Philips.'

The Colonial Surgeon said: 'They'll have to do as they're told. We're the government. We have the guns.'

Tsang raised his head again, and everyone saw it. Unease descended on the committee: as if they had remembered all those other Chinese on the edge of whose kingdom the British sat, temporary victors.

'Now,' said Darley rather too briskly, 'gentlemen, the rest of the business.'

The provision of extra hospital beds, the inspection of Chinese premises, the removal of the sick to the hospitals, the disinfection and cleansing of said premises, the committee passed them all for immediate action. There was no time to lose.

Chinese coolies battered on doors at the orders of young British volunteers – mainly military men. They intruded on Chinese homes and searched them: where they found the sick they pulled them from their beds and carted them away to the hastily improvised hospitals. They they took all the furniture out of the houses and

318

cleansed them with carbolic and lime. Those who died in the hospitals – which was most of them – were taken away and buried in a large cemetery at the western end of the island.

Philips brought more complaints to the committee. Masses of ghosts were being cast out into the island – and they could never be fed with offerings by their relatives, since no one knew where they were disposed. The dignitaries of the Chinese community warned of increasing ill-feeling. Reluctantly, Philips went back to explain to them that it was all necessary. Yet the plague kept pace with everything the British could do – though almost entirely among the Chinese. Only some of the soldiers died.

The Colonial Secretary brought Samuel into the Club for a drink, and Richards called him over to play billiards. MacVicary came past and spoke to him. He was ashamed of his gratitude, he was ashamed to have been so lonely. He was afraid they would turn on him again. It was better not to think, and there was work to do.

As May turned into June, Darley sat in his office and drew up plans for an extended drainage system. He didn't care that the Chinese clerks outside diverted the routes when they ran through the spines of dragons. He could ask for as much money as he liked: no one would dispute his budgets now.

He said to Samuel, as he had said many times already:

'Always knew something like this would happen. The Chinese can worry on about dragons if they like, all I know is, the worst-hit area is Taipingshan. We haven't had cases on the Peak, have we, or in Mid-Levels? Of course not. Drains, my lad, good buildings, ventilation, fresh water, and more drains!'

'What do you think about this rat business?' asked Samuel, 'do you think Mackenzie's on the right track?'

'No,' replied Darley and shut his mouth up. He didn't like Doctor Mackenzie and he didn't want the lad to admire him. It wasn't just that Darley's friend, the Colonial Surgeon, despised the rat-and-flea theory. It was because Mackenzie thought – and had said in public – that Mrs Darley had been mutilated.

Mackenzie was a disreputable old quack – so different from the smart young man who had dealt with Mrs Darley's problem. How could he be allowed to know anything about the cause of the plague? And why should Pink think well of him, what had Mackenzie done for Pink, compared to what Darley had done for him? Who but Darley had vouched for Pink to the Colonial

Secretary, assured him that the Lily Jackson business was at an end?

'Drains,' he said again. 'Look, if we route one here, we can run inlets from all these houses – think of the employment this'll provide, when the plague is over!'

Samuel did admire Mackenzie, who was sometimes uneasy about it. He'd decided to do the dirty on Samuel over Lily: couldn't the fellow tell? But he was working in the plague hospitals, so he didn't have much time to be uneasy.

It was among Samuel's tasks to organize the Whitewash Brigade. Like the angel of fate, he determined the visitation of streets – once every ten days in the Chinese quarter – and the next day the squads descended. On the first day, he'd gone out with them himself.

The organization of the squads was easy enough. Relations with the Chinese continued difficult. The Tung Wah Hospital urged the Governor to let it treat all the plague victims. The Governor refused.

'Of all the damn' fool things to do,' said Philips, polishing his spectacles over and again. 'Who advised him, that's what I'd like to know.'

He'd come to see Darley – Samuel knew it was because he suspected him of giving bad advice to H.E. – but Darley had actually gone to a meeting with the Governor.

Philips said: 'They talk about abolishing the Registrar-General's office – someone has to speak for the Chinese, haven't they? I'm tired of being the only man with his eyes open – haven't I worked as hard as anyone else? I can hear the discontent. How much better are the hospitals we're sending them to?'

'At least, sir,' said Samuel, 'they have proper doctors.'

Like Mackenzie, who was going to take Lily off his hands and free him from guilt.

Philips glanced at the Chinese clerk, Tsang, who was listening while he wrote.

'How good are they at curing the plague? Pink, none of our doctors knows how to deal with this. If a man has to die, he might as well die with his own people around him. How would you feel if you were dragged off to a Chinese hospital?'

Hastily, Samuel said: 'I only do what the committee decides.'

'Of course,' said Philips, 'you daren't stick your neck out.'

Samuel tried to decide if this was contempt or compassion. He wished Philips would go away.

'You must come to dinner,' said Philips suddenly, 'I've been talking to my wife about it.'

Samuel wondered if Mrs Philips had been resisting the idea. He hadn't been to the Philips house since he stopped working at the Registrar-General's Department, he had never thought she liked him. But she was a Hong-Kong lady, and he wanted her approval. She was fearless, too: she hadn't run from the plague. Of course, she had no children.

Philips wanted to get back to his argument. 'Listen, Pink,' he said, 'we sit here making dispensations for other people's sufferings. Not ours.'

And haven't I suffered? thought Samuel. But Philips was talking about the plague.

He went on: 'What I want your department to know about is the stories I'm getting back. The squads are making money out of this, threatening to drag people's personal effects out of their houses and burn them if they're not paid squeeze. I'm talking about houses where the plague hasn't been found.' He put his clean spectacles back on his nose.

'But that's China,' said Samuel. 'What can you get done anywhere in the Celestial Kingdom without paying your pieces of silver?' He remembered Tsang's presence, and wished he hadn't said this. But Tsang only glanced at them both with a bored, indifferent expression: Samuel saw it. There was an unassailability there: hundreds of years of history and wisdom and a certainty that the invader would have to go in the end, or be assimilated. He wished he could be so confident.

Philips said: 'You know we haven't any licence to sanction corruption. We have to honour our law, not clatter about their customs. What other safeguard have any of us got?'

Samuel tidied the sheaves of paper on his desk: they looked better in neat stacks. When the corners peered askew, he thought he saw Reynolds's face, and was startled. It made him feel tired. The truth of his situation lay in what Philips said: he daren't stick his neck out.

He must see Philips's challenge as another item for the desk. He got a clean sheet of paper and began to scribble on it.

'We'll look into it,' he promised. He could do this, without Darley's say-so. 'I'll write a letter to the Chinese organizations.'

It would be written with courtesy, vilifying his own attributes and abilities. That wouldn't be hard to do. He had never felt so humble.

Yet he was British, and must stand by that. It was the only safety for him.

Philips said meaningfully: 'I know how badly paid the soldiers are.'

They were indeed: along with visiting sailors they were something of an embarrassment in a colony where all the other British were of good social standing.

'Sir,' said Samuel, 'we'll do what we can.'

'Thank you,' said Philips, and left at last.

The next day, the newspapers carried a report about Doctor Kitasato's work in Japan, seeded there by Doctor Mackenzie. The Colonial Secretary was incensed. He issued a reassurance that the plague was nothing to do with either rats or fleas.

'Do you want to cause wholesale panic?' he demanded of Doctor Mackenzie when he met him at the Club. 'Rats and fleas are everywhere.'

'You can kill rats and fleas,' said Mackenzie. 'You can't kill bad air.'

The Colonial Surgeon snorted, and walked away.

Samuel got his invitation to dinner.

He stood in his bedroom and felt a strange sensation of breathlessness. He worried that he might be catching the plague – but this wasn't like illness. It was as if there was some huge, hitherto inexpressible feeling rising in him, striving to be born. He took a gulp of whisky and decided that it was only nervousness about the Philipses' dinner-party. It was going to be all right, though: Mrs Philips had invited him to bring him back into the fold. And it turned out to be a thoroughly pleasant evening, though rather unconventional, since the ladies were heavily outnumbered by men. He went home cheerful and had four hours of good sleep. Then he started awake, remembering unhappily that the Philipses had always been prepared to entertain the socially impossible.

Ah Ling said: 'They say the *gweilo* doctors are gouging out babies' eyes to use for medicine against the plague.'

'Not Doctor Mackenzie,' said Lily crossly.

Ah Ling said: 'Sometimes I worry about you, you might be possessed by them.' She placed a butterfly ornament in Lily's hair.

'By who?' demanded Lily.

'You're not quite Chinese,' said Ah Ling, 'or you wouldn't have to ask. The *gweilos*. They're not properly reincarnated – ' she shuddered, 'no wonder they're doing such dreadful things to the dead. At least that other one never comes near us now.'

'He pays the rent,' said Lily.

'The trouble is,' said Ah Ling, 'a *gweilo* saved your life when you were a baby, now that doctor has saved your life again, and he wouldn't take any money for it – what's he up to?'

'You can always go away,' said Lily, 'if you hate me so much.' She let her head drop and stared at her silken knee. Her heart jumped with terror.

'I can't,' said Ah Ling, 'I ought to leave, I could get work in Canton, but I don't want to. I suppose they've got their hooks into me too.'

'Then why did you frighten me?' asked Lily, beginning to cry.

Ah Ling undid her hair and began to comb it through again. She said: 'I have to think what's the best thing to do for both of us. The doctor does seem to be kind.'

Later, Lily noticed that a small octagonal mirror had appeared opposite the door of her bedroom. Ah Ling had put it there to repel evil influences. Lily let it be: there couldn't be any harm in it.

Darley said to Samuel: 'The Japanese are at war with China.'

It was no sensation, only another burden on overcrowded agendas. The government officials were all tired, and the Governor's wife, Lady Robinson, was dead, but she had died of sprue, not of the plague, which was the significant, the only truly significant thing.

The carts trundled along the streets, baked by sunshine, soaked with rain, carrying the bodies forcibly extracted from the charnel-dwellings of Taipingshan, the dead refuse of the hospitals.

There was no cure for plague, but it was usually the better-fed who survived. The disease swept the sickly out of the slums. It would be easier, Samuel supposed, for Darley to rebuild them afterwards. A new Hong-Kong!

'You're going to price coolie labour out of the market,' said MacVicary to Darley's face at the Club. Behind his back, he said: 'He's mad. Quite irresponsible. He ought to be sent elsewhere. I don't care where. Anywhere, as long as it isn't Hong-Kong.'

'What he can't see,' said Darley calmly to Samuel, 'is that the plague is losing us trade right now. I shall win.'

And Paul Cheung asked Samuel: 'Do I have to keep paying this policeman his three dollars a month?'

'Oh, yes,' said Samuel nervously, 'yes.'

There were rumours among the Chinese that the English troops were raping women in the houses they inspected. The government issued denials. Still, Samuel was glad that Lily's house was in the safe area of the city. He never had to ink her in for a visit.

Lily asked the doctor if she was strong enough to conceive a child yet.

He said: 'Perhaps.' He stroked his moustache and looked at her sidelong. It would be easier if that fool Pink wasn't so trusting.

'Please, Doctor Mackenzie – ' said Lily, raising her long beautiful eyes to his. He knew what she meant.

She said: 'You gave me the last baby. I know you did.' She sank her eyes modestly to the floor and waited for his judgement.

He asked: 'Is that all you want of me? A baby?'

'I don't know,' said Lily. She put her hand to her belly and felt the cold emptiness. It went all through her.

Doctor Mackenzie couldn't bear to see her look so unhappy. He put his arms round her and they went to bed together after all.

Then she loved him, all the while she opened her legs and muscles as wide as possible, made them soft and yielding and inviting for the baby.

Come, she sang into the world of spirits, come baby, come.

Doctor Mackenzie sent a note to Samuel. It read: *The truce is over.* Samuel tore it up.

Mrs Marius came to visit Lily: she met the doctor on his way out. She was pleased to see Lily so well looked after, and said so to Mrs Ellis when she next saw her.

'Alicia,' said Mrs Ellis, 'you'll be corrupted.'

'Oh,' said Mrs Marius gaily, 'I'm not a girl any more: how could I be corrupted?'

She was so happy to be married, delighted to visit Lily and spoil her with little gifts. She wasn't afraid of the plague.

'You mean to say,' said Mrs Ellis, 'that you're attracted by whoredom?'

'But Beatrice,' said Mrs Marius, 'she isn't a whore, it's all finished between her and Mr Pink.' She put her hands over her mouth.

There was no surprise on her sister's face.

'Ah-ha,' said Mrs Ellis, 'so you've known all along.' She said nothing for a long time.

At last she pronounced judgement: 'She *is* a whore. You're already corrupted.'

Mrs Marius looked at her sister who had dictated her comings and goings for so long.

'Yes,' she said, 'perhaps I am corrupted. I don't care.'

'This is the true plague,' said Mrs Ellis, 'it seeps disease into everything, into religion, morality, truth, all vitiated by that loosening of those ties that should be dearest to us. I shan't discuss the matter any more with you, Alicia.'

'Very well,' said her sister, and was a little surprised – and shocked – to find herself still alive.

Lily sent Ah Ling with a little note for Samuel.

Samuel, dear, Doctor Mackenzie says we can go to bed together again. I love you, I have never stopped loving you, believe me, if you come back to me, I'll give him up.

He wrote back: *I shall never see you again. You're a dear girl, but I have to live among my own people. I hope for your own sake that the doctor never comes to the same decision.*

Then he took out all his letters from his mother, and read through them. Perhaps he would still be allowed to get married. He could make do with one of the Fishing Fleet, if she had a kind heart.

He wished he'd had his letter from her before the port was closed. He listened, as if he might hear her words on the damp evening breeze, but all he could hear was the carts rumbling in the streets, on their way to the cemetery at West Point.

He was developing chronic indigestion.

The punkahs swept back and forth in the nineteenth-century Early English heights of St John's Cathedral. The colonialists sang, 'Oh God our Help in Ages Past.' They went on their knees:

> For our efforts in cleansing Hong-Kong,
> For the Whitewash Brigade,
> For the drains,
> For the hospitals,

For our persistence in the face of Chinese intransigence
   and ingratitude,
Lord commend us.

I predicted it, thought Darley, and wanted to cry aloud in the depths of the church, reach the ceiling with the name of the Chadwick Report. Which had recommended the destruction of insanitary quarters. And I, myself, John Darley, have planned new reservoirs. I have been obstructed by the Chinese. Who did most foolishly point to the absence of plague in their justification. And are visited now with hideous and merciless pestilence. Which they from time to time most grievously have invited.

They stood up, hymnbooks in their hands. They were spectators – though never idle ones – at a calamity which wasn't really theirs. The knowledge was uncomfortable, though they felt more unease at the thought that their immunity might not last. The men glanced at the few remaining women: weak females all and therefore endlessly endangered.

Mother in England, prayed Samuel, great ruler of the seas on whose Empire the sun never sets, whither shall I flee from thy presence? If I take wings of the morning and dwell in the uttermost parts of the sea, even there shall thy portrait hang and thy eyes shall encompass my small and insignificant being. I do earnestly repent my trespasses, oh try if there is any wicked thought left in me. And, mother, don't die, please, not just yet. In the name of God, the Almighty, Amen.

After the service, the Governor stopped and spoke kindly to Samuel, commended the work he was doing and made some encouraging reference to his future prospects before he walked away.

'There you are, my lad,' said Darley, touched him on the shoulder, and grinned. Samuel went home to cry.

That same night, he dreamed he was making love to Lily, rolling in the extreme of pleasure. By and by he realized that they were lying on a bed of splaying, thrashing noodles. There was a horrible smell of garlic.

Lily sat in the little garden at the back of her house. She had flowering plants in pots there, and a miniature tea tree, beautifully trained and gnarled. She was thinking about her baby. Her lost baby was hovering round her, begging to be reborn.

When she was alone the child's cries drowned everything else, so that now she never thought about the plague, nor of Samuel any more, and only of the doctor because she knew he would be the child's father. Nor did she think further than the baby's live birth.

A black butterfly alighted briefly on her dress, mistaking an embroidered flower for a real one. A moment later, she felt a dull pain. She began to weep and shriek: Ah Ling heard her and came running out.

'I'm bleeding,' cried Lily, clinging to Ah Ling. 'I'm not pregnant, why aren't I pregnant? Look at that Cheung, with his hare lip, even he has a son, what dreadful crime did I commit in a past life, that I'm being punished like this? Ah Ling, I must go to the temple. I must see the fortune-teller.'

'Are you crazy?' demanded Ah Ling. 'People are dropping like flies in those streets. I'm not even sure if you can go down there: the gweilos have probably had it sealed off. If you did anything except sit here and dream about babies, you'd know that yourself. Anyway, the spirits might tell the man you're going with foreigners: you don't want him to find that out, not in these days. And he's a lecher. If he's still alive. And why can't you have patience, for Heaven's sake? You've only been trying a month.'

'My baby,' said Lily, 'I want my baby.'

Ah Ling sighed. 'You're so unreasonable,' she said. 'It's hard, working for you.'

'You can go to Canton, if you like,' said Lily, pushing her away. 'I've told you that before. Then I can die in peace.'

Ah Ling said sharply: 'You're not going to die, don't try that on with me. There used to be a woman medium in the Flower-show Street. I'll send Uncle Liu down to see if she'd help you – if she's still there. Though you'd be better to wait. This is no time to have babies.'

Lily started to cry again. Ah Ling said: 'Don't cry: you'll weaken yourself. I'm too hard on you, you're possessed. You do need help. I'm sending Uncle Liu now.'

There was an emptiness about the Flower-show Street (the Chinese name for Lyndhurst Terrace), no flower vendors stood there today, and the shuttered houses refused to look at the street.

'Look,' said Lily to Ah Ling, 'the black butterflies again. They must be evil spirits.' She shuddered.

327

'The medium will banish them,' said Ah Ling hopefully, 'maybe she'll banish all the *gweilos* too.'

Lily said: 'Maybe she'll banish the doctor, maybe she'll banish me, since you don't think I'm really Chinese. Maybe I should go home.'

'Not now I've got you here,' said Ah Ling crossly, 'and she wouldn't banish you, only make you more Chinese, surely you'd like that?'

Lily stood still in the middle of the street.

'You want your baby, don't you?' asked Ah Ling.

The medium lived above a draper's shop but it was shut up.

'You're a foreigner,' she said as soon as she heard Lily speak.

'From Soochow,' said Lily quickly.

'*Ai ya*,' said the medium, 'that's a long way to come.' Lily saw the woman's speculative eyes on her and her womb cramped painfully. Of course she'd been recognized. She was afraid.

The room was ordinary and respectable: there was a bed in one corner, and a door led to a kitchen beyond. Children's voices came from there. The woman was called Mrs Ko. There was nothing other-worldly about her: she was brisk and practical. When Lily told her about the baby, she listened carefully, lighting incense-sticks at her large altar where Taoist deities looked down at offerings of oranges.

'There's a lot of work at the moment,' said Mrs Ko, 'with the *gweilos* shovelling people away. The hells are in chaos, and bad spirits everywhere, feasting on all this death.' She shook her head as if she was looking at a cockroach-infested cupboard.

'Now,' she said, 'tell me when you were born, the day, the month, and the year.'

Ashamed, and even more afraid, Lily said: 'I was a foundling. I don't know.'

Mrs Ko's face didn't change – so she *did* know already. She said: 'I'll have to speak to the king of the tenth Hell. You must be silent and reverent.'

She got a piece of yellow paper, a brush, and red ink. Lily and Ah Ling watched while she wet the inkblock and rubbed it on a carved stone. When she had enough ink, she began to write – neither of them asked what.

She kowtowed before the altar, burned the paper, and grew still: the silence seemed to envelop the whole world. After some time, she began to write with her finger in a tray of sand that she had beside her. Lily felt her pain subside. It must be good news, after all.

Still, it was hard to wait for Mrs Ko to come out of her trance. Lily held her breath.

'I've found your baby,' said Mrs Ko, looking at the tracks her finger had made in the sand. 'You're going with a foreigner,' she said.

Lily opened her mouth to excuse herself, but Mrs Ko told her to be quiet. She said: 'Your life is bound up with foreigners, poor girl: I knew that already. The one you used to live with, the one who died, he's bringing you bad luck. I can deal with him. As for the other *gweilos*, you must see to that yourself.' She tutted briefly. 'And your baby: she was your mother and she cast you out to die. Now she wants to come back as your daughter so that she can make it up to you, and so that you can love her. She has already been punished, now she must be patient. She will be born.'

'Who's going to be her father?' asked Lily.

'I can't tell you that,' said Mrs Ko.

Mrs Ko gave Lily an amulet to put under her pillow. She clutched it in her fist. Her mother wanted her after all: it was almost too much happiness.

'If the bad luck lifts,' said Ah Ling as they climbed the hill, 'you might even get a Chinese man after all.'

'The doctor's a kind man,' said Lily, 'you said so yourself.'

'He saved your life,' admitted Ah Ling. 'But don't worry, I shan't abandon you to him. I'll stay with you in your misfortune.'

There was a knock at the door. Ah Ling came to Lily and said: 'It's that *gweilo* woman. The one with the gun.'

'I'm not at home,' said Lily.

'She promises she won't hurt you,' said Ah Ling. 'She swore it. She says she hasn't got her gun. Shall I send her away?'

'No,' said Lily. 'No – let her in.'

Yet she was terrified. She stood with her hand to her face, looking Mrs Ellis up and down to see if she had her revolver after all. And Mrs Ellis had power over her. The medium had said so.

'No,' said Mrs Ellis, 'don't shrink away from me, Lily. I've come to apologize.'

'Dear Mrs Ellis,' said Lily – still warily – 'you have nothing to apologize for. Ah Ling,' she called, 'bring tea and biscuits. The

Orange Pekoe tips and milk and sugar. And the Bath Olivers.' She'd tell Ah Ling to stay, when she brought them up.

'You *are* afraid of me,' said Mrs Ellis, not without satisfaction. She hesitated, then sat down on the sinful velvet *chaise-longue*.

'Oh, no,' said Lily, sitting down too, 'how could I be, when you took me off the streets, and saved me from starvation?' She wondered what would have happened if she had starved to death. Perhaps she would have been reborn as a Mandarin with a large family, free of *gweilos*.

She didn't want to die, she really knew that. She had to be alive in this body: she was too firmly attached to this life and its complications.

'I helped you to meet your protector,' said Mrs Ellis rather grimly. 'I can't understand it, Lily – no, I haven't come here to reproach you – what was it about that man that was worth giving up your freedom for?'

'But I had no freedom,' said Lily. 'You put me in prison.'

It must be the medium's work, that she dared speak so freely to Mrs Ellis. She caught her breath and held it, all the same.

The white-eyed bird chimed into the middle of the conversation, a little peal like temple bells when the wind takes them. On an angry inpulse, Lily got up from her chair, went over to the domed cage and opened the door. Then she stood back. The pretty bird hopped to the door and came out, as it had done many times before. It flew round the room and then found the open window: the windows were usually shut before it was allowed out. It hesitated for just a moment on the windowledge, cocking its head, then spread its wings and escaped.

'It's a bird,' said Mrs Ellis, 'it has no understanding, it does according to its nature. And supposing a kite takes it?'

'It didn't want the cage,' said Lily. She was shaking now, and her mouth was dry. She felt Mrs Ellis's power wound round her after all: it felt like the tough sticky web of the poisonous spider.

'But at least,' said Mrs Ellis, 'at least with me you had your body to yourself, you were not required – and my sister too – nothing in my experience – this desire – and I have been married, you know, Lily.'

'But not all men give pleasure,' said Lily.

Mrs Ellis stared. She had simply never considered this before.

Ah Ling came in, put down the tray with the English tea things, and remained, her eyes on the madwoman. Lily felt better.

Mrs Ellis asked: 'Did Mr Jackson give you pleasure? Did the doctor? Did Mr Pink? Of course,' she said, 'you have a wide experience, haven't you: have you got a man now?'

Lily said nervously: 'I have known pleasure. Mrs Ellis, will you take some tea?'

'But with me,' said Mrs Ellis, accepting the cup, and eating a Bath Oliver, 'you had work, you could earn your living.'

'I used to work,' said Lily indignantly, 'who was it took the work away from me?'

'Oh, Lily,' said Mrs Ellis. 'The ladies decided for themselves.'

'Only because I'm Chinese,' said Lily, 'I know about the rest of them, Mrs Richards went to bed with the Governor, and Mr Richards still has his woman in Happy Valley – '

'Do you think I don't know,' asked Mrs Ellis, 'do you think I condone that?'

'And,' said Lily, 'Mrs Ellis, I wear silk here, and it's prettier and more comfortable than the clothes you made me wear. I can have time to myself. I have my pictures, my *pi pa* to play – these may seem small things to you, but they comfort me.'

She wouldn't say anything about the baby.

'Lily,' said Mrs Ellis, 'Rebecca and I are going to help nurse the sick. Will you come with us? There are trained nurses working in the hospitals, but they need women to help. There are many tasks a woman can do to help the plague-stricken, and we're willing to do them.'

'Oh, no,' said Lily in a panic.

'Lily,' said Mrs Ellis, 'I'm offering you a great opportunity.'

Lily knew Mrs Ellis hadn't really listened to anything she'd said.

'But Mrs Ellis,' she protested, 'I might catch the plague.'

'Only Chinese catch the plague,' said Mrs Ellis dismissively.

'I'm Chinese,' said Lily. 'Rebecca is Chinese.'

'Rebecca's a Christian,' said Mrs Ellis, 'and you too could entrust your life to Christ. He will keep you safe.'

'Oh, Mrs Ellis,' said Lily, really frightened now because Mrs Ellis's certainty was so difficult to resist, 'it was very kind of you to ask me: I'll always be grateful, I promise. I do feel so sorry for all those poor people who are dying. Only I have been very ill, and Doctor Mackenzie says if I don't take great care I'll fall ill again. Will you take some more tea?' She wished she hadn't had to invoke the doctor.

'Lily,' said Mrs Ellis, accepting the tea, 'I came here because I've always loved you like a daughter, even when I was angry with you. Don't make excuses. You don't like the idea of nursing the sick.'

'It's such a noble thing to do,' said Lily, 'I'm unworthy of it.' She wet her dry mouth with the nasty strong milked tea: it was a disgusting taste, she'd always thought so.

'What does it matter?' said Mrs Ellis. 'God doesn't call the worthy, Lily, you should know that. He calls the tax-gatherers and sinners.'

'I know that,' said Lily, 'but I've been very ill, and I don't want to die. Oh, Mrs Ellis,' she said, 'I have loved you. And I hated you to be so angry with me. I hope you'll forgive me.'

'Well,' said Mrs Ellis bitterly, 'maybe God will forgive all of us, because it's so hard to be a woman.'

'It must be hard to be a man, too,' said Lily.

'Never,' said Mrs Ellis. 'They suffer – yes. But are they sold, ravished, beaten, imprisoned, deformed, and cut to pieces? No. I hate men,' she said suddenly. 'I hate every one of them. I wish there were only women in the world.' She began to weep.

'No children would come,' said Lily, coming to sit beside Mrs Ellis on the purple velvet *chaise-longue* that had once been Mrs Darley's. 'There would be no children, Mrs Ellis. No babies.'

'It's impossible, I know,' said Mrs Ellis. 'But I tried, Lily, I tried to make the Hong-Kong Girls' Rescue and Educational Trust a place where women could live alone, where we'd form an ideal community without need of men. It didn't work, did it? The men came to break in and steal the women, and then you went away with Mr Pink and then Pastor Marius came and took my sister away and all the girls escaped. That was the worst thing, that you wanted to go. And now there's only Rebecca left. She feels as I do. We nursed two prostitutes who were dying of disease. Now they've gone. So we're going to nurse more sick women. And this plague was made by men. I'm certain of that.'

She wiped her face with her hand: she was running with sweat and a wet strand of escaping hair fell across her cheek. She pushed it up to the rest: it fell down again.

Lily pinned it up for her. She said: 'Doctor Mackenzie says there's a doctor in Japan who's discovered it's to do with rats. The fleas from the rats carry the plague bacillus, and they bite humans and that spreads the disease.'

'Men are rats,' said Mrs Ellis, venomously.

Lily thought: Something's destroying her from the inside.

Then she remembered that Samuel had been cruel to her when she was ill, that an evil spirit in the form of a man had brought about her miscarriage, that Mr Jackson had died and left her to starve – and was still trying to do her mischief from Hell, and Ah Kuen – Ah Kuen had destroyed her baby. And her father had abandoned her –

'You see?' demanded Mrs Ellis, her eyes on Lily's face.

'Yes,' said Lily.

Mrs Ellis put her arms round Lily. She stroked her shoulders, caressed her face. Lily sat quite still, her limbs heavy and powerless – and yet her skin crawled and her heart raced. It was a hot day, but she was chilled.

'Come with me,' said Mrs Ellis.

'Don't let her touch you,' said Ah Ling in Cantonese. 'I can't understand what she wants, but she'll destroy you. She's a demon, and you've no idea how to look after yourself. I should have turned her away at the door.'

The spell fell off Lily. She said: 'I won't come.'

Mrs Ellis sighed. She said to Ah Ling: 'You're wrong. I want her to have true life.'

She's going to die, thought Lily, and so will Rebecca. Maybe that's what they want.

She kissed Mrs Ellis goodbye. She wondered, as the missionary left, that she'd found the strength to say no to her. She stood in front of the empty bird-cage and recognized the process of change at work.

Mr Fawler presented himself at Samuel's office: Samuel had him sit down in a rickety chair.

'Mr Fawler,' he said, 'good to see you.' He wanted to say: What the dickens do you want?

'Samuel,' said Mr Fawler with quiet insistence. Samuel wished the missionary would call him Pink. 'Samuel, my church is empty.'

'That must be very disappointing for you,' said Samuel, inking in a street for the Whitewash Squad to inspect.

'I have no occupation, Samuel,' said Mr Fawler, raising his voice slightly.

'You could write a book of sermons?' suggested Samuel absently, beginning to write the day's ordinance. He'd have to go out there,

333

he thought, and inspect the proceedings, it was as well, once in a while.

'I speak good Cantonese, Samuel,' said Mr Fawler, louder still. He raised his voice for the peroration. 'I heard the voice of Jesus tell me to volunteer for the cleansing squads. They need men of honour to administer them.'

Go away, thought Samuel, don't lecture me about corruption. But he won't go, I'll have to get him out.

'We have enough people,' he said, 'and you don't know the work. It's filthy work, too. You don't know what it's like. And the Chinese hate you for doing it. If they saw you in charge of a squad, they'd never come to your church again. Why don't you ask to be sent into China: you could go to Canton, maybe?'

'They won't let me go,' said Mr Fawler. 'My missionary society doesn't want me out there. I am worthless here, Samuel,' he said, and his voice was all at once full of sincerity. 'I was cast out because of my concern for Miss Lily. And now I have nothing to do at this time of deep trouble.' His eyes were wet.

Samuel felt guilt fall on his head and blacken him like ink. He and Lily had used Fawler, deceived him, brought about his downfall. Now he himself had been admitted back into decent society – on sufferance, but he was there. Fawler was still in outer darkness. And there was a sort of nobility about the man. Again he felt that there was something inside him on the point of breaking out, something frightful.

'Pray,' he said breathlessly, terrified he might cry. 'You must pray, Mr Fawler. God will tell you what to do.' Wasn't that what God was for, to do what human beings shrank from?

Mr Fawler said simply: 'But God told me what to do. When I was shaving.'

Samuel thought he'd do anything to get rid of the man. He said: 'I'm sorry, Mr Fawler, but I can't accept God's recommendation.'

Mr Fawler gasped with pain. He said: 'I do not know you, Samuel.'

Samuel was glad. He didn't want anyone to know him, least of all himself.

The Whitewash Brigade coolies' faded blue and black clothing was spattered with lime, reeked of carbolic – the clean smell, the smell of healthy sterility. Samuel drew it hungrily into his nostrils. There was a young officer from the Shropshire Light Infantry in command of the squad, and a group of soldiers with guns, though the enemy they were after couldn't be killed by bullets.

Hammer, hammer, on the doors: the guns reinforced the white man's argument. There were still pigs grunting in first floor rooms and their ordure often dripped down on plague victims who lay in their filth and the pigs', both having been abandoned. The inhabitants went quietly on the whole, but their eyes hated. Samuel remembered Mencius's formula for winning the Empire: not to impose on the people what they didn't want.

I won't have it, thought Samuel. I don't care if they don't like it, it's for their own good.

The sick and the dead were brought out. The houses were cleansed. Samuel stood and sweated beside the officer: he watched every house search, made sure everything was done properly: while he was here no one would hold furniture and bedding to ransom. He wouldn't let such things pass. It was quite different from the time he'd gone out to inspect these premises and had felt so ill. He'd hardened now. Like Darley, he knew who the enemies were, disease and filth. It was good to have something to hate and destroy. And yet he thought: it's a disgusting, dangerous job, would it be surprising if the officer wanted to get some extra pay out of it?

The coolies went into house after house. One of them buckled and fell. He was taken off to the infirmary with the other sick Chinese. The coolies continued with their task. It had happened before, it would happen again, and, since the port was closed, this was the only work they could do. And they, too, probably wanted to buy some fish to go with their rice.

'Mr Pink,' complained Mr Fawler to the Colonial Surgeon on Sunday, 'won't let me join the clean-up squads. I made the application in a spirit of Christian self-sacrifice. And I speak fluent Cantonese.'

The Colonial Surgeon said: 'I can't interfere. Pink's doing a good job with this street cleansing, he's got his reasons, I daresay.' He turned away from Fawler.

Oh, thought Mr Fawler, they all have their reasons. If only my wife was here!

He could go to China after all. He could go alone, without the sanction and support of the missionary society.

335

He knew he didn't dare.

He went to visit Lily. He thought she'd be glad to see him. But Ah Ling told him she was in bed, resting (she was in bed with the doctor.)

Mr Fawler thought: I must be patient. I must endure.

He went back to his house and fell on his knees.

24

THE REUNION

IN the middle of August, the number of cases of plague began to fall off: the fact was discussed at the special subcommittee of the Sanitary Board.

'It could set up again. Not cool enough yet,' said the Colonial Surgeon. 'It proves it isn't rats, though,' he made a grimace at the absent Mackenzie and the distant Kitasato. 'The rats don't go away in August, do they? It's bad air coming up from the soil. We must ban excavation work between May and October: the summer is the worst time.'

'We must get the new water-treatment works in operation,' said Darley. 'There's so much left to do. And Taipingshan will have to come down.'

The priority was to get the port open. They knew that. When Hong-Kong was once more a going commercial concern, then their work would have been justified. At the moment, it wasn't paying its way. It was costing the home government money, and that at a time of economic depression.

Samuel was still paying Lily's rent so that she could sleep with Doctor Mackenzie. It didn't trouble him. It seemed fair: after all, he'd slept with Darley's wife while he kept her – and Darley was a good man, Mackenzie was a good man.

'He doesn't mind,' said Doctor Mackenzie to Lily. He came to Lily in the evenings now, as Samuel had done, making sure he washed and changed all his clothes after the day's work in the plague hospitals.

'No,' said Lily, unconcerned, 'after all, he doesn't come here.'

'I don't understand it,' said the doctor. 'I don't understand either of you. I always want to duck when I see him smiling at me at the Club.'

One evening he found Mrs Marius crying in the Government Hospital.

'Oh, Doctor Mackenzie,' she said, 'I've just brought my sister here.'

He didn't have to ask what was wrong with her. He guessed. He'd met Mrs Ellis, aproned in grey, exhausting herself among the dying Chinese, and (though he preferred to avoid her) he'd warned her she ought to take better care of herself. She'd refused to listen. Then he'd seen her yesterday, when Rebecca had been brought in to the fever hospital. Rebecca had died last night in Mrs Ellis's arms.

'I've got her a private room,' said Mrs Marius, 'My husband and I are paying for it because she hasn't any money. I went over the books at the Refuge – they haven't been eating properly – you see the money stopped coming when the girls left and no one wanted to give them any for the sick prostitutes. She was starving herself, and I never knew.' She began to cry again.

'Don't blame yourself,' he said, 'you'd have helped her if you'd known.'

Mrs Marius said: 'She's asking for Lily.'

He wanted to forbid it. He said: 'Miss Lily's still very delicate.'

'Of course,' said Mrs Marius, 'you've been looking after her health, haven't you? She's told me how good you've been to her, so different from most of the *bigoted* people here. But my sister's quite desperate to see her, and the Matron wants to keep her away. She'd do as *you* say.'

She looked up at Doctor Mackenzie: she had grown rather pretty since her marriage. He knew Lily wouldn't want him to refuse.

He went to see the Matron and pointed out that Mrs Ellis's life's work had been to save bad women. It was only fair to allow her one more when she was on her deathbed.

'If you say so, Doctor Mackenzie,' she said dubiously. She was sweet on him, but that was a two-edged weapon. It made her more likely to guess what was between him and Lily. He was sick of the colony, all of a sudden, a man could suffocate in its stuffiness. And he'd didn't want Lily to go near Mrs Ellis and her plague bacilli, yet he'd been forced to arrange it.

He thought he'd insist on paying Lily's rent.

Mrs Marius came for Lily at nine o'clock the next day. Lily was dressed in her black silk outdoor clothes, and had her hair drawn back in a chignon with no ornaments. It felt right for the occasion. She was afraid of Mrs Ellis's deathbed, and she thought Mrs Ellis might be angry with her when she came. But she couldn't tell Mrs Marius this: it would be heartless, when she was about to lose her sister. Nor could she stay away. Mrs Ellis had once included Lily in her family, and deathbeds were for families. Lily was touched and shaken that Mrs Ellis had asked for her.

The Matron came to meet them: 'She's sinking,' she said severely. 'I sent someone to your house to fetch you, but you weren't there.'

'Oh, dear,' said Mrs Marius, pushing her fringe away from her face. 'I only went to fetch Miss Lily, and we bought flowers for her.' Her voice wobbled: she caught her breath with a little high-pitched sob.

'My dear Mrs Marius,' said the Matron, softening ever so slightly, 'she's too far gone to see any flowers. You'd better go in to her, quickly.' She looked angrily at Lily. She'd visited her at the Refuge, had been thrilled by her testimonies, had later had a grey dress with black piped trimming from her, and had paid for it: Lily thought that was probably the worst wound, since several ladies far wealthier than her had been so outraged that they hadn't ever paid their bills. She slipped in after Mrs Marius, wishing the Matron did owe her money: it would give her an advantage.

Mrs Ellis lay on the bed under a thin cover. Her arms were outstretched, so that the swollen buboes in her armpits bulged through her nightdress sleeves: she breathed in short, almost snoring gasps, with long gaps between breaths, and shivered violently from time to time. A nurse was wiping her face. Her breath was foul, her eyes were closed, but red about the lids. There was a fan on the table beside her, which the nurse handed silently to Lily. She set about fanning Mrs Ellis: she knew, since she was Chinese, it was expected that she should serve.

'She's been vomiting for hours,' said the nurse. 'Now there's only a little black stuff coming up. But it relieves her for a while. And we have this ice-water to wipe her face with: it cools the fever. Your amah's fanning will help.'

Mrs Marius didn't correct her. She said: 'We'll see to her now.'

The nurse left: there was plenty more work for her to do in a plague-struck colony with trained nurses in short supply.

Lily wished Mrs Marius had told the nurse that she wasn't her amah. She felt close to tears, angry with herself, too, for minding such a thing now, at the hour of a death. She looked at the severe, frightening Mrs Ellis, who was quite helpless now, burning and shaking like dry grass thrown into the oven.

'Beatrice,' said Mrs Marius, 'Beatrice, it's Alicia. I'm here now, Beatrice, what do you want?' Lily saw the black bubbly stuff on Mrs Ellis's lips and got the basin just in time.

She took the cloth the nurse had been using and wiped Beatrice's mouth. When her hands were cold with the ice-water she found Mrs Ellis's face almost too hot to touch.

'It's true,' said to Mrs Marius to Lily, 'flesh *is* as grass.' She seemed to accept that Lily would do the little jobs for Mrs Ellis, as if the nurse had turned Lily into an amah. Lily was angry, though she didn't show it.

With Mrs Ellis's knees bent, her bare feet had come out from under the sheet: she thought they were so sad. Mrs Ellis had had such a firm step, hard-leathern on the ground. Lily had never seen her without shoes on. She'd never worn slippers. Now Lily saw that her feet were rather narrow, quite beautiful, but the soles were creased and soft and vulnerable. When the rigors came, they cramped inwards. Lily held the large fan as close to Mrs Ellis as she could, and waved it back and forth: it made her arms ache, but she kept up with it.

Mrs Marius held her sister's fiery hand. 'She grew so strange,' she said. 'I didn't know, she gave me no hint that she was going hungry, she was always so thin, how could I have guessed?' She sobbed. 'Lily, I used to play at hospitals with her. But she never wanted to be the patient, I always had to be the patient, she was always the nurse. Now I don't know what to do for her. I feel as if I shouldn't. She doesn't want me to be here, you see. She doesn't want me to be stronger than her.'

Mrs Ellis moved again, made another noise. Lily held the basin for her again, but she didn't vomit. Then tears came out of Mrs Ellis's eyes.

'She's crying,' whispered Mrs Marius.

'Perhaps she's sorry,' said Lily softly, 'she's sorry she was hard to us.'

'Oh, no,' exclaimed Mrs Marius. 'Beatrice,' she pleaded, 'speak to me.'

'I'll speak to her,' said Lily. She took Mrs Ellis's other hand, and said: 'Mrs Ellis, it's Lily. I've come to visit you, and I admire you so much. You've been so brave, you've been a wonderful woman.'

Mrs Ellis opened her eyes and looked at Lily with utter joy.

'Lily,' she said. 'You came, after all. To nurse. Good girl. God will love you.'

Her eyes closed again.

'And I'm here, too,' said Mrs Marius, stroking her sister's cheek, 'I'm here with you, Beatrice.'

But Mrs Ellis made no response to this. She lay, breathing in and out – and there was a long gap when they thought she'd never draw breath again – and then she breathed in and out briefly, her lungs labouring with the breaths – and yet she kept breathing.

They sat with her for hours, listening to that disjointed rhythm. She stopped vomiting after a while: there was nothing left to bring up. Lily thought she'd be here for ever: it didn't seem to matter. Doctor Mackenzie looked in, examined Mrs Ellis, sighed, and praised their care for her. A nurse brought them food. They sat by Mrs Ellis in turn, holding the burning hand.

Lily thought: Will God love me? He seems to want such dreadful things of people. He seems to want people to die. I don't want to die. And yet Mrs Ellis's approval – however mistaken it had been – felt like a blessing that couldn't be taken away.

Lily had come to nurse Mrs Ellis, after all, and Mrs Ellis had the plague.

'She's journeying,' said Mrs Marius to Lily. 'Journeying into God's arms. But it's such a mysterious journey: we have only faith to guide us, and it's hard to see one's sister set off on that path – already she's deaf to us, Lily, deaf.'

She began to cry silently.

Mrs Ellis opened her glazed smeary eyes, and said in a harsh voice: 'Whoever that is crying, they must go out. I don't want to hear anyone crying. I'm not going to die. I have too much work to do.'

'Of course,' said Lily, trying not to cry herself. 'Mrs Ellis, dear, you're going to live, and be an example to us, many, many more years.'

Mrs Marius stood up, and went over to the window. She held her handkerchief up against her eyes. Lily's chest ached with compassion for the younger, weaker sister.

'Mrs Marius,' she said in a whisper. 'I think she's stopped breathing.'

Mrs Marius turned. There was no one left to object to her tears. Mrs Ellis grimaced for a moment, then her face relaxed.

So quickly, thought Lily, so quickly life is over.

Mrs Marius insisted that Lily took a sedan chair home, and gave her the money for it: Lily was so tired that she obeyed. When she got home, she found Samuel waiting for her in the parlour.

'She's dead,' said Lily.

'Who?' asked Samuel.

'Mrs Ellis,' said Lily, 'didn't Ah Ling tell you?'

'No,' said Samuel, 'she hasn't told me anything.'

'Ah Ling!' said Lily angrily.

'Sit down,' said Ah Ling, 'why should I talk to him? What does he want, anyway?' She put Lily in an armchair, took her hair out of its knot and began to brush it as if Samuel wasn't there.

'So tired,' she muttered to Lily, 'you've worn yourself out tending a mad demon, now here's another one come to visit, where's the Doctor, why doesn't he throw this one out?'

'How are you?' asked Samuel, almost coldly.

Lily forgot that Samuel had ever been away. 'I don't know,' she said. 'I don't think I can make love tonight, Samuel dear, I'm very tired.'

'No,' said Samuel, 'I don't want that.'

Ah Ling said: 'You should go home.'

She began to plait Lily's hair. Lily's eyes closed. She kept them closed and talked. 'I didn't know about the plague, I didn't know what it was. I didn't have a heart for it. And now Mrs Ellis – it was me she wanted more than her sister – and now she's dead.'

Ah Ling tutted. She tied the end of the plait, and began to undress Lily, again without regard to Samuel. 'You need to sleep,' she said.

'Please,' said Lily, 'not yet, Ah Ling. Bring me some tea.'

Ah Ling said: 'You're the mistress. I suppose I have to do as I'm told. And have you eaten rice since you left this house?' She put Lily's nightclothes on her.

'Yes,' said Lily, 'in the hospital.'

'English food,' said Ah Ling rudely, '*gweilo* food. I'll make you some chicken soup. And green tea without milk. If *he* doesn't like it, he can do without.'

She went downstairs, and Lily heard the knocker.

'That's Doctor Mackenzie,' she said to Samuel.

He said: 'I'll go in a moment. I only came to say goodbye. Properly. I shan't stop paying the rent.'

She said: 'Doctor Mackenzie says he wants to pay the rent.'

'Oh,' said Samuel, 'very well. I didn't want to harm you, that was all.'

She looked at him, small and plump with his moustaches drooping over his mouth: there was a strangeness about him. She wouldn't want to touch him now.

'Do you really love me?' he asked.

'I don't know,' she said.

Ah Ling came up with Doctor Mackenzie and the food.

'I'm going,' said Samuel, in English for the Doctor and in Cantonese for Ah Ling. His cheek twitched slightly, and he held his hands clenched.

She said: 'Samuel, dear, goodbye.'

She didn't love him; he had no hold at all over her any more. It was terribly sad. She began to cry at last. She hadn't cried in the hospital, she had held Mrs Marius while she cried.

'I'm going,' he said, 'goodbye, Lily.'

He went home.

September brought a typhoon that broke houses and some of the first ships that had come back into the harbour, but few plague deaths: Mrs Ellis had been one of the last. It also brought the first ladies back to the colony: the newspaper began to report arrivals:

Mrs Adams returned from a summer spent in the Old Country yesterday: she will be reopening 'Dundrum' on Bowen Road. (And would she invite Samuel to dinner?) Mrs Smallridge has returned to her gracious home 'The Palms', Mrs Caird, of Robinson Road, has returned to our colony. Mrs MacVicary and her three daughters are coming back to their residence on Peak Road.

Mrs Darley remained in England.

Now was the testing time, now he'd find out if his acceptance was going to last. There was no going back, in any case. He'd stopped paying Lily's rent. He squared his shoulders and wished he didn't feel so tired and nervous.

He had the persistent delusion that he was being followed, though he never heard footsteps. It didn't matter. Once he stood in front of a mirror and thought he caught a glimpse of a panting, excited, predatory hot face just at his shoulder. When he looked round, there was no one there.

The post came at last: two envelopes from Reynolds, a letter with Feng's beautiful script on it, and a few communications from the Pinks' lawyers relating to their property, which was going to increase his income by two hundred pounds a year: so he could certainly marry, if anyone would have him. He supposed it would be a little while before the Fishing Fleet dared to enter Hong-Kong again. The newspaper announced no visitors travelling for pleasure. Everyone was too frightened of the plague.

Feng wrote nothing about the plague, but discussed a passage from the Classics: Samuel had sought enlightenment on it in April. Samuel was warmed by the Master's floodlike benevolence and forgiveness.

There was nothing from his mother. He wondered if he'd offended her beyond fear of forgiveness? Surely someone would have told her now that he'd given Lily up? He thought he'd have to wait. He found that very hard.

Reynolds's letters were written in April and May. They were the usual sort of thing, full of complaints disguised as jokes, the details of Reynolds's nasty brutish life in backstreet lodgings and seedy public houses, the odd rag of suspect philosophy, and pleas for money. He supposed there were no more because Reynolds had heard that no letters were getting through. He knew, then, that he found Reynolds disgusting, but he sent him money – he could afford to, especially since he didn't have Lily to maintain.

When Mrs Caird invited him to dinner he had his tailor make him an entire new suit. He was placed next to MacVicary's daughter: Mrs MacVicary kept her eyes on him throughout the dinner. He was on probation and suspect, he knew it.

It turned October, and beautiful weather. The buildings shone white and clear in the sunlight, the familiar sound of Cantonese twanged in the streets, the coolies were back with their burdens, rickshaw-pullers and sedan-bearers hurried their passengers along. Then a second typhoon struck the colony and beat about its ears for forty-eight hours. A landslip killed several Chinese in Taipingshan, and a boulder came rolling into the Darleys' garden, knocking a corner off their house. Darley moved into the Club. Again, ships were wrecked, lying on the harbour shores like toys thrown down by a careless giant child. Samuel lost half his roof and had to spend two weeks in the room next door to Darley's while it was repaired.

There was still no letter from his mother.

There were invitations to dinner-parties, however, not from Mrs MacVicary or any of the holiest in Hong-Kong, but from Mrs Richards, from the Philipses again, from the Colonial Surgeon. The Colonial Surgeon's wife had brought her second daughter back with her, a tiny girl, slightly plump, with white-blond hair. She was very shy and very sweet, and Samuel was allowed to talk to her after dinner. People had heard about his legacy.

He had brought the blue-and-white Chinese jar to the Club with him: he liked to look at it. He thought the flowers were dinner-party invitations, the gift of compassionate clouds that had rained blessing on his life. He knew that was sentimental. He didn't care.

If only his mother would write! He dreamed one night that she was dead, and the Prince of Wales had kept it quiet in order to lull him into a false sense of security. He was standing in front of a mirror; behind him was a man with a knife; he recoiled, bumped into the mirror, and smashed it. Then he couldn't see anything any more.

The roof was repaired, and he moved back into his house. He'd had to replace the curtains, and some of the furniture that had been ruined by the rain. He could afford better quality now. It was a new beginning.

He was glad to sleep in his bed again: he did an excellent next day's work. Afterwards, he called in at the Club and accepted an invitation to play tennis at the Colonial Surgeon's house on Saturday. He came home cheerful, slightly tipsy, and agreeably tired.

'An Englishman's here, sir,' said Paul Cheung. 'He says he's a friend of yours. You never told me anyone was coming to stay.'

He was irritated, the more so because he'd had to deliver the whisky bottle up to the visitor.

'You don't look very pleased to see me,' said Reynolds, 'do you wish I hadn't come?'

'How did you get here?' asked Samuel. 'Did you work your passage?'

What shocked him was not so much Reynolds's disreputability: his moth-eaten hair, his saggy clothes, his dilapidated face, but the fear, the breathlessness, the sense of danger. He felt physical repulsion for Reynolds, as if he stank, yet the man was clean enough: he had even shaved and his moustache was tidy.

'I've had a terrible voyage,' said Reynolds, 'seasick all the way. The lawyer paid me, the one who handles your affairs. I've brought you the documents relating to your inheritance. You can get the money now.' He was drinking the whisky straight out of the bottle.

It could have gone in the post, the diplomatic bag would have been a safer means of conveyance.

He asked: 'Can't you drink out of a glass?'

'If you like,' said Reynolds ingratiatingly: then Samuel wished he'd asserted himself and refused the glass. Besides, he could now see exactly how much Reynolds was drinking.

'How did the lawyer find you?' asked Samuel.

'I went to him,' said Reynolds, 'and asked him for work. He asked me to do this. And I thought, look at you, you're doing so well, you could get me a job out here, a new chance, look at your clothes,' he took hold of Samuel's jacket. Samuel pulled away.

'Don't,' said Reynolds, 'don't. You hurt me.' He came after Samuel, lurched, and fell against the new rosewood sideboard. The blue-and-white jar fell off it, and smashed on the parquet floor. Samuel saw its gaping broken mouth: something dreadful had been released from it, he knew.

'I'm sorry,' said Reynolds, 'you mustn't hold it against me. I've had such a hard time lately.'

'Don't touch me,' said Samuel. 'You've got to understand, I'm a man now. You walk in here as if nothing had changed, haven't I sent you money? I'd have sent you more.'

'I had to see you,' said Reynolds, 'you might have died in the plague.'

There was nothing he could complain of, except that Reynolds had broken the jar. He rang for Cheung, and asked him if he'd made a bed up in the study.

Reynolds said: 'Isn't that the room where Henderson hanged himself?' He began to shake. 'I can't sleep there.'

His distress made Samuel want to vomit. Finally he gave Reynolds his own room to sleep in, which meant he had to sleep in the study. But he slept badly. He dreamed he was dancing with Reynolds, Lily and Henderson. They were all wearing masks, Henderson a spaniel's, Lily and Reynolds fox-heads. He didn't know what sort of mask he was wearing, and it was difficult to look out through the eye-slits.

Reynolds didn't get up for breakfast, so Samuel went to see him before he left for work. He hated to see Reynolds's unshaven face in his own bed. His nightshirt was torn, and the room smelt.

Reynolds looked half-drunk still, but Samuel began to talk all the same.

'I had to come in now, I can't be late at the office. I will try to get you work, but you'll have to be patient.' He wouldn't, he'd pretend he was trying, and, when some time had elapsed, he'd say it was impossible and send Reynolds home with money. 'I've told the servant to direct you to a tailor's, get yourself some clothes made, and have the bill sent to me.'

Reynolds said: 'You can't have me hanging about like this, I can see that. But when I'm properly dressed, you'll take me round with you, won't you?'

'Yes,' said Samuel, 'I'll show you the city, and the countryside.'

'And your Club,' asked Reynolds, 'will you take me to your Club?'

'You'd have to behave yourself,' said Samuel.

'I'd be good,' promised Reynolds, 'I'd be a proper sahib.'

'I've got to go to work,' said Samuel. The hair had all gone up on the back of his neck, and he felt sick again.

If there was anyone he could have gone to about Reynolds, if only he could have said to Darley: 'Sir, my old tutor has turned up on my doorstep, and he's a real bounder. I don't want him to stay here, I need some advice.' But he couldn't. Shame kept his mouth shut.

He hadn't sent Reynolds to his own tailor, but to a man who dressed small tradesmen, ships' chandlers, the young griffins when they first came out to work in the Hongs. And missionaries. Fawler had patronized this shop. But it shamed him to think of Fawler, too, who had gone back to England, recalled by his missionary society. The gossip was that his wife had arranged it. The gossip was cruel and Samuel hated it.

He came home the first evening and found Reynolds drinking whisky again. It was Friday night.

'Tomorrow afternoon,' he said, 'I'm invited to a tennis-party, and I can't bring you. I'll take you to the cathedral, once you've got some decent clothes. On Sunday afternoon we'll go over to Kowloon – I've told Cheung to hire coolies – and we'll walk.'

Reynolds said: 'You're keeping me out of the way.' He laughed.

'You used to like the countryside,' said Samuel.

'At night,' said Reynolds, 'when we escaped.'

'You can't go to this countryside at night,' said Samuel, 'there are cobras and king cobras, there are bamboo snakes and pythons that can strangle a man. There are poisonous spiders. And the natives, over there, they can be hostile.'

'Are you trying to frighten me?' asked Reynolds. 'Where's your sense of adventure?'

'A man has to be responsible,' answered Samuel. He knew he sounded intolerably prim.

'And you don't want to esape?' asked Reynolds.

'Look at yourself,' said Samuel angrily, 'why should I?'

Reynolds turned away and picked up Samuel's copy of *The Sign of Four*.

'I can get you plenty of books,' said Samuel, 'I'll give Paul Cheung a list, and he can take it to Kelly and Walsh.'

'Thank you,' said Reynolds, 'that'll give me something to do.'

His humility laid a trap for Samuel: he slid straight into it and was impaled on sharp pangs of self-reproach.

He went to the tennis-party at the Colonial Surgeon's house: sweet little Miss Dottie partnered him. Her shyness was turning to giggles, and she admired his good strokes. But all the time he thought that Reynolds was there, watching, he was afraid she might see him and ask: 'Who is that shabby man who goes everywhere with you, Mr Pink?'

The Amateur Operatic Society was staging *The Pirates of Penzance*, she said she'd take part if Samuel would. He let himself be persuaded, though he was afraid Reynolds would want to come to the rehearsals.

She had beautiful blue eyes. He supposed she'd be stout later on, but he didn't think he'd mind that. If he was allowed to marry her.

Darley wrote to his wife: *I can assure you now that the plague has abated, and that it is quite safe to return here as soon as you wish. Should you wish to remain in England for a few more months, this would also be agreeable to me. I know you were anxious to spend some time with Agnes, and would like to visit the children's schools at least once more before you return. I am very busy here with the plans for the extension to Tai Tam reservoir, at least the plague has this silver lining, that all the improvements I have been pushing for*

*are now accepted without any question. You will return to a
significantly different Hong-Kong. Let me know what your plans
are.*

He signed it, and read it through. It was a cold letter. There were
no endearments, no hints of his pleasure in the reunion he was
giving her the opportunity to postpone. He thought she'd stay
away. He'd send money home, pay for her upkeep, pay for the
children's schools. He'd come home, every five years, and visit
them. He was already a stranger to them – what difference did it
make?

Samuel went to the parade ground after the service on Sunday: he
knew Reynolds was waiting for him, but he had to see Miss Dottie.
What would she think if he stayed away? And yet all the time he
flirted with her, something at the back of his mind prophesied that
he wouldn't have her. He tried not to listen. The more he saw her,
the more he wanted her. She had dimples either side of her mouth: it
wasn't as lovely a mouth as Lily's, but she had other advantages.
She seemed to think it was daring, almost wicked, to flirt with him,
but he could see that her mother had approved him. He mustn't let
anyone spoil his chances.

At one o'clock he took Reynolds down to the Praya, where they
were to board a launch for the Kowloon side of the harbour. This
was the dangerous moment, since there would be other parties
waiting to go on excursions. But their launch was ready, bumping
against the quay, and two coolies already waiting for them. He got
Reynolds into it as quickly as he could.

'It will drop us at Cheung Sha Wan,' said Samuel, 'and pick us up
at Kowloon City.' It was going to cost twenty-four dollars, but he
thought it was worth it to keep Reynolds off the ferry-boat. 'It's a
nice walk over the hills.'

'Have we got some whisky?' asked Reynolds.

'You should be careful,' said Samuel, 'drinking so much. People
who drink too much sometimes get brain-fever, out here.' He tasted
the threat on his tongue. It wouldn't do any good. 'Besides,' he said,
'if you get drunk you won't be able to walk.'

'I ought to pull myself together, oughtn't I?' asked Reynolds.
'Especially if you get me a job.' The ingratiating note was in his
voice again.

They steamed across the harbour, weaving among the boats: it didn't take long. It was still very hot by British standards, though the local people were already dressed in their quilted winter clothes.

'You're in China, now,' said Samuel as they got out of the launch's dinghy. He'd brought his revolver: it was just as well to do that.

'It doesn't look any different,' said Reynolds. The same granite rocks sat sentinel on scrubby hillsides, the same turquoise sea lapped on the yellow beach. 'There's a kingfisher!' he exclaimed. 'Look!' He was alive, then, the way he'd once been.

'Yes,' said Samuel, 'it startles you, doesn't it? Just like at home. There are pied kingfishers, too, but I like these best.'

The bird darted blue across the surface of the water and came to rest on a mooring post.

'They're quite fearless,' said Samuel. They walked up the steep hill, with the coolies coming behind: Reynolds found it a struggle. Samuel, used to the heat, could hear him panting.

'Easy,' he said, 'we'll have a rest. And drink water, not whisky.'

Reynolds did as he was told: Samuel thought he needed to be taken care of. He was at ease for a moment, then in a panic, then he steadied himself again.

'How old are you?' he asked.

'Did I never tell you?' said Reynolds. 'I'm forty.' He stared down at the sea. 'I like those,' he said, pointing to the junks. 'They're pretty.'

'I keep meaning to take up painting,' said Samuel, 'I'd like to paint the colours of the water, or the sunsets out here.'

'What's that bush with the white flowers?' asked Reynolds.

'I don't know,' said Samuel, 'it looks like a camellia, doesn't it? I know the flowers only last a day.'

A bird was singing a high, thin song somewhere over the hill. Reynolds shook himself.

'Let's go on,' he said.

The path took them behind the hills that backed Hong-Kong harbour and they could see Mirs Bay in the distance. China stretched to their left, hundreds of thousands of miles and wider than it was possible to imagine. They had to rest at regular intervals – Reynolds was sometimes so short of breath that Samuel began to be afraid he had tuberculosis. He was relieved when the clouds came over the sun. If only it didn't rain!

They stopped for a longer rest, and food, after about an hour and a half's walking. A deep peace lay over the hillside. Down below they could see patches of deep green that were rice-paddies and vegetable beds, and the roofs of houses surrounded by trees.

Samuel showed Reynolds a comfortable rock to sit on. He thought: why should it make me despair to show him simple kindness?

'Let me tell you,' said Reynolds, 'about my boyhood. Those years you asked about.'

'Your father died,' said Samuel. 'You were very poor.'

'He hanged himself,' said Reynolds. 'Do you see why I had to sleep in your bed?'

'Did you find him?' asked Samuel.

'No,' said Reynolds.

Samuel said: 'I found Henderson.'

'He wasn't your father,' said Reynolds, 'and you don't mind that other room, or you'd have moved, wouldn't you?'

'You know why I didn't want to move,' said Samuel.

'I've forgotten,' said Reynolds.

Samuel said quickly: 'It doesn't matter, not now. Your uncle paid for your education, didn't he? What was he like?'

Reynolds ate greedily. He'd finished the cold meat and bread and was at the cake. Samuel let him have it all.

'He didn't pay for anything else. We went hungry, my mother and I. But don't think we were noble and self-sacrificing. We squabbled over the food. She took in sewing, sometimes she was at it all night. Her eyesight began to go. She almost went blind, but she saw to it I had respectable clothes for school. That was her pride. I wanted to leave school and get a job, I was tired of poverty, but she made me stay on.' Reynolds finished the cake: the crumbs were all over him. He said: 'Her bad eyesight killed her in the end. She was knocked down by a hansom, in the early evening. My uncle came to Oxford to tell me. He said at least I was independent now.'

Reynolds began to laugh harshly, then he choked on a cake crumb and coughed instead. He said: 'You were lucky, weren't you? You had a good boyhood.'

Samuel said: 'Yes.' He couldn't have disagreed.

'I had a boyhood,' said Reynolds, 'with you. You gave me that. I'm grateful. If only you could give me a job. That would mean manhood, now.'

He looked at Samuel abject, horribly affectionate.

351

Samuel stood up, and he couldn't breathe. There was a picture forming inside his head – he had to fight it. He had to feel sorry for Reynolds – *that* was what he needed to experience.

He found himself fingering the scar on his forehead. 'We must go on,' he said. He instructed the coolies, who began to gather up the remnants of the meal. He noticed how neat they were in all their movements, how efficient.

He said: 'I wish you hadn't taken me to the fair.'

'Can't you let bygones by bygones?' asked Reynolds.

A rat ran across the path ahead of them, followed by a snake – Samuel recognized it as a copperhead racer. He remembered that Doctor Mackenzie had recommended a new rat poison to him. It took a week to act, and the rats didn't feel ill during that time, so that they came back and took the bait again. They died infallibly, of something similar to brain-fever. He thought he'd ask Doctor Mackenzie how to get hold of it.

'We've got to go,' he said again. Then he said: 'How can you ask me for a job? You hated colonialism, you never believed it was possible to do it properly, what about all that stuff you used to write to me?'

'As long as I survive,' said Reynolds, 'I don't care any more. I can't. If you'd been through what I've had, the last years – you don't realize.'

Samuel wished he'd kept his mouth shut. He thought he understood too well.

'If we don't start,' he said, 'we won't get to the launch before dark.'

Reynolds was exhausted by the time they got to Kowloon City. Samuel hurried him on to the launch: MacVicary was waiting for the ferry with a party of friends and family, and Samuel didn't want Mrs MacVicary to see Reynolds.

It troubled him that there was still no word from his mother, and that Reynolds had arrived instead. Who was it that chose Reynolds for him, who was that lawyer who'd been so careless about his correspondence? He hated the lawyer for standing between his mother and himself, he hated the world for making it necessary. And Reynolds – but you couldn't hate a broken man. Only Reynolds must go, the sooner the better. All the same, he let himself be persuaded to take him to the Club.

352

Reynolds, in the new clothes from the tailors, was quite passable at first: he drank brandy and soda and won a few dollars at billiards. He behaved well. It was possible to introduce him as 'my old tutor, a university man'. When Darley asked Reynolds what he was doing now, he said he was taking a vacation before he began a new job, tutoring the delicate son of a baronet. An hour later, however – after more brandy and soda – he told Mackenzie that he'd come out here to look for work, and asked Mackenzie if he could help him. Later in the evening, he told Richards that he'd come out to give Samuel some news.

'What do you mean, news?' asked Samuel, pulling Reynolds aside.

'Not news,' said Reynolds. 'Documents.'

Samuel let it be.

He stood back and watched Reynolds hunch over the billiard table, sweating heavily: the bright light exaggerated every crease in his face.

He thought someone spoke to him: 'Verminous' said the voice. He didn't recognize it, it didn't belong to anyone who was standing about. But he saw how beastly Reynolds was, with his thin fading sandy hair and whiskers. He was drunk, now, he was losing heavily. Samuel would have to pay for him.

'Why don't you get him home?' asked Darley, appearing beside him. He looked tired and miserable – Samuel thought he was working too hard.

'I shall,' said Samuel. Again, he wanted to ask Darley to help – he thought Darley would – but something kept his mouth shut. It was like those dreams when you couldn't scream or move, in spite of your terror.

He saw Mackenzie. He went over to him and asked him quietly how Lily was.

'She's well,' said Mackenzie, briefly.

Samuel asked: 'That rat poison you told me about – has it any taste?'

'No,' said Mackenzie. 'That's why it's so effective. Got a problem with them, have you? Better get rid of them, I don't care what the Colonial Surgeon says. They bring pestilence.'

'Where do you buy it?' asked Samuel.

'Oh,' said Mackenzie, 'you don't need to. I'll send some over to you. Tomorrow?'

Again he heard the voice say: 'Vermin.' It frightened him. He thanked Doctor Mackenzie and got Reynolds away before he'd done worse than spill a champagne cocktail down himself and lose eighty dollars. Samuel slipped him the money and hoped no one was looking.

'Imagine,' said Reynolds when they got home, 'if you told all those people whose son you are. Shall I tell them?'

'You're drunk,' said Samuel angrily. 'Don't talk about my mother.'

Reynolds turned round, got hold of Samuel's collar and yanked his head forward. Samuel resisted, and the collar tore off its studs. Reynolds kept hold of it, tightening it round Samuel's neck, Samuel aimed a punch at Reynolds's face. Reynolds flinched, and let go of the collar.

'If I was younger – ' he said.

'Go to bed,' said Samuel, quite coldly. He wasn't frightened, only surprised at his cold detachment. 'Don't you think you cost me enough money,' he said, 'without ruining my clothes as well?'

'You're cruel,' said Reynolds. 'You don't know how to forgive.'

'Hold your tongue,' said Samuel.

He lay in bed and dreamed that part of him was evaporating, drifting through the mosquito-net to hang in dark cloud from the ceiling. The man on the bed began to sweat, soaking his nightshirt and sheets, then to shiver: the darkness above was aware of this, took note of it.

On the other side of the wall was Reynolds, walking through his bedroom, pilfering: Samuel saw him with something in his mouth, shaking it violently backwards and forwards. It would be dead in a moment.

'Vermin,' said the voice of the darkness. 'You put bait out for vermin. You kill it.'

'No,' said Samuel, 'No.'

Doctor Mackenzie sent the rat poison the next day: Samuel locked it away in a drawer of his desk.

He had to persuade Reynolds that there was no work for him here. He made enquiries among the various schools. They asked him about Reynolds's past record: he was forced to admit the fondness for drink and women, and the sackings. The principals of the

354

Victoria College, of St Paul's College, of the Diocesan Home and Orphanage, all shook their heads and regretted their inability to help. Samuel told Reynolds, who didn't seem concerned. He went down to the P & O offices and bought Reynolds a second-class ticket back to Southampton. He told Reynolds he'd done this, and saw him dissolve in tears. He said he couldn't bear to leave Samuel again. Then Samuel was sorry for him, felt like a traitor and gave him whisky to drink.

He just managed to stop Reynolds pinching Miss Dottie's behind on the parade ground after Matins. Miss Dottie didn't like Reynolds and was cold to Samuel. He sent him down to the brothel on Queen's Road that same evening: Reynolds couldn't understand why Samuel didn't want to come with him.

While Reynolds was at the brothel, Samuel sat in his study and looked at the colourless rat poison. It was an intellectual exercise only – he knew that, a game, like a detective story.

The obvious thing to do – if anyone was going to do it – was to mix it into the sugar bowl: Reynolds took so much sugar in his tea, Samuel didn't take any at all. Reynolds would administer the poison to himself, would almost have killed himself. The solution to the problem was the sugar bowl.

But there was a further conundrum: the sugar bowl mustn't go back to the kitchen, in case Paul Cheung used the sugar for something else, or ate it himself. How could that be dealt with? One could knock the sugar bowl over by accident, though Reynolds would remember it afterwards. Yet why should that seem to have any significance? There was nothing suspicious about brain-fever, nothing suspicious about any sudden illness out here.

The poisoner could get the sugar bowl and throw the contents down the water-closet. Would he be able to carry out that movement of the hand? He'd have to be a steady-headed man, a cold man, a man who could reduce the whole business to a mechanical series of actions.

There was no such man.

It could happen like this, at breakfast time: Reynolds always came to breakfast now. He'd be sitting opposite the poisoner, stuffing food down himself as usual, and the poisoner would give him a newspaper article to read, say about Darley's reforms, or something regarding pirates – Reynolds liked to read about pirates. While Reynolds was reading the newspaper, the poisoner would tip the powder into the sugar. It would take a minute, no more. He'd already have reserved some of it for use against the rats.

It was theoretical, it wasn't going to happen.

Reynolds would pick the sugar bowl up, take the spoon, dig it into the poisoned sugar, and heap it into his cup. He liked to spoon the syrup from the bottom of the cup after he'd finished. Then there'd be the remaining sugar to get rid of. It couldn't happen till Reynolds had emptied the teapot and taken as much sugar as he wanted. He usually left the table abruptly: it would be childishly easy for the poisoner to remain behind, take the bowl up and tip it away.

25

THE UNMAKING
OF PATTERNS

THE following Monday, Reynolds didn't come to breakfast. Samuel went looking for him and found him still in bed. His eyes were reddened and dull, but he said it wasn't anything much. He'd been to the prostitutes again – that was the fourth time in the week, and he always came in drunk, so Samuel supposed he had a hangover. He sympathized, and went to work.

In the afternoon, a message came for him that Reynolds was worse. He spoke to Darley, and got permission to go home. He arrived to find Reynolds propped up in bed, staring at nothing in particular. James Cheung was fanning him.

Cheung said: 'He fell over.'

'I fainted,' said Reynolds. His voice was slurred. 'Seem to have lost the feeling in my hands and feet now.'

'I'll get the doctor,' said Samuel.

Reynolds said: 'I don't want to cause you so much trouble.'

'I've come home,' said Samuel, 'haven't I?'

'I'm glad you came home,' said Reynolds.

Samuel said to Cheung: 'Get Doctor Mackenzie.'

He sat beside Reynolds, and was distressed to see his hair falling out.

Reynolds said: 'You never wanted me here. I'm a nuisance to you. But you've got the documents, I'll go home when I'm better. I only wanted to see you again.'

Samuel said: 'I was ten, wasn't I, when you came to look after me?'

'Just ten,' said Reynolds.

'We had jolly times,' said Samuel, and hated his own trite words.

'I don't know what to do,' said Reynolds. 'I wish I did.'

357

'Oh,' said Samuel, 'I'm sure you'll find work in England.'

'That's not what I mean,' said Reynolds. He closed his eyes. The lids were creased and horrid – Samuel thought of turkey wattles or his own foreskin, they were indecent – he looked away. He felt that breathlessness again.

'Don't think about it,' he said, 'you don't need to think about it.'

'No,' said Reynolds, 'no there's no need, you're right. You've been kind to me, Samuel.'

'Don't,' said Samuel.

'You sent me money,' said Reynolds. 'You answered my letters. There's something I have to tell you.'

Samuel said: 'The doctor's here.'

Leaving Doctor Mackenzie with Reynolds, he stood outside the door, biting his thumbnail. After a quarter of an hour, Doctor Mackenzie came out to him.

He asked: 'Did you use that rat poison I sent you?'

'Yes,' said Samuel, 'I gave it to my man to use.'

Mackenzie said: 'It couldn't have got into the food?'

'I don't know,' said Samuel. 'I'll ask my man. But you wouldn't – nobody would bring criminal charges against him, would they? I'm sure he's not a poisoner.' He rubbed his hand across his forehead.

'It's dangerous stuff,' said Mackenzie.

Samuel rang for Cheung and interrogated him in Cantonese. 'He's been very careful,' he said to Mackenzie, 'he says he's a sensible man, he's angry that I should even ask. I know he's telling the truth.'

'Well – ' said Mackenzie, 'it's probably brain-fever after all. Yes. I've given him something that may help. I'll come back in a few hours. Do you want a nurse?'

'No,' said Samuel, 'the Cheungs will nurse him.'

'I've had the servant pull the shutters,' said Mackenzie, looking intently at Samuel. 'Brain-fever cases can't bear the light. And you must expect delirium.'

He went to see Lily, though it was the middle of the afternoon. He didn't much care if anyone saw him, he hated the pretence.

He asked her: 'Should I tell the police that Pink has poisoned his old tutor?'

'Are you sure?' asked Lily.

'No,' he said. Lily came to sit close beside him.

'I haven't bled this month,' she said.

He put his hand protectively over the lower part of her belly. He said: 'I gave him the poison to kill rats with.'

'Oh, don't,' said Lily, 'don't go near the police, they only make trouble. You don't understand, Ah Ling told me. Mr Reynolds will die because of the ghost.'

'What ghost?' asked Mackenzie.

'Mr Henderson,' said Lily. 'The servants exorcized the room, but Ah Ling says a suicide's spirit will only really rest if it's killed someone else in the house. Mr Reynolds wasn't there when the exorcism was done, so Mr Henderson's spirit is going to kill him. Even if it was Samuel who gave him the poison, he couldn't help it.'

'I don't want to hear about this,' said Mackenzie.

Lily stroked his forehead. 'Leave it be,' she said, 'leave it be.'

'I want to leave Hong-Kong,' said Mackenzie, 'there are still places where we could be married and live openly. We could go to Malaya, Penang, perhaps.'

'Oh, please,' said Lily. She began to cry. 'Then I could work, and no one would send me out of their house, and our baby would have a mother and a father. Please, yes.'

Samuel sat beside Reynolds, who dozed, muttered and tossed about; James Cheung fanned him. It grew dark outside, and Paul Cheung brought a dim lamp in and set it in a corner, away from Reynolds.

Samuel thought of St Paul, lying in darkness after he'd seen Christ. Only here was the darkness without the vision. Samuel didn't want a vision. The thought gave him pins and needles.

'Do you remember the boy?' asked Reynolds.

'Which boy?'

'The pickpocket took all his money, and he had to get off the merry-go-round.'

'Yes,' said Samuel, 'yes, I remember.'

'He never had any fun,' said Reynolds, 'someone else took the fun from him, do you think the man was sorry?'

'No,' said Samuel. 'He was a pickpocket, he enjoyed stealing. He didn't mean it badly.'

'He couldn't help it,' said Reynolds. 'I saw the boy a moment ago. Keep seeing things, they rush towards me head-on.' He groaned.

'It's because you're ill,' said Samuel uneasily. 'Listen, I've got to go out for a moment.'

'No,' said Reynolds, 'don't leave me.'

Samuel found himself asking: 'Why did you break the jar?'

'What jar?' asked Reynolds, and shut his eyes. Samuel went out after all, and used the water-closet.

Chinese exorcists were supposed to shut up evil spirits in jars, like the genies he'd read about in the *Arabian Nights* when he'd been a boy. Maybe the whole thing was a fantasy and there was no one in his bed. He went to see. He sighed, and sat down beside Reynolds.

'I've got to tell you,' said Reynolds half an hour later.

'No,' said Samuel.

'Don't be cruel,' said Reynolds, 'those things won't come at me if I tell you.'

'Yes, they will,' said Samuel. Now the tears came out. 'You're ill. You're not going to get better.'

'I know,' said Reynolds indistinctly, 'I'm dying.'

'I poisoned you,' said Samuel, 'why did I do it?'

He knew how strange it was that he was asking Reynolds for help. Yet now he really thought he'd get it. He was hopeful.

'It's because of what I did,' said Reynolds, 'I tried to say it when I wrote to you once. I did filthy things – I didn't understand why. Now you're doing the same. Poor Samuel.'

Samuel said: 'Oh, no, you didn't do anything. You were always good to me.' He wanted to whine like a puppy.

'Yes, I did,' said Reynolds, and it seemed to Samuel in the dimness that he saw a leer on the other man's face. 'You must remember. On the clifftop. You promised you'd never tell. I shouldn't have done it. I let the woman do it to me. Ought to have made it better.'

Samuel put his hands over his face again.

'Yes,' he said. 'It was all right then.'

Reynolds screamed: 'Get away from me!'

Samuel got up, and collided with Doctor Mackenzie in the door.

'He's delirious,' said Mackenzie. 'I warned you.'

'He's talking nonsense,' said Samuel. 'I need to be sick.'

He went out and vomited in the water-closet. Then he came back. Mackenzie was checking Reynolds's pulse.

'Is he going to die?' he asked Mackenzie.

'I don't know,' said the doctor irritably, 'I'm not the recording angel.'

'I did it to him,' said Reynolds. 'Deserve it.'

'No,' said Samuel, 'not at all. It was my fault.'

'Easy, old fellow,' said Doctor Mackenzie. 'I'll be back in two hours,' he said to Samuel. 'Not much we can do, I'm afraid. I've tried another medicine, but – '

It came to Mackenzie that if the suicide's room had really been exorcized, it would have been the only safe place for Reynolds to sleep. Then he blocked his thoughts: they were too disturbing.

'He's gone, hasn't he?' said Reynolds.

Samuel asked: 'Why did you make that up? Were you trying to make me feel better about murdering you?' He thought how dreadful the truth was, how comforting lies and pretence. That was what formalities did, they kept the unspeakable safely contained. They had to be.

'Stop that,' said Reynolds. 'Another thing – have to tell you.' His words were slurring so badly that Samuel could hardly understand him.

'No,' said Samuel. There was a thud against the shutter outside: he guessed a cockroach had flown into it. He wished it didn't have to be so dark.

'Before it's too late,' said Reynolds. 'I made the mistake. About the coat of arms. Wasn't Her Majesty, only by appointment to Her Majesty. I wouldn't have known, but see – I opened it, it was meant for you, but I opened it.'

'Oh,' said Samuel, 'you're confused. Stop talking, you're exhausting yourself, please go to sleep.'

'Jam,' said Reynolds. 'Not the Queen. The letter's in my bag, you – you can go and get it.' He caught his breath with an inarticulate moaning noise. 'Deceived you – all these years. Not on purpose. Made a mess of everything,' he said, 'smashed the jar, gave you the wrong mother. Never held a job. Poisoned jam. Preserves. Trespassed on them.' He screamed again, 'Get away from me!'

'Stop it,' said Samuel. 'Stop it, please, talk sense, please stop raving. I'll tell the doctor what I did, he'll make you better.' But there was no antidote. He knew that.

'Snakes,' wailed Reynolds, 'throwing themselves at my face.'

Samuel ran out of the room.

He wouldn't stay with Reynolds any more: he sat in his study with the whisky bottle. Reynolds was calling him, but he didn't go. He kept drinking, and he couldn't get drunk. However much he took, it didn't make any difference. At last he went back into the sickroom.

361

Reynolds was quieter now. He lay with his knees drawn up and his arms round them, as if he was concentrating himself into an essence of his own humanity, or trying to keep his life from escaping. He wet the bed. Paul Cheung had put a pad of cotton under him and was changing it from time to time.

'Reynolds,' said Samuel to him, 'tell me it was all lies.'

Reynolds mumbled: 'Dissolving. All my clothes in rags, can't keep me in any more.'

'Reynolds,' said Samuel, leaning down to him. 'Reynolds.'

Reynolds rambled on: he could just make it out. 'Hungry, when you're hungry, you don't exist, all the hands coming at you, taking your food away.'

Samuel said: 'It's your illness. No one's taking your food away.'

'Cold,' said Reynolds, 'empty. Grey as her hair here, her eyes used to be grey, too. She's coming for me. You wouldn't feed me, so now she's reaching at me with her grey fingers. You can't do anything for me,' he said to Samuel with sudden clarity, 'it's not possible to make improvements.' Then he fell silent.

Doctor Mackenzie came again. Quietly, he said: 'Not long now.'

Samuel sat in the dark: Jam, he thought, jam. Not royalty. By appointment to Her Majesty. What was he talking about, what was he ever talking about?

His mouth was dry, his lips mumbled drought against his tongue.

'Gone,' said Doctor Mackenzie, putting his finger on the silent pulse, checking the lack of reflexes, shutting the eyes. 'I'm sorry, Pink.'

Samuel said nothing.

'Will your man wash him? I'll write out the death certificate for you, and you can get a coffin in the morning. We'll have to get him in the ground quickly, in case he was infectious.' He looked at Samuel. 'As quickly as possible,' he said.

He was alone now.

He was afraid that the murderer had always been within him, perhaps that was why Reynolds had done that thing to him, on the clifftop. Unless the murderer had been born of that act, held silent till he had been able to rise up and do silent justice on Reynolds. He had really seemed to forget, that was what appalled him. It was unbelievable, but he had to believe it. And Reynolds, why had he come to Hong-Kong, had his death allured him?

362

He had the death certificate. There would be no criminal investigation, no enquiries from concerned relatives. Reynolds had no one except himself. He wondered where he could go to escape from himself. He put his head in his hands and whimpered: the tears wouldn't come to give him relief. Reynolds had called him unforgiving: Reynolds had been right.

But about his mother – he hadn't wanted Reynolds to talk about his mother. He must have guessed what Reynolds might say. But no, *that* was a lie. He'd look through Reynolds's things to see if there was a letter, but he wouldn't find one. Reynolds had been delirious, he'd babbled about jam.

He went into the bedroom – his own bedroom where Reynolds was laid out. He looked at his old tutor: death had smoothed the eyelids over. Samuel put his hand on the cold cheek. Reynolds lay still. He looked harmless in death, innocent of deceit.

He took the bag and tipped it upside down. There wasn't much in it: most of it had been unpacked and Reynolds had given Paul Cheung his old clothes to get rid of. There was a battered hat, a pipe, and a sheaf of his own letters to Reynolds.

He said aloud to himself: 'Nothing. There's nothing.' Then he found the opened envelope. It was thick and expensive-looking, and it was addressed to him, his name only, no address. It wasn't his mother's handwriting.

He put it down. He didn't want it.

It lay there, another secret, another unwelcome answer. He was sick of it all. He thought Lily was lucky to have had no parents.

He took it up again, he pulled the letter out. He didn't recognize that handwriting either. It couldn't be the letter from his mother. He must be safe.

Dearest Samuel, it ran, *dearest, dearest child, my only son –*

He whispered: 'It's not her writing.' He read on.

Dear heart, I am dying. When you get this letter you will know that I am already dead. It is almost Easter, Good Friday already, but I fear that I shall never see Easter Sunday. I am dictating this letter to my maid – I can trust her. She will see that it gets to the lawyer, who will send it on to you.

When you were born, I promised my father that I would never tell you who I was. He had no right to demand that, and now I'm breaking my promise. I was always a headstrong girl, though God knows I have made up for it in years of painful obedience.

363

If ever a child was a love-child, it was you. I should have married your father, there were no real objections, except that he was a junior Hong-Kong civil servant, and I was an heiress, the daughter of Sir Jabez Denniston, whose success in manufacturing jam led him to believe he was entitled to marry me into the nobility.

'Jam,' said Samuel, 'jam.' He began to laugh, gasping for breath. He saw a Jubilee jam glass, engraved with the royal coat of arms.

Your father and I believed that once a thing was done – in other words, we ran away together. My father fetched us back and refused to let us marry. I cannot describe to you the pain I endured. Your father's leave was up, and he had to go back to Hong-Kong without me.

Samuel stood up, walked three times across the room and back.

Later he married, but the marriage wasn't happy. As for me, as soon as you had been born my father married me to the Marquis of Ramscraigs and was satisfied. He sent you to the Pinks, and used you as hostage for my good behaviour. He imposed a treaty on me: I was allowed to send you presents, and you would be provided for. You would be found work. You would inherit a respectable sum of money after his death. My father is a hard man, but he keeps his promises, and cares about his own blood. He cares too much, in fact, too much to have ever abandoned his plans and allowed us to be happy. I was given only a few hours with you before they took you away.

Samuel went to get himself a glass of whisky, but he came back into the bedroom to carry on reading.

To this day he is a healthy man, while I lie dying of cancer. I know – I made the doctor tell me. My father has been here, he will come again, this letter must be written before he comes, for he mustn't know that I have given the secret away.

There was no Married Women's Property Act when I was married, and so all my money passed into my husband's hands. Ramscraigs wasn't capable of discovering that I was no virgin. He was seventy when we were married, already crippled and half-crazy, yet he only died three years ago, at the age of ninety-five. Why do men live so long? He made me work for my title. Though we could afford the help of nurses, he made me wait on him. I had to obey. And yet he was a pauper when he married me, that was why he allied himself with jam, preserves and ketchup – how he used to taunt me! My father still congratulates himself on the alliance.

I had to agree to everything, for your sake. That is why I hoped you would be happy. Perhaps the love of this Chinese girl is what you need. Perhaps you cannot be happy. How should I know? I don't know. Your father sends me reports: he feels great affection for you. But I am no longer in a fit state to advise you. I can only hope that we meet in another world – who can tell? It is Good Friday after all: there may be an Easter Sunday for us all.

Your father is John Darley – there, now I have told you everything. I love you, dear boy, as well as a mother may love a child she has never seen. I yearn for you. But I am too tired – there is so much pain. This letter has taken several hours to dictate, and it must be posted before my father comes. Farewell.

It was signed: *Your loving Mother, Victoria Ramscraigs.*

Doctor Mackenzie's death certificate was accepted without question, and Reynolds was buried the day after his death in the Anglican cemetery overlooking the Happy Valley racecourse, where he lay alongside all the others whose stay in the colony had become more permanent than they expected. Samuel was drunk – but respectfully so – at the quiet funeral. He had been drunk ever since he'd read the letter, and he wanted to stay drunk forever.

He had no picture in his mind of the other Victoria, the Marchioness of Ramscraigs. He had the biscuit-tin with the portrait of the Queen. Darley might tell him what she looked like, only he didn't want to ask. He didn't want to go to work and see Darley. He didn't want Darley to be his father. He wanted his father to be dead, his mother to be alive, he wanted to be John Brown's son.

The truth was that he'd known her as the Queen while she was alive – how could he remake her, now that she was dead, into a jam manufacturer's daughter? And he hadn't recognized the hand-writing. The whole thing could be a hoax. Only there was no one to tell him: he could hardly go and ask Reynolds in his grave, and he might make a fool of himself if he asked Darley – *that* was a good reason not to ask Darley.

He kept drinking. At eight-thirty it became quite clear to him that the letter was a hoax. Someone had done it to him on purpose, to confuse him. It was probably the Prince of Wales. He felt an intense hatred for the Prince of Wales with his legitimacy. He resented the Queen for failing to acknowledge him. Reynolds *had* been right, his vision of the world had been right, it was all founded on falsehood

365

and cruelty. He thought of Miss Dottie, who had shrunk away from Reynolds. He hated her primness. He'd wanted to belong to the British Empire, and it was trying to spit him out. He'd tell them all, he'd jump out of his own accord.

He took his sedan down to the Club: he knew what he had to do there. He'd drunk enough whisky to make it possible.

He walked through into the billiard-room: there was Darley, there was Mackenzie, MacVicary, Richards, Caird, and the Dean. And the Colonial Surgeon: he especially wanted the Colonial Surgeon to hear.

'I'm a bastard,' he said loudly to the Colonial Surgeon. 'You don't want someone like me hanging round your daughter.' The Colonial Surgeon flushed red and drew five paces back from him.

'Pink,' said Darley, hurrying across the room, 'go home.'

'I'm the Queen's son,' he said. He saw Darley's mouth gape: no, Darley hadn't known that. 'Her son with John Brown. She went to bed with John Brown and had me. I wasn't supposed to tell anyone about it.'

Now Mackenzie had arrived, had put a hand on his arm. He saw it but he didn't feel it. The drink surrounded him with a fuzzy protection, like the halo round a gaslamp in the rain. He laughed at Darley's silly, astonished face.

'His friend's dead,' said Darley to the other men, 'poor Pink, it's all been too much for him.'

'No it hasn't,' said Samuel, 'and I won't go home.'

But Darley and Mackenzie had hold of him: he wished he could jump up on the billiard-table and fend them off with a cue, but it was too late, and he could see, even with his swimming head, that he'd have some problems with the long overhanging set of lights.

'Pink,' said Mackenzie, 'come on, be a good fellow.'

He said: 'That's the way you talked to Mrs Ellis, when she found you in bed with Lily. As if she was mad. I'm not mad.'

Darley and the Colonial Surgeon stared at Mackenzie, who said: 'You're overwrought, and drunk. You'll feel better in the morning. Look – I'll take you home.'

It was all wrong, he'd wanted them to gather round him, shout at him, abuse him even, he didn't care. But here he was with Darley and Mackenzie and the Colonial Surgeon was slipping away to join the other men on the opposite side of the room.

He shouted: 'Don't pretend you can't see me. You'll be talking about it for years, the night Pink went mad at the Club. But I'm not mad.'

'No, just drunk,' said Darley wearily.

'I'm letting you down,' he said to Darley, 'aren't I?'

'Come home,' said Darley, pushing him towards the door.

There was Mackenzie on one side of him, and Darley the other side, and they were too strong for him. He began to sob.

'That's better,' said Mackenzie.

'Oh,' said Samuel, 'you think you know what's best for me – ' by now he was on the stairs, the backstairs, and they were hauling him away, 'you'll put a strait-jacket on me, that's how you keep the world in good order. I know all about it. I saw through it, and I didn't want to believe it. I wanted to be part of it, but I can't. I'm nobody.'

'What's all this stuff about the Queen?' asked Darley, 'I thought your mother was sending you a letter.' He sounded so matter-of-fact that it was impossible not be believe him. Samuel stopped struggling.

'You can let go of me,' he said. 'I suppose you're taking me straight to the lunatic asylum?'

'Don't be a fool,' said Mackenzie.

'I killed Reynolds,' said Samuel. 'You knew that, didn't you, Mackenzie? I don't know why you wrote the death certificate. You could have got me hanged. I gave him rat poison in my house. I don't want to go back there.'

Darley said: 'I don't care if you killed Reynolds twenty times over. He was no good. He was a bad joke your grandfather played on your mother. I knew it as soon as I set eyes on him. Just as long as no one finds out. I do care about you wrecking yourself.' To Mackenzie, he said: 'We'll have to pretend he's ill. We can say he's got malaria. He'll have to stay in bed for a week, then people might forget about this.'

'I don't want to go home,' said Samuel.

'My house,' said Mackenzie. He instructed the bearers.

Samuel let himself be persuaded into his chair and carried uphill to Mackenzie's house. He felt sick, and there was something that raged at his own passivity.

'Good lad,' said Mackenzie, when they got there.

'Damn him,' said Darley, sitting down with a thump in one of Mackenzie's green armchairs, 'he's not a good lad. He's forever in trouble.'

There was a mirror on the wall, heavily framed in mahogany. Samuel went to it and looked at himself, then at Darley. He had the same nose, the same chin. He knew Darley was distressed, since he saw the same lines of pain in his own face. He'd thought this room was hell once, when Lily was so ill. Now it felt like a purgatorial waiting-room where the guilty were kept, pending sentence.

'What was my mother like?' he asked Darley. 'I've never seen her picture. I thought I had, of course.'

'You really believed – ' said Darley.

'It was the coat of arms,' said Samuel: he hated the words, 'on the letter. Reynolds saw it, when the lawyer gave him the job.'

'Reynolds,' said Darley. He moved his mouth disgustedly. 'Poor lad,' he said, 'poor lad.'

Mackenzie poured out whisky for himself and Darley, and Watson's aerated water for Samuel. 'Drink it,' he said to Samuel, 'you won't have such a bad headache tomorrow.'

Samuel said: 'I didn't want you to be my father.'

Darley looked away from him.

'I'm sorry,' said Samuel, 'you've been good to me, I can see you care. She said you cared.'

'She was lovely,' said Darley, 'and brave. I thought I'd die of wanting her. But I told you, lad – a man gets over things like that. He finds things to do.'

'He kills his feelings,' said Samuel miserably, 'the way I killed Reynolds.'

'Feeling isn't everything,' said Darley, 'feelings have to be kept in bounds. A man has to discipline himself, or there's no point to his life. He has responsibilities.'

And yet Samuel could see how unhappy Darley was. 'I can't bear them,' he said, 'I can't bear my responsibilities.'

'We share them,' said Darley. 'We all share the responsibility, out here.'

'I knew,' said Samuel unsteadily, 'when I told them I was the Queen's son, I knew then that it wasn't true.'

'Have some more water,' said Mackenzie. Samuel drank.

'Too many lies,' he said. 'I want to go away.'

Darley said: 'People forget the sort of thing that happened tonight. They forgive it. We all know, out here, what it's like. You're not born to the climate. The summer we've just had. You did good work, with the plague.'

368

'I've killed a man,' said Samuel. 'I can't leave that to lie and get on with my job. I can't take responsibility for other people's lives when I've killed.'

Mackenzie said to Darley: 'Why don't you let him go?'

Darley said: 'He's my son.' He stared at Mackenzie as if Mackenzie had been talking gibberish. He asked Samuel: 'What made you kill Reynolds?'

'When I was a boy,' said Samuel, 'he – I can't say it.' He put his hands to his head: he thought he could feel something cracking in there. He said: 'If only I'd told him I didn't want it.'

'Don't,' said Darley, quickly, 'you don't need to – poor lad.'

'You can say that,' said Mackenzie, suddenly angry, 'look what you did to your wife.'

'A man makes mistakes,' said Darley, 'it's part of responsibility. We're none of us perfect.'

Mackenzie said: 'A man can take too much responsibility on himself. Why shouldn't he go away? I'm going. With Lily. I'm going to marry her.'

Darley asked nastily: 'Do you want to take him to make three?'

'I loved her, too,' said Samuel, 'that was the feeling I killed.'

Mackenzie asked: 'What do you want to do?'

'I want to be forgiven,' said Samuel, 'It'll take a long time. You see, he wasn't all bad. That's what makes it so difficult. I think I'd like to paint. I'd like to paint light. Light on a wall.'

Darley asked: 'Are you good at painting?'

'It doesn't matter,' said Samuel. 'I don't want to be good at anything. I shan't go back to England. I could go to Java, or Tongking, and paint there. I could live on my income.'

He thought about the shadows on the wall of the cave: they were so confusing, and the answers, even when they came, didn't explain anything. He felt desolate, at the same time strangely hopeful.

'You're going to waste your life,' said Darley. 'What about all my years of service, don't you think they're worthwhile?'

'A man does his best,' said Samuel. 'You do your best. I wish I could stay. But to administer the law – the law says a murderer must hang.'

Violently, Darley said: 'You're out of your senses. You agree with me, don't you, Mackenzie, temporary insanity, that's what we can call it.'

'No,' said Samuel, 'no, you don't understand. I haven't got to

369

hang. It would be too easy to die. I have got work to do. It's harder to live – but she said there might be an Easter Sunday – '

'She,' said Darley, 'you mean your mother.'

'My mother,' said Samuel.

Darley sighed. Samuel never forgot the expression on his father's face at that moment, though, since he didn't become a particularly good painter he never managed to paint it: there was grief, and bitterness, and a reluctant sort of satisfaction.

EPILOGUE

He sent in his resignation, and left for Java at the end of the month. He settled in Batavia and lived there till he died among the Chinese and the Arabs and the Dutch whose ladies walked about in sarongs and consumed enormous platefuls of food from the *rystafel*. Paul and James Cheung came with him. Darley visited him there about once a year, till he was sent to become the Governor of an African colony. Darley died of yellow fever in 1901.

Mrs Darley became a suffragette and was arrested once, for setting a pillar-box on fire, but released from prison on grounds of ill-health: all the same, she lived to cast her vote several times. Mrs Marius went to Peking with the Pastor after the Boxer Rebellion, and the couple spent the rest of their lives there. They had four children. Mr Fawler was sent into one slum circuit after another, where he did sterling work among the poor. His wife worked alongside him.

Doctor Mackenzie and Lily went to Penang with Ah Ling: they were married by the captain of the steamer on the way there. Lily and Ah Ling had a dressmaking shop in Penang and after the doctor died in 1920 they moved to Singapore and set up a luxury department store. Lily's daughter, Meiling, married a well-off Chinese and had five children. They all moved to America at the outbreak of war, and thus escaped the Japanese occupation. Lily lived till 1959, when she was eighty-nine years old. By that time she had twelve great-grandchildren and the family was very rich.

In 1897 Samuel married an easy-going Dutchwoman, but they never had any children. Instead, they took in orphans – starting with an escapee cabin-boy, then a young Chinese slave-girl whom they bought and adopted, then a pair of twins born to a dying prostitute, and so on. He gave shelter to anyone who was needy, which sometimes caused trouble, as he was particularly fond of the undeserving. His grandfather Sir Jabez died in 1898; his substantial legacy helped Samuel to carry on this way of life.

He sold some of his landscape paintings, but they were thrown out when his customers could afford better things, or allowed to be eaten by tropical insects. Only his Chinese adopted daughter kept as many as she could. She liked to remember him, old and bent, mixing colours for the sky, or for a patch of sunlight on the earth. He took so much trouble over it, as if those were the only parts of the work that mattered. Then he would look out beyond the canvas and his eyes were just as bright, or brighter: his paintings had no such special quality.

THE public events described in this book do correspond to actual events during that period, but apart from the Governors of Hong Kong, Queen Victoria, and people who are referred to peripherally, such as Sir Paul Chater, the Sassoons, and the Rustomjees, etc, I have invented my own cast. None of the main characters represent any actual people alive at the time. For the sake of simplicity, I have rendered the name of the Bodhisattva Kwan Yin in the Mandarin form throughout.

ACKNOWLEDGEMENTS

MANY people have given me help with writing this book. First and foremost there is Martin Palmer, who has been so generous with his time and special knowledge of China – though any blunders I may have made have been my own. My agent, Bill Hamilton, has been equally generous with his time, encouragement and valuable feedback, and I also want to thank my editor, Elsbeth Lindner for her helpful comments. Then there is Ursula Price, librarian at the Hong Kong Government office in London, Lindsey and John Mullaney, the staff of Caversham Library, Derek Beaven, Judith Wavell, Sally Garforth, Chandran Nair and, last but not least, my sometimes patient and always supportive family.